O. W. S.

MW01675242

Garibaldi and Italian Unity

SALZWASSER VERLAG

O. W. S. Chambers

Garibaldi and Italian Unity

Reprint of the original, first published in 1864.

1st Edition 2022 | ISBN: 978-3-75259-204-7

Verlag (Publisher): Salzwasser Verlag GmbH, Zeilweg 44, 60439 Frankfurt, Deutschland
Vertretungsberechtigt (Authorized to represent): E. Roepke, Zeilweg 44, 60439 Frankfurt, Deutschland
Druck (Print): Books on Demand GmbH, In de Tarpen 42, 22848 Norderstedt, Deutschland

GARIBALDI

AND

ITALIAN UNITY.

BY

LIEUT.-COLONEL CHAMBERS.

LONDON

1864.

PREFACE.

From information obtained during a residence in Italy, the writer became convinced that there was much unknown in the history of General Garibaldi, particularly with regard to the part he took in the transactions that led to the disastrous affair of Aspromonte. The facts relating to this expedition have been entirely misrepresented; the true story, hitherto unknown to the public, is here for the first time given to the world.

In the following pages the writer has endeavoured to give an account of the services rendered to Italy by Garibaldi between the Spring of 1859 down to the close of 1863; no previous history comes down later than the early part of the year 1861. The history of the growth of the little State of Piedmont into the Kingdom of Italy, having been already fully described by others, the author has made frequent extracts from the best works on the subjects, such as Count Arrivabene's "Italy under Victor Emanuel," Captain Forbes' "Campaign of Garibaldi," and Admiral Mundy's "Palermo and Naples."

During the time this work was in the hands of the printers, the writer proceeded to Italy and has but lately returned to England; this must be an apology for any inaccuracies, which, in consequence of the writer's absence may have occurred during its progress through the press.

PRIORY HOUSE,

EVERTON, LANCASHIRE, *April*, 1864.

CONTENTS.

CHAPTER I.

CHAPTER II.

CHAPTER III.

CHAPTER IV.

CHAPTER V.

CHAPTER VI.

CHAPTER VII.

CHAPTER VIII.

CHAPTER IX.

CHAPTER X.

CHAPTER XI.

CHAPTER XII.

CHAPTER XIII.

CHAPTER XIV.

CHAPTER I.

Political parties in Italy previously to 1859—England, the freest Republic in the world—Present condition of Europe—France, Poland, and Hungary—Garibaldi summoned by the King from Caprera—Is informed of the secret alliance with France—He accepts from the King a Corps of Volunteers—Volunteers increase—Finds himself at the head of a little army—Doubts the sincerity of the Emperor's professions—Napoleon desires to make the Mediterranean a French Lake—Garibaldi's Volunteers fight with the Austrians—Urban defeated and retreats—Gen. La Marmora prevents volunteering—Garibaldi enters Rome—Issues a Proclamation to the Lombards—The Battles of Solferino and San Martino—Disgraceful peace of Villa-franca—Cavour resigns — Napoleon's Treachery—Garibaldi issues an Order to the People—Cavour suggests sending Garibaldi as Commander-in-Chief to Florence—Mazzini declares in favour of Victor Emmanuel—Garibaldi proposes National Rifle Associations—Jealousy shewn by the King to Garibaldi—He resigns his command—Proclamation to his companions in arms—An instance of Treachery towards Garibaldi.

PREVIOUSLY to 1859, the Northern Italians were divided into two great parties, the Austrian and the National. The latter was subdivided into three chief sections, viz.:—Republicans, who looked to Mazzini as the only faithful apostle of liberty; Liberals, whose desires fell short of the schemes of Mazzini, and who regarded General Garibaldi as the tried champion of Italian freedom; and lastly, the followers of Cavour, who knew and trusted the great statesman whose life was devoted to effecting the aggrandizement of his country.

During the brief existence of the French Republic, Mazzini, the friend of Ledru Rollin, had hoped that the lamentable condition of Italy would excite the active sympathies of her powerful neighbour; however, the siege and capture of Rome by the army of the Republic, appears not only to have banished from his mind every such expectation, but also to have substituted a well-grounded suspicion of any offers, made by France, of sympathy or assistance. It was, in fact, a matter of accusation and reproach against the party which regarded General Garibaldi as its leader, that it evinced too great a leaning towards France, and as far too anxious to introduce into Italy, French authors and French modes of thought.

Undoubtedly, both before and after the establishment of the Empire, the party in question hoped to see in France, not the despotism which reduces a people to the condition of a well-drilled camp, but a nation intelligent and free, guided by a chief able and willing to carry into effect the generous desires for Italian freedom, so constantly expressed by the orators and writers of France.

Taking into consideration all the changes the French people had passed through in succession, it seemed that, possibly, a strong government might be for a time the best thing for the real happiness of the French people. Napoleon might be in earnest in his expressed wish to grant and carry out constitutional liberty in France; it was at least only just to try before condemning him:

"Hope springs eternal in the human breast."

And hope, even in the matter of French Government, is not always disappointed. This hope was not wholly unfounded. The President of the French Republic had been elected Emperor of the French by universal suffrage, to represent in himself the natural sovereignty of the people. How ought this to have altered the position of the nation? What is a Republic but the acknowledgment of the national sovereignty of the people, and the faithful execution of their wishes?

Such was the reasoning and such the hope of a large section of Italians. We have since seen how far they were well-grounded. It matters not much what the form of Government may be, if the spirit of freedom be kept alive among the subjects, and respected by the Prince; as Garibaldi himself has often said, Monarchical England is the freest and purest Republic in the world. So doubtless it is, but fortunately our own Royal Family, unlike their clumsy imitators on the continent, respect the freedom and institutions of the people. What is the result? the result for them is that no other Royal Family in Europe can boast of such true loyalty, or such entire devotion from its subjects as the monarch whose truest glory and pride is her love for those free constitutional institutions which form at the same time the surest foundation of her own throne and dynasty, and of the unity and grandeur of her people. Who did not hope when the electric wire flashed across Europe the mournful intelligence of the 14th of December, 1861, when the grief of an entire nation was only exceeded by the grief of the widowed Queen, that at so touching a proof of the perfect sympathy which exists, and can only exist between a free people and a constitutional sovereign, true on each side to themselves and each other, the despots of Europe, seeing the love, the happiness, and even the power lost to them, might have relented? Alas! it was not so! like the King of Egypt in the olden times, they hardened their hearts and are doing what is evil in the sight of the Lord.

What is the actual condition of Europe? France lies oppressed by a despotism, Prussia is in a similar position; both Poland and Hungary are yet red with blood, and Rome has become a mere den of thieves. Spain is sunk in the grossest superstition and idolatry. In the Tablet Newspaper, only the other day, the astounding statement was made that the Church of Rome was no longer intolerant, and that the charge of intolerance could be brought with equal justice against every Church in the dark ages. Can this be true? Can the Leopard change his spots? Let us see. Here are also papers from sunny Spain; Why do they contain such long lists of imprisonments? Of what crimes have these poor people been guilty? They have well merited their fate, is the response; they have dared to read for themselves the great God's message of mercy and pardon to fallen man. Of such deeds as this consists the so-called toleration of the Church of Rome, in the 19th century.

There was no reproach so freely pressed upon the Garibaldian party, by the officials at Turin, as that they encouraged and introduced into Italy, French literature and ideas. The astonishment, therefore, of Garibaldi may well be conceived when, on being summoned from Caprera to Turin, in April, 1859, and admitted to an interview with the King, Cavour, and La Farina, he was informed of the secret alliance concluded with France. He started, and said,—"Mind what you are about! Never forget that the aid of foreign armies must in some way or other be dearly paid for! As for the man who has promised you his aid, I heartily wish he may in the eyes of posterity, redeem the evil he has done to France, by assisting in the redemption of Italy." The King assured Garibaldi that Napoleon desired to see Italy happy and free, and that he had for that reason only, consented to the marriage of his daughter with Prince Napoleon. Cavour told the General that the long expected day was at hand, and that his services were demanded in the cause of liberty. Garibaldi, with pleasure, accepted the command of the Cacciatori delle Alpi, a Corps of Volunteers which had been formed by General Cialdini, through the unceasing activity of the Marquis Giorgio Pallavicini, and of his Secretary, La Farina. Committees were established in almost every town in Northern Italy. Their organization was admirable, being entirely conducted by the National Society of Turin, under the management of Giorgio Pallavicini. Agents and sub-committees were appointed in the towns subject to Austrian sway, and by their exertions the emigration of Volunteers increased every day, until at the end of April, on assuming the command of the Cacciatori, Garibaldi found himself at the head of three Regiments of Infantry, one company of Genoese Sharp-shooters, and a squadron of Guides. From that time the Cacciatori were recruited rapidly; they completely established themselves in Lombardy, and at last became the nucleus of National insurrection. Although General Garibaldi, entertained great doubts respecting the desirability of the French alliance, and of the sincerity of the Emperor's professions towards Italy, well remembering as he did the history of the Crimean war, and the peace so hastily concluded to suit the interests of France, and France alone,* he deemed it his duty to support the Government with his whole energy, and with all the means at his disposal. Besides this, he felt a debt of deep gratitude to Cavour, to whose influence alone he well knew he owed his summons from Caprera, and the happiness of being allowed to fight for the freedom of his native land.

Those who, now that they can review the past, are strong in condemnation of this part of Cavour's foreign policy, which, in their opinion, caused the cession of Nice and Savoy, and the more recent affairs of Sarnico and Aspromonte, will do well to remember that the plans of the Italian Prime Minister were such as at that time most Statesmen would have considered enlightened and prudent. It must always be remembered that Lord Derby, not Lord Palmerston, was then in office, and that any alliance with England was thus rendered very difficult, if not impossible.

With regard to the cession of Nice and Savoy, Garibaldi has now only to say, that France was paid to overflowing for the aid she rendered; and therefore that to talk of gratitude being still due to her for it, is simply absurd; and in regard to Sarnico and Aspromonte, he has to express his profound conviction that had Cavour's life been spared, they would have been utter impossibilities. Moreover he firmly believes, that before the death of Count Cavour, no one could be more fully satisfied of the

* The Emperor's Speech of 5th November, 1863, in which he calls attention to the sincere and cordial acquiescence of Russia in his own annexation of Nice and Savoy, and avowed the alliance that existed between Russia and France from the termination of the Crimean war to the present time.

hollowness of the French Alliance, than was that universally lamented Minister. This Alliance was viewed with extreme disfavour by the party of Mazzini. They feared that the interests of Italy would be made subservient to the projects of French ambition, and that the honour of their country would be sacrificed. They spoke of it as an unholy alliance, they issued a proclamation in which it was stated truly enough, that the independence of a people can never be secured by the faithless, grasping, and dishonorable protection of foreign tyranny, and they besought the Italians not to delude themselves with the hope of gaining liberty and independence under the auspices of Napoleon, who could not establish in Italy by force of arms, that liberty which in France he had drowned in blood. They warned the Italians also, that the Emperor would try to divert the thoughts of his subjects from liberty, by the fascination of conquest and territorial aggrandizement, and that the sole object of his expedition, was to secure, as the price of his assistance, a part of the Italian soil for France, and to establish in Italy a branch of his dynasty, and so realize the oft-quoted Napoleonic idea that the Mediterranean must become a French lake. This proclamation was published early in March, and for the reasons therein mentioned, Mazzini and his followers declined to aid in carrying on the war. The difference of opinion that existed between Garibaldi and Mazzini is shown in the following letter from the former:—"I am delighted with the March of our affairs, and only want a hint to move. I believe ——— will end by going with me, in spite of some lingering Mazzinianism he has got into his head." General Garibaldi wrote few letters at this time which did not contain tributes to the patriotism of Cavour.

With the events of the campaigns on the Lakes, all Italians are familiar, but as that is not the case in England, it may be as well to insert here a short statement of the places successively seized by the Cacciatori. On the 6th of May, Garibaldi led his newly formed battalions from Brogolo to Casale, and on the 8th they fought their first fight—which was rather a series of heavy skirmishes with the Austrians than a battle—some few miles to the West of Casale. On the preceding day the General had received his formal authorization from the King, as Dictator, to enlist volunteers; and on the 9th of May he led his troops northwards again to Verrua. From the 12th to the 21st of May, the Cacciatori were incessantly skirmishing with the Austrians, under Urban, and on the last-mentioned day entered Arona. On the 22nd they crossed the Ticino and stood upon Lombard soil, entering Sesto Calende with the apparent view of resting there. The General, however, altered his plans, and pushed on to Varese which he barricaded, leaving only one company in Sesto Calende. On the 25th General Urban attacked Varese with 7,000 men, but was signally discomfited and obliged to retreat. The next point for Garibaldi to make for was Como itself. He had not 4,000 men with him, and Urban barred his way with 10,000. But this force was unable to prevent the Cacciatori from defeating them, and entering Como on the 2nd of June. On the 3rd Garibaldi outwitted Urban at the Villa di Medici. On the 8th the Cacciatori, always in advance, entered Bergamo by sending an expedition down the Lecco branch of the Lago Maggiore, and thence to Brescia and Lago di Garda.

At the commencement of his short and brilliant campaign, General Garibaldi issued a proclamation to the Lombardo-Venetians; in which he charged them to hold themselves in readiness, and entreated them to raise no other standard than the Tricolour, and no other cry than that of Viva l'Italia! From the first, the encouragement given by the Government to Garibaldi's volunteers was but slender. A letter from Turin of the 3rd of May says: "Very few volunteers arrive here; for General La Marmora throws impediments in their way. With him the law for the formation of the legion of Garibaldi, is one of suspicion."

The Official bulletin of the 20th of May announced Garibaldi's entry into Varese, and stated that the arrival in Lombardy of the first troops destined for its liberation caused great enthusiasm among the population, who declared at once for the King of Sardinia and the National Cause.

When Garibaldi entered Como, the town was one blaze of illumination. The inhabitants flocked to join his standard, for the rapidity and daring of his exploits had drawn the eyes of all Europe upon him: he had conducted his men with Cæsarean dispatch from position to position, until at length the Sardinian tricolour was flying over the ancient towers of the town. With 3,000 men this intrepid chieftain had left Varese, which he had seized after a desperate conflict, and rapidly pushed forward further into the enemy's territory. San Fermo, the position taken up by Urban, was one of great strength; but such was the impetuosity of Garibaldi's troops, that notwith standing the formidable resistance of the Austrians, and the consequent sacrifice of life among his own officers, he was again victorious, and the advantages gained were sufficient to enable him to carry out his ultimate object, and enter the capital of the province, where he was received with great enthusiasm.

Upon entering Lombardy, Garibaldi issued the following proclamation:—"Lombards! you are called to a new life, and you will respond to the appeal as your fathers did of yore; the enemy is the same and as pitiless as ever; your brethren of every province have sworn to conquer or die with you; it is our task to avenge the insults, the outrages, and the servitude of twenty generations; it is for us to leave to our children a patrimony, freed from the pollution of a foreign domination. Victor Emmanuel, chosen by the national will for our supreme chief, sends me to organize you for the patriotic fight. I feel deeply the sanctity of this mission, and I am proud to command you. To arms, then! bondage must cease! he who can seize a rifle and does not is a traitor! Italy with her children united, will know how to reconquer the rank which providence assigned her amongst nations." The difficulties Garibaldi had to encounter were very great, often apparently insurmountable;. Count Arrivabene, for instance, in his work, "Italy under Victor Emmanuel,"* pointedly describes the situation:—

"On the 9th of May, Major Corte, one of Garibaldi's most trusted officers, had an interview with Count Cavour, and had the promises then made been kept, the General's little army would have been swelled by the four battalions of Cacciatori delli Appennini, which the lukewarm Colonel Boldoni (to give him the mildest epithet) organised, or disorganised at Acqui. There is no avoiding the inference, that the great officials at Turin hated the Volunteers, and, indeed, feared them as well; because, though they had loyally accepted the programme of Unity with Victor Emmanuel, they knew that they were not the men to become slaves to the ruler of Imperial France."

Another witness, an officer in Garibaldi's camp, writing from Como, June 24,† gives further evidence as follows:—

"The Sardinian Minister had promised Garibaldi 10,000 men, well armed, with a battery, and a squadron of cavalry, but he broke his promise, closed the enrolment as soon as 4,500 men had enlisted, and then left them without either cannon or horses, with the exception of a few Guides."

And again:—

"There is something apparently supernatural in the life of the daring Italian leader, few Generals could have so wonderfully escaped from the grasp of an overpowering enemy, who felt certain of surrounding him, and, indeed, had taken all the necessary means to that end. The ability shown by Garibaldi in this campaign, and in subsequent operations, was, no doubt, the result of his experience; and the successes he obtained are mainly to be ascribed to that power of comprehensiveness which he possesses in so high a degree. Being an excellent mathematician, he at once studies the ground on which he is going to operate, calculates all possible combinations of strategy and tactics, and acts accordingly. Endowed with the greatest determination, he never hesitates; his plans being once settled in his mind, he strikes instantly,

* Vol. 1, p. 103. † Vol. 1, p. 54.

dares all issues—and succeeds. In this campaign his communications with the Sardinians were almost always cut off without the Austrians being aware of it. He always acted alone, his principal aim was to spread the insurrection amongst the Lombard population; and he pretended to fall back upon the advancing Franco-Sardinian army, in order to advance more rapidly. With the true intuition of military genius, he perceived that by gaining the lake of Garda, and occupying the mountain districts, the Austrians would be obliged to send a considerable force in pursuit of him, and that this would help the allied forces in case a reverse should retard their progress towards the Mincio. The means resorted to by Garibaldi, in order to lead his adversary astray, were no less ingenious, and always succeeded. His plan was to deploy as many forces as he could spare in opposite directions. When he first arrived at Como, he sent one officer with one hundred and fifty men to Ciro, then ordered three others to lead each of them twenty or thirty men on three different roads to attack the Austrians whenever they could meet them, without, however, engaging themselves too much. He thus made the enemy believe that he was at the head of numerous troops, and the Austrians were easily kept in error. This system had also the advantage of impressing the people of the country with his superiority in numerical strength, and of inducing them to take up arms against the oppressors of their country. The effect of this skilful plan was, that when General Urban retired on Monza, he was quite convinced that General Cialdini's division was operating with Garibaldi; whilst, in fact, the first-named General was then engaged at Palestro with Baron Zobel. To act upon Urban's mind, Garibaldi now and then sent telegraphic messages to Cialdini from different places, knowing they would be intercepted by the Austrians. In one sent from Como, he said, 'Help me! Urban will attack me again to-morrow—I cannot resist.' From Verese he had telegraphed, 'I am obliged to fall back on you; send the cavalry to support my backward movements. Neither Cialdini, nor any other General of the allied armies, was within the reach of such telegrams. There was, however, a General who read them, but who never suspected that their only object was to deceive him. It is to be hoped that it will be now explained, how it was that the Austrian General, Urban, at the head of ten thousand excellent troops, never succeeded in isolating and surrounding 3,000 Cacciatori delle Alpi."

And yet again *—

"On the 4th of June, the Austrians felt certain of victory, and Urban telegraphed to Milan that he had at last surrounded Garibaldi, and hoped to have him dead or alive before the day closed. Garibaldi concentrated the whole of his forces on a narrow height, crowned by the villa of a Milanese family. On the memorable day in question, palisades and chevaux de frise were put up by the Cacciatori, and while this was going on, the Austrians were watching from the plain, and not even trying to check the proceedings; for they showed an intention on the part of the Garibaldians to remain, which was what Urban desired; and it soon became evident that Urban's intention was to surround the Villa the next day, and cut off all hope of retreat for the conqueror of Varese and Como. To induce Urban to believe that he intended to accept the fight, Garibaldi, as night came on, made a great display of blazing bivouac fires, and ordered his men to march up and down behind them; then, taking advantage of the night, he gave orders for a retreat. Silent, with their bivouac fires still burning, the Cacciatori passed unnoticed close to the Austrian outposts, struck along the arduous mountain path into the deep gorges, and after a long, difficult, and fatiguing march of many hours, through rivers and ravines, arrived at Como whilst Urban was anxiously awaiting the moment of attack. Another time, when the Austrian General had concentrated ten thousand men on one point, Garibaldi, though his corps scarcely numbered three thousand, trusting in his bayonets, ascended the hill and fell upon the Austrians like an avalanche, and entirely defeated them, allowed them no rest, compelled them to run through the streets of Como, and forced them in complete disorder from the town, leaving behind them their ammunition, commissariat carriages, and a great portion of their material."

It was not till some time afterwards that at last a battery, sent from Turin, reached Garibaldi.

In a proclamation to the inhabitants of Brescia, Garibaldi said:—"The joyous demonstrations with which you have received the Chasseurs of the Alps, give new proof of your patriotic enthusiasm. You have shown that as zealous guardians

* Vol I. p. 53.

of your recovered independence, you are resolved to defend it with your lives, and to consecrate it with your blood; the enemy leave, wherever they go, traces of their barbarity and their execrable domination, now finally overthrown. Then unfurl the tricolour banner, the idol of our hearts, and you will command the love and the courage of your country. Let the glorious Italo-French armies, in delivering you from your enemies, find you worthy of your liberators." That portion of the English Press most opposed to Garibaldi and the Italian cause, was forced to confess that, though badly supplied with everything necessary for a campaign, and entirely without canvas, he was ever in advance of the Allies, crowning himself with glory.

In the meantime, the allied armies were not idle. The victory of Magenta had placed Milan in the hands of the liberators, when Napoleon issued his well-known proclamation to the Milanèse people. That proclamation concluded with these words:—"Remember, that without discipline there is no army. Animated by the sacred fire of patriotism, be soldiers to-day, that to-morrow you may become the free citizens of a great country."

Then followed, on the 24th of June, the furious battles of Solferino and San Martino; and within a few days afterwards, to the sorrow of all true Italian patriots, was concluded the inglorious Peace of Villa Franca.

The campaign of Garibaldi in the Valtellina was that of a great general, and all his plans were conducted with skill. His officers and soldiers were so well trained that a year later they were enabled to conquer the Kingdom of Naples. And the skill and daring shown by their leader was so much appreciated by the enemy, that when Colonel Corte was sent to inform the Austrian General, Hayn, of the armistice concluded at Verona, the latter cordially expressed his admiration of him. The Austrian officers encamped on the Stelvio spoke of him in the highest terms of praise, and thought him a truly wonderful man: as for the Croats, they firmly believed that he was the son of the

Devil. Upon the declaration of the Peace, Count Cavour, apparently maddened at the conduct of the French Emperor, resigned office, and was succeeded by Rattazzi, as Prime Minister. Garibaldi then went to Victor Emmanuel's head-quarters, to give up his own commission, and those of all the officers of his corps; but his Majesty would not accept them. "Italy still requires the legions you command," answered the King, "and you must remain:" so he remained.

There is no doubt that the peace of Villa Franca disappointed and surprised Cavour. Mr. Dicey tells us that* "Cavour was bitterly opposed to the treaty of peace, and sooner than be obliged to sign it he resigned his office." During the war the country had such confidence in the Government, that all Parliamentary institutions were suspended for the time; and the Government had such confidence in Cavour, that the negociations between the French and Sardinian Cabinets were, to a great extent, carried on by Cavour privately; so much so indeed, that it is doubtful whether he ever left any full record of them behind him. The Rattazzi Ministry had no settled plans, and not knowing what was best to do, did nothing. The Sardinian envoys were recalled from the Duchies and the Romagna; Garibaldi was requested to resign the command of the Æmilian army; the vote of the different Provincial Parliaments, for annexation to Sardinia, was neither refused or accepted; the nomination of Prince Carignano to the regency of the provinces was declined, and Buoncampagni, who had not been asked for, was sent in his stead. The organization of the Sardinian army also was neglected, and the incorporation of the Lombard Provinces with Piedmont was conducted so inefficiently as to cause great discontent. The policy of Napoleon towards Italy had indeed been treacherous. In nothing that he had achieved had he gained the confidence of the Italians. His words were deemed enigmas, his deeds regarded with suspicion, his most solemn

*See Mr. Dicey's Memoirs of Cavour.

promises bore no weight with a people who felt that they were betrayed at the very hour when deliverance was within their grasp. Unfortunately since the luckless day when the treaty of Villa Franca was signed, the conduct of Napoleon had been dark; a more inauspicious affair than that transaction had never been recorded by history. It left nothing complete, and everything to be settled; all those manifestations of sympathy which were exhibited towards him when it was supposed that the French came as liberators, ceased on his second appearance at Milan; no more bouquets, no more ovations, no more crowns. His troops were looked upon then as the obedient janissaries of a capricious sultan; there was silence accordingly, there was vacancy; in vain the French regiments entered the cities, trumpets sounding and drums beating; the windows remained closed, and the inhabitants kept silence, or perhaps a single form was seen—that of a beautiful woman in deep mourning—at once a satire and a protest against the cowardly and treacherous peace. The two emperors disposed of Lombardy exactly as though the King of Sardinia had no existence. Francis Joseph yielded it to Napoleon, who passed it on to Victor Emmanuel. Was it for this that the Piedmontese Sovereign gained the battle of San Martino; that Garibaldi cleared the mountain tracks of Lombardy of the Austrians; that two Sardinian divisions covered the left wing of the French army, and contributed to the victory of Solferino? Was it for this that the Piedmontese army was upon the point of taking Peschiera, and that Garibaldi cut off the enemy's communication with Germany by the Stelvio? It is now almost universally supposed that wherever the French went they did everything; the ally was only an annoyance. As in the Crimea, so in Italy, the French contrived to throw their allies into the shade, and to monopolize to themselves the attention of the world.

The Emperor's own account of the matter, addressed to the senate and the other bodies of the State, who flocked to St.

Cloud to offer their official congratulations, was that he found it impossible to carry out the great work he had commenced, and, therefore, he recoiled before its magnitude; that by the time he arrived before the walls of Verona the struggle had assumed such formidable dimensions he dared not continue it. But it was not fear of Austria that stopped the French army. Solferino had given a death blow to Austria, and an insurrection was on the eve of breaking out in Hungary.

Garibaldi, on his part, issued the following order of the day: 'Whatever may be the march of existing circumstances, Italians must neither lay aside their arms nor be discouraged. They ought on the contrary to increase in number in the ranks, to testify to Europe that, guided by their King, Victor Emmanuel, they are ready to face again the vicissitudes of war, whatever they may be. Perhaps at the moment we least expect it, the signal of alarm may again be sounded."

Meanwhile the Grand Duke of Tuscany had fled, and his subjects wished for annexation to the Northern Italian Kingdom, then in course of formation. The fable of the faggot of sticks had not been lost upon them; but Napoleon, at this time, refused to give his consent to the arrangement. Cavour, who though out of office was frequently consulted by the ministers, suggested sending Garibaldi, as commander-in-chief of the army of the Centre, to Florence, in order that should any Italian counsels prevail, the inhabitants of the Centre, who could bear arms, might join that corps.* Garibaldi, on his part, placed his services unreservedly at the disposal of the ministers, departed at once for Florence, and issued the following proclamation: "Italians of the Centre! it is only a few months since we said to the Lombards, your brothers of all the provinces have sworn to

* It is certain, however, that if Canrobert's Corps had marched into Tuscany, as was expected, it would have been received with cries of "Long live Prince Napoleon our king." To check this, however, Senator Plezza was sent to Garibaldi to induce him to accept the command of the Tuscan army, which General Ulloa, who was accused of being one of the chief supporters of Prince Napoleon, had disorganized.

conquer or die with us, and the Austrians know whether we have kept our word. To-morrow we shall say to you what we then said to the Lombards, and the noble cause of your country will find you drawn up on the first field of battle, eager as we have lately been, and with the respect of men who have done and will do their duty. Returned to your homes, forget not amidst the embraces of those who are dear to you, the gratitude which you owe to Napoleon and to the heroic French nation, whose sons, wounded and mutilated, still suffer on the bed of pain for the cause of Italy." Wherever he went in the course of his tours of inspection, there seemed to be but one feeling, he was received with the most perfect ovation it is possible to conceive. The letters written from Florence at that time stated that the whole country was filled with joy, but his first object always appeared to be to postpone proffered hospitalities, and to cheer and comfort the wounded soldier by his presence.

At this time Napoleon wished to impose Prince Napoleon, as King, upon the Tuscans; but with Garibaldi in their midst, it was most unlikely that the Tuscans would meekly submit to dictation, or after Villa Franca, look favourably upon the cousin of the French Emperor. The Duchies of Central Italy had a formidable army, and this army was now commanded by Garibaldi. The General declared himself delighted with the demonstrations of the people; accepting them not for himself, but for his King, he recognized them only as intended to glorify the principles he represented—love of Italy, her glory, independence, and nationality.

Mazzini now declared his adhesion to the new state of things, and, frankly accepting the policy of the King, professed himself willing to renounce all personal views, touching the form of government, and promised that if the King could and would only make Italy one, and free, he should receive the support of the democratic faction which he represented. This declaration was very well received by the Italians, and many journals took occasion to observe how marvellously happy was the situation of Victor Emmanuel; for that he rallied around him men of all parties, however widely divided they might previously have been.

Garibaldi, in a letter from Bologna, proposed to purchase a million of rifles by means of a subscription which he himself headed with 5,000 francs, and which met with a cheerful reception by Italians generally. Meanwhile, however, his popularity aroused the jealousy of the Commanders of the regular Sardinian Army. General della Marmora gave proofs in Lombardy of his firm resolution to remove all national elements from the army; he had dissolved and taken up the victorious Cacciatori, and endeavoured to form the army into a purely Piedmontese institution, and by these means the popular discontent was daily on the increase. As an instance of the harshness of Della Marmora, the following anecdote may be mentioned:—One of the most rising painters of Italy, laying aside his easel for the rifle, enlisted as a private soldier in the Cacciatori in the beginning of the war; he was always first among the foremost, distinguished himself in every action, and rose by the bravery he displayed on the battle-field, step by step, until before the end of the war he had attained the rank of captain.—He then returned to his profession, and asked not for a pension or effective rank, but only that he might be allowed to keep his honorary rank and uniform—his request was refused, the principle being not to recognise the nominations of Garibaldi. Such measures as these, though they might be according to rule, yet were very short-sighted; they disheartened every one who did not belong to the clique, and in fact, nipped in the bud that Volunteer movement, which might, by proper management, have been made most serviceable. This discouragement began very early. At the end of the year, when the army of central Italy was being formed, orders were given to dismiss all the Volunteers from Central Italy, so that they might serve in their own province. As many as 18,000 or 20,000 of these passed through Modena, and received their pass and a franc to return, but not one could be induced to enter the regular army, so sickened were they of their Piedmontese experience, but all were ready to follow Garibaldi. General Fanti on resigning the superior command of the army, caused himself to be nominated Minister of War at Modena, and then in order to gain authority over Garibaldi demanded and obtained the suppression of the Ministry of War at Bologna, at which place Garibaldi was Commander-in-Chief. He thwarted Garibaldi in every possible manner, and even sent confidential messages to officers under the General's command, warning them not to execute the orders of their immediate chief. It was probably this which filled the cup, already full to overflowing, and induced Garibaldi to resign. It was correctly stated at the time in the *Daily Telegraph*, that the resignation of Garibaldi, and the simultaneous appointment of Buoncampagni, exhibited in startling colours the utter prostration of Sardinia before its Idol in Paris, and shewed plainly enough upon whom the whole ardour of Italian enthusiasm had been lavished. A hundred times over had Garibaldi fought the battle of independence and liberty in behalf of his native country—day and night he has devoted himself to the noble cause—there was no danger he had shunned, no toil, no fatigue, no rational expedition he had refused, to compass the ends of freedom—his life had been in danger, and he had proved himself the hero of a series of conflicts, (which with him are almost synonymous with victories;) in Rome, in Spanish America, in the fastnesses of the Alps, he had never flinched before an enemy, but had carried death and defeat wherever he had unsheathed his sword, and called on his devoted battalions to follow him. He had attached to himself a nation of patriots, because they believed him to be penetrated with a deep sense of the humiliation to which his country was subjected—they saw in him an ardent aspirant for her emancipation; when his hour was overcast, all felt it was with the contemplation of the misery of his countrymen; and Garibaldi was trusted as a true friend, and fêted with imperial honours whenever he appeared in public. No man stood higher in the estimation of his countrymen than the gallant Captain, who drove back the Austrians from the lake of Como, pursued them up the valley of the Valtelline, and was first to arrive on the banks of the Garda. Since that day, however, a collapse had taken place, Garibaldi resigned with mysterious promptness, and the only consolation he had bequeathed to his comrades and fellow-countrymen, was the assurance that he should resign for their good, and a promise that his sword would be ready to aid the common cause when an opportunity arose. Sensible men, however, must have thought seriously when they read the apologies put forward for his resignation, and they must have felt their hearts quake at the thought of the miserable confusion in which the affairs of Italy had been thrown.* By the military law of Piedmont, an officer, to give up his commission, must not state his reason for doing so. Unfortunately, knowing what had taken place, the head of General Garibaldi's staff wrote a private letter to his beloved chief, begging him to forward the writer's resignation along with his own, and stating his reasons for making the request—Garibaldi had left—a fact of which the writer was unaware when he forwarded the letter, and it fell into the hands of a very different General—the offender was instantly summoned to Florence, he unsuspectingly obeyed the order with military promptitude, and was instantly placed under close arrest. He had greatly distinguished himself in the campaign on the lakes, being seldom absent from his great leader's side, and had only recently recovered from fever, brought on by over-work and over-anxiety in the discharge of his duty—and what was the consideration now accorded to him for his past services? After a fortnight's imprisonment, he was liberated, with the loss of his commission, as an act of personal grace and favour from the King to Garibaldi himself.

* The correspondent of the DAILY TELEGRAPH writes:—If I were to give you only the extract of the papers relative to the retirement of Garibaldi, they would fill several columns, the circumstance is universally regretted, many predicting the most fatal consequences to the national cause, and it has, indeed, created the most profound sensation.

Garibaldi was by his valour, constancy, and daring, the idol of the Italian troops, and, by his virtue, an example which influenced the habits even of his commonest soldier. No man has in our days been so universally adored: the women loved him for his chivalry; the great mass of the people for his intrepidity and simplicity of character, and to follow him was to follow honour and virtue. In central Italy he was the most splendid personification of the national sentiments: a separation from him was for all a sad misfortune, inasmuch as many believed the National cause was abandoned and lost for ever. It was to check such a belief, and to prevent it from gaining ground, that Garibaldi issued the following Proclamation to his companions-in-arms in Central Italy:—"Let not my temporary absence cool your ardour for the holy cause that we defend. In separating myself from you whom I love as the representatives of the idea of the Italian deliverance, I am downcast and sad; but consolation comes in the certainty that I shall very soon be amongst you again to aid you in finishing the work so gloriously begun. For you, as for me, the greatest of all possible misfortunes would be not to be present whenever there is fighting for Italy. Young men, you who have sworn to be faithful to Italy and to the chief who will lead you to victory, lay not down your arms; remain firm at your post; continue your exercises, and persevere in the soldier's discipline. We desire to invade no foreign soil; let us remain unmolested in our own; whosoever attempts to gainsay this—our determination—will find that we will never be slaves, unless they succeed in crushing by force an entire people ready to die for liberty. I say again, do not lay down your arms; rally more closely than ever to your chiefs, and maintain the strictest discipline. Fellow-citizens, let not a man in Italy omit to contribute his mite to the national subscription, and let no one fail to clean his rifle, so as to be ready, perhaps to-morrow, when we may obtain by force that which to-day they hesitate to grant to our just rights."

"You ought not to thank me," he said, in answer to an

address from the National Guard "for the little I have done for you: I did it solely because it was the duty of a good citizen. If events had responded to my desire, I should certainly have done more. Unfortunately, we are living in the midst of a diplomatic armistice; but when the day comes in which we shall be forced to engage in the tempest, I will again be with you on the battle-field: only I repeat, for what I have done and for what I am still to do nobody ought to thank me. I obey only the dictates of my heart, and I fulfil the duties devolving upon me as an Italian. Permit me to thank you for this gratifying demonstration. I highly esteem the National Guard. When we have a million of armed citizens at home, and can dispose of 200,000 soldiers upon the battle-field, we shall no longer need the intervention of others—we shall be able to manage our own affairs."

A correspondent at Milan, writing to the *Times* in December stated that the resignation of Garibaldi had by no means checked the subscription for arms. That not a day passed on which the General did not receive numbers of letters from Italy as well as from abroad, announcing new subscriptions; every one wrote and expected an answer. In the mean time, the Garibaldi subscription had become more and more a demonstration, as well as a practical means of arming Italy. Even the Venetians had consented to take part in it, in spite of the Austrian police and Austrian system of espionage.

The Florentine correspondent, of the *Times* observed that if credit were given to all the rumours which were whispered about, it might have been thought that at the bottom of all the scandal arising from the silly conduct of the Tuscan Government, there were plotters and schemers acting upon suggestions from the Cabinet of the Tuileries. The whole battalion Paggi, mostly composed of the Cacciatori delle Alpi, had been bodily dismissed from the service of Central Italy, and in the other regiments the elimination continued. There was a regular razzia against the popular leader, although patriotism was quite the fashion in Italy; it was, in fact, more difficult than could be imagined to act as a true patriot; Garibaldi, however, had carried the self-denial, modesty, and disinterestedness of the patriot, to a point where it becomes almost a fault; his whole career had been one succession of sacrifices, not only of his own personal interests, but also of his own views and opinions. Animated by the most ardent love for his country, and for freedom, he never hesitated to submit every other consideration to the progress of the national cause; sincere and noble-minded himself, he believed in others as he did in himself. Although nurtured in the traditions of the free municipal life of ancient Italy, he forgot his own predilections to rally round the cross of Savoy when it first appeared in the field as the emblem of Italian unity and independance. In 1848, when the capitulation of Milan dispelled this fair dream, he retired to Rome, where there was still a chance of doing something for his beloved land, and held out, in spite of difficulties and disappointments, when every one else had given way. Although his upright nature instinctively divined the anomaly of a union with the man against whose soldiers he had tried to defend the freedom of Rome and the independance of Italy, he hastened where there was again a chance to fight for the national standard; unheeding all personal vexations and personal jealousies, and overcoming all obstacles thrown in his way, he followed his task in the mountains of Lombardy, until he imposed silence on his detractors and defeated the intrigues of others; although he had, as usual, been dismissed when he was no more required, instead of resenting the ingratitude, he was thankful for the opportunity thus given to work in a new field, and he went to Central Italy, which wanted an army. His name attracted thousands from Lombardy and Venetia, and, in a short time, the Romagna and the Duchies had more soldiers than they wanted. When the work was most prosperous, jealousy got alarmed, and Fanti was sent there to reap where he had not sown; one word from Garibaldi, and the Piedmontese inspector would have had to remain on the other side of the frontier. Instead of this, Garibaldi carried his patriotic magnanimity so far as to declare that he was superseded by his own consent, and the work he had so prosperously begun, he continued. When, in spite of his self-denial, it had become impossible to maintain his unnatural position, instead of using his power and getting rid of the intruder, he calmed the irritation of his troops, and went to Turin, where he not only gave in his resignation, but did all in his power to prevent the disbanding of the army in the Duchies and the Romagna. Feeling the importance of the movement, and seeing the disgust excited in the country by the narrow-minded and weak policy of the government, he thought it was his duty to bring the real state of things before the King, who, in his mind, was and is the ark of the union. Such is the simple story of these transactions. It cannot but force upon the mass of Italians, who are foreign to Piedmontese party intrigues, the conviction that those who claimed the lead as statesmen were unfit for the post, as they had their own personal interests more at heart than the common cause of their country.

The desire of the Emperor Napoleon was to form a kingdom in central Italy for a member of his own family; the great obstacle to this scheme was the spirit infused into the people by Garibaldi, the large armies he had raised, and the political action of the Garibaldini. At this crisis, the exertions of Guiseppe Dolfi, a man universally known and respected among an extensive circle of his townsmen had great influence in Florence. It was well known to every person in Florence that whenever Dolfi might choose to step into the Great Square before the Palazzo Vecchio, he could command 3,000, 4,000, or even 10,000 men. This man advised his friends to promote by all the means in their power, annexation to Piedmont. A writer at Milan stated that the dissatisfaction was not against Piedmont but against the Piedmontese ministry. In order to understand how this change was brought about, it must be borne in mind that the annexation to Piedmont meant for central Italy, as well as for Lombardy, the union of Italy. And so paramount was this aspiration, that everything else disappeared before it, and no sacrifice was thought too great to obtain this object. It was indeed no trifling sacrifice of old pride and ancient civic vanities when Milan, Florence, Parma, and Bologna resolved to forego their ancient and cherished dislikes, and adopt as their common object annexation to Piedmont. Certainly it was not any especial love for Piedmont, or reverence for Turin which inspired them with this vehement desire; it was not that they desired to become Piedmontese, but that they yearned to become Italians.

As an instance of the official jealousy of which Garibaldi and his Volunteers had been the object, a case may be mentioned in which this feeling was shown to such an extent, that it might not only have caused serious embarrassment and loss, but total destruction to the captain and his troops.

In the course of the Campaign on the Lakes, Garibaldi received instructions from the King to attack the Austrians* at a certain point, being informed also that the manœuvre was necessary to the plan of the campaign, and receiving a promise that he would be supported by the Piedmontese army. Garibaldi, although he had grounds for suspecting that when the time came this friendly aid might be some distance off, obeyed the directions, using the greatest caution in advancing against the

---

* A letter from a Garibaldian officer to the author, states, "You may freely assert that had the General obeyed on June 15, 1859, the order he had received from the King, he and all his soldiers would have been irretrievably lost.

In confirmation of this statement, I quote the following from *Garibaldi and the Italian Campaigns*, by Colonel Exalbion :—"For three or four days Garibaldi was supposed to be lost—either cut to pieces or forced to fly into Switzerland. It was asserted that Garibaldi had been betrayed into that false position by a promise to send him reinforcements, and that the promise was purposely broken in order to get rid of a man who had it in his power to become dangerous, and to destroy the reputation of the volunteers, and take away from the people all idea of conquering by their own efforts, leaving them no hope save in the regular army. The destruction of Garibaldi's troops would, it was said, extinguish all idea of a national war for a long while to come."

enemy. It was well that he did so, for as he had anticipated, he found himself entirely unsupported, and had he attacked in earnest, he and his little army must have been entirely destroyed.

Well knowing how badly he was supplied with everything, the French Emperor sent to offer supplies from the French Camp. Garibaldi, however, answered by expressing his sense of the kindness of his Imperial Majesty, but declared that his own King would supply all required. When spoken to afterwards on the subject, he observed, "You forget the deep debt of gratitude which I owe to Cavour for his having enabled me to serve once more my own Italy." To have confessed the trick might have seemed a reproach to that statesman, and it is well known he was not the one to blame. So great, indeed, were the difficulties Cavour encountered at the Turin war-office respecting the employment at all of the defender of Rome, that he afterwards, in one of the last speeches he ever made in the Italian Chamber, himself described them as very nearly insurmountable. Alas! this good understanding between these two great men was soon now to be destroyed; for we are approaching the melancholy history of the cession of Nice and Savoy.

CHAPTER II.

Count Cavour's Ministry formed, and Garibaldi returned as Member for Nice—Subscriptions for the National Rifle Fund—Suspicions of the sincerity of the Emperor of the French—Lord John Russell states that the Sardinian Government had no intention to cede Savoy to France, and Cavour assures Garibaldi of the same—Garibaldi refuses to accept the rank of General of Division in the French army, but prefers to remain a subject of King Victor Emmanuel—Garibaldi unanimously returned for Nice—Speech of Garibaldi—Manifesto of Lubonis—Garibaldi denies the legality of the transfer of Nice—his departure for Nice—Justification of the Annexation—Change of Garibaldi's feelings towards Cavour—The "Economist"—Enthusiasm for Garibaldi at Milan—Funeral of General Guaglia—Result of the Elections favourable to Piedmont—Sketch of the four political parties in Italy—Sketch of the old Piedmontese party—The Moderates and Sir James Hudson—The Garibaldian party—Cavour never intended the unity of Italy, but the aggrandisement of his own country—Garibaldi prefers any alliance to a French one—Garibaldi's introduction to Mazzini—Defence of Rome—Jealousy of Victor Emmanuel towards Garibaldi.

In the early part of January, 1860, the King accepted the resignation of the Ratazzi ministry, and charged Count Cavour with the formation a new cabinet. Garibaldi was returned, almost unanimously, member of the Chamber for Nice. His reception there had been most enthusiastic; he was overwhelmed with addresses from the people, and the authorities testified their respect by presenting him with a sword of honour.

The success of the subscriptions for the National Rifle Fund increased daily; almost every municipality in Lombardy followed the example given by Milan, and subscribed a smaller or larger sum, according to its means. The cities of Central Italy soon began to do the same; Bologna having given 20,000 francs,

Forli 5,000 francs, the towns of Venetia sent their mite; and even the remote provinces of Friuli and Istria contributed to arm the volunteers whom they sent to fight for their country. The most remarkable and significant feature in this subscription was, however, the general participation of the lower and poorer classes. It was this class who contributed most, in proportion to their means, (4,000 of them having contributed as much as 3,000 lire), while the wealthier classes rather remained behind; and it was remarked by Garibaldi, in his address to the people of Prato, in Tuscany, that in Italy it seemed that misery alone had something to spare.

At the same time, thousands of peasants were to be seen on Sunday flocking into the towns, bringing their contributions to Garibaldi's fund for the purchase of one million of muskets. They also wore in their hats the ticket for the vote of annexation to Piedmont, which was, in fact, as regards the people, almost unanimous. When first Garibaldi was summoned from Caprera, he expressed, both to the King and Cavour, doubts of the French Emperor's sincerity, but he was then informed that this was an error, and that the ruler of France was the true friend of Italy. Lord John Russell appears to have expressed the same opinion in the House of Commons; in 1859, when a rumour had been current for some weeks that as soon as peace should be signed, and Lombardy should be ceded to Sardinia, France would ask Savoy, as compensation for her expenses in the war, Lord John assured the House that the Emperor of the French had made no such demand, that he did not intend to make any addition to the frontiers of France, and our Foreign Minister considered that any addition whatever to the frontiers of France, however insignificant, following on the war, could not fail to rouse the suspicions and jealousies of Europe.

On the 17th of July, 1860, referring to the nature of the communications which had passed between Sardinia and England, Lord Russell stated that he had inquired of the Sardinian Government whether there was any engagement, or any intention, to yield Savoy to France, and the answer he received had been, that there was no engagement on the subject, and that Sardinia had no intention to cede Savoy to France. To Garibaldi Cavour gave a distinct denial that there had ever been any engagement or intention to give up either Nice or Savoy, and he even said that he "had never dreamt such a thing." It will be remembered also that when the Emperor of the French passed the Ticino and entered Milan, he solemnly proclaimed his pure disinterestedness in endeavouring to break the Austrian yoke, and in the most emphatic language that could be used repudiated the slightest suggestion of aggrandizing designs;* and on his return to Paris he used the same language, boasting that France alone, of all nations of the world, was capable of making war for an idea. Even so recently as the commencement of the Session of 1860, and certainly more than once during the following autumn, he assured our ministers, to allay their incipient suspicions, that no bargain or agreement had been made between France and Sardinia relative to the cession of Savoy. But now it may be said to be matter of history, and that before a single French soldier crossed the Alps in 1859—nay, even as far back as the 17th of January in that year—a definite and written agreement for that purpose had been entered into, and was signed by the Emperor's own hand. When the existence of some such compact for the transfer of Savoy became too notorious any longer to be denied, he assured Lord Russell, and authorized him to assure the House of Commons, "that however confident in the justice of his claim, he would not take any steps to carry it into effect without first consulting the great powers of Europe." Shortly afterwards, however, he finally accepted the cession, and proceeded to

---

* "The Emperor, in his proclamation to the people of Italy, from his head-quarters, at Milan, on the 8th of June, 1859, said:—" Your foes (who are mine) have tried to lessen the universal sympathy all Europe felt in your cause by giving out that I only made war for personal ambition, or to aggrandize the French territory. If there are men who cannot understand the epoch they live in I am not of that number."—See *Times* of July 18, 1860.

occupy the territory; and he exchanged his promise of waiting to consult the great powers for a cynical expression of his hope that some of the great powers would favorably examine his claim.

By arrangements between France and Sardinia, the civil and military functionaries of the provinces ceded to France, in passing under the French dominion, were to have preserved the same rank and pay as under the Sardinian Government. Garibaldi would, therefore, have obtained the rank of General of Division in the French army; but he at once most decidedly declared his choice was Italy, and that he intended to remain a subject of King Victor Emmanuel.*

A letter from the *Times* correspondent, writing in April, stated "that the only plausible defence of the Government was in these pithy words, 'Needs must, where the —— (Emperor) drives.'" Napoleon either actually compelled the Piedmontese to belie and almost to forswear themselves at every stage, or so misled as to involve them in reiterated flagrant contradictions or misconceptions—this latter, with Count Cavour's acuteness and fertility of resources, appears the less probable.

The election of a Deputy to the New Chambers at Nice was fixed for the 25th of March, and proved a blank failure, because the *Avenir* and other papers in the French interest had announced that the annexation of the country to France was a settled matter, and that the election of Members to the Piedmontese Parliament was, therefore, an idle ceremony. That announcement was, however, formally contradicted by an official proclamation, placing, as it were, the fate of Nice in the hands of its people, by promising an appeal to the public suffrage; and then, on the second election day, the voters rushed to the polling places in great numbers and returned Garibaldi all but unanimously. On that day, Nice voted not only for the General, but also for Italy. Garibaldi took his seat in the House, his

* *Times*, March 30th, 1863.

fair, or rather fox-coloured hair and complexion, and lion-like face, presenting a strange contrast to the countenances of the civilians around him. He professed to have come to do stout battle for his native city in the House, and to combat the annexation scheme by words as he would be too happy to fight against it by might of arm. It was announced in the Royal Speech that, out of gratitude to France, a sacrifice was necessary, and that the King had made the one which was dearest to his heart.

The *Times* correspondent conveys the best picture of the scene in the Chamber on that day. The General had taken his seat in the Chamber, and sat motionless hour after hour, exhibiting a rare power of endurance and composure under the infliction of the endless twaddle of some of his colleagues. Towards half-past four, the President of the Council of Ministers, Count Cavour, unexpectedly entered and took his place at the ministerial board, when almost instantly a deep ringing voice called out "Domando la Parola," the customary form by which a deputy expressed his wish to address the house—General Garibaldi was on his legs—a profound silence ensued, when the General in a few clear and fluent words begged leave to interrupt the present discussion for a short time while he put a question to the Minister of Foreign Affairs. The President of the Chamber offered a few remarks relative to the condition of the House, which was not yet legally constituted. Count Cavour broke in with great alacrity, and in a visible state of irritation, contending that no discussion was allowable before the Chamber had constituted itself, except on the subject of the verification of powers, adding with warmth and even a certain asperity, that even if a question were asked he would not answer it. Garibaldi insisted, upon which Cavour turned to the President and invited him to put the previous question to the vote of the Chamber. Deputy Robandi addressed the House in very passionate tones, pleading the urgency of the present situation, and contending that if the Austrians were at the gates of Turin, it would be idle to say that Parliament ought to remain inactive because the members were not formaly introduced to one another. Now the French were at Nice. Deputy Mellana observed that even if in the unconstituted state of the House it was not lawful to deliberate as to the purport of a question, there was, however, no reason why the question itself should not be put, and begged that freedom of speech should be given to the General—he added that it stood written nowhere in the constitution that the House could not deliberate in its present state. If the Chamber only existed after the verification of powers, why had it been sworn on Monday last? and if deputies were no deputies till their election was approved, why had the King on that day addressed mere nonentities? Rattazzi alleged precedents as arguments against any deliberation previous to the constitution of the Chamber. The House then divided, and after speedily disposing of the motion, adopted the previous question by a considerable majority. Thus was Garibaldi foiled in his first attempt to take up the cause of his native City. It was soon known that Savoy and Nice would be called upon to pronounce on their own destinies by universal suffrage, in about eight days, and if Nice could be made by fair means or foul to vote for annexation to France, there was an end for ever of Garibaldi's Parliamentary opposition, nevertheless, Cavour could not fail to have a "*mauvais quart d'heure*" before this Savoy and Nice matter was settled. On leaving the Carignano Palace Garibaldi was heard saying with anguish—"It is well the world should know the fine Parliament we have."

By the 7th of April, a great many of the Æmilian and Tuscan deputies had left Turin for their own homes, and some, indeed, left almost immediately after the Royal sitting, the general impression being that no very important discussion would take place previously to the King's journey to Central Italy, for which the 15th or 20th of the month was appointed. The short incident of Garibaldi's question, however, ought to have proved how rash it was for representatives of the people to reckon on the inactivity of the House. The harsh and flippant tone adopted by Count Cavour on this occasion left in men's minds an impression bordering on dismay. "Nice is sacrificed" people murmured, "and not one word to be said about it."

About this time the Provisional Governor of Nice, for the King of Piedmont, Lubonis, put forth a manifesto, by which the feelings even of the most apathetic were outraged. In the royal speech the King said he had "*stipulated*" a treaty (now, "*stipulated*" in Italian is not the same as "*concluded*"); and he also said that the negotiation was still subordinate to the suffrages of the people and the consent of the Parliament; yet, before any appeal to the people or any discussion occurred in the Chambers, the King withdrew his troops and his Governors, and Savoy and Nice were instantly occupied by French soldiers. The Governor's proclamation ran as follows:—"All uncertainty is at an end. By a treaty of the 24th of March last, the valorous King Victor Emmanuel had given up Savoy and the territory of Nice to France. Before the august word of the King, all uncertainty as to our future is dispelled. All opposition must break and become powerless against the interests of the country and the feeling of duty; nay, more, it would meet with an insuperable obstacle in the very wishes of Victor Emmanuel. Let us hasten and confirm with our votes the annexation of our country to France—let us become the echo of the intentions of the King—let us range ourselves round the throne of the glorious Emperor Napoleon III. —let us surround it with the fidelity characteristic of our country, a fidelity of which, up to this day, we have given such luminous proofs to the dynasty of Victor Emmanuel."

On the 12th of April, Garibaldi rose in his place in the Chambers, and in a firm clear voice began by reading the fifth article of the Constitution, by which no sale or barter of any part of the State can take place without the consent of Parliament. He explained to the House that the vote which had been put to the provinces, Nice and Savoy, was neither legal or valid without the sanction of the Chambers. Nice came into the power of the House of Savoy in 1388, and in 1391 a compact was made with Count Amadeus VII., by virtue of which the count could not part with' either the city or any part of the territory or people; but in the event of his releasing the people of Nice from their vote of allegiance, the latter were free in their choice of a new sovereign, without being therefore amenable to the charge of rebellion. The treaty of the 24th of March, by which the province was ceded to France, was not only an infraction of the old charter of Nice, but is also a violation of the right of nationality. They were told that the exchange of two small trans-Alpine provinces against Æmilia and Tuscany was a desirable bargain, but the sale of a people is always a deplorable transaction, and the Italians of the Centre had but a poor earnest of the account into which the rights and wishes of a people were taken. If the Government depended on the vote of the population, why should the vote of Nice be appointed for the 15th, while that of Savoy was to come off on the 22nd? The moral pressure then being exercised upon Nice rendered an appeal to universal suffrages a mere derision. Garibaldi then spoke of the intrigues of the French police—of briberies and threats—and of Lubonis's manifesto, and he ended by moving a resolution that the vote of the people of Nice should be put off till Parliament had fully deliberated on the subject. The motion was lost, and the House then adjourned.

On leaving the Chambers Garibaldi was received with the greatest enthusiasm by the vast crowd assembled outside, and was actually carried away in triumph. He said himself, with his usual modesty, that he might better trust his powers in handling a rifle than in addressing a house filled with some of the greatest literary celebrities in his country. He left for Nice on the following morning. Nice is a fair city, and an Italian city; it had fought bravely for the common cause—its citizens had no more desire to become Frenchmen than had the citizens of Turin. And indeed their deputy protested, in their name, against their being expelled from the Italian brotherhood. And it must be considered that this was something more than the cession of a province—it was as the sale and transfer of a land of faithful friends. There was great sorrow all over the province, while Garibaldi in singleness of heart and in ignorance of state-craft, was fighting the fight alone, and uttering words that echoed in the minds of his Italian compatriots. The first act of the first Italian Parliament was to ratify the sale of the people of Nice.

Mr. Dicey, in his able Memoirs of Count Cavour, admits that it is difficult to acquit Cavour of virtual dishonesty towards Italy and towards the ceded provinces. The common English justification is, that necessity knows no law, and that Cavour, knowing that Italy was in the power of France, had no choice except to accede to any demands of the French Government. This justification is more simple than satisfactory; it is by no means clear that there was such an absolute necessity of yielding to France. France could not make war against Sardinia in order to annex Savoy and Nice; and, short of making war, there was no way by which the annexation could be effected without Sardinia's consent. If, then, the cession was a political crime, as it is commonly represented to have been, it would seem that nothing but absolute necessity could excuse it.

Terrible as was to Garibaldi the loss of his beloved Nice, it was as nothing in comparison to the revolution of feeling towards Count Cavour; he was unable any longer to feel either gratitude or affection towards one whom he thought had wilfully deceived him from the first, and had compromised the honor of his King and country. Is it a question,—Who gave Cavour (the Constitutional Minister of a Constitutional King) either at Plombieres, or any where else, permission to cede provinces to France or any other country, and this without consulting Parliament, or making the slightest stipulation respecting their future rights? Was such power ever, in this world, allowed to the Plenipotentiary of a constitutional state before? The loss of Nice itself gave not half the grief to Garibaldi that did the feeling that such a fearful inroad had been made into the national independence of Italy, and such a terrible breach in her constitutional liberties. The *Times* correspondent asserted that, "Cavour, accustomed as he was to the exercise of very absolute power within the Cabinet, in which he frequently took two or even three portfolios upon his own shoulders, to rouse and to lull at his pleasure—to browbeat, and sometimes even to bully the Parliament—Cavour never stopped to consider the nature of a promise which bound him to the sale or barter of rational beings, and gave himself as little concern about it as if they were dumb cattle. There is hardly an Italian able to explain to me how it was that Count Cavour was betrayed into that shameless declaration, that "he had never dreamt of giving up Nice and Savoy."

The *Economist* argued that the annexation of Savoy to France was a grave fact, and gave rise to graver reflections. The act itself was grave enough, the manner in which it had been accomplished, and the language in which it had been announced, were graver still. This article pointed out what conclusions must be forced upon the conviction of Englishmen by the whole course and tenor of the proceedings taken by France in this affair; that their opinion of Victor Emmanuel and Cavour must be sadly lowered by their tame complicity in what appeared, at least, like an underhand intrigue, a shabby bargain, and an unwarrantable cession; henceforth said the writer, there could be no more cordiality or intercourse towards the Emperor, because there could be no confidence in his intentions and no trust in his word.*

* It is, however, asserted that the *Times* and *Economist* were only half informed; the most current English justification of Cavour is that he was in earnest when he stated that there was no intention of abandoning Nice and Savoy. It was the King who had made the agreement with the Emperor for the cession, unknown to Cavour, and his Majesty pleaded that, having made a promise, he felt it binding on his honour. Cavour sacrificed his own popularity to save that of the King. But supposing this be the correct version, where was kingly honour when the deputation from Nice was received at the palace with assurances that all rumours of the cession were groundless, and that their King would be the first to protest against such a measure, and where was it when Garibaldi was written to in similar terms!

When Garibaldi passed through Milan on his way to Turin, whither he had been summoned by the King, he most anxiously wished to avoid all demonstrations. In spite of every precaution, however, when his presence became known he found the staff and many officers of the National Guard, who greeted him in the name of the national force of Milan. He made an appropriate answer, in which he pointed out the importance of the National Guard in any national struggle exerting the organization of that force. The municipality of the town, with the Podesta at their head, came to welcome him. He received them; and then feeling tired withdrew to his room, but only to leave it again; for the news of his arrival having spread, crowds of people assembled in the evening in the Corso di Porta Nouva, where he had taken up his abode. The band of the National Guard arrived, and a demonstration began such as had not been witnessed since the first days of joy in the preceding month of June. The broad corso was full of people, cheering and shouting almost without interruption; an illumination was imprôvised all along the high street. Garibaldi was obliged again to come forward to the balcony: the sight of him seemed to revive the best traditions of Milanese enthusiasm. He addressed the crowd, telling them he took the ovation less for himself than for the great principle which he represented, "the idea of a free united Italy;" he exhorted the people to persevere in their endeavours to realize this great idea, and not to lay down their arms until Venetia should be free and Italy united. The enthusiastic crowd forgot everything—the delicate health of Garibaldi and the foggy night included—until the General reminded them of the cold, and asked to be excused. Hours after he retired the demonstration continued: it was as if the crowd had long restrained its feeling, and would not let pass an opportunity of venting its enthusiasm and real sentiments.

The authorities of Central Italy wrote to the committees which had been formed for the Garibaldi subscriptions, asking to have the produce of that subscription. The committees of course refused to give up their trust, which the subscribers intended to be at the disposal of Garibaldi. Garibaldi was for some time the centre of ovations at Turin, and had to pass his time in receiving deputations and haranguing the people, for Turin evidently was not willing to be behind any other Italian town in this respect. The liberal party there gave him a dinner, at which a number of Members of the Parliament were present. It was in connection with the establishment of the new political society, called "La Nazione Armata." The committee of the *Liberi Comizii*, composed chiefly of members of the Parliamentary Left, appealed to Garibaldi to become a member of that society. His answer was, that he had no wish to belong to any of the committees in existence, but he desired all Liberals to unite and arm. The two committees decided to unite, and nothing could be better than such a union of all the liberals, and if there was any name to bring it about, it certainly was that of Garibaldi, and if all had been as patriotic and upright as he, nothing would have been easier. For one fact might have made Garibaldi's position clear in the eyes of Europe, namely, that his name sufficed, even in Piedmont, to banish, at least for a time, anger, jealousy, and disunion; he electrified the masses wherever he shewed his countenance, or only suffered his name to be whispered.

The burial of General Quaglia, the President of the Chamber, gave rise on Easter Sunday to an affecting incident. The funeral was appointed at six o'clock in the evening and among the Members of Parliament following the body the vast assembled crowd singled out Garibaldi. At the door of the church of San Filippo 5,000 persons were thronged together. No sooner had the body with the chief mourners entered the sacred edifice than all at once a deafening shout broke from the assembled multitude. The cry was, "Viva Garibaldi!" "Viva Italia!" The General, who was far from expecting this ovation, endeavoured to escape from it by running into the church after the body, but the people closed around him, beset the church door, and pressed so hard that it was with the greatest difficulty, and only by the strongest exertion on the part of some of his friends, that the General, relinquishing his former purpose, succeeded in disengaging himself, and escaped for refuge into the neighbouring Palazzo Carignano, closely followed by the sovereign people, whom he was obliged to address from a window, representing to them how unbecoming it was to disturb the mournful ceremony which had called them together by any demonstration totally foreign to it. The crowd then quietly dispersed.

The result of the elections in all the four provinces of Tuscany, Parma, Modena, and the Romagna, was, that the people decided for annexation to the Sardinian Kingdom, and utterly rejected both the claims of their hereditary sovereigns, and the scheme which had lately been put forward by the Emperor of the French. Up to this day, Piedmont had been utterly at the mercy of France, and had taken good care not to avow the conduct of the Central Italians; but the King's answer to the Deputies of the Central Italian assemblies in the preceding September, and the pitiful shifts of his ministers (Rattazzi & Co.) left no doubt as to the perfect and absolute inability of the Piedmontese statesmen to uphold the annexation vote. When, however, Count Cavour came into office, undeterred by the threat of France to withdraw from the contest and to leave Sardinia to contend alone against Austria and Naples, he, on behalf of his country, boldly accepted the position, and declared that if the Tuscans should persist in their desire to annex themselves to Piedmont, the King of Sardinia was resolved to accept them as his subjects. In the face of M. de Thouvenel's despatch, the Count declared that he accepted beforehand the contingency of the annexation. The next phase, therefore, of this strangely shifting question promised to be, that Northern and Central Italy would constitute themselves a single Power, in the face of the express or tacit disapproval of every one of the great Powers except England.

Before entering into the stirring events at this period, related in the next chapter, we ought to understand the relative political divisions of society that were then in Italy. In 1860, four parties existed in Italy; first, the old Piedmontese party; second, the self-called Moderates; thirdly, the party of Garibaldi, called the Garibaldini; and fourthly, the party of Mazzini. The old Piedmont party can be dismissed in a very few words, for it was and is a party that believed in a King of Piedmont—never in a King of Italy—it was alternately the slave of Austria and France, and perfectly content to be so. It still consists of a few nobles and priests, with their adherents—yet encumbered with their old traditions—speaking the patois of petit Piedmont. They are, in fact, as the *Times'* correspondent in 1863, described them, a party for whom the clock has stood still since Charles Albert proclaimed himself a constitutional King. For genuine primitive conservatism there is no nobility at all equal to the old-fashioned Piedmontese nobility! There are families whose houses have grown too large for them, but who are blind to the fact that the town has grown too small for its population. People who will rather allow their premises to go to decay than misdemean themselves by receiving a rental, and would a thousand times sooner burn their property down to the ground than permit Jew or Protestant to become tenants—nay, it is a fact, there was lately a young noble at Turin, who being coaxed to go out in the evening by his newly married wife, bade his footmen light the links and torches of the good olden times, because he had actually never made out by eyesight or hearsay that the streets were lighted with gas after eight o'clock. A few scores of worthy families of this description made up, what was called in Piedmont, before 1848, La società, and not a few of them have resisted all change. Anyhow, the genuine noble keeps true to the almanack of the year of grace 1815—before National Guards, Chambers, annexations, and similar vagaries were heard of—they were accustomed to identify their cause, almost their own persons, with the reigning house—they knew they had their place at court, in the army, and in the state—they looked upon office as their birthright, not to be taken from them by any political innovation, they accepted amalgamation and fraternization with the Italian races, and learnt, with well-bred condescension, that they were of one blood and one family with them. They hardly inquired to what extent all this would alter their position, but were well-determined that it should in no way change their nature, their manners and customs, their tenets and prejudices. This class seldom alludes to politics, and never complains; but it keeps aloof from stirring life, muses and broods, or idles and trifles existence away. Sometimes it indulges in a fit of contradiction—takes up the Pope's cause and the Priests', out of mere spite, caprice, and bravado, and young men, bearing the names of the noblest patriots, take pride in affecting the darkest die of retrogradism. They are too honorable to conspire—too loyal to rebel; but they fret, and protest, and mutter threats which are never meant to be carried into effect. The real, sorrowful fact is, that this old-fashioned Piedmontese società is ill educated. They have been brought up by monks and nuns, and their ignorance and prejudices are something appalling. Even at the present day most of the scions of noble houses are sent for their schooling to colleges of the Loyola brotherhood, in France. The girls, if no nuns are at hand, are educated in a kind of domestic nunnery. Italian books are never read; and as to French literature, the respectable families have a pious horror of it. Hence, there is but little culture for the young, and none whatever for the adult. The young ladies employ their energies in embroidery, while the older ones take snuff and talk scandal. Summer or winter, town or country, bring very little variety to the quiet tenor of their existence. Access to their drawing-rooms is not very easily obtained, and is hardly worth the trouble of obtaining, for the society there is very stiff and formal. Victor Emmanuel, as the *Times'* correspondent wrote, was at heart of this party, but possessed "no refined tastes—no very reputable companions

The key to a Piedmontese heart, from the King to the peasant, is the Piedmontese dialect."

It is to be hoped, however, that the days of this clique are numbered, and that the time is fast approaching when a different state of things may be expected. Let us not forget that the great City of Manchester, within our own time, was not represented in the Imperial Parliament of Great Britain. Two noble lords did all in their power to prevent the formation of the Liverpool and Manchester Railway; and a hundred other trifles tend to prove that once England, as well as Italy, contained a party like that of old Piedmont.

The Moderates are a party who believe entirely in the French alliance, and hold that the liberties of Italy can only be secured through the sovereign will and good pleasure of his Majesty Napoleon III. This is the party which in 1859, when a victorious career lay before them, made peace because peace was necessary for the interests of France. The head of this Moderate, or French Party, was Count Cavour; but from the peace of Villa Franca to the 14th of January, 1860, the head of it was, of course, Rattazzi—and the nature of the acts of his Government has already been shewn. Sir James Hudson, the late English ambassador at the Court of Turin (who is a most accomplished gentleman, and was a worthy representative of the British nation, and a firm friend to the liberties of Italy), was the devoted admirer of Count Cavour, referred all questions to him, and to him alone, and regarded the terms "Cavour" and "Italy" as synonymous. Yet it was no proof of his influence with that great statesman that, at that very time, Cavour threw himself body and soul into the views of the Emperor of the French, to the almost utter exclusion of English influence. It is, however, to the credit of the Moderates, that very early in 1860 they dispatched agents to Sicily, with the view of ascertaining the true state of affairs in that island, and of discovering if it would be possible to free it in any way from Bourbon misrule. The messengers returned to their employers in Turin with the information that any project of the kind was utterly hopeless. They reported that though there had been and was a tendency to insurrection amongst the lowest classes, yet generally the people really appeared very contented, and certain defeat would attend any expedition from Piedmont, be the commander whom he might. The correctness of this account was not only believed by the ministers, but even at the time by General Garibaldi himself, who was summoned to Turin to be offered the command of the National Guard, and who was informed of everything which had taken place, the information being conveyed with all the red-tapism and dogmatism imaginable. In Turin he was also assured, that as any expedition must certainly prove an entire failure, no plan of the sort could receive their support; and that if he were foolhardy enough ever to allow himself to be drawn into anything of the kind, when the moment of defeat arrived, no effort whatever would be made to free from a well-earned imprisonment those who had not perished under the bayonets of the victorious Neapolitan soldiery, or fallen by the hands of military executioners; in fact, it was well understood by all parties that the promoters of any such enterprise were to be abandoned to their fate, whatever that fate might be.

The Garibaldian party had for their chiefs the Deputies Mordini, Crispi, Caroli, Bertani, the Marquis Pallavicini, and many others, while they fearlessly claimed to have in their ranks an enormous preponderance of all that was enlightened and intelligent in Italy. In the first place, their argument has been that the alliance between Italy and France could never be genuine; that France having a government nearly despotic, would never view with friendly eyes a neighbouring state struggling to acquire free institutions. France was much more powerful than Italy in any combined war; she, in reality, commanded the forces of both countries, could make peace at her own pleasure, and to suit the interests of France alone, which interests being those of a despotic empire, had often proved antagonistic to Italy. The Peace of Villa Franca, the cession of Nice and Savoy, the more recent commercial treaty with France are but illustrations.*

The Moderate party was very fond of saying that it was Count Cavour who originated and maintained the French alliance. But what was the policy of Count Cavour? The thing most remarkable about it, was the facility with which he adapted himself to circumstances; and even when events turned out entirely different to his previous expectations, the ease with which he availed himself of them, and yielded to what he believed to be the true interests of his country; for instance, in the early part of 1859, Count Cavour had never dreamt of a United Italy—whatever intention he might or might not have had regarding the cession of Nice—but he had dreamt of one thing, and that was the aggrandizement of Piedmont, and it was this which led to the agreement at Plombieres, now matter of history; by this agreement Cavour stipulated for Piedmont the acquisition of the whole Valley of the Po as far as the Adriatic, embracing the Lombardo-Venetian kingdom, the Duchies of Parma, Modena, and the Legations, making up a North Italian state of at least 12,000,000 souls. In return for this aggrandizement Sardinia céded to France, Savoy and Nice, and allowed France to build up a Central Italian state in Tuscany and the Cisapennine part of the Papal territory in behalf of Prince Napoleon.

Now, to obtain all this territory the sword of Garibaldi would prove most useful. He was accordingly summoned to Turin. His active support was gained, and from him the agreement at Plombieres was carefully concealed. The spirit infused by Garibaldi and his party into the whole of North Italy rendered it difficult, if not impossible to carry out these plans; a united Italy not being compatible with the Mediterranean French lake scheme. Peace was hastily patched up—Cavour, then out of

---

* The Emperor obtained the freedom to trade with 1,800 miles of coast, in exchange for 600 on his own side.

office, was opening his eyes to the possibility of a *United Northern Italy* at least, and he contrived to have Garibaldi sent to Florence to organize the armies, which is so necessary to independence of action.

Cavour, accordingly, accepted the new position, and reaping where he had never sown, at once declared his acceptance of the annexation and all its responsibilities. Those who are anxious to tread in the footsteps of Count Cavour, would do well to remember that before his death he was well sickened of the French alliance, which, however necessary he might have considered it to the development of his plans in 1859, he considered by no means necessary in 1861. After his full and entire reconciliation with General Garibaldi in the latter part of April, 1861, he observed quietly to more than one person, "*Any alliance now rather than the alliance of France.*" In 1861, he believed in the possibility of a united Italy, and felt now how little chance there was of Napoleon ever peacefully quitting Rome. Perhaps, in their last interview, Cavour, for the first time in his life, really understood and did full justice to the noble character of Garibaldi. The fourth party in Italy in 1860 was very small, but powerful in comparison to its numbers, from the intelligence of its members, and its ceaseless activity: this was the party of Mazzini; formerly its principles had been republican, but it has been shown that it had now accepted those of a constitutional monarchy, and sworn allegiance to the crown of Victor Emmanuel. Garibaldi never joined the Mazzini party; they, however, joined themselves to him, forming to the Garibaldini an extreme left, affording them much the same kind of support that the radical members in England sometimes give to the Government of Lord Palmerston, although on many points they may totally disagree with him.

"I have nothing to do with men or political parties," one day observed Garibaldi,—"my country and nothing but my country is my object. Columbus was not more delighted at the cry of 'Land' after so many wanderings through the dreary wastes of the Atlantic, than I was at hearing the word country pronounced, and on seeing in the horizon the first pharos lit up by the French revolution of 1830."

In 1833 Garibaldi was first introduced to Mazzini, who succeeded in imbuing him with his own views. At that time Mazzini was engaged in risking an attempt for the republican cause, and in this he involved the aid of his new friend—it was afterwards called the rash enterprise of St. Juliano—and signally failed. The first time General Garibaldi ever saw his own name mentioned in a newspaper was to read in the Peuple Souverain that he was condemned to death—he had therefore to leave his country, and he took refuge in Montevideo, which state he saved, defended it alike from Rosas and all comers, and only left it after its freedom had been established, and its prosperity secured. Before he left for Europe he himself refused, and on behalf of the Italian Legion declined the rewards and grants of land offered, stating they did not, when asking for arms, and offering their services to the Republic, contemplate receiving any other reward than the honour of sharing the perils of the children of the country which had afforded them hospitality. They obeyed, whilst acting thus, the voice of their conscience: having satisfied that, which they considered simply the accomplishment of a duty, they desired no other price or recompence. On the 27th of March, 1848, he left South America, and landed at Nice on the 24th of June,—all Nice flocked to welcome him, and volunteers from every quarter joined his standard. He was now convinced that a constitutional monarchy afforded the best hopes for the prosperity of Italy, and consequently, Piedmont, the only Italian state which had even the shadow of a constitution, received the offer of his allegiance and his sword; and his programme was then as now, "United Italy, with Rome for the Capital!" It was not until the French attacked Rome that Garibaldi entered it,—with Mazzini's Government he had nothing to do,—that which he did undertake was to keep the enemy from the gates, if possible.

The splendid defence of Rome by Garibaldi is matter of history, and it is also well known that had he had his own way there, the French might have been thoroughly defeated, whereas his ardour was checked by the refusal of Mazzini to give him the troops he asked for, on the ground that if completely defeated France would be the mortal enemy of Italy. This serious error on the part of Mazzini, deprived Garibaldi of a glorious victory, and rendered his success fruitless. It was a fatal error, but yet excusable in a man who had placed all his hopes in the French democratic party, but for Italy it was a source of incalculably evil consequences. Garibaldi's plan, had it been adopted, would have changed the history of Italy; there would no longer have been a question of a French or any other than an Italian occupation of Rome. After this check, all General Garibaldi could do was to preserve Italian honor, which certainly has never suffered in his hands. These circumstances are referred to because so many misconceptions have existed in England respecting the early connection between Garibaldi and Mazzini, and the extent to which this connection might be likely to influence his future conduct. Mazzini has been much and unnecessarily maligned by those who are ignorant of his real character, but one fact greatly to his honor may be mentioned, which is, that the last 30,000francs he possessed he sent in the autumn of the year of which we are writing, to Garibaldi, to assist him to bring the Calabrians to Naples.*

---

* See a leader in the *Times* of October 7th, 1862.

CHAPTER III.

Official efforts of the Government to suppress the expedition of Garibaldi—Comments of the "Times" on Garibaldi's expedition—Heroism of Garibaldi—Letter from Garibaldi to Dr. Bertani—He writes to the King on the state of Sicily—Proclamation of Garibaldi to the people of Sicily—Same to the Italian army—Little army of Garibaldi in Sicily—First Battle—Garibaldi assumes the title of Dictator of Sicily—Onward march of the Liberators—Garibaldi enters Palermo, and defeats General Lauza—Carelessness of the Sicilians as to form of Government, and their confidence in General Garibaldi—Relation by Admiral Mundy of the Bombardment of Palermo—Admiral Mundy is selected as a Mediator between Generals Lanza and Garibaldi—Dishonorable conduct of the Royalists—Articles of the Convention, and their final adoption—Civil and Military Administration—Educational Estblishments—Ugo Bassi—Monarchical form of Government—Banishment of La Farina.

We now approach that great event, the invasion of Sicily by Garibaldi, which is the next chapter in the history of this patriot. On returning from Sicily, as we saw in the last chapter, Mazzini's agent reported that it would be dangerous to attempt anything in that quarter; still it was not considered impossible that great good to the Italian cause might be effected if Garibaldi decided to undertake the expedition, and throw the weight of his immense prestige into the scale. Mazzini promised him support, and all the money he could collect in England and in other countries. Garibaldi was to be left perfectly free in every way to act as he himself thought best for the interests of Italy. It is but common justice to state that nothing could be more straightforward and open than the conduct of Mazzini in this matter. He accepted Garibald's own programme, gave him all the information in his power, and unconditionally supported him. Garibaldi thinking it was the duty of all Italians to aid and augment the number of combatants against oppression, and though he had not advised an insurrection, yet that from the moment his Sicilian brethren threw themselves into the struggle, he was bound to assist them, after much consideration finally decided to join in the enterprise.

The negotiations with the ministers at Turin, respecting his taking the command of the National Guard, were broken off, he even resigned his commission as general in the Piedmontese service. Dr. Bertani held for him at Genoa, money to the amount of £40,000 collected in the different towns in Italy; subscriptions were also made in England, an Italian Unity Committee was formed in London and other towns, and the expedition of the thousand was prepared. The *Times* correspondent wrote at this time—"That he was told, though he would never believe it, that the utmost had been done to estrange the heart of King Victor Emmanuel from his self-sacrificing leader, by rousing up in the upright, but perhaps, over-confiding mind of the King, a jealousy of the 'Nizzard adventurer,' akin to the feelings of Saul for young David. There were those even who asserted that the King evinced some vexation as he proceeded on his ovations through Central Italy, whenever the name of the hero of Varese happened to be coupled, in the people's outcry, with that of the conqueror of San Martino." Well aware was Garibaldi of all that was reported, and confident in his own boundless devotion and loyalty to his king and to Italy, he fearlessly trusted to that alone to overcome every difficulty of the sort, and attributing in a constitutional monarchy whatever was wrong to the ministers, he replied only to those about him, in the following words:—"I go to conquer fresh thrones for King Victor Emmanuel, or to perish in the attempt." And so, from a country house near Genoa, on the night of the 5th of May, 1860, Garibaldi, against the consent of the Government at Turin, and, as they solemnly stated without their knowledge,* started to make private war, though intended, ultimately, for the advantage of Italy, against the King of Naples, at that time an ally, and at peace with the new kingdom of northern Italy. If, in this desperate venture, some who had stood at Rome by Garibaldi's side, and afterwards attended him on the heights of Aspromonte, were found absent, let those who would blame them read carefully over Mr. Gladstone's account of a visit to the Neapolitan prisons, and if this is not satisfactory, refer to the "Exiles of Italy," and ponder well on every statement therein contained. It was never the risk of death by the General's side that kept back any who had ever served Garibaldi; it was the fear and the apparent certainty that, if they escaped the Neapolitan soldiers and the military executioners, they would have to pass the remainder of their existence in the loathsome dungeons which have now been so often truthfully described. It must also be remembered that Garibaldi had 1,000 volunteers only, and that he was to be opposed to 128,000 well-trained, and well-appointed regular troops.

Count Cavour and the Piedmontese Government had ordered all arms and ammunition which had been deposited at Quarto, near Genoa, to be seized, and had also given orders for the port of Genoa to be watched. The Government, in fact, made every possible protest against this act of General Garibaldi, which

* It is, however, certain that Cavour knew, though he disapproved of the proposed expedition,—he might not know any of the details, but he felt that it was not for his comfort to have Garibaldi either at Nice or in Turin during the period when he was finishing the session of Nice and Savoy. He preferred, consequently, that the General should be in a difficult position in Sicily. Previously to the sailing of the Marsala expedition. Cavour took forcible possession of all the arms and money which the General had deposited in Milan, under the charge of the Committee, for the purchase of the million of muskets; neither arms or money were at any time restored to Garibaldi. Cavour well knew that the means at Garibaldi's disposal were so scanty as to make success very difficult. The most intimate friend and confidant of Cavour was La Farina. A person in whom he took a great interest, wished to join Garibaldi the day before the departure of the General, La Farina telegraphed to his friend not to join Garibaldi, as the expedition would terminate nowhere but at the bottom of the sea.

might involve the new Italian state in serious difficulties. Garibaldi's soldiers seized two steamers of the Genoese Company (Rubatino and Co.) the *Piedmonte* and the *Lombardo*, which were in the roadstead at Genoa, and once outside the port, they steamed along the coast, picking up the volunteers at various points previously fixed upon. The Director of the Company lodged a complaint in due form, and immediately telegraphic orders were received from Turin to watch the coast, and to seize all the arms they could discover; but all the volunteers had already embarked. The Sardinian Government, at the same time, sent out the fast screw-frigate, *Maria Adelaide*, under the orders of Admiral Persano, in pursuit of the expedition.*

The *Constitutionnel*, at this period, published an article signed by M. Grandguillot, which asserted that the reply of Count Cavour to M. Thouvenel proved that Piedmont as well as France "energetically blamed the audacious attempt of Garibaldi." M. de Carafa forwarded a circular on the part of the Neapolitan Government to the diplomatic corps, bitterly accusing the Piedmontese Government of having, notwithstanding its promises, allowed bands of volunteers to be enrolled, armed, and dispatched to Sicily,—that this violent attack against international law exposed Italy to sanguinary anarchy, and compromised the whole of Europe. The Marquis de Villa Marina, in the name of Sardinia, protested against this accusation as false and injurious; and the official *Piedmontese Gazette* published an article refuting the accusation of Ministerial connivance in the affair. The article said that the government disapproved of the expedition, and attempted to prevent its departure, by such means as prudence and the laws would permit. The Sardinian ships of war had orders to prevent a landing, but could do no more than

* Admiral Persano's official orders were to capture Garibaldi. It is, however, supposed that Cavour shrank from the obloquy which the arrest and trial of the popular General would have brought upon him, and that his secret instructions were not in accordance with his official ones.

the Neapolitan vessels, which were cruising in the Sicilian waters. Mr. Diecy was correct when he wrote that there was no greater error than to suppose that the whole history of the Italian revolution, was an elaborate scheme of Machiavellian ingenuity, forecast, and devised by Cavour. At the commencement of 1860, there was nothing further from Cavour's thoughts, than the annexation of Southern Italy. While Victor Emmanuel was making his triumphal entry into Tuscany, the first tidings came of the Sicilian insurrection. He had not left the Duchy of Parma, at the conclusion of his royal progress, when the rumour spread that Garibaldi was about to join the insurgents. Of the insurrection itself, the Sardinian government thought little, and with reason. Mr. Dicey says, from what he could learn in Sicily, some months after the revolution, the native insurrection was practically suppressed by the royal troops, and it was only the announcement that Garibaldi was approaching, that kept together the insurgents at all till they had effected the landing at Marsala. At the time, Cavour had little belief in the success of the expedition. The insurrection had taken place against his judgment, and without his sanction: possibly he would not have regretted its failure.*

Garibaldi, as the correspondent of the *Times* writes, was ever ready for self-sacrifice, and embarked at Genoa, as it was supposed for the coast of Sicily, or of the neighbouring southern kingdom. Appalling as such a report was to all the lovers of the Italian cause and to the personal friends of the heroic guerillero, there were many sufficiently confident in the fortunes of that daring patriot, in the prestige of his name, and of the effect of his landing, both on friends and foes, to anticipate for him a better fate than that which awaited Murat on the Calabrian shores. If Garibaldi succumbed in the attempt, he would most

* Count Arrivabene, who was with Cavour at the time, writes—"I have every reason to believe that Count Cavour, far from having encouraged the project of Garibaldi, tried all he could to prevent it. A practical man, as Cavour was, could not have had great faith in the result of an expedition which everybody thought at the time to be mere madness."

assuredly sell his life at a very high price, and the bitterness which has lately filled the cup of his existence inclines people to think that a glorious death would not have been for him the worst of contingencies.

The *Times* of the 12th of May contains a letter to the effect that this enterprise was beyond the limits of either praise or blame. The man, the cause, and the circumstances, were so extraordinary, that they must be judged by themselves. Success would have stamped Garibaldi as a general and statesman of the highest rank; defeat, ruin, and death would cause him to be remembered as a Quixotic adventurer of dauntless courage but of feeble judgment. The expedition to Sicily would in future be ranked with the landing of William of Orange in England, or with Murat's landing in Calabria; all that was certain was the heroic courage of the man by whom the attempt was made. It was possible that if the communications with the mainland were cut off, the insurgents would have been able to hold their own against the troops already in the island, but in case the king was at liberty to use the whole strength of the state in coercing the refractory province, the *Times* thought the cause which Garibaldi had espoused was a desperate one.

"What would be mere rashness and stark madness," wrote the *Times*, "in another, is no more in Garibaldi than faith in his own good star. In him, mere impulse in action is better than other men's caution and fore-thought." Again, "The tone in which Garibaldi spoke to those who urged upon him the desperate character of his enterprise, touched upon that sublimity which may seem akin to madness; to those who called his attention to the chances of meeting with the Neapolitan cruisers, he talked about the feasibility of boarding the Neapolitan frigates, and taking possession of them one after the other; he also remarked that a navy was the very thing he should want the most, and that they would be very useful. Those who well knowing his devoted love and affection for his eldest son, implored him almost on their knees to spare the youthful Menotti, and not to cast a blight on a life which he had given, and to remember how little was to be hoped from the tender mercy of a king of Naples, so closely allied with Austria. The only response gained was—"I only wish I had ten Menottis, in order that I might risk them all."

Garibaldi was despaired of in the fearful straits in which he had put himself at Varese less than a year before. He had not more than a handful of men with him at Velletri. Yet he drove the father of this very Bourbon whom he now assailed in ignominious flight; a flight which, but for the pressure of the besieging French force around Rome, would never have stopped except under the cannon of the Neapolitan forts. Nay, was not King Ferdinand within an inch of falling into the hands of the adventurer, and gracing with his presence a triumph which might have given altogether a different turn to the disastrous vicissitudes of 1849. The destinies of Southern, and, indeed, of all Italy, hung on the cast of a die. Was not the deliverance of one half of Italy little short of a miracle? Is there a limit to the might of a wonder-working Providence? Such were the remarks that rose uppermost, wherever two or three were gathered together to discuss the one event of the day.

General Garibaldi had written the following letter to Dr. Bertani before his departure from Genoa:—

"Genoa, May 5th.

"My dear Bertani,—As I am once more about to take a share in the events which are to decide the destinies of a country; I leave the ensuing directions for you.

"To collect all the means you may obtain to aid us in our enterprise; to give the Italians to understand that if we receive proper assistance, Italy will be consolidated in a short time and with little cost, but that a few barren subscriptions will not acquit them of their duty. That part of Italy which is free to-day should have not 100,000 but 500,000 men under arms, the latter number being by no means out of proportion to the population;

on the contrary, it is a proportion attained even by states which have not their independence to secure by conquest. Let Italy have such an army, and she will have no need of foreign masters, sure to eat her up piecemeal under the pretence of giving her Freedom. Remind them that wherever there are Italians fighting against their oppressors, there all brave men should be sent, supplying them with means for the journey. That the Sicilian insurrection should be aided, not in Sicily alone, but wherever her enemies may be met. I never advised this Sicilian movement, but since these brethren of ours are fighting I deemed it my duty to go to the rescue. Our war cry will always be 'Italy and Victor Emmanuel.' I hope, even out of this crisis, the banner of Italy will be borne without dishonour.

"Yours affectionately,

"G. GARIBALDI."

The Minister-at-War in Turin, had, after the peace of Villa-Franca, rewarded the bravery of the Cacciatori delle Alpi by dissolving them: from the remnants of this force the thousand who landed at Marsala were selected. They were all volunteers, though serving as soldiers. They belonged to the classes which in England are conventionally termed respectable; indeed, 420 serving in the ranks were the sons of gentlemen, and in Lombardy it was a dishonour to be at home while Garibaldi was abroad. Colonel Cairoli, the second son of a widowed mother, had fallen in 1859; this loss Garibaldi never ceased to deplore. Three younger brothers of this gallant soldier, hearing of the secret expedition, hastened to Genoa with their mother, who was still in the deepest mourning. It was she who presented the youths to the General, claiming for them their brother's place by his side; and as if that were still insufficient, she presented Garibaldi with 30,000 francs (£1,200), for his expedition. Before leaving, Garibaldi had also written a letter to the King, stating that the cry for help which had reached him from Sicily had touched his heart, and the hearts of some hundreds of his old soldiers. Garibaldi said he knew that he was going to embark on a dangerous undertaking; but he trusted in God, and in the courage and devotion of his companions. Their war-cry would always be "Long live the unity of Italy! Long live Victor Emmanuel, her first and bravest soldier!" Should they fall in the enterprise they were about to undertake, he trusted that Italy and liberal Europe would not forget that it had been determined by the most unselfish sentiments of patriotism. Should they succeed, Garibaldi would be proud to adorn the crown of his Majesty with a new, and perhaps its brightest jewel, on the sole condition that the King would prevent his advisers from handing it over to foreigners, as had been done with Garibaldi's native country. He (the General) said that he durst not communicate his project to the King, for he feared that from the great devotion which he entertained for him, the King would have succeeded in persuading the General to abandon his enterprise.

During the voyage Garibaldi remarked, that were the Neapolitan ships to discover the expedition they might easily escape by steaming either in the direction of Sardinia or towards Africa, but that he would never have recourse to such measures, unless the enemy were in great force, and should they encounter only the two frigates their guns were ready, and he would also show his Cacciatori how to board the enemy's vessels.

It is hardly necessary to narrate the landing at Marsala in detail, so often has it been described—no sooner had he put his foot on shore than he was saluted as liberator. He at once issued the following proclamations:—

1. "To the People of Sicily.

"Sicilians, I have brought you a body of brave men, who have hastened to reply to the heroic cry of Sicily. We the survivors of the battles of Lombardy are with you, all we ask is the freedom of our land united, the work will be short and easy, To arms then! he who does not snatch up a weapon is a coward or a traitor to his country; want of arms is no excuse, we shall get muskets, but for the present any weapon will do in the hands of a brave man. The municipalities will provide for the children, women, and old men deprived of their support. To arms all of you! Sicily shall once more teach the world how a country can be freed from its oppressors by the powerful will of a united people.

"G. GARIBALDI."

2. "TO THE NEAPOLITAN ARMY.

"Foreign insolence reigns over Italian ground, in consequence of Italian discord. But on that day when the sons of the Samnites and Martii, united with their brethren of Sicily, shall join the Italians of the North, on that day our nation of which you form the finest part, shall reassert its ancient position as preeminent among the nations of Europe. *I, an Italian* soldier, only aspire to see you drawn up side by side with these soldiers of Varese and San Martino, in order jointly to fight against the enemies of Italy.

"G. GARIBALDI".

Garibaldi was thus, on the 11th of May, established in Sicily with his little army of 1,002 Italians, five Hungarians, and only six small pieces of cannon; a few stand of arms, and a moderate amount of ammunition. Though Medici was to follow, it seemed probable that the matter must be settled one way or the other before assistance could arrive. Crispi and La Masa hastily organised a body of some 1,200 peasants. With these small numbers, the Liberator was opposed by upwards of 50,000 men, with a numerous artillery, strong fortresses, and a fleet of 900 guns to succour them. He was face to face with 28,000—rather heavy odds. The Neapolitan General Lanza had in the meanwhile announced, in a pompous order of the day, his intention to crush the firebrand of Italy—the outlawed fillibuster of South America. At ten o'clock on the 15th of May, the first action commenced by Garibaldi's attacking the Neapolitan force in their strong position. His military genius, and unequalled quickness in manœuvring, staggered the Neapolitan General, while the bayonets of the Cacciatori and the fire of the *squadre*,—who, by Garibaldi's orders, had outflanked the enemy,—decided the first fight on Sicilian ground in his favour, and the battle of Calatafimi was won. The action lasted three hours, and the band of heroes paid dearly for their victory—Menotti, the son of the great Manin, and Baron Stocco, being among the wounded.* After the battle, Garibaldi issued a proclamation to the soldiers of Italian liberty. He said that he had counted on their bayonets and had not been deceived. While he deplored the hard necessity of being compelled to fight against Italian soldiers, he confessed that he found a resistance worthy of men belonging to a better cause. He called on them to rally round the glorious banner of redemption.

From Calatafimi to Palermo the liberators marched on, constantly fighting and conquering, and carrying out, under the guidance of Garibaldi, the most admirable strategical plans. The Cacciatori knew not what flinching was; the Sicilian *squadre* soon acquired a better organization, and became familiar with the bullets of the enemy. Garibaldi's plan was to slip into Palermo on its southern side, passing through the line of ten thousand Neapolitans, massed at Monreale and Parco, the two points on which Palermo can be easily defended.

When the General was at Parco he heard that three English naval officers were driving through a neighbouring village, and sent one of his attendants to request them to visit his headquarters. They accepted the invitation, and informed Admiral Mundy† on their return that Garibaldi was standing in the middle of a large enclosure, amidst a group of fifteen or twenty followers. Garibaldi having invited the officers to be seated, offered refreshment, and entered into friendly conversation with them. He spoke of his affection and respect for the English people as a nation, and of his hope that before long he should make the acquaintance of the English admiral. He then bade adieu to the Englishmen.

---

* Italy under Victor Emmanuel.

† See Mundy's Palermo and Naples.

The General crossed the mountains to Palermo by following goat tracks; his guns were carried on men's shoulders. He suddenly appeared with his troops on the opposite slopes. So far was General Lanza from imagining that the "filibuster" was close upon him, that he received the first intimation of the enemy's presence in the suburb of the city, while probably he was dreaming of the total destruction of the patriotic band. On hearing of their arrival he hastened to the Termini Gate, where the riflemen of Garibaldi had already taken up a strong position. The 12,000 Neapolitans who defended the city were dislodged in less than four hours and Garibaldi occupied the Piazza del Pretorio. Before night the General was in possession of the whole town, with the exception of the royal palace and the forts. Admiral Mundy states that on the 21st of May he hoisted the Neapolitan flag at the main, and fired a royal salute, which was immediately returned by the guns at the citadel. At eleven he landed, in full uniform, with his staff, to pay an official visit to his excellency General Lanza, the Royal Commissioner Extraordinary of his Majesty the King of the Two Sicilies. On the evening of Garibaldi's arrival before Palermo, messengers had arrived from General Bosco giving an account of the supposed dispersion of the Garibaldians. Lanza ordered out the band on the Marina, and gave a supper in honour of the success, sending off a steamer to Naples to convey the joyful news. At midnight he dismissed his guests, congratulating them on the happy dispatch of their antagonists. Before morning, however, an aide-de-camp, rushing into Lanza's bedroom, exclaimed, "Garibaldi is in the town."

Such was the confusion caused by his arrival, that out of a population of more than 200,000 inhabitants not one was to be seen in the streets, nor was there a vehicle abroad save that which he occupied. Troops, however, there were in plenty; they were posted at every corner, and were in appearance a fine soldierlike set of men. The equipment of the Artillery was especially remarkable for its efficiency. Skirmishing now began, and Admiral

Mundy mentioned one skirmish in which Garibaldi was victorious from the following stratagem :—The Neapolitans began the attack, and their opponents fell back in large numbers as if completely routed; in reality, they were kept steadily advancing on their hands and feet, up the side of a hill; and when close enough they sprang to their feet delivered one volley and charged with the bayonet and drove the Neapolitans *pêle mêle* down the hill, in which descent they suffered great loss. The excesses of the Royal troops were horrible; houses were burnt down, and women and children murdered without any other motive than revenge and robbery. The ruffians, however, paid dearly for these atrocities afterwards.

At Salemi, Garibaldi issued a proclamation in which he stated that he considered it necessary that the civil and Military powers should be concentrated in one person, and in the name of Victor Emmanuel, King of Italy, he assumed the dictatorship of Sicily.

Up to this time the people of Sicily had heard little, and cared less, of the King of Piedmont; but they would have accepted any government that Garibaldi, their liberator and idol, recommended to them; so certain were they that he would in every way consult their best interests. There is no fact in connection with this expedition more insisted upon in the letters from Sicily of the learned Hungarian, Francis Pulsky, than the absence of all mention, or, even thought of Victor Emmanuel on the part of the Sicilians, at this time. I have mentioned several times that Victor Emmanuel was nearly unknown in Sicily, it was Garibaldi's prestige which lent a ray of popularity to the King. And M. Durana Brager, writes: "Quant à il Rè Galantuomo il n'en fut pas plus question que de l'Empereur de Chine'—also "Quoi que l'on en dit, les évènements accomplissaient bien plus aux cris de 'Viva la libertà' qu'à ceux de 'Viva il Rè Galantuomo.'"

It was evident that no other leader could have succeeded in the island. Sicilians of various political opinions all agree that they would have gratefully accepted any government the liberator proposed to them, and they accepted that of Victor Emmanuel on the assurance that they would enjoy the same constitutional freedom as the English did, and that in Victor Emmanuel there was no deceit.

A Sicilian leader came one day to the General, informing him that ammunition was becoming very scarce, and asked, "What shall we do?" "Go home, if you like," was the reply. "If you join me, you must learn to live without bread, and to fight without cartridges."

The bombardment of Palermo, and what ensued upon that occasion, is admirably related by Admiral Mundy. Disturbed early on the morning of the 27th of May by the discharge of musketry, the Admiral looked out of the port, and he observed a body of Neapolitan troops retreating at the double from the guard-house towards the gate of the citadel. The whole of the Neapolitan squadron opened an indiscriminate fire of shot and shell upon the town, which was very soon in flames. By noon, Garibaldi, had established his head-quarters in a central position. The bombardment was continued with considerable skill, and the fleet delivered fire upon their countrymen till midnight put a stop to the siege that had been continued during the whole day. The next day, General Lanza wrote to His Excellency General Garibaldi: "Since the English Admiral has let me know that he would receive with pleasure on board his vessel two of my Generals to open a conference with you, at which the Admiral would be mediator, provided you would grant them a passage through your lines, I, therefore, beg you to let me know if you will consent thereto; and if so (supposing hostilities to be suspended on both sides), I beg you to let me know the hour when the said conference shall begin. It would likewise be advantageous that you should give an escort to the above-mentioned Generals, from the Royal Palace to the Sanita, where they would embark to go on board."

"What must have been the distress of the Royal Army, remarks our gallant countrymen, before the *alter ego* of the Sovereign could have condescended to pen so humble a letter as this! The man who, up to the present hour, had been stigmatised by epithets degrading to human nature, and denounced in proclamations as a pirate, rebel, and filibuster, now elevated to the title and rank of 'His Excellency,' and of 'General!' It was equivalent to the recognition of his character as an equal, and an acknowledgement of his inability to subdue him by force."

An intimation was conveyed, both to General Lanza and his great opponent, that the Admiral would receive the negotiators at any hour after noon; but, to his utter dismay, he states, he heard a loud report of musketry, and this was succeeded by heavy guns from two of the men-of-war steamers. It was just the hour of noon, at which time the arrangement had been distinctly made known by messengers despatched to every barricade, and to the posts occupied by the Royal forces. It seemed a contemptuous defiance of every understood law of honour. The Royal troops retained the ground they so dishonourably gained; and Colonel Carini, whilst standing on the top of a barricade with a white flag in his hand, and restraining the Garibaldians from firing, was severely wounded. The whole affair was planned to surprise and capture Garibaldi. When Garibaldi and his son were standing at the landing-place, waiting the arrival of the Neapolitan Generals, several musket-shots were fired at him from the citadel, though the cutters were at the steps below him, with the English white ensign flying. As the distance across the inlet is not more than three hundred yards, any fair marksman with a rifle must have killed him on the spot. Garibaldi waved his handkerchief directly the shots were fired, and they were not repeated.

General Garibaldi and the Neapolitan Generals, Letizia and Chretien, came on board the *Hannibal*. Garibaldi was the first to step on the quarter-deck; the royal officers having insisted on his taking the precedence. The proceedings opened by his requesting that each article of the proposed convention might be read to him separately, on which he would at once determine whether it was admissible or not. This was accordingly done, and the 1st, 2nd, 3rd, and 4th, were agreed to without comment. They ran as follows:—

"1. That a suspension of arms should be concluded for the period about which the parties should agree.

"2. That during the suspension of arms each party should keep his position.

"3. That the convoys of wounded from the Royal Palace, as well as the families of the *employés*, should be allowed to pass free through the town, in order to embark on board the royal ships.

"4. That the royal troops in the palace, and the families of the refugees in the monasteries in the neighbourhood, should be allowed to provide themselves with their daily provisions.

The delivery of the 5th article brought about the storm.

"5. That the municipality should address a humble petition to his Majesty the King, laying before him the real wishes of the town, and that this petition should be submitted to his Majesty."

To this General Garibaldi replied—"No." Then drawing himself up, he added—"The time for humble petitions, either to the King or to any other person, is past; besides, there is no longer any municipality. '*La municipalité c'est moi!*' Pass on to the sixth and last proposition." Astonishment and indignation were depicted on the countenance of General Letizia on hearing these words. Folding up the paper, which lay spread before him on the table, he exclaimed, "Then, sir, unless this article is agreed to, all communication between us must cease."

Garibaldi, who, previous to the consideration of the 5th point, had maintained a phlegmatic demeanour, now denounced in unmeasured terms the want of good faith—indeed, the infamy—of the royal authorities, in allowing the Italian troops to be attacked while a flag of truce was flying. By this treacherous manœuvre they had severely wounded one of the bravest of his officers, and acquired a position in advance, which they still retained, in defiance of every principle of military honour. But perfidy such as this could not succeed; eventually it would recoil with terrific effect on the heads of the authors of it. Garibaldi had now risen from his seat under the belief that the negotiations had been brought to a close; but General Letizia announced to his adversary that he would agree to the expunging of the 5th Article from the convention, though by so material a concession he should incur the displeasure of the Royal Commissioner. The 6th, and last Article, was then accepted without comment.

"6. That the troops in the town should be allowed to receive their provisions from the Castello. An armistice was agreed to until noon on the following day."

Before taking their departure, General Letizia and General Chretien asked the Admiral for a few minutes private conversation. The Admiral strongly recommended these ardent diplomatists to proceed at once to Naples, and explain the state of affairs to the Sicilian Government; pointing out that, from the readiness shown by General Garibaldi to acquiesce in any proposal having for its object the stoppage of the shedding of blood, he would certainly agree to a prolongation of the armistice till they returned from Palermo. He then requested General Letizia to express to the Royal Commissioner the mortification he had felt at the unaccountable conduct of the Royal troops in advancing upon the insurgents after a truce had been proclaimed. This breach of good faith had compromised the British flag, and was an injustice to himself after the great responsibility he had taken, and the efforts he had made to meet the wishes of the King's Commissioners in support of constituted authority.

On re-landing, the Neapolitan Generals invited Garibaldi to accompany them in the Vice-regal barouche, to the nearest street leading to the Pretorio; an offer which was accepted unhesitatingly, though not without misgivings on the part of the staff of the Dictator.

On arriving at the great square of the "Quatro Fontani," Garibaldi addressed the assembled multitude. His commands were to be up and doing. To-morrow would be a day of life or death. The whole population must work during the night; he and his handful of soldiers must have rest. The barricades must be enlarged, multiplied, and strengthened. The *squadre*, now designated Cacciatori dell' Etna, and every able-bodied man, must be armed and at his post, in readiness to renew hostilities at the expiration of the armistice, and the first act must be to drive the foreign mercenaries from the advance position they had treacherously gained under cover of a flag of truce. At night the city was splendidly illuminated. Before noon the next day, the admiral received information that there was to be an extension of the armistice for three days, in order to allow time for General Letizia to proceed to, and return from, Naples. He was now a suppliant before the Dictator, who, standing on the vantage ground, gained by yesterday's proceedings, assumed the tone of the despotic ruler of the Provisional Government of Sicily. In his walk to the head quarters of this extraordinary man, Letizia had seen the mighty efforts made during the preceeding night by the inhabitants; he had witnessed priests, women, and children, working at the defences, and monks carrying the crucifix before them everywhere, exhorting the people to fight in the sacred cause of liberty. The royal troops had fought well, but for many days they had been short of provisions and water. The number of dead was great, and 500 wounded remained in the palace above: at dusk the city was again illuminated. On the 1st of June, by the terms of the convention, signed by General Lanza on the one side, and Signor Crispi (Secretary of State for the New Provisional Government), on the other, the finance, or royal mint, was delivered over to the insurgents. In this way they obtained possession of more than one million five hundred pounds sterling cash: this money allowed arrears to be settled, and gave an ample surplus for the purchase of arms and ammunition for the Dictator. In the afternoon, Garibaldi made a tour of inspection, round the town, walking among the cheering, laughing, crying thousands; the people threw themselves forward to touch the hem of his garment, as if it contained a panacea for all their past sufferings; children were brought, and mothers asked on their knees for his blessing. Garibaldi was all this time calmly smiling, taking up the children and kissing them, trying to pacify the crowd, listening to complaints, of houses burnt and property destroyed, giving good advice, comforting and promising that all should be paid for.

Garibaldi now wrote to his agent, Dr. Bertani, at Genoa, authorising him to make advances, and negotiate a loan for Sicily, as he had immense means to satisfy all claims.

He now devoted himself to the civil and military administration, evidently convinced that at any rate he had bought a long lease of the Island.*

To alleviate the sufferings experienced by the poor, money and food were distributed to the most needy every morning, at the gate of the royal palace; and his own aides-de-camp, each in turn, superintended this distribution. He also wrote a letter to the ladies of Palermo, in which he stated that "he wept not at the sight of the misery and misfortunes to which this unhappy city had been condemned, not with indignation at the recent butchery, nor for bodies mutilated by the bombardment, but at the sight of victims and orphans, exposed to die of hunger. "At the Orphan Asylum, eighty per cent. of the inmates perish for want of nourishment, and yet a very little would suffice to feed these beings, created in the image of God. But here I stop. I leave the rest to be understood by your generous hearts, already palpitating with emotion, at the spectacle of such misfortunes."

* Trois ou quatre jours se passèrent ainsi Garibaldi coupant taillant administrativement, législativement, militairement, financièrement et le tout carrément et promptement. Les décrets se suivaient avec une rapidité inouie et certes on ne peut accuser ses Ministres d'avoir occupé des sinecures."—(See *Durand—Beager.*)

Garibaldi, who believed that neither war or any other cause affords the slightest excuse for a government neglecting the moral and intellectual improvement of the people, took possession of the Jesuits' College, and turned it into a school for all the little dirty and ragged outcasts that were to be found in the streets of Palermo. The improvement of these children, in a short time, was wonderful. No one would have recognized them: he had them carefully clothed, cleaned, and taught, and they soon became healthy and well conducted, and likely to become respectable citizens, and intelligent men. He also founded schools for girls, and many other similar institutions, in various parts of the island, almost all of which have, unhappily, been suffered to fall into decay by the Government. Many other schools were founded, suited to the religious, moral, and intellectual wants of the different classes of the population. While he was attending to all these institutions, he did not forget to institute a national militia, in which all between seventeen and fifty were called upon to serve: those between seventeen and thirty, in active service; those between thirty and forty, in their own provinces; and those between forty and fifty, in there own communes. He also instituted a Free Press, and named the first paper the *Independente*, and trusted the press would be the first to attack him, if he ever proved false to the principles he then advocated. He sent for Gavazzi, who had been his chaplain at Rome, and said—"Go preach the Gospel of Jesus Christ, and proclaim salvation to the people, through the merits of our redeemer alone;" he also issued a proclamation to all good priests, begging that they would prove by their conduct, that the true religion of Christ was not entirely lost in Sicily; and recalled to them the venerated name and example of the martyr, Ugo Bassi.* The first religious ceremony in Sicily, that Gari-

* "He possessed," says Garibaldi, "at once the simplicity of a child, the faith of a martyr, the knowledge of a scholar, and the calm courage of a hero. I had him constantly by my side, for though unarmed he was an excellent horseman, aud was constantly repeating to me in the midst of the hottest fire, 'General! pray send me where there is danger, instead of sending any one

baldi attended, was to return thanks to the GOD OF BATTLES for his first victory. Preparations had been made to receive him in the church, and cushions placed for him to kneel upon, but with that deep humility which forms so striking a trait in his character, the victorious General knelt on the outer step of the church, before the eyes of his assembled army, and an enormous crowd, composed of all ranks of the people. The officiating priest might almost be pardoned for saying to the assembled multitude,—"Let all behold how the victor humbleth himself before Him who alone giveth victory."

The "Madman's Freak" had now succeeded: the possession of the government; the formation of a Sicilian army of 20,000 men; the organisation of a National Militia; the formation of educational establishments, and a free press: all these were now "accomplished facts." Up to this time, since landing, Garibaldi had received from the main land, only one hundred recruits since his arrival at Marsala, on the 31st of May.

Garibaldi's conquest of Sicily was significant of something

more useful than I am.' Bassi accompanied the Italian legion in all its peregrinations. His powerful voice fascinated the people. If ever Italy comes to be united, may God restore her the voice of a Ugo Bassi! When Rome had fallen, when nothing was left for me but exile, hunger, and misery, Ugo Bassi did not hesitate a moment to accompany me." On parting—for the only hope of mutual safety lay in that—the General said to Bassi, grasping his hand, "Heaven preserve you! we shall meet again." "Yes, in Italy or heaven," was the answer; continuing, after a pause, "We shall not meet again on earth; I feel a conviction that I shall soon seal with my blood my devotion to our cause. Heaven is fairer still than Italy, and there is everlasting rest." "Nay, speak not thus," said Garibaldi, "please Heaven you yet shall live and bless our victorious armies." "As God wills it, my General," replied Bassi; "that day shall assuredly come for Italy, and you and I shall equally rejoice whether here or there." They parted, and met on earth no more. Bassi was taken prisoner by the Austrians, handed over to the Inquisition, and suffered much. He was ordered to confess his heresy and rebellion. He answered he had been guilty of neither, and by God's help he had been faithful to Him and to his country. On being reminded that his Holiness the Pope had excommunicated him, he answered, "As a spiritual chief there is One greater than he, who has said, the '*curse causeless shall not come.*' The outward insignia of the priesthood is yours to give or to withdraw, but the consecration which is from above is as unchangeable as He who gave it." It is said that on the day of his execution he observed, "Even now the shadows of death have rolled away, like the vapours of the morning; one step more, and I shall hail the sunrise." He was shot under circumstances of unusual barbarity. He walked composedly to the side of the grave that they had dug for him, exclaiming, "I die without remorse,—I die for God and my country;" and bravely met his death with the name of his Saviour on his lips.

more than mere hatred of the Neapolitan Bourbons; it was the first notable exhibition for nearly two centuries, of the devotion of a whole people, to the cause of moderate constitutionalism, equally remote from republican license and irresponsible despotism, statesmen wouid do well to mark the character of this extraordinary achievement. We cannot without admiration read of the calm determination with which Garibaldi and his friends cling to that representative system of Government, for the establishment of which, in Sicily it was necessary to expel the Neapolitan tyranny amidst all solicitations, and under all pressure, to which he was subjected; he never for a moment swerved from his first object, to extend and strengthen the constitutional kingdom of Victor Emmanuel. The argument offered by Great Britain of the advantages of constitutional monarchy over every other form of Government, produced the conviction and steady zeal of Garibaldi and his party. Contributions flowed into his treasury not from England alone, but from every other people who laid claim to civilization. The calm and wise disposition which leads men of sense in every country to prefer lawful rule and right supremacy, to the extremes of popular violence, and the exaggerated folly of despotism, found in Garibaldi a new representative; he was essentially the champion of order, he repudiated with equal determination the figment of divine right, and the sanguinary dreams of socialism. The principles which he avowed, and for which he risked life and reputation, form the political creeds of multitudes in every nation, and therefore towards him men's eyes were directed, and in his successes they saw the triumph of their own convictions.

But from this time, Cavour's policy was to be exchanged for one of active sympathy. The insurrection had taken place without his sanction, but the revolution was a great success.

Cavour considered that the interests of Northern Italy demanded a leader; he attempted to take thatcharacter upon himself. In the meanwhile, Garibaldi was received officially by Admiral

Persano, on the part of the Sardinian government. He was considered by the Admiral as the *de facto* Viceroy and Ruler of the Island. Great antagonism existed between Cavour and Garibaldi, on the subject of the immediate annexation of Sicily to Piedmont. The Dictator was determined to rule absolutely in the island, until he could organize a sufficient military force to free Naples, and so hand over both together to his King; while Count Cavour, with equal pertinacity, had fully resolved to govern Sicily by his own agents, in the name of Victor Emanuel. For this purpose he had sent over from Piedmont a tried friend, the Signor La Farina, who through the persuasive eloquence of Admiral Persano was permitted by Garibaldi to hold the reins of government. The Dictator, however, never intended for a moment to relinquish the executive power: and while he allowed the installation of Count Cavour's nominee in due form, he gave him unmistakeably to understand that he was to occupy himself solely with financial and commercial affairs. La Farina first remonstrated, and then rebelled. A quarrel ensued, but the question was soon solved as to where the real power lay; for an order was issued by the Dictator, and the contumacious functionary was seized by an armed force, in the dead of the night, and shipped off to the Maria Adelaide, the flag ship of Admiral Persano, with a recommendation to quit the country with all convenient speed. Thus ended the vexed dispute of immediate annexation.

Captain Forbes says, "Every thing had prospered, save that a large portion of the civil government, under Piedmontese influence, had endeavoured to usurp the Dictatorial power, and agitated for immediate annexation. La Farina commenced his intrigues without delay, and Palermo and its ruins were adorned with bales of blue bills, imported from Turin,—'Vote for immediate annexation under the Constitutional Rule of Victor Emanuel.' Many of the Sicilians, who never imagined that they were thwarting Garibaldi, fell an easy prey to the Piedmontese agents. As remonstrance was unavailing, and was only mistaken for weakness by La Farina, no other course was open to the Dictator than the one which he adopted."

This will explain the increased distrust felt by the General towards Cavour. It must be admitted that Cavour acted always with a view to his country's good, but unfortunately he often sought to attain his object by means which to Garibaldi were utterly incomprehensible.

CHAPTER IV.

Intrigues of La Farina—Bombardment of Palermo—General Lanza's interview with Admiral Mundy—Defection in the Neapolitan fleet—Letter of Garibaldi to the Queen—Garibaldi in danger of losing his life. Napoleon urges Victor Emmanuel to prevent Garibaldi crossing over to the mainland—Garibaldi refuses to obey—A Republican attempt suppressed—Oath of fidelity taken to Victor Emmanuel—Garibaldi's kindness to the poor—His apartments in the Lighthouse—First arrival of the Volunteers on the Calabrian coast—They are attacked by the Royalists—The use of the Neapolitan Navy offered to Garibaldi against the Austrians—Loss of the "Torino"—Capture of Reggio—Romantic Scene—Dr. Tommasi Liborio Romano—Entry of Garibaldi into Naples.

Garibaldi when he undertook the conquest of Sicily acted against the will of the King and Cavour. His intention, however, was to transfer the island to his Sovereign so that when he declared himself dictator it was only to hold it in the name of the King. Notwithstanding the annexation of Savoy and Nice, La Farina who was well known to be the representative of Cavour, was dispatched by that Minister to Garibaldi ostensibly for the purpose of assisting him in that critical juncture. He was received by the General on the representation of the Piedmontese Admiral, and immediately established in office. Garibaldi, however, soon discovered the new minister to be spending large sums of money upon agents from Turin, whom he had employed to intrigue with a view to deprive him of the dictatorship. No doubt, in all this, La Farina considered he was acting for the good of his country. With the exception of these intrigues everything was progressing favourably in Sicily. A convention for the final evacuation of Palermo was drawn up just 26 days after the arrival of the "Filibuster" at Marsala—within which period Garibaldi had, with his little army of 1,007 warriors, defeated 28,000 troops, and seized the capital by a spirited and well timed *coup de main.* The British Admiral's dispatch to our Government perhaps gives the most correct account of the bombardment of Palermo.

"The scene, as reported, is most horrible. A whole district, 1,000 yards (English) in length, by 100 wide, is in ashes; families have been burnt alive, with the buildings, while the atrocities of the royal troops have been frightful. In other parts, convents, churches, and isolated edifices have been crushed by shells, 1,100 of which were thrown into the city from the citadel, and about 200 from the ships of war, besides grape, canister, and round shot. The conduct of General Garibaldi, both during the hostilities and since their suspension, has been noble and generous. The convention which Garibaldi signed, declared that the royal troops should be sent away from the city, with their arms, baggage, and matériel, receiving all the honours of war, as soon as a sufficient number of transports could be procured.

"On the 6th of June, Rear-Admiral Persano, with the *Maria Adelaïda*, anchored in the bay. On the next day 15,000 Neapolitan troops, infantry and cavalry, marched towards the Mole to be in readiness for embarcation. At the entrance of the Toledo, the eldest son of Garibaldi, mounted on a black charger, took up a position in front of the principal barricade, and these vanquished hosts of disciplined men defiled before him."

On the 19th of June, General Lanza came on board the *Hannibal*, attended by the whole of his staff, and thanked the British admiral heartily for his conduct during the terrible crisis through which they had been passing. He was saluted with nineteen guns on leaving the ship. When Garibaldi came on board the ship of Admiral Mundy, he expressed the lasting esteem and gratitude he entertained for him, and the love he bore for England and the British people; their sympathy with the cause of Italian regeneration, and with the oppressed in every land, had made, he said, the great English nation the admiration of the world. He assured the admiral of his desire to mitigate the horrors of war, and to stay the effusion of blood. He alluded, with great satisfaction, to the admiral's having brought the English squadron to an anchor so near the shore, to the great peril, as he believed of the ships, in order to afford a refuge to the non-combatants who were fleeing from the surrounding destruction. This magnanimous proceeding, he said, had been felt and acknowledged by all parties, and could never be forgotten. The admiral, however, had not told him the whole truth, for he had stationed a well-disciplined little craft at the rocks, which were close to the Toledo, for the purpose of saving Garibaldi's own life should a stroke of adverse fortune compel him to seek refuge in some ark of safety. When the admiral returned the visit of the General, he found him occupying a large suite of apartments at the end of a lofty terrace, on the extreme left wing of the royal palace, commanding a magnificent view of the adjacent country. Garibaldi was truly glad to see the gallant admiral, and expressed himself as equally pleased with a visit he had received the previous day from the French Rear-Admiral. Of the French nation and people he spoke in kind terms; but he was unable to believe that their Emperor had any true regard for Italy.

Admiral Mundy being now ordered to Naples, went to bid adieu to Garibaldi, when the latter again repeated his expressions of affection and admiration for the British nation and government, and said that he should soon meet him at Naples, upon which city he was going to march. He afterwards wrote the admiral a most affectionate letter expressing sentiments of deep gratitude, and thanking him for his services, in the name of Palermo, of Sicily, and of all Italy; and he concluded by praying that Providence might ever protect that noble vessel, her valiant crew, and the esteemed and generous sailor who was her commander.

Garibaldi now dispatched Prince San Giuseppe* to London, and Prince San Cataldo to Paris, to plead his cause. At this juncture we hear for the first time of defection in the Neapolitan fleet. The *Veloce* was brought into Palermo by her captain, with her entire complement of arms, ammunition, and crew, and the *Duca di Calabria* and the *Elba* were captured on the Neapolitan shores. The Cabinet at Naples, terrified by these startling events, was now willing to purchase the goodwill of Europe, by granting to Sicily a separate government, and even offered to abandon the island if it could only obtain guarantees for the immunity of the king's territory on the mainland. Its distracted envoys were bowing and vowing in Turin, London, and Paris. Garibaldi summoned to his aid all the resources that Sicily could afford. He hired steamers, bought arms and ammunition, and made every preparation to renew the campaign. Early in June, Colonel Medici was ready to leave Genoa with this expedition, which he divided into two parties: one under his own command, and the other under the command of Colonel Corte. The latter embarked with 900 men on the evening of

---

LETTER FROM GARIBALDI TO THE QUEEN.

A distinguished Sicilian, Prince Pandlfini, was afterwards apopointed by the Dictator to represent the interests of Sicily at the English Court, and entrusted with the following letter to her Majesty:—

"Your Majesty,—Called by my duty to my Italian fatherland to defend its cause in Sicily, I have assumed the dictatorship of a generous people, who, after a long-continued struggle, wish for nothing but to participate in the national life and freedom under the sceptre of the magnanimous prince in whom Italy trusts. The envoy who presents himself to your majesty in the name of the provisional government which now rules the country, does not pretend to represent a special and distinct state, but he comes as the interpreter of the thoughts and sentiments of two millions and a half of Italians. By this title I beg your Majesty to deign to receive him, granting a kind audience and attention to what he may respectfully urge upon your Majesty in behalf of this most beautiful and noble part of Italy."

"Palermo, July 22."

Garibaldi also wrote the following letter to the Countess of Shaftesbury:—"Dear and most Gracious Lady,—Amongst the greatest fortunes of my life the most surpassing assuredly is, that of having secured for my country the sympathy of the generous ladies of England. May I beg of you, most kind and corteous lady, to be the interpreter of my gratitude with those most valued and dear friends to whom Italy owes so much. With all the feeling of my heart, I am, your most devoted servant,"

"G. GARIBALDI."

the 7th of June, on board the American clipper *Charles and Jane:* this vessel, with the contingent on board, was captured by a Neapolitan frigate, which towed the rebels into the bay of Gaeta, under the guns of the Neapolitan fortress. The unfortunate clipper lay in this precarious situation for twenty-two days, whilst Medici himself, with better fortune, reached Palermo in safety. The American minister at Naples compelled the government of Francis II. to surrender the prize, and Colonel Corte and his men were enabled to reach their destination in safety.

On the 20th of July the battle of Milazzo was fought. The total force under Garibaldi's disposal was about 4,400 men and three guns,if such a name may be applied to two old ship twelve-pounders and a six-pounder cast in the 17th century. General Bosco had under him four regiments of rifles, amounting to 4,800 men, the 15th Régiment of the line 1,000 strong, two squadrons of Dragoons, and five pieces of Artillery, in all, about 6,500 men and twelve field pieces remarkably well mounted. He had also great advantages in position. On the other side all felt unbounded confidence in Garibaldi, who might be said to exercise a spell that enchanted every heart, altogether without parallel amongst modern commanders, who are too apt to neglect the cultivation of the affections of their soldiers, and to place confidence only in the strictness of military discipline. Amongst the Garibaldians the word of their chief was law —wherever he appeared victory followed. This battle, however, nearly cost Garibaldi his life and Italy her existence. He owed his life to Colonel Missori, who shot, with his revolver, three Neapolitan dragoons that assailed him, and the horse of a fourth. Upon Garibaldi being summoned by the officer in command to surrender, he instantly drew his sword and seizing his assailant's bridle exclaimed "Surrender yourself! I am Garibaldi." More than once during the fight the fate of Italy hung trembling in the balance, and it was without doubt Garibaldi's hardest fought battle in Sicily, for it was universally allowed that Bosco's troops made a more determined resistance and fought with greater resolution than the Austrians had ever displayed in Lombardy against the Cacciatori.

On Garibaldi being requested after the battle to write a bulletin, he replied, "No; if I write an account I shall be compelled to say that some did better than others. You are at liberty to write if you please; but the best thing you can say is, 'that the action commenced at daylight, and in the evening we had possession of the town.'" During the action the General had been slightly wounded; and finding his shirt soiled, he took it off and washed it himself in a neighbouring brook, and hung it upon the bushes to dry, whilst he partook of his frugal repast of bread, fruit, and water. Then sitting down on the ground, bare backed, he smoked his cigar, and, rapt in thought, contemplated the drying of his garment. Thus in war and in repose did he share alike danger and hardship with the humblest of his followers. By the unremitting exertions of the medical department, under the personal superintendence of the General, the wounded soldiers, amounting to nearly 800, on whom the thoughts of the General were now concentrated, were conveyed into the temporary hospitals formed in the churches and public buildings of the city. Colonel Anzano of the Neapolitan staff, came with full powers to treat with Garibaldi, who received him with his usual affability; but when Anzano endeavoured to intimidate him by hinting that the steamers in the bay were able to compell him to abandon the city, Garibaldi told him plainly that the whole Neapolitan fleet would not make him swerve from the terms he had offered. The colonel, finding he had made a mistake, relented, and the convention was signed. Garibaldi was always most generous to those whom he had conquered. As soon as the Colonel had made his submission, he enquired of him whether he thought he wished to humiliate his brethern? He allowed General Bosco to embark with all his troops for Naples, simply giving his word of honour that he would not for three months bear arms against the National forces; and General

Bosco who had boasted that he would annihilate Garibaldi and his ragged volunteers, was now obliged to walk to the place of embarcation through a double row of these very men, at the head of his own defeated troops, leaving to the conqueror 44 guns, half a field battery, large quantities of ammunition, 94 mules and 45 horses.

The Neapolitan Cabinet was now convinced of the perfect hopelessness of attempting to oppose the further progress of Garibaldi in Sicily. The flower of their army had been sent to the island; picked battalions under the man who most deservedly enjoyed the highest military reputation in the service, had been vanquished.

The Emperor of the French sent an autograph letter to King Victor Emmanuel urging him to use all his influence with Garibaldi to prevent him crossing over to the mainland, because the King of Naples had promised Baron Brassier to grant a constitution, carry out reforms, and adopt a national Italian policy, based on an alliance with Piedmont. The alliance referred to in this letter was now pressed upon the Cabinet of Turin by that of Naples, with an ardour only equal to that with which a similar proposition had been made in December last, when urged by Turin on Naples. The King of Piedmont, therefore, wrote a letter to General Garibaldi, in accordance with the desire of his Imperial ally, and sent it by Count Giulio Litta. In this letter he tells Garibaldi that he did not approve of his expedition, but was entirely averse to it. That the very grave circumstances in which Italy was placed, rendered it necessary to enter into direct communication with him. That if the King of Naples would consent to evacuate the whole of Sicily, it would be wise for him to abandon any further enterprise against the kingdom of Naples. But that in case of the refusal of the King of Naples, he expressly reserved to himself entire liberty of action, and declined to make any comment upon the General's projects. Yet, in the face of this letter, Count Cavour had written, on the 19th of June, to his agent in Sicily, La Farina, "that the Sardinian Admiral

Persano was to aid him in everything, without compromising his flag."

Garibaldi understood perfectly that French diplomacy had been exerted to influence the man whom he wanted to make the monarch of a free and united Italy, independent of the patronage of France. He, therefore, at once resolved that nothing should for one single moment be allowed to interfere with him in carrying out the work of national redemption throughout the whole of the Neapolitan kingdom. He, therefore, in reply, wrote a letter full of devotion and affection to the King, declining, however, to obey the royal request. His mission, he said, was too noble to be relinquished. He had sworn to Italy to accomplish it—he must keep his word—he could not sheath his sword until he had completely accomplished his programme, and made his Majesty King of united Italy. Count Trechi, one of his aides-de-camp, who had previously held a similar office in the service of the King, was dispatched with this letter, instructed to offer the fullest explanations, and use to the most respectful and affectionate language; but to say, at the same time, that Garibaldi's programme and war-cry, "United Italy and Victor Emmanuel," were unchanged and unchangeable.

Garibaldi drove up to the Royal Palace, at Messina, in his usually quiet manner, and established himself there before the crowd had any distinct knowledge of his presence. No sooner, however, had they become aware that their hero was amongst them, than they beseiged the palace with such shouts of admiration and joy, that Garibaldi was compelled to appear repeatedly at the window to satisfy their enthusiasm. In the evening he addressed the multitude from his balcony, urging them to be ready to make all necessary sacrifices to preserve what they had acquired, telling them that he could not then remain amongst them any longer, and that he earnestly desired them to have confidence in themselves, and not to rely too much upon him.

Captain Forbes truly observed that Garibaldi exercised a kind of magnetic influence over the populace, which made them regard him as a kind of link connecting them with the Deity, and as a sort of father who could pardon their most grevous transgressions, and one who, though only human, was nevertheless of a nature infinitely superior to them.

In the evening Garibaldi addressed the inhabitants from the balcony of the palace. He had been repeatedly obliged to rise during dinner and show himself at the window, in answer to the incessant cheering that rose from the street beneath, which was so densely thronged that it seemed paved with human heads instead of stones. Resting his elbows on the balcony, his noble weather-beaten countenance radiant with goodness, realized the ideal of an apostle of old, half human, half divine, who had undertaken some earthly mission.

General Bixio had been dispatched with his brigade to the district of Mount Etna, to trample out a small spark of Communism which had been kindled in Bronte. Garibaldi, however, notwithstanding his mild and forbearing disposition, had no more idea of being trifled with by the Ultra-Democratic party than by that of Cavour, and he could not have selected a better man than Bixio, who, arriving with his brigade at the focus of the movement, shot the ringleaders, and imposed a fine upon the commune, observing, with great justice, that the inhabitants should have taken up arms and resisted this band of brigands and adventurers.

The Dictator next raised a loan to be levied on the municipality of Palermo, on Thomas and Bishoffskeim (Paris and London, bankers), so that he could assume the offensive without embarrassment. He was now at the head of an army of about 25,000 regular troops, whose *morale* was excellent, and whose faith in their leader almost amounted to "a religion." Owing to the vast supply of Enfield rifles, which he owed to the energy with which Colonel Colt had fulfilled his contracts, the whole force was supplied with that weapon, whilst 40,000 muskets were stowed away in the arsenals ot Messina, ready for service in the Calabrias, and seventeen mountain howitzers and field guns were also ready for the use of the various divisions. Since the expulsion of La Farina, and the arrival of Dopretis, there had been great improvement in the internal administration of Sicily.

Although the country was not yet formally annexed to Piedmont, an oath of fidelity to Victor Emmanuel was taken by the Prodictator and all the officials of the government, which had all the good effects to be derived from annexation without causing any embarrassment either to the King or Garibaldi. All taxes were duly paid, property was respected, and with the exception of the occasional appearance of brigands in and near Bronte, who were always speedly checked by Bixio, the cause of order was triumphant throughout the island, and the Dictator inaugurated the campaign with the main body of his army without any misgivings as to reactionary movements or civil disorder. The fortresses of Messina, Syracuse, and Agosta still remained in the possession of the royal troops, although it had been solemnly agreed that they should be evacuated. Notwithstanding however, they were virtually in the power of the Garibaldians, for it was certain that, although the royal troops might make a resolute defence, they never would adopt an aggressive policy. In the Royal Palaces, Garibaldi had retained all the servants of the old viceroys, thinking that it would be unjust to dismiss them. The only change he made was to order the service to be conducted in as simple a manner as was consistent with the dignity of the Dictatorship. They were also informed that he required nothing for his own dinner except a little soup and a plate of meat and vegetables. During the first few days after his entry into Palermo many men were brought up before him to receive their sentence of death. He gave them however, a full and free pardon for all previous offences, merely telling them to respect for the future the majesty of the law. We have seen that Garibaldi had caused enormous subscriptions to be raised in Italy and other countries, the greater part of which money was entirely at his own disposal, and every farthing spent in the public service. We have also seen that he had found £1,200,000 in the treasury of Palermo, all of which he caused to be spent for the good of his country; what was necessary for his maintenance at the royal palaces he accepted as inseparable from his position as Dictator, and the pay which he allowed himself out of the public treasury was 8 francs a-day, and it is supposed that the following would not be an incorrect account of his wardrobe in Sicily:—One old Piedmontese general's uniform,—a relic of his campaigns in the Lakes,—two pairs of grey trousers, an old felt hat, two red shirts, a few pocket handkerchiefs, two neckties, a sabre, and a revolver, a kit which his daily allowance of eight francs did not do much to improve, owing to the simple fact that after an early hour in the morning there was never by any chance a single carlino to be found in the pocket of his Excellency.

Garibaldi's hostility to the injudicious distribution of alms upon undeserving objects, and to that false charity which serves only to encourage habits of idleness, and rather increases than diminishes destitution, was as decided as that entertained by any British magistrate. But, alas for human frailty! the General was not perfect; and here we have the only instance in which his practice clashed with his principles. It was, indeed, a difficult task for him to refuse to alleviate the sufferings even of a man, but to reject the supplication of a woman or a child was an impossibility. Hence, the little pocket-money he allowed himself frequently melted away before the morning had passed, and often was he compelled to borrow small sums from his friends, which he always punctually repaid out of his next day's allowance.

The following extract from Captain Stewart Forbes will be sufficient to show the arduous nature of the duty Garibaldi had taken upon himself, which was not only the deliverance of his country, but also what is of far greater importance, the regeneration of the people from the demoralization consequent upon four centuries of Bourbon misrule:—"The venality of the official system, bequeathed by the late Government, is playing havoc in the Treasury. For instance:—A, a very disinterested commercial traveller, arrives with 30,000 shoes from Marseilles, and offers them at really a remarkably low figure to Garibaldi. The latter is delighted with the chance of having his army well shod, and sends him to B, the Secretary of State; B sends him for the price of the shoes £500, another £500, which he does not present to A. Imagination will fill up the rest."

For some days previous to his departure from Sicily, Garibaldi, leaving his staff on board the vessel to be in readiness on any emergency, established himself at the lighthouse, with a few of his intimate friends, ostensibly for the better superintendence of the military operations, but in reality, as Captain Forbes supposes, to avoid the crowd of adventurers that followed his person, causing him great annoyance by their inopportune solicitations to supply him with ships and arms, or by officiously pressing upon him offers of personal service. During his residence in the lighthouse, the General received a visit from Captain Forbes, who found him just awakening from his siesta, domiciled in an incommodious room, or rather closet, scantily furnished with a box, two stools, and a low tressel bed. Nor could the General's little room boast of a table. His trusty sword and a spare shirt were hung upon the walls, and a South American saddle and a poncho were lying in a corner. He offered a stool to each of his visitors, and taking a seat upon a corner of the bed, he assured them that the day would soon arrive when it would be decided whether the result of his enterprise was favourable, or whether he had miscarried in his undertaking. He regretted the meddlesome policy of diplomatists; but spoke in the warmest terms of the sympathy he had received from the British nation.

On the day that the battle of Milazzo was fought, Garibaldi's camp was altogether destitute of the usual luxuries and advantages, the General being quite content to sleep on the bare ground, the sea shore, or even on the pavement of the street, with no other pillow than his saddle. He could never understand that a soldier required more than what he deemed sufficient for himself. He more than once washed his own shirt, and prepared his own frugal dinner. After the battle of Milazzo he was discovered by Alexandre Dumas slumbering, with his staff, in the porch of a church, exhausted with fatigue, his head upon his saddle. Near him lay his scanty supper: a small loaf of bread and a jug of water. The lives of every one of the General's staff, from the chief to the subordinate, seem to afford a better theme for romance than for history. Their highest honour was the approval of the General; they sought no reward save the glory of their country.

So great, indeed, was the enthusiasm with which Garibaldi was regarded by a portion of the peasantry, that they attributed to him almost divine attributes, contrasting strangely with the superstition of the Neapolitan soldiers, who believed that he had sold his soul to the devil to purchase a transitory temporal success in this world, alleging in support of their belief the facility with which, as they affirmed, he was able to shake the rifle balls from his person.

Garibaldi's activity was now wholly directed towards preparing for the safe landing of his army on the Calabrian coast. This was not an easy enterprise, as a large Neapolitan force was supposed to be massed on the opposite shores, ready to check the landing of the volunteers, should any be attempted.

The influx, however, of patriots from Calabria by no means abating, Garibaldi was prevailed upon by them to dispatch a body of 200 men, on the 8th of August, to the Calabrian shore, with instructions to surprise, and if possible, to capture, a strong fort which was stationed upon the coast, directly opposite to Cape Faro.

A south-west wind springing up towards sunset, drove dense masses of clouds towards the Calabrian coast. The moonbeams were unable to penetrate the darkness of the ensuing night, and a thick veil of mist overhung the entire line of the coast of Sicily. Everything was favourable to the enterprise the General had so long contemplated. Majors Missori and Nullo were entrusted with the command of this perilous expedition. At nine o'clock they received Garibaldi's final instructions, and before a quarter of an hour had elapsed all were on board, and ready to weigh anchor. Then arose a loud and unanimous complaint from the soldiers who were not among the chosen few. They clasped the hands of Major Missori, and conjured Major Nullo not to leave them behind. It must, indeed, have been a touching sight to witness their grief, and to hear their earnest supplications to be allowed to accompany the expedition. Order was, however, soon restored, for the sense of duty was uppermost in the hearts of all. It was precisely half-past nine when the expedition weighed anchor.

Either owing to the darkness or to the influence of that current which in all probability gave rise to the ancient fable of the whirlpool of Charybdis, the boats were unable to approach the coast at the point intended, so they came to shore and disembarked a little to the left of the fort. Missori, trusting to the darkness of the night, made a forced march along the rocky paths of the coast. A signal had been previously concerted with Garibaldi to acquaint him if the expedition should prove successful, all were waiting with anxiety for the light which was to be the signal of success, when the rattling of musketry followed by the roar of cannon, burst upon their ears.

The corps was marching in the direction of the fort when it was met by a patrol of Neapolitans who at once opened fire and put the troops in the fort on the alert, it was therefore, impossible to surprise the garrison, and Missori could do nothing but lead his men across the mountain paths of Aspromonte and gain the high land of Calabria. Taking advantage of the night they pushed through the narrow ravines of the Finmara and gained the mountains unobserved by the outposts of the army. The

Neapolitans believing that Garibaldi himself had landed with a considerable force, did not venture to move forward at random towards the mountains.

Making their way through the defiles, Missori and Nullo spent many days, marching from village to village, everywhere spreading the revolution and preparing the people for the triumphant progress of Garibaldi through Calabria. General Briganti sent Missori a dispatch containing a haughty demand to surrender: Missori answered that the soldiers of liberty were ready to receive the supporters of tyranny whenever they dared to give battle.

In the meantime, Garibaldi seemed endowed with ceaseless activity; he was giving directions everywhere; yet he found time to occupy himself with politics and superintend the organization of his army and navy, and to receive deputations. He was the very soul of that great movement, and from daybreak to nightfall his busy hand and brain were almost incessantly at work.

De Martino, one of the ministers of Francis II., sent a deputation to Garibaldi, offering him 50,000,000 francs, and the use of the Neapolitan navy for service in a war for the liberation of Venice, if he would consent not to cross the Straits; this mission, of course, fell to the ground. These were not the only attempts the Neapolitans made to get rid of Garibaldi. Two men were arrested at Messina on suspicion of being implicated in a plot, the successful issue of which would have cost the General his life. A Calabrian also confessed that he had been sent on a mission to assassinate the General.

Garibaldi, on the 18th of August, embarked for the conquest of the kingdom of Naples, which was defended by a well-organized army of at least 80,000 men. The right cause was on his side. The majority of the Neapolitan population gave him their sympathy, and what is of far greater importance, he was supported by that prestige which is more efficient than any material power. Four thousand men embarked with Garibaldi on board the *Torino* and the *Franklin*. The General was in the latter vessel, which by his own personal labour, he saved from foundering, for she had sprung a leak, and in less than an hour had made several feet of water. The Neapolitan fleet was looming in the distance keeping night-watch over the city of Reggio. Two diversions, organized at Messina and Cape Faro to draw away their attention, were crowned with success. Two vessels, well manned and supplied with ammunition, had been stationed at the above-named ports, apparently ready to weigh anchor at any moment, should occasion require it. To keep up the delusion they occasionally fired their guns, which were re-echoed from the high rocky coasts of Calabria, for here the mountains of Aspromonte run down abruptly to the sea.

At this point the General disembarked, and all was successful with the exception of the loss of the *Torino*, which her pilot in his anxiety ran upon a sand bank, from which she never moved.

Garibaldi with his characteristic energy was the first to land. There was no apprehension of opposition from any Neapolitan force at this point. Fishing boats wherever they were found were pressed into the service.

Before four, to the great astonishment of the peasantry, every one had disembarked.

In a fruitless attempt to save the *Torino* they were attacked by the Neapolitan ship of war *Fulminante* and two other vessels, and before they could escape to the mountains out of range of fire they lost three men.

The Neapolitans then opened a heavy fire upon the ill-fated craft, and before midnight they boarded and burnt her, the flames serving to light up the midnight march of the invaders.

The *Franklin* being an American vessel was allowed to retire unmolested to Messina.

It is to be remarked that, like Pizarro in his invasion of Peru, all means of retreat were cut off from Garibaldi, both in this instance and in his conquest of Sicily, by the burning of his ships, but confidence in his success under such trying circumstances serves only to prove the greatness of the man.

Nothing can exceed the wild beauties of the Calabrian coast at this point.

A range of steep rocks rising abruptly from the sea and running far into the interior where they joined the mountains, afforded a position best calculated for Guerrilla warfare.

The General surprised Reggio and gránted the same terms of capitulation which he had done at Milazzo. The garrison was then placed on board the Neapolitan ships. The reception of Garibaldi and his troops was most enthusiastic, every family in Reggio according to their means and position claimed a certain portion of the officers and men as their guests. The spoils consisted of 26 heavy guns and field pieces, and 500 stand of arms, besides a large quantity of coal, ammunition, provisions, horses, and mules. Captain Forbes was invited by Colonel Nullo, who commanded the guides, to ride out with him, an invitation which he readily accepted, as he was desirous of making a call at Villa San Giovanni. The recent lamented death of Colonel Nullo, in Poland, gives a melancholy interest to this incident. We are indebted to Captain Forbes for the following description :—"The inhabitants of the various villages we passed all told us that the Neapolitans were falling back and that my destination was clear, so we cantered on heedless of danger, revelling in the beauty of the scenery, when on entering the town we found ourselves to our astonishment, in the midst of a couple of squadrons of lancers. Instead of giving themselves up as prisoners at once, my six companions drew their revolvers and coolly summoned both squadrons to surrender. The officer replied by asking 'Who and where are your troops? Oh! replied Nullo, 'They are in ambush all round, and unless you surrender immediately they will open fire.' Well, said the officer, 'you had better come and talk to our general.' Nullo went on to see General Melendis, to whom he told the same story and reiterated his demands. Melendis asked where Garibaldi was and offered to go and treat with him. Nullo merely said, that he could not permit it, but would send back to inform the General of his request, and at the same time wound up this consummate piece of presence of mind by ordering Melendis to withdraw his lancers over the bridge, which he considered the advance post of the two armies. The lancers were accordingly withdrawn, and two guides were posted on the bridge to represent the Garibaldian army, whilst one was sent back to look for Garibaldi and bring up the troops with all possible speed. The night proved cold, and Captain Forbes was lightly clad. He had left Garibaldi sleeping in the stubble of a corn field, wrapped in his blanket, and had gone to procure a bed and some supper, with the intention of returning before dawn. Captain Forbes continues: "A more romantic scene than that I left behind, it would be difficult to conceive, and as I rode through the cordon of Calabrians, clustering round their watch fires, in their quaint velveteen breeches and jackets, their jaunty and fantastic sugarloaf hats with a superabundance of ribbon, their weapons of every shape and make; numerous priests, too, mingling with them like ghosts stalking abroad in the night. The dark sea murmered in the abyss, and formed a picture more like a fairy tale than an incident of real life."

A French Garibaldian officer, named Colonel Paul de Flotte, was unfortunately shot while endeavouring to storm Salino. In the three days of '48, he had been the commandant of the barricades against Cavaignac, and was subsequently a member of the Chamber of Deputies at the time of the *coup d'etát.* The following is an extract from Garibaldi's order of the day:—"De Flotte was a noble son of France. He belonged to the whole of mankind; for that country was his wherever a suffering people was struggling for liberty. De Flotte died for Italy, and fought for it as he would have fought for France."

In compliment to the patriotic exertions of the Calabresi, Garibaldi exchanged his wide-awake for one of their peculiar sugar-loaf hats, which excited uproarious applause. All his staff followed his example, a measure which not only identified them with the population, but proved an infallable claim upon their hospitality. Religious sentiment had great influence in Calabria, as throughout all Italy. They not only protested against civil despotism, but also against the despotism of Rome. They were by no means inimical to religion, but were determined to uproot priestcraft and its concomitant miseries. One of the great features of this army was its sobriety. No one ever heard of a Garibaldian being drunk, consequently discipline was easily maintained.

Count Cavour, finding that General Garibaldi was everywhere successful, organized a secret committee at Naples, which took the name "Comitato delle Ordine," and consisted of Cavour's agents, under Silvio Spaventa, Belleli, and Leopardi. This latter had been appointed as minister to Berlin. He agitated for immediate annexation to Piedmont, and had endeavoured to usurp Garibaldi's authority at Sala. Dr. Tommasi, of the Cavourian party, had the audacity to read to General Garibaldi an address, tantamount to saying that he was a very fine fellow; but that he was not wanted at Naples, where they were going to organize a provisional government, and to annex that city immediately to Piedmont. At the same time he presented to the General a printed list of its members. Garibaldi, answered this flippancy with stern dignity; and this well-meaning, but ardent partisan, received a severe lesson. This is mentioned as serving to illustrate the audacity of the Cavourian intriguers, and the length to which they were prepared to go. There is no denying that their conduct was not only ungracious but ungenerous to the last degree; and this it was which paved the way for that wretched system of intrigue between the two factions which was so speedily to follow Garibaldi's entry into Naples, where his presence had now become a necessity, to prevent not only a civil war in the streets, but a disruption which might create infinite mischief to the national cause. Dr. Tommasi had promised Cavour to stir up a revolution in Naples, and he and his friends of the Cavourian committee, boasted they would shed the last drop of their blood in the prosecution of their design for the immediate annexation of Southern Iatly and Piedmont; they utterly failed, however, in their promise. To check this party a second committee was organized, of which Dr. Bertani was the very soul and life, and the ascendancy of Garibaldi was secured throughout the whole of the Neapolitan kingdom. Such was the position of affairs which preceded the arrival of the Liberator in the Neapolitan capital.

Don Liborio Romano had visited Alexandre Dumas on board his yacht, the *Emma*, then lying in the Bay of Naples, well knowing he had been sent there by Garibaldi to watch the course of events, and use his utmost endeavours to hasten the revolution. Dumas had secretly spread abroad Garibaldi's manifestoes, distributed arms and ammunition, and he became, in fact, an active agent of the national propaganda. To such lengths did he go, and so open were his acts, that the French admiral and ambassador intimated to him, that if the Neapolitan government should order his arrest, they would protect neither his yacht nor himself. Dumas, however, pursued his course as before. Don Romano, seeing that success would attend the General, went, as has been said, to see Dumas, declared himself to be an ardent Garibaldian, and offered him his co-operation for his country's good. On the 5th of September it was decided that King Francis II, with his queen and court, should leave Naples the following day for Gaeta. The royal proclamation, in which the king bade adieu to his subjects, which was written by Don Liborio Romano, was full of dignity; but on the very same day, three hours before the departure of his royal master, the very man who had penned that proclamation dispatched the following telegram to Garibaldi: "To the invincible Dictator of the Two Sicilies. Naples expects you with anxiety, to confide to you her future destinies.—Entirely yours, Liborio Romano."

On the departure of the court not a man in the whole of that city was seen to mourn: not one bade a last farewell to the departing king; and, but for the presence of the ministers and courtiers, the porticoes of the Royal Palace would have been entirely deserted. The ministers whom the king had left behind to provide for the public tranquility, assembled at the house of the president of the expiring cabinet, and they there decided that Prince d'Alessandria (then sindaco of Naples), should go at once to Salermo, with General Lazepano, to see Garibaldi, and make the necessary arrangements for his entry into the capital. Meanwhile fresh attempts had been made by the leading members of the Ordine, or Cavouridio Committee, to urge the expiring ministry and municipal council to organize a kind of provisional government, and at once proclaim the annexation of Naples to Piedmont, in the name of Victor Emmanuel; this, however, was not more successful than any of the previous attempts. The 7th of September ought never to be erased from the memory of the Italians; for on that day Garibaldi determined to enter the capital, in spite of its fortresses, which were still in the possession of the royal troops. The evening before he left for Naples he thus expressed himself: "I shall be loyal to Victor Emmanuel; I love him as my life. I have served him without an oath. I shall do all in my power to procure the annexation of Naples to Sardinia, under the government of the king; but this I must be allowed to do in my own manner. I must also endeavour to obtain for this measure the entire support of the people." He also, at the same time, issued a proclamation to the people of Naples, stating that as soon as the syndic, and the commander of the National Guard of Naples, which he expected, should arrive, he would promptly present himself to them.

To this proclamation Liborio Romano replied by the following telegram:—

"To the invincible General Garibaldi, Dictator of the Two Sicilies:

"The people of Naples are awaiting your arrival with the utmost impatience to hail you as the redeemer of Italy, and to place in your hands their own destiny and the guidance of the commonwealth Subject to your authority, I shall remain responsible for order and public tranquility. Your own words which I have made known to the people, give the securest pledge for the success of my undertaking.

"Awaiting your further orders—I remain, with profound respect, LIBORIO ROMANO."

Instead of dispatching a courier, Garibaldi considered it the better course to take his orders himself. He accordingly determined at once, to enter the capital which the King had left but a few hours before. He left in a special train of four carriages at half-past nine in the morning for the capital, and he, Cosenz, and thirteen of the staff represented the National army. A few English amateurs and National Guards occupied the remaining seats. At every station the enthusiasm increased, and the roofs of the carriages became crowded with National Guards, who decorated them with flags and evergreens. The vast populations of the Torre del Creco Resina and Portici took complete possession of the line, and the little party was obliged to halt at every station and proceed at a snail's pace to avoid destroying the masses of human beings, in which women and children, citizens and National Guards swayed to and fro in ecstatic confusion. At Naples, order was maintained in the interior of the station, but outside, the scene baffled all description, horses and carriages, lazzaroni and ladies, national guards and gendarmerie, rival committees and royalist partisans were heaped confusedly together, and rendered egress apparently impossible. Missori, Millo, and one or two others rode briskly in advance, Garibaldi followed in an open carriage with Cosenza, and he was greeted with a deafening chorus of vivas, kept up without intermission until he drove into the courtyard of the Palace of the Queen Mother, at the foot of the Toledo. Though nothing could have been more enthusiastic than the reception given to him by the population, and though many of the houses were bedecked with the tricolor and cross of Savoy to the seventh story, the aspect of the troops with few exceptions, and more especially those quartered in the Castello Nuovo was sullen and by no means reassuring. On more than one occasion as this handful of men passed under the very muzzles of the royalist guns it appeared to his friends that Garibaldi was tempting Providence by his extraordinary boldness. One wanton shot from a crowd would have resulted in a general conflagration: one chance ball might have condemned Italy to another decade of servitude, as with Garibaldi would in all probability have perished the hopes of the present generation. He escaped, and was addressing the populace from the Palace window, before one-half of the town knew of his arrival.*

Another account gives the following description of the incident:—"Garibaldi arrived a little before noon; Don Liborio Romano was waiting to receive him at the station. The General shook hands with him, and thanked him for having saved the country. They entered the carriages which were waiting outside the station: that which carried Garibaldi took the head of the column, and rapidly made its way to Naples. The forts were still in the possession of the Neapolitan troops. At the approach of Garibaldi, some of the artillerymen made a sort of hostile display. The General the moment he saw this, stood up in the carriage, with his arms crossed, and looked steadfastly upon them. The artillerymen then gave him the usual military salute. But when they came up to the Grand Guard, the officer there ordered the soldiers to fire, but they refused to obey. In conformity with the usual custom of king and conquerors, the General proceeded immediately to the

* When Garibaldi entered the city without a single file of his own men to back him, and saw the artillerymen beside their guns, lighted match in hand, waiting but the word of command to fire, Garibaldi turned his eyes with a long gaze towards the Royal Palace, that stronghold of secular tyranny, and as the carriage in which he sat came fully within the range of the guns: "Drive slower, slower—more slowly still," was the order that he gave. And the hostile soldiery amazed, almost terrified into admiring sympathy with the man they were there to crush, flung down their matches, and waved their caps in the air with an impressive shout of "Viva Garibaldi."—See *Social Aspects of the Italian Revolution.*

palace of the archbishop. As soon as the *Te Deum* was sung, Garibaldi invited Romano to get into a carriage with him, and they drove off to the palace of Angri, where he, and his aides-de-camp and staff took up their quarters.

A thousand voices proclaimed the downfall of the Bourbon and the national gratitude for the Liberator. Garibaldi appeared at the window, when the shouts were redoubled, and thus was the emancipation of Naples accomplished, without costing a single drop of her blood.

CHAPTER V.

General Cosenz forms a Government—Proclamation to the Neapolitan people—Proclamation to the Royal troops—Interview of Garibaldi with Mr. Elliott—Departure of the remainder of the Royal troops for Capua—Captain Forbes—Garibaldi urges Mazzini to leave Italy—Refusal of Mazzini—Conversion of Mazzini to the principles of Constitutional Monarchy—Possibility of Cavour having reason to suppose the French would not offer substantial opposition to his schemes—The Confessional—Gives land for an English Church—Two appointments of Garibaldi found fault with—Colonel Peard.

The Dictator at once organized a government, a matter of considerable difficulty, if we consider the discordant elements which at that time rent asunder the people of Naples. At this juncture the Cavourian party made a bold effort to secure their ascendancy. They organised a provisional ministry, and introduced a few liberal and Neapolitan nonentities to mask their designs. Having assumed the title and authority of government, they issued a decree appointing Garibaldi Dictator of the Kingdom of Naples, and placarded the walls with lists of its members. Orders were, of course, issued for the arrest of the authors of this impertinent assumption of authority. An incident which would be scarcely worthy of remark, if it were not a good illustration of the hourly increasing difficulties which Garibaldi had to encounter.

General Cosenz, a Neapolitan subject, was instrusted by the Dictator with the disagreeable task of forming a government. He selected men of all shades of opinion, but none of the partisans of extreme parties. By noon he had succeeded: he was well acquainted with the men who could be best trusted. Liborio Romano, of course, retained his post of Minister of the Interior; General Cosenz became Minister of War, Pisanelli was charged with the portfolio of Justice, and the Marquis D'Afflitto accepted administration of the Public Works. In the meanwhile the Marquis Villa Marina, the Piedmontese, Ambassador to Francis, the second and the Piedmontese Admiral Persano, had arrived at Naples, to negotiate with the Dictator. To the Ambassador he observed that he would see the King in Naples much sooner than he expected. One of his first and most important acts was to decree that the Neapolitan navy should, from that day, form part of the Sardinian Squadron, under the orders of Admiral Persano. He therefore told Admiral Persano that he asked him, in the name of Victor Emmanuel, to accept the command of the fleet; and the same evening he dispatched a steamer to Genoa with the offer of the prodictatorship to the Marquis Pallavicini, the companion of Silvio Pellico in Spielberg, and a stanch friend of Italy and the King. These acts tend more than anything else to show that his policy was the unity of Italy under Victor Emmanuel; the manner and time of its accomplishment remained for him to decide.

On his arrival at Naples, the following proclamation was issued by Garibaldi:—

"People of Naples,—The opposition of strangers, interested in our humiliation and internal discord, has heretofore impeded the constitution of our country into an united kingdom. This day Providence seems to have brought so much misery to a conclusion. The unanimity of all the provinces, and the constant triumph of our arms, are guarantees of the approaching close of the misfortunes of our land. One step remains, nor do I doubt the issue, for how can our present prosperous condition be compared with the scanty resources of those brave men who have placed us in our present happy situation. The easy nature of the enterprise is clear to all, but my desire is to avoid the unnecessary effusion of Italian blood, so I exhort you to attain this great object by mutual forbearance. Your courage is well known to me, but let us preserve peace among ourselves, and reserve the sword for the enemies of Italy. Accept, then, that right hand which has never served a tyrant, nor the enemies of our fatherland. In conclusion, I again exhort you to avoid mutual jealousy, to reserve your strength for our enemies, and with you I am ready to die for the glory of Italy."

"GARIBALDI."

During the formation of the ministry the Dictator issued the following proclamation to the people of Naples:—

"People of Naples,—

"It is with feelings of the profoundest respect and love that I present myself before you in this centre of a noble and long-suffering people, whom four centuries of tyranny have not been able to humiliate, and whose spirit could never be broken by a ruthless despotism. The first necessity of Italy is harmony and social order, without which the unity of Italy is impossible. This day Providence has conferred that blessing upon you, and has made me its minister. The same Providence has also given you Victor Emmanuel, whom from this moment I will designate the father of our country.

"The model of all sovereigns, he will impress upon his posterity the duty that they owe to a people who have, with so much enthusiasm, chosen him for their king. You are supported by the clergy, who, conscious of their true mission, have, with patriotic ardour and truly Christian conduct, braved the gravest dangers of battle, at the head of our Italian soldiers. The good monks of La Gancia, and the noble-hearted priests of the Neapolitan continent, have one and all assisted us in the good fight.

"I repeat that harmony is the one essential thing for Italy; and let us freely forgive those who, having disagreed with us, are now repentant, and are willing to contribute their mite to build up the monument of our national glory.

"Lastly, we must make it apparent to all that while we respect the houses of other people, we are determined to be masters in our own house, whether the powers of the earth like it or not.

"GIUSEPPE GARIBALDI."

Many persons qualified to speak on this subject consider that Garibaldi made the same mistake here as he had before in Sicily, and that the proper course for him would have been to keep by the sword what he had won by the sword, until his infallible judgment prompted him to transfer it to his Sovereign. A dictatorship and a civil government have been proved to be utterly incompatible, especially with a people to whom a strong government is a necessity. Sicily, since Garibaldi's departure, had been heaving and surging under the weak but well-meaning Depretis. There zealous partisans of all parties were raising questions which they never should have been allowed to entertain, and the disorders developed under the government of La Farina were again beginning to break out, for want of a pro-dictator of sufficient nerve to repress them. All business was suspended in Naples for two days after Garibaldi's entrance, the entire population roused themselves into a state of excitement bordering on madness; Sunday, the second day, being the national festival of "Pie di Grotta," was worse than the first; but luckily on the previous evening Garibaldian troops had begun to arrive, and a proclamation from the Minister of Police, requesting the unwashed to reserve their energies for Venice, served somewhat to pacify them. In one point, however, they deserve some credit, that is to say, that when the tumult of Sunday night was at its highest pitch, and it was announced from the windows of the Palazzi Angri that the Dictator was asleep, that portion of the Toledo was instantaneously cleared, as if by magic, and in spite of many temptations, they never afterwards re-assembled. No cases of robbery occurred, the far-famed Lazzaroni being apparently inoculated by the virtue of their idol.

"The manner in which order was maintained," says Admiral

Mundy, "amidst such a scene of wild fanaticism, was indeed a miracle almost as great as the entry of the Chieftain into the city, yet not a drunken person was to be seen, and upon its being made known to this impassioned throng that the Dictator was retiring to rest the orgies were at once discontinued and quietude restored. No words can express the frantic joy of the people, or the madness of the scene."

Orders had, however, been dispatched to bring up troops with all possible speed, both by land and by sea, for the proximity and number of the royal forces, as well as the intrigues by which Garibaldi was surrounded, rendered his position anything but desirable. The fortress of St. Elmo, which overlooks and commands the town, was still in the possession of the royalist garrison, whose intention seemed very indecisive, as the soldiers remained faithful to the King, and were desirous to put in execution the royal command of bombarding the town, and the officers, on the other hand, wanted a quiet life and a speedy surrender. The alarm of the townspeople was, however, relieved by the capitulation of the garrison on the ensuing evening.

Garibaldi issued a proclamation to the royal troops, in which he told them that if they did not disdain him for their companion in arms, he was only too desirous to fight by their side against the enemies of their country. He exhorted them to put aside discord, which was the chronic misfortune of their fatherland. He told them that Italy, trampling upon the fragments of her chains, pointed to the north, and that the path of honour lay towards the last lurking place of tyrants; and concluded by assuring them that he promised them nothing more than to make them true soldiers of liberty.

Garibaldi now hoped to be able to complete the revolution without more bloodshed, and wished to preserve rather than to destroy the remainder of the Neapolitan army. He entertained the same feelings with respect to the civil administration. He was determined neither to abase the Republicans nor to exalt the Annexationists, but to endeavour if possible to heal their differences, and soothe that rabid bitterness of feeling which, if encouraged in either party, might lead to the most deplorable results. If parties, however, should go to extremes, he held martial law to be the just and proper remedy.

No sooner was one ministry created than intrigues were hatched to destroy it. Garibaldi was grieved at the waywardness of his children, but would not chastise them; he knew his army was available on any real emergency, and that he could, at any moment, coerce them by force of arms. The intriguers, however, took advantage of his well-known patience, and by their detestable conduct rendered civil government, if not impossible, at least most difficult. He was also soon at war with the whole of the drivers of public carriages, on account of their cruelty towards their unfortunate horses, which was brought under his notice in the following manner:—The day after his arrival one of his staff was separated from him in the crowd, and wishing to rejoin him as quickly as possible, jumped into a cab. The driver struck the horse with the butt-end of his whip upon a sore upon the shoulder, and when indignantly remonstrated with, did so again. This was too much for the young Garibaldian, who instantly struck him, saying he would teach him how to behave in such a brutal manner to a dumb animal. The General's fondness for animals is well known to amount almost to a passion; and at Caprera neither whip nor stick is, under any circumstances whatever, allowed to touch horse or dog. And here he was ably supported by Mr. Adam Smith, agent to the London Society for the Protection of Animals. Another evil, which early attracted his notice, was the almost infinite number of impudent beggars who thronged the principal streets of the city. This evil was found to be too deeply rooted to be thoroughly eradicated; but all that law and regulation could do was done in good earnest. The state of the prisons, also, received immediate attention, and all underwent the most thorough cleansing. In that of St. Maria Apparente, nice, large windows were made, in places that before had only contained little slits in the wall, and the terrible dungeons of the Castle of St. Elmo, though now well aired and swept, were ordered to be entirely disused. Part of the diplomatic body had followed the King to Gaeta; but the French ambassador and the Papal legate remained at Naples, and their presence was felt in the mysterious influence they exercised on the Bourbonic party of the capital. The latter of these diplomatists lost no time in forming conspiracies against the Dictator's Government.

Baron Brennier did not conspire, but he took no pains to disguise his dislike of the new rulers; and one senior French naval officer on the station, less prudent than the rest, candidly and publicly confessed that he considered Garibaldi "L'ennemi de Dieu."

On September the 9th, Mr. Elliot received a telegram from Lord John Russell desiring him to express to General Garibaldi the hope that no attack would be made upon Venetia. As Mr. Elliot, English ambassador to Francis II., could not enter into direct official communication with the Dictator, it was arranged that a visit should be paid by Admiral Mundy to the *de facto* ruler, and that when he returned the visit on board the *Hannibal*, Mr. Elliot should be there to meet him. "When I," (writes the admiral), "called on the General I found him engaged in conversation with Lord Llanover and others, and being much fatigued from incessant work he was lying upon the bed in easy slippers, but otherwise habited in his usual uniform. Lieutenant Wilmot having announced that I was present in the anti-room, the Dictator remarked that it would not be becoming in him to receive the Admiral without his boots, so he commenced pulling them on, and had just succeeded in dragging the first over his foot when I entered the room. We were both much amused at this little disorder of dress, but immediately holding out his hand, he said, 'I am indeed glad to see you. I told you, admiral, when we parted at Palermo, that we should meet again at

Naples.' On my saying I wished to speak to him privately, he requested Lord Llanover and his companions to leave us together. When alone I informed him that Her Majesty's Minister had a communication to make to him from Lord John Russell. On hearing this name, before I could finish the sentence, he exclaimed, 'Lord Russell is an excellent man, and a true friend of Italy,* I proceeded to say that if he would come on board the *Hannibal* the following day Mr. Elliot would meet him in my cabin, and would there make known to him the message from Her Majesty's Government. Garibaldi, in his usual quick way, replied, 'Certainly: anything you wish I am always ready to do. I will get a boat from Admiral Persano, and be on board the *Hannibal* at eleven o'clock, if that hour will suit. I shall be glad to make the acquaintance of Monsieur Elliot, who, I believe, is connected by marriage with Lord Russell.' I thought it strange that this circumstance, so entirely of a family nature, should have been known to the Dictator, and from whom could he have learnt it? The city was again illuminated at night, and the effect, when viewed from the sea, was extremely beautiful. On September the 10th General Garibaldi and Mr. Elliot met on board the *Hannibal*, at eleven o'clock. After I had made her Majesty's Minister and the Dictator acquainted with each other, I requested the latter to desire his attendant staff to leave the cabin, as Mr. Elliot was desirous of a private conversation, and Captain Farquhar took them on the lower deck to watch the gunnery exercise. Mr. Elliot having expressed to General Garibaldi the astonishment with which, in common with all the world, he had witnessed the marvellous results he had accomplished with such trifling means, informed him that though he could have no official relations with him, he should remain at Naples until he received further instructions from Her Majesty's Government. This information appeared to give great satisfac-

* For an account of a testimonial presented last autumn to Lord Russell, by the people of Milan, see *Times* of October 9, 1862.

tion to the Dictator, who said he fully understood that official intercourse was not practicable. Mr. Elliot then informed him that Lord John Russell had charged him to express the hope that no attack would be made upon Venetia, as, in his Lordship's opinion, it would be calculated to bring the greatest calamities upon Italy. Garibaldi replied by stating that he would make no concealment of his plans, which were plain and straightforward. He intended to push on at once to Rome, and there place the crown of united Italy on the head of King Victor Emmanuel, upon whom would devolve the task of the liberation of Venetia, and in which he would himself be but the lieutenant of his Majesty. If that liberation could be accomplished by purchase or by negotiation, so much the better. He added, he was sure that Lord John Russell in counselling the abandonment of Venetia did not fairly represent the generous feelings of the people of England towards the Italian nation, although he cheerfully recognized the obligation Italy was under to Her Majesty's Government for the sympathies they had exhibited in regard to Rome. Rome is an Italian city, and neither the Emperor or anyone else has a right to keep me out of it. It will be remarked that Garibaldi made a difference between Rome and Venice. Rome is the capital of the country, that must be had at all risks. He will never abandon the Venetian cause but was content to wait for it and to obtain it by purchase if possible."

At sunset on September the 11th, the rest of the royal troops marched out of the city towards Capua: there was a sullen determination and defiance in the look and bearing of the men which plainly showed that they bore no sympathy towards the cause of the Dictator.

Captain Forbes says: "On the 12th instant Depretis arrived from Palermo. Alarmed at the strife his weakness had fostered he now came to proclaim his own incompetence. He had countenanced annexational intrigues which Crispi, the Minister of the Interior, and the other Garibaldians in his government had determined to oppose, even by force, if requisite, believing that Garibaldi was yet Dictator of the island, and that he, and not M. Cavour's agents, had the right of annexation; and further, that it was for Garibaldi, and Garibaldi only, to deliver up the kingdom, which he had won with his sword, to the future King of Italy.

"The Cabinet at Turin, jealous of Garibaldi's prestige, wish to strip him of his power, without even allowing him the gratification of resigning it into the hands of Victor Emmanuel; and these are the reasons which obliged Garibaldi to start for Palermo on the night of the 16th, to calm the Palermians, and establish another pro-dictator, Mordini, a man who had wise, moderate, and statesman-like views, as well as great eloquence and perfect command of temper in debate. In the meantime Suton was left pro-dictator at Naples, and Turr remained in command before Capua, well knowing that, come what might, his army was staunch and his generals might be relied upon. What with the intrigues of partisans, place hunters and itinerant politicians, who have the effrontery to imagine they are competent to advise him, Garibaldi had to endure what would break down any intellect save his; his unswerving integrity alone enables him to carry out 'sa tache sublime.'"

"In his downright honesty we have the secret of his unparalleled successes. He cannot lie; and if he could, why should he? From the hour when he first dreamt of 'Italian unity,' he declared war to every obstacle in his path, whether priestly or princely. When he saw an Italian prince lead on against the Austrians he hastened to join him. Though Europe dared not oppose a French occupation of Rome, he did, by his uncompromising hostility to oppressors, whether foreign or domestic; he revivified the nation and inaugurated that spirit which has emancipated sixteen millions. Three millions of his countrymen are yearing in Rome, and Venetia, and because he is bold enough to avow his determination to finish his task, haggard diplomacy desires him to be more circumspect. What, in the name of heaven! has diplomacy ever done for Italy since it condemned her to half a century of misrule at the treaty of Vienna? Garibaldi has nothing to conceal. He sees the Rome of the Popes made the hot-bed of intrigue against the rising liberties of his country, and though she is bristling with French bayonets, he declares she shall be the Italian capital. Having nothing to be ashamed of, he knocks boldly at the door, and says: 'What are you doing in Casa Nostra?' not that he need or would attack the French garrison; for their position has become, if not irk-some, impossible; he only wishes them to clear out on the first opportunity. In a word, he would and will see the dream of his life completed in an Italy of the Italians. Garibaldi returned this morning from Palermo, having thoroughly succeeded, and left a determined anti-annexationist, until Garibaldi orders it, pro-dictator, Mordini, by name, so that peace may now be hoped for in the island. One cannot help wishing that good old Ruggerio Settimo had been able to accept Garibaldi's former offer; eighty-two years old, he wisely declined; but it was a generous tribute, on the part of the General, to one who has loved his country well, and who was Prime minister during the English occupation, and was again borne to the surface in 1848, when he headed the Sicilian Government."

Count Arrivabene says, "A real cause of annoyance to Garibaldi was the discontent of those who wished to hasten the annexation to Piedmont, a feeling which manifested itself more and more every day, hampering the regular march of public affairs, and opposing the organization and stability of the Dictatorial Government. The party which caused these embarrassments, a party composed of those patriots who emigrated to Piedmont in 1848, or who had been condemned by the tribunals of Ferdinand II, and which was called the Piedmontese party, was not disheartened by the defeat which it had already sustained; its members, though, no doubt, honourable men, wanted to get into power, and did not possess sufficient philosophy to stand on one side and await the solution of the political question; whether rightly or wrongly, they were accused of desiring to demolish the influence of the Dictator, and to ensure the supremacy of their own party. To judge from facts, it would appear that the action of this party was carried so far that Garibaldi thought it necessary to send out of the country Silvio Spavento, who was believed to be the most intelligent, and active leader of the Piedmontese Propaganda. At this time Dr. Bertani was appointed Secretary General to the Dictator.* Soon afterwards letters appeared in the official gazette at Naples, repudiating the idea of any reconciliation between Garibaldi and Cavour, and stating that the General could never be on terms of friendship with a man who had sold an Italian province.

The reader who has traced all the underhand intrigues organized by the agents of Cavour against the authority of the Dictator, cannot fail to perceive that no amount of personal dislike could have increased, to any extent, the antagonism of the policy of Cavour towards Garibaldi, though happily, as has before been said, all this was changed before the death of that minister. To increase the difficulties of Garibaldi, Mazzini now made his appearance at Naples. Garibaldi could not, with the slightest appearance of justice, banish from the country the man who had obtained so much important information on the state of affairs in Sicily, by which service he had rendered great assistance to the cause of the revolution in that island. Mazzini was also one of the earliest and strongest supporters of the unity of Italy.

It must always be borne in mind that in the middle ages Italy was the Italy of popes and municipalities, and that the unity of the Italian family never had been so much as dreamt of, and that for the first time it was presented in a tangible form before the minds of the Italians in the pages of a newspaper edited by Mazzini himself. Mazzini declared, again and again,

---

*Mr. Dicey says, that Cavour must have been more than mortal, if he did not harbour feelings of resentment against Garibaldi, and undoubtedly Cavour was in some degree at least, influenced by personal feelings in his subsequent policy towards the ex-dictator.

that he had forsaken all his republican ideas and accepted, without *arrière pensée*, the programme of Garibaldi. His residence in Naples, and an erroneous supposition of his possessing influence over the Dictator caused great discontent, in consequence of which, Garibaldi accepted the resignation of Dr. Bertani, and appointed the Marquis Pallavicini to the pro-dictatorship of Sicily. Garibaldi had offered him this office in the beginning, and had the Marquis accepted it then, he would have avoided much subsequent annoyance both to himself and to the Government. One of his first official acts was to address to Mazzini, with Garibaldi's approbation, the following letter, requesting him to leave the country without delay:—"Self-denial has always been the virtue of the generous, I believe that you are generous, and I now offer you an opportunity of displaying your generosity to your fellow citizens. As representative of the republican principle, and an indefatigable defender of that principle, your presence among us cannot fail to arouse the mistrust of the King and his ministers. This is why your presence in this country creates embarssment to the Government and danger to the Nation, by compromising that concord which is indispensable to the advancement and triumph of the Italian cause. Even without intending it you divide us; perform then an act of patriotism by leaving these provinces; add a new one to the many sacrifices you have already made for your country—a sacrifice which she demands from you as a token of your love for her, and for which she will be eternally grateful. I repeat it, even without intending any mischief, you divide us, and it is necessary that all the national forces should be united in one band, I know that your words preach concord, and I doubt not your acts are in unison with them; but all do not believe you, and there are many who misuse your name with the parricidal intention of hoisting a hostile banner in Italy; honor commands you to put an end to the suspicions of some and to the intrigues of others. Show the sincerity of your patriatism by leaving Naples, and you will carry with you the praises of all honest men."

Naples, October 3, 1860.

Mazzini, however, refused to comply with this request, and in a letter he wrote a few days afterwards, he says: "I think that I ought to represent and support, in my own person, the right of every Italian to live in his own country when he does not attack its laws; because it would appear to me that by voluntarily exiling myself I should be guilty of insult: firstly, to my country, which cannot, without dishonouring itself in the eyes of Europe, render itself guilty of tyranny; secondly, to the King, who cannot fear an individual without admitting himself to be weak and insecure of the affections of his subjects; and, thirdly, to the men of your party, who cannot be excited at the presence of a man declared by them to be alone and abandoned, without standing convicted of self-contradiction, because the desire comes not, as you think, from the country which labours and combats under the flag of Garibaldi, but from the Turin Ministry, to whom I owe no debt. Lastly, because on arriving I received a declaration from the Dictator of this country that I was free in the land of the free." He goes on to state that he had accepted monarchy, and that if ever he took up his old flag again he would honestly avow it, and publicly too, both to friends and enemies.

It is probable that he would have greatly increased his reputation by gracefully and promptly yielding to a request which would have elicited from all parties a well-merited admiration for his patriotism, and gained for him the lasting gratitude of the government of the Dictator. On the other hand it might have been remembered that even during the "Lombard campaign of 1848, Mazzini stated that to assure the independence and unity of the country, he would sacrifice not indeed his republican faith, but all action for it, and he only asked Charles Albert to "dare all, raise the banner of unity, and call the nation to arms, and to call into court the testimony of deeds on the eve of the campaign of 1859. Mazzini stood aloof from Garibaldi, exposing and protesting against the scheme of Plompreres, the details of which he knew and published; yet immediately after the peace of Villafranca, when Cavour despairing, sent the following telegram to Baron Ricasoli, not quite suitable for ears polite: "Peace with Austria; I resign; Dukes back; all to the devil," was the time selected by Mazzini, to support the royalty of Piedmont. On the 20th of July, 1859, he wrote: "Liberty and National Unity! Let this be the sole cry that bursts from those who will not allow Italy to be a dishonoured slave. What was the aim of those who separated themselves from us, and gave themselves to the French Alliance? Their aim was like ours, one free Italy, independent from all foreigners. Let all disputes cease, in the name of the honor of Italy let us unite; accursed be he among us who cannot cancel the memory of all mutual reproaches and accusations in the great principle that by uniting, we may and ought to save our country!"* Mazzini wrote a letter to the Neapolitan papers, in which he stated that he and his were firm to the monarchy, that the word republic had never been heard from his party for two years, and that the only difference of opinion was that he preferred the programme of Garibaldi to that of Cavour. It has been stated a hundred times at least, that Garibaldi was surrounded by Mazzinians, that his staff and personal attendants were without exception selected from that party; so little truth was there in this assertion, that Captain Forbes mentions, that after Dr. Bertrani's resignation, he was unable to get a letter conveyed to Garibaldi; his messenger waiting uselessly for hours, only because Bertani was supposed to share Mazzini's views, but to return: All things tend to prove the respect that Garibaldi entertained for constitutional freedom. It was his personal desire that Bertani should accept office, on account of the great service he had rendered to the national cause, in the admirable manner in which he had organized the Sicilian expedition. The moment that he discovered that he had lost the confidence of the Neapolitans by the republican

* See the Italian Movement and Italian Parties, by James Stansfeld, Esq., M.P., one of the Lords of the Admiralty.

tendencies that were imputed to him, Garibaldi immediately accepted his resignation, and caused, as we have seen before, the Marquis Pallavicini to be appointed to the pro-dictatorship.

The General had written to the King to explain to him why he considered that the policy of Cavour was not at that time beneficial to the country, and giving the reasons he entertained as to the necessity of the removal of that minister from office. In his reply the King said that he was a Constitutional Monarch, and, as such, could not withdraw a minister who was acceptable to the majority of his subjects. It must be remembered that up to this time Victor Emmanuel had no authority in the kingdom of Naples, and that Garibaldi, as Dictator, held absolute sway over that kingdom. The General acquiesced, without reserve, in the constitutional view of the question, and, as is much to be regretted, his Majesty had not always acted consistently with the sentiments he expressed on that occasion. Notwithstanding this Garibaldi lost no time in making all necessary arrangements for the annexation of Naples to Piedmont, for his patriotism was too pure to allow any disagreement between himself and the King to stand in the way of the national cause. Garibaldi had, during his stay in Sicily, organized his men, forming them into four divisions called the 15th, 16th, 17th, and 18th divisions of the army of Italy, the whole called L'Armata Meridionale, the fourteen divisions of the Piedmontese army being supposed to form the nucleus of the national forces. Of course when he became Dictator of the two Sicilies this army was greatly augmented, and Garibaldi had written to the Government desiring them to confirm his orders, and to authorize the consolidation of the two services into a national army. It is not easy to comprehend how so reasonable a request could be denied, for we have seen that when Nice and Savoy were annexed to France, Napoleon absorbed the forces of those two provinces into the Imperial army, and even offered to Garibaldi the rank of General in that service. Garibaldi was delighted with the King's promise in reply that he would accept his army as part of the national forces, and permit his officers to retain their rank in the new Italian army, subject, however, to the approval of a mixed commission that was to be organized for that purpose.

Most of the officers that at that time surrounded his person can testify to the affectionate anxiety of the General for the arrival of the King.

Mr. Dicey, in his "Memoirs of Cavour," says: "The invasion of the Papal States by a Sardinian army was the master-stroke of Cavour's political genius. It had become imperatively necessary to stop Garibaldi's progress, to restore Sardinia to the position of leader in the Italian revolution, and to annex Naples, without delay, to Northern Italy."

Count Arivabene says: "That the sudden change in the policy of the French Emperor was brought about by causes not generally known in England. Dr. Bertani had offered to a French exile, Colonel Charras, the command of a division intended for the Papal States. This was known to Cavour, who saw at once the advantage he could derive by suggesting to the Emperor that the French colonel, at the head of a republican force organized by Bertani, would be a sort of defiance to the Napoleonic rule. Farina and Cialdini were commissioned by Cavour to impress on Louis Napoleon, that if he did not allow the Piedmontese army to cross the Papal frontiers at once, the army of the revolution would do so in a few days. The Emperor was evidently convinced of the force of this argument, and gave in his adhesion. The growth of Lamoricière's army on the extended and defenceless frontier of Tuscany, was a position dangerous to Sardinia, and it was important to check its formation. All these objects could be attained only in one way, and that was by the invasion of the Papal States. The one apparently fatal obstacle to the plan was the presence of the Imperial army.

It is possible, though the evidence appears to contradict it, that Cavour had private reasons for knowing that the French would not offer any substantial opposition to the scheme; but it is more probable that he relied upon the conviction that the Imperial Government was as unwilling as himself to see a revolutionary movement inaugurated in Italy under the guidance of Garibaldi, and that the advance of the General to Rome would have placed France in a most difficult position. There was, therefore, a great chance that the Emperor would only protest against the measure, and would not withdraw his protection from Italy, which he had hitherto afforded her, by preventing any interference on the part of Austria. The stroke was a bold one, but was crowned with success. With but a few days' notice the Sardinian armies crossed the Papal frontier, scattered Lamoricière's army, captured Ancona, (on the 29th of September), and added some of the finest and most celebrated provinces in Italy to the new Italian kingdom. Thus, when at the head of his victorious army, Victor Emmanuel passed from the Papal States into the kingdom of Naples, Garibaldi could no longer claim alone the title of the Deliverer of Italy. The revolution was defeated by its own weapons, and again the policy of Cavour became the policy of Italy.

On this subject Mr. Stansfeld writes:—"On the 10th of September, 1860, after the invasion by Garibaldi of the Neapolitan states, Cavour wrote to Baron Talleyrand, 'If we are not at the Caltolica before Garibaldi we are lost; the revolution will invade Central Italy. We are forced to act.' Again, in a circular of M. Thouvenel, of October, 1860, I find these words: 'Signor Farini (sent by Cavour), has explained to the Emperor, at Chambery, the very embarrassing and dangerous position in which the triumph of the revolution, to a certain extent personified in Garibaldi, threatens to place the government of his Sardinian majesty. Garibaldi was on the point of freely traversing the Roman States, raising the population as he went, and had he once passed that frontier, it would have been utterly impossible to prevent an attack on Venice. The government of Turin had one mode left open to it in order to prevent that eventuality, and that was to enter the Marches and Umbria as soon as the arrival of Garibaldi had produced disturbances, and re-establish order, without infringing on the authority of the Pope, and if need were, to give battle to the revolution in the Neapolitan territory, and request a congress to immediately decide the destinies of Italy.'" "Now certainly," continues Mr. Stansfeld, "these professions of motive cannot be said to be very creditable to Cavour, and they look as unlike as possible to the arguments of a patriot having the accomplishment of his country's unity above everything else at heart." Garibaldi acted in a very different spirit when, on the 27th of September, he announced to the people the success which had crowned the Sardinian arms. The General addressed the populace from a balcony of the palace, in the following laconic speech:— "People of Naples: Our brethren of the Italian army, commanded by the gallant General Cialdini, combat the enemies of Italy, and conquer. The army of Lamoricière has been defeated by those valiant men. All the provinces enslaved by the Pope are free. Ancona is ours. The valiant soldiers of the army of the North have passed the frontier, and are on Neapolitan soil; we shall soon have the good fortune to clasp their victorious hands." It is of this period that Count Arrivabene writes:—"In politics the question of the outs and the ins will always exist, and be at times a source of embarrassment. It was, therefore, natural enough that the new opportunities suddenly opening to the intelligence of the Neapolitans should arouse an eagerness for power among those who, saturated with pride and vanity, think themselves wronged because they are set aside by their political adversaries. Many of the opponents of Garibaldi, and of his government, were doubtless honest men, but the long years they had passed in exile had left them ignorant of the real wants of their country. Most of them were, besides, far from popular. Openly hostile to the Dictator, they encouraged an agitation which might have proved fatal to Southern Italy, had not the popularity of

Garibaldi kept it in check." These people, be it remarked, were the Piedmontese or Cavour party. So far was the General from giving any encouragement to extreme opinions, that, notwithstanding his desire to relieve the distress that was then prevalent, he refused to allow Louis Blanc to open national workshops, stating that he withheld his assistance from him purely on account of his republican principles.

An officer on the General's staff wished to return to the treasury the amount of his pay. "Don't do that," was the answer of Garibaldi; "give the money to your wife, and beg of her to spend it, not in actual charity, but in giving employment to the poor. For instance, embroidery for dresses would employ young girls, ornaments of little value, excepting from the workmanship, would give occupation to men." These suggestions were immediately complied with. The English residents at Naples had previously had no church of their own, though, of course, service was allowed to be performed at the British Embassy. The English, knowing well the religious feeling of Garibaldi, requested him to permit them to purchase land on which to build an English church. "Nay," he answered the deputation, with one of his own smiles,* "I must refuse your request, and in my turn proffer one, which is, that you should select the plot of land you think the most suitable for your church, and accept so small a mark of sympathy from the government of the Sicilies." When his chaplain applied to him the day previously to know when he could receive the English deputation, he answered, "To-morrow;" adding, in a tone of half reproach, "And when was it that the occupations of Garibaldi, however numerous, ever prevented his making leisure enough to receive an English deputation?" The supposed miracle of St. Januarius had been performed twice a year, when theatres

* This gift of Garibaldi's was only confirmed by the Government at Turin, after the death of Cavour in 1861, by Baron Ricasoli, and the first stone of the church was laid on the 15th of December, 1862, by the Duchesse de St. Arpino. The spot chosen is in the quiet but central Grada San Pasquale, at the back of the Riviera di Chiaja.

used to be closed for fifteen days, both ceremonies occasioning a loss of thirty days' wages to all performers and persons connected with public places of amusement. Garibaldi issued an official ordinance, worded so as not to be offensive to the prejudices of the people, which stated that actors must, like other people, have an opportunity of gaining their livelihood, and that thenceforth theatres, and all other places of public amusement, would be closed for two days only during the year, in honour of the patron Saint.

He also caused sermons to be preached in the churches by Gavazzi and others, and collections to be made on behalf of the wounded. The subject of the first sermon was the Life of Jesus Christ. The request of the General was that they would at all times preach Christ's Gospel. The Diodati New Testaments (from the press of the British and Foreign Bible Society) were sold by thousands in the streets, and not only to foreigners and to the people of Naples themselves.

The Confessional he considered was an institution well adapted to the early ages, when the perception of right and wrong was almost unknown, but at the present period destructive, in many cases, to family repose, and he carefully explained that it was against the abuse only that he protested.

Towards the middle of September, Garibaldi had permanently established his head-quarters in the magnificent palace of Caserta, the summer residence of the ex-royal family. He always rose at three o'clock in the morning, attended to the business of the state, consulted with the ministry, and received his numerous visitors, without distinction of noble or peasant. One morning a poor woman, being prevented by the body guard from entering the room of the General, who was at the moment engaged with the chief of his staff, wept so bitterly that her lamentations reached the ears of the General. Garibaldi suddenly appeared in the ante-room, and asked her what she wanted, and at once granted her petition, forbidding his guard, at the same time, to refuse admittance to any person that desired an audience with him.

After his ministerial duties were over he would frequently climb up the steep rock of St. Angelo, where he would spend hours in gazing upon the Neapolitan camp, the tortuous windings of the Volturno, rolling beneath his feet, and the ramparts of Capua, scarce perceptible in the far distance. It was there Garibaldi studied the future field of his operations. At noon breakfast was served, and in the evening he returned to the Palace to dine. Two of the appointments that Garibaldi made about this time have been subjected to much misrepresentation; the one was the selection of Alexandre Dumas for the superintendence of museums and excavations, when the small palace of Chiatamone was granted to him as a residence for that year only. When we remember the services which Alexandre Dumas had rendered to the national cause on board the *Emma*, when she lay in the bay of Naples, and the fact that he received no payment whatever for his services as director, the office being of a purely honorary nature, and the director living in his new abode entirely at his own expense, owing at the end of the first week the Hotel de Crocelles a thousand francs for breakfast and dinner; when he paid the bill, and sent for his cook from the *Emma*, it can certainly never be said that a house rent free for a few months was an exorbitant remuneration for having risked his life and his yacht in the cause of Italian independence. The other appointment so much objected to, was that of Colonel Peard, who was nominated to the command of the English Legion. Colonel Peard is a gentleman of good family and fortune, who once held a commission in an English Militia regiment, and who must, therefore, have acquired some elementary military instruction before he went to Italy. Like many others of our countrymen he was heartly grieved at the dismal picture of Italian affairs so aptly pourtrayed by Mr. Gladstone, and so instead of ingloriously confining himself to giving the Italians nothing better than mere sympathy, he entered the corps of the Cacciatori as a private soldier, and encountered the dangers of the Lombard campaign. His manner being quiet, gentlemanly, and unassuming, he speedly won the respect of his officers and eventually the esteem of Garibaldi, who, immediately after the battle of Milazzo, gave him the rank of Colonel. On the march to Naples, he was for some time entrusted with the telegraphic communications, and greatly distinguished himself by the ingenuity and address which he displayed in that department. When the English Legion arrived at Naples it was immediately placed under the command of Colonel Peard.

Mr. W. B. Brook, in his amusing little work, "Out with Garibaldi," tells us that as soon as the ships having the British Legion on board came into port, the gallant colonel visited each in succession, and read aloud his commission, and, in whatever light that appointment may have been subsequently regarded, no reasonable doubt can be entertained as to his popularity at that time among his countrymen, who regarded it as a compliment conferred alike upon both him and themselves. During the former Italian Campaigns, Peard had particularly distinguished himself, and there was hardly a man of the legion who had not heard in some way of the deadly rifle of that sternly-visaged and powerful old man.

Such was the man, then, whom the English Volunteers, on arriving off Naples, greeted with those thundering cheers that cause so much surprise to foreigners, who are totally powerless to imitate them. Regarding the subsequent management of the English Legion there is much to be said on both sides; composed of totally discordant elements, and hastily sent out, it would indeed have required a very able officer to command them with satisfaction to everybody.

CHAPTER VI.

The Battle of the Volturno—False report that they were assisted by the Piedmontese—Superiority of the Garibaldian over the Piedmontese military costume—Danger of Garibaldi—Address of the King to the people—Extract from "Blackwood's Magazine"—Proclamation of Garibaldi to the people of Naples—Letter of the "Times" correspondent relating to the King and Garibaldi—Capitulation of Capua—Culpable neglect of the King to Review the Volunteers—Garibaldi uses all his influence to compel the people to vote for annexation—Similarity of Garibaldianism to a religion—Return of Persano from Gaeta—Entry of Victor Emmanuel into Naples.

On the first of October was fought the battle of the Volturno. About four in the morning the outposts of Milbitz and Medici were driven back along the whole line; another Garibaldian brigade was also so vigorously assailed that, for a time, it lost ground, being unable to cope with the overwhelming forces that were hurled against it. A little after three in the morning Garibaldi left the palace of Caserta, with his staff, and arrived at Santa Maria before four. A desultory sound of musketry had been heard at early daybreak: the mist which is wont to cling to the lowlands on either side of the river was heavier than usual, and well calculated to conceal the Neapolitan attack, now rapidly assuming a general character, while the furious cannonade at Saint Angelo announced that something more than the usual morning skirmish was commencing. The sound of a heavy cannonade was, moreover, heard in other directions.

Bixio had dispatched in all haste a telegram to the purport

that a strong column was straining every nerve to dislodge him from his position. The royal army had evidently formed a determination to take the bull by the horns, and carry all before them by the weight of their columns. Garibaldi at once perceived the gravity of the situation, and never throughout his varied career did he give greater proof of that instinct which forms so striking a characteristic of his military genius, than during the long struggle in which, with only eleven thousand men, he resisted the combined attack of 30,000 Neapolitan troops, massed in the short line from San Tamaro to St. Angelo, whom he entirely routed as soon as his reserve, which scarcely amounted to 5,000 men, arrived on the field. The Garibaldians thus won the day entirely by their own exertions.

The story that was then current in Europe, that the Piedmontese army had arrived just in time to turn the fortune of war in their favour, is utterly destitute of foundation, although it may find some supporters at the present day. It is true that one battalion of Bersaglieri, 200 strong only, was sent by the Piedmontese Ambassador, but it did not reach the field of battle till the day after the battle was fought. It would, indeed, be a matter of some difficulty to point out the Garibaldian divisions that gained most glory on that memorable day. Captain Forbes tells us that by eight in the evening all the wounded were in hospital. The General himself slept at St. Angelo, and returned to Caserta at two o'clock the next morning.

Captain Forbes, who was present, describes the small party of Piedmontese as looking uncommonly gay and serviceable. On the 2nd of October, he says, they were laden like packhorses, and contrasted strangely with the Garibaldians, who had no other incumbrance than ninety rounds of ammunition; they were soon compelled to abandon their shakoes and knapsacks, and adopt the Garibaldian kepis, and great-coats. Though men of great strength and activity, they could never be expected to compete with the Garibaldians, whose only incumbrance was a flannel shirt and a pair of trousers, while the Sardinians, on the other hand, were clad in close fitting tunics, which rendered all active movement exceedingly difficult, nor was it any easy matter to keep in its proper place the extraordinary head-dress that their military regulations compelled them to wear. It was impossible to avoid wondering how much longer it would be the fashion in European armies to retain such a uniform as is best calculated to unfit the soldier for muscular exertion. How long will people be in recognizing the important truth that military success depends as much upon the freedom of the soldier's limbs, as upon the excellence of the arms that are put into his hands? Here is an example in the light troops of Piedmont, the far-famed Bersaglieri. They were so hampered with these unnecessary encumbrances that they were totally unable to march more than twelve miles a day without rest. Suppose, now, that two men equally skilled in the use of the bayonet were engaged in a struggle with that weapon. The one is a Garibaldian unimpeded by the encumbrances we have above-mentioned, the other a Piedmontese as I have described him. Who can doubt the result of the contest? Suppose, again, two armies on the field of battle, the one representing the Garibaldian and the other the antiquated principle—the one marching thirty miles a day with ease, the other scarcely able to complete fifteen. Who can doubt the result?

But to return to our subject.—The Royalists are said to have lost in the recent battle about 10,000 men, and the king, despairing of success in the field, withdrew with the remnant of his forces to Gaeta. Garibaldi was unwilling to renew the attack, hoping that the king, seeing the desperate state of his fortunes, would abandon such a hopeless contest, and spare the further effusion of blood.

At dinner the General lavished enthusiastic praises on his men, especially the Calabresi, who had, in the recent battle, outshone their comrades in deeds of heroism.

Two incidents that occurred in the recent battle may not be uninteresting to the reader.

Garibaldi having arrived at early dawn at a spot near the field of action, was moving towards the castle of St Angelo when he was surrounded by the enemy. Without further protection than his staff and a few outriders, it soon became apparent that he must either cut his way through his enemies or surrender at discretion. Subjected to a pelting storm of grape and musketry, but favoured by the mists that still clung to the banks of the Volturno, and by that never-failing good fortune which seems to give him a charmed existence, the General seemed in a fair way of escape, when one of his carriage horses was struck by a ball and fell dead. At the same moment the coachman of the carriage following Colonel Missori's was killed. Garibaldi and his party jumped out, and finding themselves by good chance near one of the water courses, instantly jumped into it, and succeeded after a brief skirmish, in gaining the slopes of the mountain near St. Angelo, with the loss of only three of the party. After four hours' hard fighting Garibaldi in turn became the assailant, and leading on his entire available force, drove back the Neapolitans at the point of the bayonet, retook the batteries and position near the river, and thus ended the first act of the battle. Another, but somewhat trivial incident occurred when two squadrons of Neapolitan dragoons made a daring attempt to capture one of the Garibaldian guns. They charged bravely through the open fields, but when the spoil seemed just within their grasp, they were received by an unexpected volley of musketry that made them reel back in dismay and take to headlong flight. This repulse seemed to come out of the ground, for not a man was to be seen. Garibaldi had been on a reconnoitring expedition, and observing the advance of the cavalry, had laid himself down with his men in the furrows, and bade them reserve their fire till the troops were upon them.

Armed by the constitutional power granted by the Deputies of Turin, the King was authorized to accept those provinces which manifested a desire to form part of the Constitutional Monarchy of united Italy. He came to meet Garibaldi, who was about to present him with half the Italian Peninsula.

It should be remembered that the conquest of Naples was accomplished in utter defiance of the Law of Nations, for if there be any truth in the doctrine of Divine Right, then this was an act of the grossest injustice. But if, on the other hand, the love of their subjects is the only secure tenure by which kings can hope to rule, then this was a righteous act, and Garibaldi was fully justified in making private war against the king of Naples, and transferring his kingdom to Sardinia.

The king told them that he addressed them at a moment that would ever be memorable in the annals of Italy; that he appealed to men who had changed the face of the country, and had in his name sent to him numerous deputations from every class of society, entreating him to secure to them the blessings of unity, order, and freedom. He urged upon them his consciousness of the duties that were demanded by Providence of an Italian King. That he would prefer to lose his crown than to be guilty of any want of fidelity to the word he had pledged to them; that he had secured freedom to them at an epoch that was most inauspicious, and that he fondly hoped that this seed that he had sown would take root, and developing itself into a mighty tree would spread its branches abroad, and embrace every member of the Italian family. He assured them by representative franchise, by popular education, by the freedom of trade and industry, he would endeavour to increase the well-being of his people. That he wished all due respect to be given to the Catholic religion, but that he also desired liberty of conscience for all his subjects. He told them he considered his magnanimous ally at the Tuilleries to be deeply moved with the misfortunes of their country. That the Italian soldiers had fought nobly beside the invincible legions of France, and that it was indeed natural that the events that had recently occurred in Central Italy should arouse the minds of Southern Italians, the excitement even in Sicily breaking out into open insurrection. He reminded them of the blessings that were secured to them by the heroism of Garibaldi. "Was it," exclaimed his majesty, "within my power or my duty to prevent them?" He went on to say, that the fall of Naples had strengthened in his heart the opinion that monarchs should build their thrones upon the love of their people. That the new government of the two Sicilies was inaugurated in his name; but that some of its acts caused grave apprehensions that it would not, in all respects, be a sound interpreter of the policy which was represented by him, as it was feared throughout all Italy, that under the shadow of a glorious popularity a faction might muster which would be ready to sacrifice the triumph of the national cause to the chimeras of an ambitious fanaticism. That in the present emergency any culpable neglect to restrain with a strong hand any act of indiscretion that would compromise the safety of the commonwealth, would be a sign rather of weakness than of forbearance.

In conclusion, the King gave them his assurances that he did not come to impose his will upon them, but to see theirs respected, and he hoped that his conduct would tend to reconcile in every nation of Europe the progress of the people, with the stability of the throne. He was convinced that he had fulfilled his duties as a King and as an Italian, and that his policy might not perhaps be useless in reconciling throughout Europe the progress of the people with the stability of the throne. He knew, he said, that in Italy he closed the era of revolutions. In this address the King alluded to the question as to whether he ought not to have checked Garibaldi's expedition to Sicily. What disclosures could not the Neapolitan Ambassador at the Court of Turin make of the official assurances of Count Cavour in the name of the King, and the reiterated assurances that every nerve had been strained to check the movement?

Did not the Marquis of Villa Marina, the Piedmontese ambassador at Naples, protest against the accusation that the King had connived at Garibaldi's expedition, as false and injurious? Did not the Official Piedmontese Gazette state that the Government had attempted to prevent the departure of that expedition, that the Sardinian ships of war had received orders to prevent a landing, and that the King's Government understood and respected the principles of international law, and considered it to be its duty to make that principle respected in the state for which it was responsible?*

It is believed by many that from the beginning there was a collusion between the king, Cavour, and Garibaldi. This, however, is not the fact, and there are many and powerful reasons to prove the contrary. The truth seems to be that from the first moment that the expedition seemed likely to prove successful, the king had made up his mind to secure the spoils.

In another part of this proclamation the king alludes to the Mazzinian party, who had certainly rendered him good service, but the scanty sympathy they received from the Government of the Dictator has already been shown. Bertani was deprived of office, and returned to Genoa; Mazzini was requested to leave Naples; Louis Blanc was refused permission to open workshops,

---

* "Blackwood's Edinburgh Magazine" for October, 1863, has an article entitled "To-day in Italy," the following extract is taken from it:—"After Garibaldi had left for Sicily, Cavour continued to confer and consult with the Neapolitan Envoy at Turin, so, in a like spirit, he accompanied his friendly remonstrances to the Tuscan Court by an organized conspiracy, destined to bribe the Government officials and corrupt the army. To make the Grand Duke give himself his own checkmate was the craft of the wily statesman. Nor with such an opponent did the game call for any high exercise of skill. To wring from him, one by one, a string of concessions, and cry 'Too late' over each as he yielded it, was the sure and safe tactic by which they worked. Angered and insulted, the Prince lost patience at last, quitted his capital and his state, and never returned to them! We see in these transactions the same duplicity that never left Cavour in every political emergency. When La Farina, convinced that the democratic spirit of Italy must be summoned in the event of a war with Austria, informed Cavour by letter of the formation of the 'National Society'—a sort of self-constituted parliament—Cavour's answer was this, 'Go on—only remember this, that if I am attacked about you by the diplomatists, or questioned in the Chamber, I'll deny you as though I were St. Peter.' That some at least of the great states of Europe regarded the conduct of Piedmont at this epoch with indignation, is easily shown. 'Lo Piémont,' said the French Emperor, 'malgré nos conseils, voudra poursuivre une politique d'agrandissement.' In another place it is said the Emperor sent for M. Sauli, and said, 'If your master's country be really at the mercy of the democracy, it is time for the other states of the Continent to consider what relations can be maintained with it.' Cavour's answer to all remonstrances on this subject is so characteristic that it deserves to be quoted. 'What right have you,' asks he, 'to inquire why we have not prevented the disembarkation of the Garibaldians, so long as the whole Neapolitan fleet has failed to do so?"

and finally, the Marquis Pallavicini, the avowed and determined opponent of any approach to Mazzinianism, was made pro-dictator by Garibaldi. The king proclaims Italy for the Italians, and almost tells them in the same breath that he knew that in Italy he closed the era of revolutions.

Rome and Venice are Italian cities, and in proclaiming Italy for the Italians it is presumed that the king had no intention to exclude them. Yet one of these cities is governed by the Pope, with the assistance of a French garrison, and the other by the Emperor of Austria. The only right that the king could possess to either of them could be derived from the free-will of the people themselves, notwithstanding the necessity of employing force or diplomacy in obtaining possession of them. There can be no right to either Rome or Venice, which is not based upon the popular will, now this will must be expressed in each instance by some overt act of disapprobation of the existing governments, and an open avowal of their preference to the rule of the king, and this is what most people would call a revolution; so that before Italy can be for the Italians, there must be at least two more revolutions, despite the objection Victor Emmanuel may entertain for the word.

On the 4th of October, the king issued a further proclamation respecting further operations in Southern Italy. He told the soldiers that he was satisfied with them, because they were worthy of Italy—by arms they had vanquished their enemies, and by their conduct the calumniators of the Italian name. The king said, that the mercenaries whom he had restored to liberty would speak in honourable terms of the Italian soldiers throughout every country of Europe, since they had learnt that God recompenses those who serve him, and not those who trample upon the liberties of nations. He reminded them that it rested with them to establish a strong Italian monarchy to secure the liberty of the people, whose duty it was to assist them with order and concord. That day by day would that glory which had for eight centuries blazed around the cross of Savoy, be increased under the auspices of the Italian army. The king concluded by telling them that he would take the command of the army in person, and that his fondest desire was to be foremost amongst them whenever there was danger.*

On the 11th of October the future King of Italy first put his foot upon Neapolitan ground. On the previous day the conqueror of the two Sicilies had called upon the people of Naples to vote by universal suffrage for or against the annexation of Naples and Sicily to Piedmont, announcing to them at the same time the arrival of the king, in the following words:—"Tomorrow Victor Emmanuel, King of Italy, the elect of the nation, will appear amongst us and break down that frontier which has for so many centuries divided us from the rest of our country. Let us then worthily receive the messenger of Providence, and scatter in his path the flowers of concord, as the pledge of our affection—no more political colors, no more parties. Let Italy be united (as the people of the Metropolis have wisely determined she shall be) under the king, Galantuomo, who is the symbol of our regeneration and of the prosperity of our country.

GARIBALDI."

The *Times* Correspondent tells us that there is no doubt but that evil counsellors had shaken the confidence of Victor Emmanuel in the purity of Garibaldi's designs, but that subsequent events must have made him see the error into which he had been led, and that he must now be anxious to heal the wounds which his distrust had inflicted upon the frank but extremely sensitive nature of Garibaldi. For the last few days,

---

* Victor Emmanuel has the credit of roughing it as much as any one. I was, therefore, somewhat surprised at finding him travelling with four or five most deliciously padded open and close carriages. They were all drawn up together in the road before his quarters, and there was no difficulty in inspecting them. The one he arrived in a day or two ago was a Clarence, lined with a gorgeous blue silk, and made with many conveniences, something in the style of Napoleon's celebrated chariot, taken at Waterloo.—See *In the Track of the Garibaldians*, p. 96.

he goes on to say, the General has been making as it were, his dictatorial testament, making those last dispositions which he thinks necessary to recompense those who have suffered or distinguished themselves during the war. Those who have lost limbs or property will be recompensed, although whether the Piedmontese war department will recognise the promotions and nominations of General Garibaldi, is a matter still to be discussed, for the union of southern to northern Italy has been so unconditional, that not even this point was insisted upon by Garibaldi. Another last disposition of Garibaidi is, that the families of all those who have fallen in battle and those who have suffered imprisonment or exile under the late government, should receive pensions from the state; further dispositions are to be made by the minister of the interior, that all those who have suffered by the inevitable consequences of war, in their property, may be indemnified in proportion to the damage they may have sustained. To recompense soldiers of merit, the national domains are to be employed, and the property existing in mortmain. An hospital of invalids is likewise in course of establishment; the first idea of Garibaldi was the palace of Caserta, part of which was to remain a royal palace, where there would have been sufficient room for Victor Emmanuel to repose after indulging his favourite pastime of shooting: the rest was to be appropriated to the invalids of the national war of independence. The idea was to leave to those invalids the charge of the gardens, woods, and preserves, so that the king would have been even in his pleasure, surrounded by those to whom he owed his South Italian kingdom. This poetical idea was, however, given up, as it was apprehended that it would not be to the taste of the king, who is most jealous of game, and who had enjoined one of the last messengers sent him by Garibaldi to take good care of the game in and about Caserta.* In consequence, another royal palace

* This was supposed to be in consequence of General Garibaldi having given to his son, and some of his staff, permission to shoot in the preserves at Caserta; Garibaldi himself was residing in the palace at the time, as Dictator of the Sicilies.

was chosen for the purpose, and the Palace of Quissiana, near Castellamare, has been selected. Garibaldi attends every day at Naples, concentrating his own attention on doing, in the short time left to him, as much good as possible. * * He visited the large hospital of St. Giuseppe: he was not one of those routine commanders who merely pass through the hospitals. When he came he came as a friend, not asking common questions, but stopping before every bed. He had a kind word for every one; a caress with his hand for every burning head; a shake of the hand, and a word of thanks, for every one he has met once before. A visit of his did more to heal than many a plaister and bandage, and even where all hope was lost, the sight of him was consolation. At his very last visit, a touching scene occurred in a room in the hospital of the incurables. Garibaldi was stroking the feverish forehead of a young Venetian who had but a few hours to live, and asking him what he could do for him, "Don't forget my country" was the reply of the agonized youth. From what precedes, you can see that Garibaldi's hospital-visits are affairs of hours not minutes, so that although he arrived at noon, it was nearly four o'clock before he left the hospital. While he was there, there were even greater crowds than usual beseiging the door to get a look at him. Another time Garibaldi holding in his arms and fondly caressing a dying boy—notwithstanding all his usual self-control—burst into tears, exclaiming, "Can even liberty be worth all this?"

Great attention was directed to the hospitals, although at first some difficulty existed in procuring for them a proper amount of attention. One day Garibaldi sent his chaplain to pay them a nocturnal visit to see if the nurses were doing their duty. He found them all asleep. Another time Madam Mario, going to a cupboard that had been for some time in disuse, found there forty dinners which ought to have been served to the sick. Doubtless the intention of the nurses was to sell them for their own profit. In a little time, however, all this was changed.

When the king arrived at Teano Garibaldi had concentrated at Calvi the whole of the forces he had brought up from St. Angelo two days before. He had sent in advance Colonel Missori, and then Count Trecchi to convey his respects to the king, and to receive his commands. On the following morning Count Trecchi and Missori came to inform him that Cialdini was within an hour's march, and that the king was following close behind. Garibaldi left immediately with his staff, and in the course of three quarters of an hour he came in sight of the head of the Piedmontese column. He clapped spurs to his horse, the Piedmontese advancing presented arms to Garibaldi, and opened their ranks to allow him to pass. Cialdini pushed forward, and Garibaldi jumping off his horse embraced him affectionately, after exchanging a few words, Garibaldi remounted and hastened to meet the king, who was not far behind, leading on his own division; as soon as he perceived the red shirts he took a telescope and recognizing Garibaldi, put spurs to his horse and galloped towards him: Garibaldi did the same. When they were within ten paces of each other the officers of the king and Garibaldi shouted, "Long live Victor Emmanuel," Garibaldi advanced, taking off his hat, and in a tone somewhat hoarse from emotion, greeted him as "King of Italy." Victor Emmanuel put his hand to his kepi and then held it out, and the General, with equal emotion, replied, "Sire, I thank you;" their suites meanwhile had mixed together. Passing a group of officers Garibaldi saluted them, among others were Farina and General Fanti, minister of war. Count Arrivabene tells us that Garibaldi was reviewing Eber's and Bixio's brigade, at the foot of a hill, known as "Santa Maria della Croce;" when the king appeared at the head of his staff, Garibaldi advanced to meet him. It was a singular sight. The elegant and splendid uniforms of the Piedmontese officers contrasted strongly with the coarse garb of the Garibaldians. The General himself wore his wide-awake, a plain red flannel shirt, half covered by his American grey cloak, and a pair of black trowsers. At his side hung his famous English sword, which had done such service at Calatafimi and Melazzo. The king complimented the General by saying that without his daring expedition the unity of Italy would not have been a reality for ten years. "It may be, sire," answered Garibaldi; "but I would not have attempted my expedition had not Victor Emmanuel been the most noble and generous of kings." On parting from Victor Emmanuel, the Dictator said to one of his generals: "I did not shrink from telling the king that he is surrounded by a set of men who are not the warmest friends of Italy. I tried to persuade him that *what has been said about the influence which Mazzini and his friends exercised over me is a mere calumny. 'How could I have insisted upon sending Mazzini into exile when he had done so much for Italian unity?'* I observed to Victor Emmanuel, and his majesty agreed that I was right."

Now comes the annexation, which Garibaldi wished should be made unconditionally, and he took every possible means to insure this result. Every man privileged to vote had first to produce his paper from the mayor, showing that he was entitled to vote; he was then admitted through a file of the National Militia, up a flight of steps, to a platform, on which the urns were fixed. The urns to the right and left of the central vase, which were several feet distant from it, bore the words "Si" and "No" painted on them respectively, in a large type. Up to one of these the voter had to walk, beneath the gaze of a dozen servitators, to thrust in his arm, and draw out a card. Of course this was open voting in the clearest sense of the word, as voters had to deliver up their papers of identification, and so their names and calling were, of course, known. Under regulations such as these, it may fairly be doubted whether a plebiscite by universal suffrage can be received as a correct representation of the real feeling of a nation. Owing to this arrangement, and the openly expressed wish of the Dictator that every one should vote for the annexation, no reasonable doubt as to the result could be entertained.

On October the 15th, six days before the voting, the General issued the following proclamation, being the first official intimation of his intentions regarding the future government of the kingdom he had conquered:—

"People of Naples,—The Two Sicilies, which owe their redemption to the blood of the Italians, who have elected me as their Dictator, form an integral and indivisible part of Italy. On the arrival of Victor Emmanuel, our constitutional king, I shall surrender into his hands the dictatorship which the nation has conferred upon me.

"Given at St. Angelo, Oct. 15, 1860."

We have already seen that all the influence which Garibaldi could command was exerted to procure votes for the annexation which he had pre-determined in his mind should take place. The only defence which it is possible to make for him is, that he thought he was acting for his country's good. He was placing affairs in the hands of ministers who bore a great dislike to him, and he must, therefore, be acquitted of all self-interest or personal ambition in the transactions to which we have referred. Indeed, did he ever during the whole course of his life show the slightest trace of either? Admiral Mundy tells us that perfect order reigned in every department, but that according to his opinion it would have required in any person a strong moral courage to make a public avowal of enmity to the unity of Italy.*

Captain Forbes tells us that now there was no Bertani to father their sins, so that the Dictator himself was made the target of the Piedmontese faction, who strained every nerve to blacken his character: of course he was so immeasurably superior to his calumniators that their shafts fell harmless at his feet. After his proclamation he received the division of the

* The General is said to have rebuked one of his oldest friends for not having, on the first election day, voted for the king, in the following terms:—"You have done wrong. I understand a republic as the supremacy of popular will in opposition to the single pleasure of the sovereign. I have done everything in my power to realise the wish of the Italians, and unite them under the sceptre of Victor Emmanuel, and you ought to do the same."

army which was stationed at Caserta. Galloping along the ranks he sought the glance of his old companions of the first expedition, whose instinct told them that this was, in all probability, the parting farewell of their chief, at least for that year. Gathering the officers around him, he was scarcely able to speak from emotion. His rare eloquence fled before the tears of his companions, and a few hoarse words, thanking them for the fidelity with which they had supported him, were perhaps more thrilling than any oration could have been. "My old comrades, we have done much in a short time, and I thank you, in the name of our country, of which you have deserved so well. Convey my thanks to the soldiers under your command." To the British brigade, which had just arrived, he remarked, "With pleasure I see around me the representatives of a nation which from the beginning has done so much for our cause, which has helped us in every way, and to whose powerful voice we owe, in a great measure, the upholding of that principle of non-intervention, which is the best security for our national independence."

Military operations on Garibaldi's part now ceased. The Piedmontese had undertaken everything north of the Volturno, and the garrison of Capua was too weak to make any offensive movement. Garibaldi went every day to Naples to conduct the final acts of his dictatorship, now so rapidly drawing to a close. Captain Forbes tells us that even the king's mind was in a measure warped by the animosity often poured into his ear by the enemies of the General. With respect to the aspect of affairs at Capua at this period, we have it on Garibaldi's own authority, that General Ritucci refused compliance with his request to evacuate the citadel, and so to spare the further effusion of blood. Garibaldi said that he had caused batteries to be raised on Mount San Angelo, on the railroad, and on bridges to be thrown across the Volturno in preparation for the assault upon the fortress. What was not known is this: King Victor Emmanuel wrote to Garibaldi urging him to slacken the bombardment, to extend his lines so as to invest the place, and then to permit matters to rest for the present. When he arrived at Garibaldi's camp he told the General to act upon his last arguments. This was done, and in two days after Capua was free. It has, however, been asserted that the troops marched from Ancona, through the Abruzzi, to save the Garibaldians, and to extricate the General from a most serious embarrassment. What the General's men did in two days, he could have ordered them to do a month before, but the king's letter, he asserts, prevented him. At Teano, in spite of Garibaldi's efforts to make the inhabitants cry, "Evviva il Rè d'Italia Vittorio Emmanuele," they yielded but a feeble compliance to his orders, and then shouted more lustily than ever, "Evviva Garibaldi." On the first of November he went to Naples to present the Hungarian Legion with their colours, which they had earned so nobly. He said—"This is a memorable day for you, for it cements the alliance of two nations, and establishes the fraternity of the people. To-day you have destroyed that principle of egotism which has kept the nations separated, and thus has facilitated the servitude of all. The people with whom you have fraternised to-day have the same enemies who threaten you. Your cause is theirs, and theirs is yours. But before fighting against this enemy outside, you have internal enemies to beat down, and I will tell you that the chief of them is the Pope. If I have acquired any merit with you, I have acquired that of telling you the truth frankly and without a veil. In using this privilege I tell you that your chief enemy is the Pope. I am a Christian, as you are: yes, I am of that religion which has broken the bonds of slavery, and has proclaimed the freedom of men. The Pope, who oppresses his subjects, and is an enemy of Italian independence, is no Christian: he denies the very principle of Christianity—he is the Anti-Christ. This truth you must spread among all those who are near to you, for it is only when all Italians shall be thoroughly convinced of this truth that Italy will be really free and united." Admiral Mundy informs us that he subsequently, accompanied by the pro-dictator, the

Marquis Palivicini, and the Marquis Villa Marina, the Piedmontese ambassador, addressed the assembled multitude from the balcony of the Palace of the Forestieri, announcing the speedy arrival amongst them of the king of their choice, and he terminated his discourse by the following severe words against His Holiness, which, wonderful to relate from so bigoted and superstitious a race, were received without a sign of disapprobation: "Personal ambition has blinded the Pope, and causes him to oppose the national movement, so great, so noble, and so pure, which stands alone in the history of the world. It is the Pope-king who retards the complete liberation of Italy, he is the sole, the true obstacle to our unity. I am a christian and I speak to christians, and I love and venerate the religion of Christ, because Christ came into the world to free mankind from the bondage for which God had not created him?" Scarcely had six months elapsed since Garibaldi landed in Sicily in defiance of a battery of 900 guns and an army 120,000 strong, yet not half were now living to answer the muster-roll, and amongst these survivors might be perceived many an honourable scar. The great Italian idea, though a subject of division to many, had nevertheless swept everything before it. He rendered a willing homage to those through whom he had accomplished his mission, telling them that it was because they were well known by him, that he undertook with them an enterprize regarded as impossible by all. He told them that he knew that with men like them he might attempt everything. That this apparently impossible work they had accomplished, but many of those who had gone with him were now absent, their bones lay bleaching on the field of battle. The same day Garibaldi distributed medals among the survivors of the thousands who had landed at Marsala. The Dictator, surrounded by his staff, and attended by many ladies of the Southern aristocracy, alluded in terms of touching eloquence to the sad loss they had sustained since their disembarkation on the shores of Sicily. The names of this heroic band were called out alphabetically, and the medals were distributed and fastened to the breast of each by the hand of the Duchess of Vendino. Many of these heroes were very young, one being a mere child of but thirteen years of age, yet he had born the brunt of the storm at Calatafimi and Mellazo, and had come unscatched out of the conflict. Alluding to the fallen, the General observed, that their names would never be forgotten. Let their families, he said, keep these medals as heirlooms to be handed down to the latest posterity, as memorials of the valour of their ancestors. Turning to the survivors the General reminded them that all was not yet accomplished, and that he called upon them to be ready at all times to lay down their lives for the national cause.

It had been arranged that Victor Emmanuel should make his triumphal entry into Naples on the 8th of November, after having given a reception to the Garibaldians assembled at Caserta. His majesty, however, neglected to receive them. About 22,000 men survived the casualties of the Volturno, and we may roughly estimate the killed and wounded at 3,000; 1,000 prisoners, about 8,000 laid up in the hospitals with fever or opthalmia. Of these 22,000 men, 10,000 might be considered first-class troops, capable of any service, and ready to endure any hardship. They were also willing to fight, as their chief told them, without bread and ammunition, and could, without difficulty, march thirty miles a day. The remainder, though they could not, with justice to the first class, be considered equal to them, were, nevertheless, far superior to the average of ordinary troops. Within the space of six months they had, without assistance, accomplished more than what any man would have deemed possible, under ordinary circumstances. Notwithstanding the systematic falsehood of the Turinese press, in representing these men as republicans and Mazzinianists in the worst sense of the word, their religious and political faith can, nevertheless, be embodied in the magic name of Garibaldi; for no body of troops could be found, either in France or in Piedmont, who would more cheerfully suppress any attempt of establishing a republic.

There may indeed be found among their ranks many men of republican sentiments, but this must be attributed to the oppression which they endured for so many years under the Bourbon monarchy. It can never be said that they would not willingly stifle every private desire in deference to the will of their leader, than whom the King of Italy has not a more devoted subject. With them Garibaldianism is quite as much a religion as was Mohammedanism with the followers of the prophet of Arabia.

The studied insult which was offered to Garibaldi and his followers, brought to maturity those seeds of discontent which had already been sown far and wide by the hauteur of the Piedmontese. They had been ordered to Caserta for the special purpose of being reviewed by him, and this was the second time he had deceived them, after making them wait for hours in anxious expectation. All this time the King was flirting at Capua, and it may very reasonably be doubted whether he ever intended to review them at all. Most certainly he had a right to do as he pleased. Though nothing would have induced this portion of his army to remain in Naples during the winter months, when no active operations could take place, it would have been politic, and certainly kingly, to have sent them to their homes, happy and contented, instead of irritated and annoyed, especially when it could have been accomplished by a few kind words and a generous acknowledgment for that which their chief had won for him. Towards evening the king sent to ask General Garibaldi to act for him. Perhaps these circumstances served, if possible, to increase the enthusiasm with which they received their chief, who had yet to make Italy, and might possibly afterwards find it a more difficult task to keep his king on the throne than he had done in placing him there. Though the pouring rain was enough to damp the most buoyant spirits, still all knew well that this was the parting farewell of their slighted chief. They were far too much exalted by his presence to care to give the slightest indications of the just contempt they entertained for their sovereign, and in contemplation of future glory they were willing to forget the wrongs of the present.

It seems quite certain, however, that if any open hostilities should now be proclaimed between Garibaldi and the king, the General would be supported by the greater number of the South Italian army, in spite of the gross misrepresentation of the Piedmontese journals. One of Garibaldi's volunteers, describing the present position of affairs, says that he could perceive an hourly increasing dislike manifesting itself in the Piedmontese against the conqueror of Calatafimi, Mellazo, and the Volturno*.

On the 6th of November, Vice-Admiral Persano returned from Gaeta. As soon as the French admiral observed that Persano occupied a position at the entrance of the river, he sent an officer to inform him that he could never be allowed to take active measures. The Sardinian admiral answered that he had received instructions from his king, which he must obey, and as further opposition was not offered by the French squadron, it was supposed that force was never seriously contemplated. Two days afterwards, however, when the Piedmontese squadron commenced the attack upon Gaeta, Admiral de Tinon proved himself to be in earnest by ordering the *Bretagne* to fire a shot across the bows of Persano's flag-ship, letting him know, at the same time, that he could never permit him, under any circumstances, to approach within 3½ miles of the French squadron, which then lay at anchor under the fortress. The effect of this act of foreign intervention was to foster civil war for many weeks throughout the land, and was mainly instrumental in encouraging Francis II. in that obstinate resistance, in which

* Garibaldi, as Dictator, had given a pass to an English gentleman, Mr. Bicknell and his party, to visit any part of the camp. On arriving at the Piedmontese quarters the officer in command demanded: "Whose pass is this?"—"Garibaldi's." "Whose signature is that at the bottom?"—"Brigadier-General the Count of ——" "And who is he?"—"The officer who signs all the passes that are issued at the Garibaldian head quarters." "Well, I won't arrest you; but I don't recognise Garibaldi's passes, or anything that is connected with him; and I advise you strongly, if I let you go, never, on any account, to return here, for if you do you will most assuredly get yourself into great trouble."

we must all acknowledge he showed a heroism worthy of a better cause.

On the 7th of November Victor Emmanuel made his triumphal entry into Naples. Everything forboded ill. The day was dark and stormy, and dense clouds that had long been gathering from every quarter, now burst in torrents of rain. Arriving at the station the king entered the royal carriage, placing Garibaldi on his left, and the Marquis Pallavicini and Signor Mordini, the two pro-dictators of Southern Italy, in front. An immense crowd thronged the streets; a stranger however, would, probably, have been led to enquire which of the two personages seated in that carriage was the king, not to say that evvivas for the hero of Palestro were wanting, but those with which the Neapolitans greeted the name of Garibaldi were undoubtedly more numerous. Had Victor Emmanuel been envious, he would have had reason to regret his first entry into Naples by the side of so popular a companion. It is said, he might have received at the hands of the king any favour he chose to ask; this statement, however, cannot be quite free from error, as may be gathered from the following incident.

Fanti and Farini had both suggested to the General that it was quite possible that Piedmontese rule might not meet with very general approbation in Naples, and that his volunteers might not be encouraged as much as he could wish. The General, therefore, asked three things of the king in return for the two crowns he had given him—namely: 1st. To be appointed governor of Southern Italy for three years; 2ndly. That the decrees he had signed during his dictatorship should be ratified, so far as they were in accordance with the constitutional laws of the country; and, 3rdly. That the rank conferred by him, by virtue of his dictatorship of the Two Sicilies, on his companions in arms, should be recognised by the new Italian Government. A peremptory refusal was, if we are informed aright, given to the first request. The two last the king's ministers were disposed to grant, but upon certain conditions to be named by themselves. When told that the king iutended to give him an order, Garibaldi answered, that a soldier who fought for his native country should desire no richer ornament than a laurel wreath to be exchanged for another and a fresher, the next battle won.

In the end, the king renewed the royal promise he had previously made, that Garibaldi's volunteers should be incorporated with the regular army, and be subjected to the scrutiny of a mixed commission—a promise which was afterwards broken by his ministers. Under all these circumstances, it is not surprising that Garibaldi declined the offers made to him by the king. The king offered him apartments in any palace in the kingdom of Naples he liked to name. He also promised him that when his daughter should marry he would give her a wedding portion. He proposed making his eldest son, Menotti, one of his aides-de-camp, offering him at the same time the grand cross of an Italian order. Under all the circumstances it will not excite much surprise that these offers were refused. General Cialdini had endeavoured, it was said, to bring about a reconciliation between Cavour and Garibaldi, but it can never be supposed that in this Cavour was in earnest. For if he were, why was General Fanti permitted to accompany the king? The conduct of General Fanti at Florence, and General Garibaldi's resignation of the command of the army in Tuscany in consequence of that conduct, will be fresh in the remembrance of our readers. Yet now General Fanti was chosen to regulate the future destinies of the southern army, although he had always been the greatest adversary of the volunteers, and was believed to be the bitterest foe of Garibaldi himself. On the arrival of the king, his Majesty, as a devout Catholic, attended to pay his devotions at the shrine of St. Jannuarius, Garibaldi did not kneel, but remained standing apart a few paces behind: the king was in his handsome uniform, Garibaldi in the old red shirt in which he had gained two kingdoms for Victor Emmanuel. Mr. Brooke says, "as the evvivas of the populace rang through the damp air, I thought Garibaldi seemed by far the more popular personage of the two, and I rejoiced that it was so. What born king on earth is as great as he in his sublime simplicity of character and spotless purity of intention? I asked myself that day, and found no answer. The visit to the relics was soon over, then bold Victor Emmanuel strode down the middle aisle, his plain bluff features set in iron rigidity, never moving a muscle; and as Garibaldi walked close to him, we had an excellent opportunity of comparison. Garibaldi, with his broad thoughtful brow, deep sunk clear eyes, in whose depths no shade of dishonest purpose ever lurked, and calm self-possessed demeanour; and the king with his dragoon's stride and bold glance, with nothing beyond this particularly noticeable about him. These two men, the born king, and the kingly subject, were, indeed, contrasts. Then, as Garibaldi walked down the aisle, the people literally rushed upon him, kissing him, and clasping the very hem of his red jacket like devotees; and then set up once more a wild shout as of long pent-up enthusiasm. The king afterwards presented himself at the balcony of the palace with Garibaldi by his side." In the evening the king had announced his intention of visiting the theatre of San Carlo, in state, and about nine o'clock he entered the house, attended by his staff. "There appeared," writes Admiral Mundy, "to be an absence of that real enthusiasm which such an occasion should have inspired. In the first place there was mismanagement at head quarters. It had originally been arranged that Garibaldi should accompany the king, and a seat had been placed for the Dictator on the left of the royal chair; but a few minutes before the arrival of his Majesty, and when excitement was at its highest pitch, a lackey entered the royal box and carried off the Dictator's seat. It became immediately known throughout the house that Garibaldi would not be present, and low murmurs of disapprobation were distinctly audible amongst the throng. It was at this inopportune moment that the doors of the royal box were thrown open, and the elected King of the Italian people marched leisurely to the front. His attitude and manner were essentially martial, the defiant expression of his countenance bearing testimony to the heroism of his nature. The boldness of his look, and I may add the severity of his aspect, did not quite comport with the part he was now called upon to act."

At eleven o'clock on the 8th of November, the king, attended by his minister of state and the superior officers of his staff, received the Dictator in the throne room of the royal palace. Signor Conforti, the minister of the interior under Garibaldi's government, then made the following address to the king, which was composed by the Dictator :—Sire,—"The Neapolitan people in public meeting assembled, have by an immense majority proclaimed you as their king. Nine millions of Italians are united to the other provinces, which have already long been smiling under the happy rule of your Majesty, and by this unity has been verified your solemn promise, that Italy shall belong to the Italians alone." King Victor Emmanuel replied in his usual laconic style, and thus began the constitutional rule of Piedmont, and ended the dictatorial functions of Garibaldi in the Peninsula. At the same time Garibaldi issued a long address to his companions in arms, from which the following is an extract. "To my companions in arms — Providence has given Victor Emmanuel to Italy. Every Italian should unite himself to him. All should gather close around him. By the side of the Re-Galantuomo every strife should disappear, and every rancour be dissipated. Once again, I repeat my cry to you, to place arms in the hands of all! If the month of March, 1861, does not find a million of Italians under arms—Oh! then, Poor Liberty! Alas! for an Italian existence. Italians of Catatafuni, of Palermo, of the Volturno, of Ancona, of Castelfidardo, and of Isernia, and every man of the land who is neither a slave nor a coward—come one and all, cluster closely around the hero of Palestro; and under his ægis will we hurl our united strength upon the crumbling ruins of tyranny. Receive, young volunteers—honourable survivors of ten battles—one farewell word. It comes radient with affection from the depths of my soul. I leave you to-day but for a short time only. The hour of battle will again see me among you, by the side of the soldiers of Italian liberty. We shall soon meet again to march towards the north, carrying thither freedom to our brethren, who are still doomed to wear the chains of the stranger. Yes, brethren, we shall soon meet again to march together to new fields of glory.*

GIUSEPPE GARIBALDI."

The king speaking to General Garibaldi, observed—"So you are resolved to return to Caprera?" "Yes, Sire;" was the answer. The king then continued—"But how do you intend to get there? there are no steamers running in that direction." "If any necessity occurred, I would ask my friend Admiral Mundy to give me a passage on board an English ship," answered Garibaldi. In the end, the Dictator returned to Caprera in an American merchant steamer, the *Washington*. The courtiers who came in the suite of Victor Emmanuel heaped a number of petty insults on the Dictator. Those to whom the General had granted apartments in the royal palaces, received from the Piedmontese officials immediate notice to quit. Orders signed by him were referred to the ministers for confirmation, and when he sent for a carriage to the royal stables to convey him to the station, the master of the horse sent him a message that he had none at his disposal, and recommended him to take a fiacre. It must be remembered that Garibaldi remained dictator

* One day Garibaldi was asked how he could really speak of the king in the terms of actual admiration which he often used; he answered, "In the first place I have seen the king fight for Italy. In the second, in speaking of a monarch, it is usually supposed that it is the kingly office which is implied. This in England and Italy, guarded as it always ought to be by the responsibility of ministers answerable for the acts of the Government to Parliament elected by the people, ought to approach perfection. Thirdly, when I was an exile and earned my bread as a tutor, I had to teach that the Egyptians were the first people who rightly understood the rules of Government, they never blamed their kings, but praised their virtues, loading at the same time with imprecations those of their ministers who gave them ill counsels and suppressed and disguised the truth. In Egypt the plan answered well."

of the two Sicilies until the day before he left; therefore, as a matter of right, the carriages of the ex-king of Naples belonged for the time at least to him. Count Arrivabene, one of the most devoted admirers of Cavour, is compelled to confess that that minister, under the evil influence of the so-called party of order, had determined from the very outset to humble the party of action in the dust.*

When Garibaldi became aware that the question was a mere struggle for power, he could not do otherwise than leave the country he had with so much heroism delivered from the iron grasp of its oppressors. Basso, his private secretary, was obliged to inform him that all the money which he (though only the day before Dictator of the richest provinces of Italy) had at his command was thirty pounds, saved by him with the greatest economy during the campaign. "Do not be anxious, Basso," answered Garibaldi, with a smile; "we have at Caprera plenty of wood and corn, which we will send to Maddalena for sale." Garibaldi returned to Caprera a much poorer man than he had left it, nearly as poor indeed as when he wandered in exile in the South American forests.

On the evening of the 8th, Admiral Mundy received a visit from Colonel Missori, sent by the General to inform him that he hoped to pay him a farewell visit before he quitted the bay. Colonel Missori spoke of his master in terms of great affection, and did not hesitate to say he was dejected and low in spirits, from a belief that his followers would not be honorably treated by the Sardinian Government. Admiral Mundy refused to form

---

* An Italian paper contained the following:—Delicate rewards for Garibaldi.—Montezemolo, who took part in the cession of Nice, goes as Governor to Sicily. Cordova, the most determined enemy of the General, dismissed for his offensive intrigues against the Dictator, returns to direct the Home Department in Sicily. La Farina (whose name needs no comments) is Councillor of State. Farini, the author of the circular that gave the mortal blow to his army, is to be Governor of Naples. Scialoja, expelled by Garibaldi, is to be Minister. Silvia Spavento, ditto. Fanti is to supplant Garibaldi in the command of the army, and Cavour is at the summit of this pyramid of power. Garibaldi humiliated, withdraws to his hermitage; his volunteers must live as they can, many are wandering about mutilated, ragged, and neglected.

any judgment upon the intentions of a Government which had not yet been installed twenty-four hours, and recommended Missori to look forward with hopefulness to the future destiny of his late companions in arms, who, whatever might be the opinion of the justice of the war, had immortalized themselves in history by their self-denial and heroic bravery. After leaving the palace, General Garibaldi established himself at the Hotel d'Angleterre, and at dawn on the 9th he rose, and wishing to leave Naples without the people being aware of his intention, he embarked at once before dawn of day, almost unmanned by the grief of the faithful followers who were forbidden by fate to accompany him; and at six in the morning, while the guns of the *Hannibal* thundered forth the honors due to his rank, Lieutenant Wilmot informed the Admiral that General Garibaldi was in his cabin; he was dressed in his usual costume, but without a sword. Looking out of the windows and pointing to an English merchant vessel that was discharging her steam, he said in a melancholy tone, "There is the ship which is to carry me to my island home, but, Admiral, I could not depart without expressing steadfast faith in the honour of the British flag." Garibaldi then invited the Admiral to pay him a visit at his cottage in Caprera. Of General Cialdini, he spoke in the warmest terms of affection and respect; the name of the king had not been introduced. When Garibaldi took leave his previous animation departed. He became dejected, and his whole manner was that of a man in intense suffering, paying a farewell visit.

"It is the last that I make before leaving Naples. Your conduct to me since our first meeting at Palermo has been characterized by so much kindness and generosity, that it can never be eradicated from my memory. It is engraven there indelibly: will last during the whole of my life." Admiral Mundy replied, "I certainly had endeavoured to treat him with that courtesy and consideration which was amply his due, both from his own humane conduct and from the acquiescence he had given to every proposal I had made. After a visit of twenty minutes' duration the ex-dictator stepped into his little skiff, rowed by four boys, and returned to the *Washington*. The vessel turned her head and steered a direct course for Caprera, just as the cannon from the forts fired their morning salute in honour of Victor Emmanuel." To the account of his visit, the English admiral adds an account of the appearance of Garibaldi. "The whole expression of his countenance is one of great benevolence and intelligence, without the least approach to fierceness, yet there is not wanting a look of profound astuteness. There is at the same time a simplicity and even a tenderness in his manner and address which is most captivating, whilst his general bearing and attitude are marked with dignity and composure. No person of moderate observation could be engaged, even in a short conversation, with this remarkable man, without being struck with the clear silvery tone of his voice and the originality of his style." The correspondent of the *Times* writing during the campagnes on the lakes, in 1859, says, "I could scarcely believe that the quiet, unaffected, gentlemanly man who entered and sat down with us, was Garibaldi. A child would stop him in the street to ask him what o'clock it was, but the man condemned to immediate execution would never, after a look of that calm determined face, waste time in asking mercy upon earth. During our long interview he spoke much of passing events, excepting his own share in them. He has the calm manner and appearance of the English gentleman and officer; it was only when he spoke of the generous sympathy of the people of England with the sufferings of Italy that his Saxon-like calmness gave way: then, as he assured us again and again how thoroughly it was appreciated by Italians of every class, and how grateful they were for it, he showed that the warm blood of Italy burned in his veins. My impression had been that his operations were more the result of rash impulse than military calculation; but it was palpable that, strong as may be his impulses, they are thoroughly under control. Bold and enterprising even to apparent rashness, he is, no doubt, but he is also cool and calculating; and as I watched him on the opposite side of the table, telling the ladies of his voyages to China and the antipodes, as pleasantly and calmly as if in a London drawing-room, while at any moment he might be interrupted by the fire of an overpowering Austrian force brought by railway to his outposts, I felt no doubt that he had made arrangements for the very worst, and knew well how to put them into execution. But what impressed me most was the mental calibre of the man. I met him with the idea that he was little more than a dashing popular military leader; I parted from him with the conviction that his warlike career is a mere episode in his history, and that his true greatness will be seen in the political regeneration and government of his country." We are informed by the correspondent of another of our daily journals that the natural dignity and lion-like majesty of his countenance rather incline a beholder to overrate his real stature, which is certainly not above the middle size. Mr. Brook writes:—"I never in my life saw a face like Garibaldi's—so dignified, so resolute, and so perfectly self-possessed in his every lineament—with the eye of an eagle, the brow of a Grecian sage—his smile is the sweetest and most re-assuring in the world." Thus far respecting the appearance of Garibaldi. While the English legion were in bivouac one night, they were joined by Garibaldi, with the whole of his staff, who slept amongst them, with a little straw for his pillow, and to their minds he could never have seemed greater than when he lay sleeping on the ground in their midst, with their colonel by his side.

The king did not make himself popular at Naples. Count Arrivabene says that, on his departure, the arduous burden of the government fell upon Farini, whose mission in Southern Italy proved a complete failure. He chose for his advisers men who did not enjoy the confidence of the people; the very men who had obstinately opposed the hero of the day; the great warrior whose influence had increased in proportion to the wrongs which, according to the general opinion, had been inflicted upon him. It is certainly not my intention to underrate the difficulties which surrounded the newly established National Government, which were, without doubt, at that time very considerable. We next come to the trial of the Duke of Cajanello, which Count Cavour himself confesses to have been foolishly got up, and was, according to him, an act of gross oppression and injustice. Notwithstanding, however, the Duke was only restored to liberty in November, 1861, when every Italian of sound political judgment had expressed grave disapprobation of the illegal proceedings. No doubt brigandage by this time had advanced rapidly; still, it is difficult to justify General Cialdini shooting seven men at Somma without the shadow of a trial, and committing the town of Ponte Landalfo to the flames.

Many other facts might be adduced to prove that unjustifiable severity is not to be attributed to the Bourbons alone. Thus, says Count Arrivabene, did the central government of Turin heap error upon error. Captain Forbes states, "Nearly two months have now elapsed since Garibaldi retired from the dictatorship of the Two Sicilies, and left to the Piedmontese the delicate task of consolidating the kingdom. The promise that the Garibaldian volunteers should be incorporated with the army of Italy, and then be subjected to the scrutiny of a mixed commission, was broken by a decree reversing this order, and requiring them to undergo a similar inspection even before they were admitted into the service at all. Thus were the brave Garibaldinians sent to their homes burning with indignation at the ingratitude that had been shown to their chief, while the remainder had to wring concession after concession from an ungracious government, which has already felt the necessity of retracing its steps, and sought to appease those whom it had slighted by granting them, at first three months', and eventually six months' pay. The following anecdote shows that Garibaldi was aware of the feelings entertained towards him by the government. Shortly after his return to Caprera, a gentleman having a claim upon the government of Naples during his dictatorship, waited upon him at Caprera, and laid all the papers before him. The General pronounced the claim perfectly just, and said that he had every reason to believe that the ministers would do him justice. "Would you, then, General," said he, "do me the favor of giving me in writing your opinion of the justice of my claim?" "Most certainly, if you wish it, for it is your undoubted right; but, let me advise you, as a friend, to present your claims at Turin on their own merits. In that case, I feel certain they will be acknowledged, for I am convinced they have every wish to do full justice. If, unfortunately, my name and opinion are introduced, *I fear that the claims will be at once condemned*, however certain of success, they may be allowed to rest on their own merits." Towards the end of December the king sent General Turr to Caprera with a necklace for Garibaldi's daughter and a letter for the General.

Thus ended the year; a year for ever glorious as having seen the successful attempt of a true and noble-hearted hero to make Italy one and united.*

---

* An account of the General's visits to the hospitals at Naples has already been given. A visit to those in Sicily may, however, be interesting. The following is taken from the letter of a young American surgeon, given in "Dwight's Life" of Garibaldi. He says:—"One of the most moving sights it has been my lot to witness, was Garibaldi's visit here the other morning. As he entered the different wards it seemed as though an electric shock had been communicated to all the inmates, after the first joyful cry, E lui! E Garibaldi! E il Generale, a dead silence prevailed, all eyes were fixed upon him as he passed from bed to bed, taking the thin wasted hands in his, or pressing his own upon many a feverish brow, making each patient feel that he was his General's favourite son, and that from him he might expect all that a father's tenderness could give—all his own men were known to him; he called them by their names, remembered where and how they were wounded, promoted this one, promised honourable employment to others disabled for military service, granted permission for others to go home, providing them with ample means. When he came to the Sicilians he inquired kindly into their wants and conditions; ordered that the pay of one should be doubled, that another should be pensioned, and so on. But perhaps the most interesting scene of all was his visit to the Neapolitan wards, where we have eleven wounded prisoners, who have petitioned to enter our ranks. After being told that they were wounded at Calata Fimi, he said 'then you are brave men, truly! You have been misled: taught to look upon us as enemies. I am fortunate to have you for my soldiers, for my brothers.' These men strong and stalwart as they were, wept like little children, and in Garidaldi's eyes were tears—one felt why it is that he is so loved, so idolised by all."

Garibaldi's government of Naples has been so much attacked that we give the following letter, which describes its condition on the 12th of September:—"There is much to be done here, and Garidaldi is doing it well. It is impossible to take up a journal, or move about in the midst of the vast crowds which throng the capital, without feeling that a master spirit is here. Long before the city has shaken off its slumber the dictator is up and driving about. Yesterday he went to visit Nisida, and surprised the British library on his return with a visit, at half-past six o'clock a.m., wishing to purchase some books. During the day he is hard at work, and the following are some of the fruits of his labours. All political prisoners are to be liberated immediately. All custom-house barriers between Sicily and the Neapolitan continent are abolished. Twelve infant asylums, one for each quarter, are to be established in the capital at the public expense, and are to be municipal institutions. Secret ministerial funds are to be abolished. The trial by jury in criminal cases is to be established. The order of Jesuits with all their dependencies is abolished in the territory of the two Sicilies, and their property declared national. All contracts on property for the benefit of the order are annulled. The burial of the dead is henceforward absolutely forbidden within the walls of a city.

The Official Journal of Naples of September the 9th, published a series of decrees, amongst others that "All the acts of public authority and of administration are to be issued in the name of His Majesty, Victor Emmanuel, King of Italy, and all the seals of state of public administration and of the public officers are to bear the arms of the royal house of Savoy, with the legend, Victor Emmanuel, King of Italy." The public debt of the Neapolitan State was recognized, the public banks were to continue their payments, as also the discount bank, according to existing laws and regulations. Passports for the United Italian States were abolished, &c., &c. On the 14th of September he placed all the ships of war and commerce, the arsenals and materials of marine, by decree, at the disposal of Sardinia, putting them in the hands of Admiral Persano. The Neapolitan navy, which had deserted all together to Garibaldi, was very respectable, taking a place in respect to material at least above the second rank in Europe, and fell little below that of the United States, the number of vessels amounted to 90 carrying 786 guns, with a compliment of upwards of 7,000 sailors; of the vessels twenty-seven were steamers, one of these carried sixty guns, eleven were frigates armed with ten guns each, eight corvettes with eight guns each, besides seven smaller vessels, each with four guns. Of the sixty or more sailing vessels, the largest was armed with eighty guns. There were five frigates carrying an aggregate of 252 guns, or about fifty each. Amongst the rest were bomb and mortar boats in considerable number, and others armed with Paixhan guns. In one of his last speeches in Naples Garibaldi said, "Amongst the Indians two geniuses are recognized and adored, one of good and the other of evil. Well, the genius of evil for Italy is the Pope King. Let no one misunderstand my words—let no one confound Popery with Christianity—the religion of liberty with the avaricious and sanguinary politics of Italy. You whom I now address—you the educated and cultivated portion of the citizenship, you have the duty of educating the people—educate them to be christians, educate them to be Italians. Education gives liberty, education gives to the people the means and the power to secure and defend their own independence. On a strong and wholesome education of the people depend the liberty and the greatness of Italy." Soon after General Garibaldi's return to Caprera, a paragraph to the following effect went the round of the journals in England, France, Germany, Italy, and the United States, and is given at page 445 of Dwight's life of General Garibaldi. "But a pleasing surprise came on his arrival at the Island of Caprera to enliven the mind of the Italian hero. The modest cottage, his modest cottage, had during his absence been changed into a handsome and elegant casino. The avenues were well marked out, and instead of the nakedness of the ground, the wild and uncultivated aspect in which he had last seen it, he observed marks of recent cultivation, plantation of trees, and hedges well arranged, convenient and well made roads. Garibaldi, full of wonder, went about trying to imagine and divine what magical hand could have made so great a change. He even almost began to doubt whether it was the Island of Caprera. Entering the house and looking about in every part, he found in the centre a lagre and commodious hall, and supported from the wall a large and beautiful portrait of Victor Emmanuel." Now this is entirely incorrect, the cottage at Caprera was in a very bad state when the General returned from Naples, and hardly a chair in the house, so much so that the officers of the American ship, Washington, gave him the chairs in their cabin; the name of each person is placed upon the chair that he gave.

CHAPTER VII.

Commencement of the year 1861—Garibaldi writes to the Glasgow Committee—Sardinia merged in the kingdom of Italy—Rome officially declared the seat of government—Garibaldi arrives at Turin—Proposal to grant him £4,000 a year—He declines—Cavour and Garibaldi in the Chambers—Cialdini writes to Garibaldi that he had become his adversary—His reply—Becomes reconciled—Death of Cavour—Mr. Stansfield, M.P., on Italian unity—Cavour had predicted in 1829, that he would be a minister of the kingdom of Italy—The farm at Caprera—"To Rome with Garibaldi"—Anniversary of the restoration of Italy—End of the year 1861.

THE year 1861 opened quietly. Garibaldi was still at Caprera. The following letters prove, however, that he was by no means in a state of inactivity. He felt that unless Italy were kept perpetually before the eyes of the world, what remained still to be done for the completion of its unity might be forgotten. In January he wrote to the "Glasgow Garibaldi Fund Committee" in the following terms:—"Gentlemen,—The conflict between the two opposing principles of good and evil—the first represented by Christ, who came to bring freedom to all mankind, and the second by the tyrants and the false priests who conspire to keep the world degraded and enslaved—rages more fiercely than ever in these our own times, because the second principle, which has been dominant for so many centuries, is now menaced by the re-awakening of our people. Justice compels me to declare that, as regards Italy, England is the representative of good, and that she deserves our deepest gratitude. May God bless the people of England, who, while they proudly and vigilantly guard the liberty of their own country, are ever ready to grant unreserved hospitality to the unfortunate; and, strong in the consciousness of their own freedom, have dared to speak out boldly, and, by so doing, have given to us comfort and support. Glasgow, in addition, was the first to send us material aid in the hour of our greatest need. I beg of you, gentlemen, to accept these few words of gratitude for all the good which you have done to our cause."

The General also addressed the following letter to the Central Committee of Genoa. "The Central Committee ought, every day and at every instant, unceasingly to repeat to all the committees, and to endeavour by every means to penetrate every Italian with the idea that in the spring of this year, 1861, Italy must have a million of patriots under arms, as the surest means of making us powerful masters of our own destinies, and worthy of the respect of the world, whose eyes are now fixed upon us. I believed it right to warn the volunteers, however, that no enrolment is formed, or advised by me for the moment."

The Turin Parliament was opened by the king in person; Garibaldi's name was not mentioned, but the king stated that a general of world-wide renown had led the armies of Italy to victory, and those few words alone were all that the king thought proper to devote, in a long speech, to the liberator of Naples. One of the first things that Parliament did, was to merge the kingdom of Sardinia in the kingdom of Italy, so confirming Garibaldi's words, "King of Italy." Rome also was officially declared by Parliament the seat of the new monarchy. If the kingdom of Italy was to be a reality, the king of Italy must be king in Rome. The Papacy also having chosen to put itself forward as a rival power to Italy, the triumph of the national cause demanded the demolition of the temporal power of the Pope. Turin, from its geographical position, could hardly be the capital of the Neapolitan provinces, while the traditional jealousies of Northern and Southern Italy, would yield more readily to a central government at Rome than at

Turin, or elsewhere. Cavour stated that the ideas of a nation were few in number, and that to the common Italian mind the idea of Italy was inseparable from that of Rome. An Italy of which Rome was not the capital would be no Italy for the Italian people. For the existence, then, of a national Italian spirit, the possession of Rome as the capital was an essential condition. "The choice of a capital," said he, "must be determined by high moral considerations—on which the instinct of each nation must decide for itself. Rome, gentlemen, unites all the historical, intellectual, and moral qualities which are required to form the capital of a great nation. Convinced—deeply convinced—as I am of this truth, I think it my bounden duty to proclaim it as solemnly as I can before you and before the country. I think it my duty, also, to appeal, under these circumstances, to the patriotism of all Italian citizens, and of the representatives of all our most illustrious cities, when I beg them to cease all discussion on this question, so that Europe may become aware that the necessity of having Rome for our capital is recognised and proclaimed by the whole nation. So far as I am personally concerned, I shall go to Rome with sorrow. Having but little taste for art, I am persuaded that amidst the splendid monuments of ancient and modern Rome, I shall regret the formal and unadorned streets of my native city." He admitted, also, that the solution of the Neapolitan difficulties was bound up with the Roman question: the government would energetically suppress any disturbances in Naples, but the most efficacious means to that end would be the solution of the Roman question.

Early in April, Garibaldi arrived in Turin, it was believed to be present at the discussion in the Chamber of Deputies on the affairs of Southern Italy. He was received with the greatest enthusiasm by the people, but suffered severely from a violent attack of rheumatic fever, and was confined to his bed the day after his arrival. Bulletins of his health were issued every day, and for some time the greatest anxiety prevailed.

On the 15th of April, while still suffering greatly from pain and fever, and a close prisoner in consequence, Garibaldi wrote a letter to the president of the chamber, in which he referred to his actions in proof of his devotion to his king and his country, but said that the manner in which the Southern army had been treated had filled his soul with disdain. He concluded by proposing a project of law for a vast national armament, basing it upon the old Piedmontese statute, which only required putting into force. He observed, speaking to some English visitors, that it was to prevent the necessity for war that he wanted the government to arm the nation, saying, with a smile :—"Diplomacy will be perfectly polite towards us if we have 700,000 men under arms and ready to fight, this would be the best seconding of the parliamentary declaration that Rome is our capital, and the Pope would be perfectly safe in our hands; we should allow neither disrespect towards him or towards those who followed him. France would then discover that we had a right to Rome, and England would rejoice to find in Italy a strong and loyal ally, with institutions similar to her own." A bill was brought into parliament with the consent of the ministers, to grant Cialdini a thousand pounds sterling per annum, in consideration of his services to the Italian cause; all the partisans of Garibaldi voted for it, and another bill was brought forward granting to General Garibaldi £4,000 a year, and the title of the first citizen of Italy. Whether General Garibaldi would or would not have accepted this grant it is difficult to say. He certainly would never have done so from the ministers who, as he believed, had misgoverned Naples. But the fact of being granted by an act of parliament, placed it in a very different light. Both in Sicily and Naples he often regretted that he had not more money to give away. It would have increased his power of doing good, and all his friends and his party were prepared to urge him to accept it. When this became known, Cialdini wrote to the chambers declining the grant to him, and it was reported that he did not act in that manner without having ascertained that his doing so would be agreeable to at least one member of the cabinet. Garibaldi's friends then thought it the most prudent course that the General should likewise decline the grant, which he accordingly did without delay. On the 18th of April, though in a very unfit state to leave his bed from pain and fever, he was present as member for Naples, in the Chamber of Deputies, and was received with such an outburst of applause, that the business of the chambers was temporarily suspended. Baron Ricasoli then requested the ministry to state their motives for disbanding the army of Southern Italy. General Fanti, the minister of war, defended the measures which had been taken. He said that it was impossible to incorporate all the Garibaldian officers with the royal army so as to permit them to retain the rank they had previously held.

General Garibaldi alluded to the disturbed state of Naples, and almost accused the ministry of having fomented civil war in Southern Italy. He said he was there to defend his companions in arms. Words of conciliation had been brought him, but they were only words, and he was a man of deeds. "When," he continued, "my country is at stake *I shall always yield;* but can I shake hands with a man who has made me a foreigner in my native land. The minister of war has stated that he saved Central Italy from anarchy. I appeal to those who governed the country. There never was any danger of anarchy. I do not want to bandy personalities; but I must defend my own honour." Then after an eloquent defence of the volunteer army, he continued: "These are glorious facts to record, and that glory was not darkened until this cabinet extended its cold and baneful hand over the south." Count Cavour here rose, in great excitement, and said a few words that were inaudible amid the cries of "Order, order." General Garibaldi continued: "I thought I had purchased the right of speaking the truth to the representatives of the country by thirty years' service." The President (M. Rattazzi) here interposed: "Speak; but do not offend others." General Garibaldi: "I speak of the horrors of a fratricidal war." Count Cavour exclaimed (passionately): "No one desired civil war. I cannot allow such words to pass." General uproar. The President put on his hat and retired. After the lapse of a quarter of an hour the sitting was resumed. The President (Rattazzi): "I am compelled to blame General Garibaldi severely for the words he has used. I must recommend him to be more moderate, or else I must condemn him to silence." General Garibaldi: "Then I promise I will not speak any more of the ministers." Resuming his speech, he spoke with great moderation; he entered into a full defence of the southern army, and said that the three divisions of volunteers, as decreed, were not sufficient for a national armament. He also entered into the history of the grievances of his companions in arms.

General Bixio observed that the division between General Gairbaldi and Count Cavour was a great misfortune; Count Cavour acknowledged the immense services of the volunteers, saying that they had proved that all Italians knew how to fight and to die for their country. The Government had done all in its power to increase the regular army, though he had not examined General Garibaldi's project, he would second its being taken into consideration. He could understand the General's feeling respecting Nice and Savoy from his own grief on that occasion.

General Garibaldi then continued:—"I am satisfied with Count Cavour's explanation, but there are means of appeasing our political dissensions. I am sure Count Cavour loves his country, let him therefore use his influence in support of my bill for arming the country; let the volunteers of the army of the South be recalled into service; thus we shall be reconciled."

General Garibaldi's very imprudent visit to the Chamber, so far as his health was concerned, brought on as might be expected an access of fever, which again confined him to the house for some days, but no one who saw him during the next day could help being struck with his perfect and entire satisfaction and pleasure at his reconciliation with Cavour; he said, "They tell me Italy suffered from our dissensions, it shall not be my fault if ever we have another:" and speaking of the warmth of the first part of his speech, he said, laughing: "After all, it was not half so violent as many speeches in the English House of Commons, at the passing of the Roman Catholic relief bill, the reform bill, &c. &c., and I was grieved at the neglect shewn to my brothers in arms. I spoke from my heart." Two days afterwards, Garibaldi held a conference with the chiefs of his party and superior officers. The General informed them that he was satisfied, and it was decided to accept the policy of Count Cavour, and to repose confidence in his future intentions.

On the 23rd of April, General Garibaldi, still confined to his room, was talking with the Marchioness Pallavicini and another lady, when a letter was placed in his hands. He read and answered it without delay, conversing with the ladies all the while, and requested Colonel Corte, who entered at the moment, to leave the note at Cialdini's hotel.

The letter of General Cialdini's in question was as follows:—"All my affection for you has disappeared, and I have become your political adversary. We are not disposed to bear your tyranny. You are reproached with having given orders to Colonel Tripoli to receive us with musket shots. I have heard your words and those of General Sivtori in the Italian Parliament, and following them up to this conclusion, I arrive at the secret idea of your party, which aims at rendering itself master of the army and the country, threatening us, if unsuccessful, with civil war. I do not know what the country thinks of this, but I can assure you that the army fears not your threats; it is only afraid of your government. You have reason to boast of your great and marvellous enterprise, but you exaggerate its results. When we arrived, you were at the Volturno in a very bad condition. The fall of Capua, Gæta, Messina, and Civitella del Tronto, was not brought about by your operations. Fifty-six thousand Bourbon soldiers were beaten and dispersed by us. Our army and fleet took sufficient part in the work of destroying more than half the Neapolitan army, so share with me the feelings of disgust and grief which the intemperance displayed by you and your party have raised in my mind." Reference was also made in this letter to Garibaldi having gone to the Chamber in a red shirt. Some people thought Cialdini might have remembered it was in that dress he gained two crowns for Victor Emmanuel, and entered Naples by his side. Garibaldi wrote in answer:—"Strong in my conscience as an Italian soldier and citizen, I will not descend to justify myself against these accusations, as by so doing I should fail in respect to the king and his army. I know nothing of the orders said to have been given by me to Colonel Tripoti. I gave orders that the Italian soldiers of the Northern Army should be received as brothers* although I knew that that army had come to put down the revolution, which, according to the words addressed by Senior Farini to Napoleon III., was personified in me. I believe that, in my quality of deputy, I have stated to the chamber a few of the wrongs which the Southern Army has sustained at the hands of the ministry. I believe I had a right to do so. The Italian army will find in its ranks one soldier more when it has to fight against the enemies of Italy. You are well aware of this. All that may have been said of me is a calumny. It is not true that when on the Volturno we were in a bad condition. As far as I know, the army has applauded the free and moderate words of the soldier deputy to whom the honour of Italy has been an object of worship all his life. If any one is offended with me for speaking in my own name only, I wait calmly for satisfaction to be

* Garibaldi's address respecting the Piedmontese army.—"People of Naples, our brethren of the Italian army, commanded by the gallant General Cialdini, combat the enemies of Italy and conquer. The army of Lamoriciere has been defeated by those valiant men. All the provinces enslaved by them are free. Ancona is ours. The valiant soldiers of the army of the North have passed the frontier and are on Neapolitan soil. We shall soon have the good fortune to clasp their victorious hands." For the state of the Garibaldian army on the Volturno, the reader is referred to the account of Captain Stuart Forbes, R.N., who was there and saw it.—*See page*, 119, &c.

demanded for my words. I desire the establishment of a national monarchy." Respecting his dress, the General stated his belief that in a free country every one was at liberty to dress as he liked. The excitement which these letters caused in Turin was very great. Garibaldi's reception whenever he appeared at the window was most enthusiastic. The few words he uttered to the people were those of peace and concord, but always requesting them to arm as the best and only means of obtaining lasting peace, and, above all, to rally round the constitutional monarchy. It was supposed by many that General Fanti (whose conduct in 1859 the reader will remember, and who, during the winters of 1860 and 1861 had proved, in many ways to be referred to hereafter, his dislike to the volunteers), was well aware of the contents of General Cialdini's letter before it was sent. On the evening of the day that the General received it, a young English peeress remarked in society what a shameful composition it was; the General hearing the remark, although not addressed to him, observed, "Hush; I cannot allow such words to pass. Cialdini is a brave man, and has fought the battles of Italy. I cannot permit another word to be spoken against him here." A playful demand to know the thoughts of another visitor having elicited a reluctant answer that it was feared General Cialdini would not in future love the General much, and that it was hoped he was not jealous, "What matter," was the answer, "if only he love Italy."

The Chamber of Deputies agreed, by a large majority, to take into consideration the project of Garibaldi in reference to arming the nation; the ministry voted in favor of the resolution. The Italian papers mentioned the joy manifested by the people that Garibaldi and Cavour had become reconciled, and before the General left Turin, he had a long and friendly interview with Count Cavour; explanations were entered into on both sides, it was believed that respecting Venetia, Garibaidi placed himself unreservedly in the hands of the ministers. Italy had to gain possession of her capital, before she would fitly begin the enterprise of rescuing her outlying province. Garibaldi expressed the greatest pleasure at the idea of a reconciliation with Cialdini, and, in fact, met and shook hands with him most cordially; he was unable to obtain the fresh air necessary for his recovery in Turin, the people coming in crowds from the country to see him, and every mother wanting him to kiss and take her baby in his arms, this from his wonderful love of children and great good nature, was no punishment to him, but it interfered with his recovery, and he left for the country house of a friend, and then, finding that things continued to progress to his satisfaction, returned to Caprera. This was at the end of April. Not a month had elapsed before an event took place which filled all Italy with grief—the death of Cavour. It was on the 30th of May that he was taken ill. Engrossed with Neapolitan affairs at the period when he was stricken with mortal illness, the recollection of them haunted his fevered brain, and even a few hours before his death he murmured "I will have no state of siege," which he continually repeated, whilst his last hour was approaching. The mistakes he had been led into by the so-called consorteria of political exiles he willingly confessed, and he had already set to work to have them repaired, when his exertions were cut short by the hand of death.* It was shortly before his illness that he declared, "In future any policy in the world rather than an alliance with France."

Mr. Dicey informs us, "There is no evidence to show that Cavour was sceptical in his religious creed; there is as little that he devoted much thought to it. In his domestic relations, as a childless and wealthy bachelor, he was neither less nor more moral than the men amongst whom he moved." Speaking of Cavour's policy, Mr. Dicey says, "That he had no doubt Cavour considered the maintenance of his own authority essential to the welfare of Italy, and that to maintain authority he would not have been scrupulous as to the measures he adopted." Cavour's

* See Count Arrivabene's Italy.

fondness for office and public life are also often referred to, and of these Garibaldi had certainly no wish to deprive him. He held the same language at Turin as he had done when he left Naples: "Do what you will, so that you make Italy one. Only let justice be done to my companions in arms, and let Naples be governed in a constitutional manner. All that he demanded is justice for the future. Fanti, even, was perfectly welcome to the sweets of office." All his own previously formed plans were abandoned, or made subservient to those of Cavour, and the *Dirritto* contained constant notices that no enlistments were authorised by him.

An attempt has recently been made to give to the so-called moderate party the merit of planning a United Italy. Mr. Stansfield, one of the Lords of the Admiralty, whose recent efforts to reform his department have already earned for him the gratitude of the English people, says, "Italy has already accomplished of her unity so much, that no policy save that of an absolute completion of the task is any longer to be dreamed of or suggested, and considering, too, how predominantly the credit and the practical fruits of that success have, in the opinion of the world and in the possession of power, enured to the benefit of the Moderate party, it would seem natural to imagine that they, too, must have had the unity of their country long in view, and that they can have differed only from the National party as to the policy best adapted to the attainment of a common object; and yet I believe the acceptance of the idea of Italian Unity, as an object of practical statesmanship, by the leaders of the Moderate party, must be admitted to be of a very recent date.

"I will go back to Gioberti, who was the founder of that party: in the Sardinian Chambers on the 10th of February, 1849, on the eve of the short campaign which ended in the defeat of Novara, Gioberti said—'I consider the unity of Italy a chimera: we must be content with its union.' And if you look to the writings, the speeches, the acts, of all the leading men of the

Moderate party until a very recent period, you will find them all, without exception, not only not propounding or advocating unity, or directed to its accomplishment, but explicitly directed to a different solution. You will find the proof of what I say in Balbo's "Hopes of Italy;" in Durando's "Essay on Italian Nationality," advocating three Italies, north, centre, and south; in Bianchi Giovini's work entitled "Mazzini and his Utopias;" and in Gualterio's "Revolutions of Italy." Minghetti, Ricasoli, Farini, each and all have been the advocates of a confederation of Princes rather than of a united Italy.

Let me come to Cavour. An attempt has recently been made to claim for him the credit of having since the days of his earliest manhood conceived the idea of making himself the minister of a future united Italy. In an article in the July "Quarterly," by a well-known pen, a letter of Cavour, written about 1829 or 1830, is cited in implied justification of this claim. He had been placed under arrest a short time in the Fort de Bard, on account of political opinions expressed with too much freedom. In a letter to a lady who had written condoling with him on his disgrace, he says:—"I thank you, Madame la Marquise, for the interest which you take in my disgrace; but, believe me, for all that, I shall work out my career. I have much ambition—an enormous ambition; and when I become minister I hope to justify it, since already in my dreams, I see myself Minister of the Kingdom of Italy." Now this is, I need not say, a most remarkable letter, and of the greatest interest, as showing the confidence in his own future, at so early an age, of one of the greatest statesmen of our times. But no one acquainted with the modern history of Italy, and familiar with its recognised phraseology could read in this letter the prophecy of that unity which is now coming to pass. The "Kingdom of Italy" is a well-known phrase borrowed from the time of Napoleon, and has always meant until facts have enlarged its significance, that the kingdom of northern Italy, whose precedent existed under Napoleon, which was the object of Piedmontese policy in '48 and '49, and one of the explicit terms of the contract of Pombier's in '59. It is rather a curious inconsistency in the article in question, that in itself furnishes ample evidence that the unity of Italy was no part of the practical programme of the moderate party. "Cavour," we are told, "founded in 1847 with his friends, Cesare Baldo, Santa Rosa, Buoncampagni, Castelli, and other men of moderate constitutional views, the *Risorgimento*, of which he became the editor; and the principles of the new periodical were announced to be "independence of Italy, union between the princes', and people's progress in the path of reform, and a league between the Italian States." Again, after saying that it was Ricasoli and the leaders of the constitutional party who recalled (in '49) the Grand Ducal family to Tuscany, and that Geoberti proposed the return of the Pope to Rome. The writer goes on to say, "It was an immense advantage to the restored princes to have been thus brought back by the most intelligent and moderate of their subjects. All that the wisest and most influential men in Italy asked, was a federal union of the different states in the Peninsula, upon a liberal and constitutional basis, from which even the House of Austria was not to be excluded.

I must trouble you with one more quotation. At the Conference of Paris in 1855, after the Crimean war, Piedmont was represented by Cavour, who brought before the assembled statesmen the condition of Italy, but unable to enter fully into the Italian question, he addressed two state papers on it to Lord Clarendon. His plan—at any rate, for the temporary settlement of the question—was a confederation of Italian States with constitutional institutions, and a guarantee of complete independence from the direct interference and influence of Austria; and the secularization of the legations with a lay vicar under the suzerainty of the Pope. At that time he would have been even willing to acquiesce in the occupation of Lombardy by Austria, had she bound herself to keep within the limits of the treaty of 1815.

Now, you cannot, I think, have failed to note the glaring inconsistency of these praises of what is called the moderation of Cavour, with the assumption to him and to his party of the whole credit of Italian unity, and the theory, now too prevalent, that no other party has contributed anything but follies and excesses, impediments, not aids, to the accomplishment of the great task. I believe such ideas to be as profoundly ungenerous and unjust as they are evidently self-contradictory, and I believe that they will be adjudged by history to be, so far as they are in any degree in good faith, superficial, partial, and utterly incapable of serving as any explanation of the method of the evolution of the great problem of Italian nationality.

Now let another witness be called into court; the late Prime Minister of Italy, Farina, on the authority of the *Turin Times* correspondent, who wrote, September 12, 1861. "You have not forgotten that in the Æmilia, Farini used, with great bitterness, to complain of the worthlessness of the Moderate party in time of trial and strife."*

But to return, on the death of Cavour, Baron Ricasoli was appointed prime minister in his place, and Garibaldi remained at Caprera amusing himself with endeavouring in every way to improve his farm. An English gentleman who visited Caprera in June, said that he was in good health and devotes his time to agriculture of the most practical description, breakfasts and smokes his cigar, then works until evening, after dinner an hour's smoking and conversation, then writing until a late hour. Such is the picture drawn in June, 1861, of the man who, in June, 1860, was upsetting tyranny and exciting all Europe to rouse themselves to war. In July he addressed a

* Count Cavour wrote from Paris in 1856 to M. Rattazzi the following:—"I have seen Mr. Manin, he is a very good man, but he always talks about the unity of Italy, and such other tomfooleries." Also La Larina, Cavour's agent in Italy in 1860, published in that year the following explanation of his differences with General Garibaldi:—He stated "I believed and still believe that the only salvation for Sicily to the constitutional government of Victor Emmanuel." This explanation was published before Garibaldi crossed to the mainland, and had Cavour gained his point and obtained annexation, the kingdom of Naples would now have been under Bourbon rule.

second appeal to the ladies of Italy on behalf of their poor countrymen, begging them to form visiting committees and raise subscriptions for the purpose of morally and materially bettering their condition; bread, labour and education, he said, were the requirements of the poor. He had previously addressed a long letter to the Marchioness Pallavicini, requesting her to become the Lady President * of a Philanthropic Association for assisting and visiting the poor, and for founding schools in the Neapolitan dominions and other parts of Italy including Turin. The General was thoroughly convinced that the surest means of raising the character of the people was to confer on the women (the mothers of the nation) the benefits of an enlightened education. In some of the schools for orphans, and the very poorest, they were to be partially clothed and fed. The General himself took the greatest interest in all the details, and continues even now to do so,† he maintained also, that the ladies who occupy themselves with such matters, are gainers, for that much of the illness among women in the higher ranks of life, arise from the want of fixed habits of employment, and nothing is so likely to enlarge and strengthen the mind as the thought that is constantly required to benefit others with success. "Let once the power of mind over body be successfully invoked, and vigor both of body and mind will be the result: work and industry is in obedience to God's great law. Those who seek to evade it and consult only their own gratification usually suffer in health and comfort, while the consciousness of having done their duty will double all the pleasures of domestic

* To the Ladies' Committee Garibaldi wrote sometime afterwards: " In the name of our country, I offer you my sincerest thanks; May God bless you and those foreign associates, who so lovingly and so nobly co-operate in this holy work; you are striving to restore to our country that highest Christianity which selfishness and deceit has cast into the mire. Permit me to bow reverently before the female liberators of my country, who are at the same time conferring a service on all humanity."

† At Varignano during a day of great suffering, the General being visited by one of the ladies connected with the schools, he asked the first thing after his dear children, meaning the pupils, receiving a favourable report of them, he turned to his visitor and said, God will bless you for your goodness to these little ones, and when you are on your death bed you will not regard as wasted, the hours you have spent amongst them, my heartfelt gratitude you know you possess.

intercourse." He also expressed his conviction that woman was appointed by Providence to take the first part in the destruction of despotism and superstition.

In August, the General was again attacked with rheumatic fever and confined to bed for several days. He was very much grieved at what was taking place in Naples. He made it the subject of long conversations with the companions of his solitude and with his frequent visitors, Italian and foreign, who urged him in vain to leave the island. This he declared he would not do, unless compelled by the course of events. He continued meanwhile to receive numerous letters and addresses, and requests for advice from all quarters.

Great complaints were made early in August about the distribution of orders and decorations to Garibaldi's army at the conclusion of the campaign. The government accordingly ordered a list of those recommended for rewards to be made out. This list was carefully examined, name by name, and approved by Garibaldi himself, and was sent to the Minister War, General Fanti. After a tedious delay, General Valfu, being then director general at the war department, issued the first list. It was immediately noticed by the Garibaldian general that several names were omitted. This error was rectified; and, at last, at the end of August, the official gazette contained a further list of the rewards to the officers and men of Garibaldi's army. There had also been some confusion relative to the publication of an order originally proposed by Garibaldi, and agreed to by the King, who signed the order at Naples, but never carried it into effect; by which the numerous officers and men who deserted from the Italian army and joined the army of the South should be pardoned and restored to their proper rank. This was also at last set right, and His Majesty signed again the act necessary for their pardon and restoration.

It was only through a singular oversight that this act of justice had been so long delayed. On Sergeant Borece being tried by court-martial at Genoa for deserting from the Marines, the judge-advocate demanded that he should be sentenced to two years' imprisonment, but his counsel appealed to Admiral Persano, the president, and pleaded that the sergeant had only deserted in order to join the expedition to Sicily, and was carried away by admiration of Garibaldi. The president and the other officers accepted the excuse, and restored Borece to his rank. Such relaxations of strict discipline are allowable in times of revolution, and will never injure the service of any country. If Garibaldi was constantly thinking of the Neapolitans, they on their parts equally loved him. This opinion is confirmed by the correspondent of the *Times*, who wrote from Naples:—"The reports from the provinces speak generally of the enthusiastic manner in which the fête of Garibaldi was celebrated, while here in the city anecdotes are continually related which go far to prove that San Guiseppe (Garibaldi) is on the eve almost of being substituted in the devotions of the Neapolitans for San Gennaro."*

---

* The People of Naples to Garibaldi.—The *Nationalites* published the following letter from the people of Naples to Garibaldi:—"The People of Naples to their Garibaldi.—Every day, every hour, every moment, we bless thee, dear Joseph our father; you reign in our hearts; our children have learned thy name and mingle it with their prayers. You are the father of the people. Quite alone, without regarding weariness or difficulties, without thinking of any interest of your own, you have shed for us your generous blood. Our hope in thee is eternal, as is our gratitude, and will be handed down from sire to son till the end of time. May the breezes bear to Caprera the echo of our acclamation 'Viva Garibaldi!'"—*Times*.

The Times Correspondent at Naples wrote on the 8th Sept.:—"For once my letter will present itself blushing all over with satisfaction. The Garibaldi Fête is over, and I have not an unpleasant fact to record; on the contrary, everything that is agreeable. The 'trades' looked highly respectable, each carried its banner, and all the members as they moved along sang some popular and patriotic hymn; as, 'The Cross of Savoy,' or, the 'Bandiera;' but the Hymn of Garibaldi, before they could get half through, seemed to rise with choking impatience on their tongues. * * * * I saw not a single soldier yesterday except as a happy spectator, and guards of public security stood about with their hands in their pockets—the people themselves preserved the public peace. It was a magnificent spectacle to witness a population of 500,000 persons so happy and so orderly, and it is a great fact that not one arrest was made. Were facts otherwise I would quickly tell you, for I never deceive you to support a party. I must note another circumstance. I heard but one name, with very few exceptions, shouted yesterday, and that name was 'Garibaldi.' He is a species of human tarantula; he has bitten the people, who all are subordinate to his will. I have known a civil tumult in the Toledo, which threatened evil consequences, stilled by a band playing his hymn. It reminded me of the effect of music according to mediæval tradition; all began to dance and sing. Such a man is himself a power, and Italy must not lose him in the prospect of coming events. The party of action may be rash, injudicious, too little calculating, but they will be shortly a necessity, and Garibaldi is their chief. In two days 14,000 handker-

Caprera began by degrees to assume a comfortable aspect. Garibaldi's farming answered; he had received presents of improved farming implements from America, England, and other countries; and he actually bought a little more land and planted

---

chiefs with his head stamped upon them were sold to the poorer classes, and on the last day perhaps as many more. A placard at the top with the words '*A Roma*' spoke the national impulse. * * * * I went down to the Villa Reale, which was converted into a fairyland. Forty thousand lamps were hung in festoons throughout the entire length of the gardens, or glittered like golden fruits among the trees. Thousands of people stood, or walked, or sat about listening to a fine band which was ranged round a fountain, and here and there tables with refreshments were laid. It was a happy, happy scene, such a one as I had never hoped to see in Naples. * * * * The procession closed with a battalion of the National Guards, fine, soldier-looking, well-dressed men, who, despite my doubts, have worked well, and have done honour to their country. A Northern Italian who was with me was in ecstacies at their appearance and with the demonstration. 'After all,' he said, 'the South will save Italy;' meaning to say that the impulse to advance on Rome will be given here, and I do not think he is mistaken, for Rome is a necessity to Naples, without it she is the tributary of Turin, at least in appearance and will be always exposed to the savage invasion from the hirelings of that son of a saint in Heaven, and of the descendant of St. Peter. Underneath the brilliant spectacle which presented itself lay two prominent ideas, to which crowds gave expression as they shouted 'Garibaldi!' and '*A Roma!*' Garibaldi is the personification of the wishes of the people. He has proclaimed an united Italy, and they will have it; but they cannot have it without Rome, and therefore the party of action, whose demonstration it was yesterday, are loud in their protest against the French occupation of their capital, and are clamouring to march upon it. There were hundreds of flags in procession, and all bore the inscription, '*A Roma!*' Hard-working operatives, who are the bone and muscle of the nation, are at the head of the movement. Seated in their workshops, they brood over the one idea; the very activity of their lives awakens their martial activity, and persuades them that there is no organization, no peace, without Rome, while the sufferings which continued agitation inflicts, point to the possession of the Eternal City as the true remedy for want, the real source of prosperity. If yesterday, therefore, commemorated a great fact—the expulsion of the Bourbons and the restoration of the liberties of the Neapolitans—it inaugurated a new era, which will become remarkable by acquisition of a capital. I was struck by the enthusiasm with which the two ideas I have noted were connected—'To Rome with Garibaldi!' He is felt to be the necessary leader of the great movement. Laying aside all party feeling, I verily believe that the South would rise *en masse* to follow him.

Cialdina is acting wisely and energetically; he has reconciled parties, and has beaten down the reaction *for the present*, but he is too much under the control of the central Government ever to become the leader of the movement, and, though highly popular, could never command the enthusiasm of the people as Garibaldi would. All the antecedents of the latter point him out as the man who should direct the march on the road at the first milestone of which the Southern Italians arrived yesterday; and it is just at this moment that rumours are circulating to the effect that Garibaldi is going to America. They may be possibly circulated with a motive, but whether they be so or not, he is daily becoming a greater necessity for Italy, and God knows how soon the popular opinion of frenzy may demand him as its chief. Garibaldi cannot, must not, leave Italy. I am becoming prosy, so let me now describe another and the last phase of the fête—the illumination, which was more brilliant than any spectacle of the kind I ever witnessed. Beginning with Santa Lucia, flags waved from every window, and lights, some in festoons, dazzled the sight. At the Marine barracks was stationed the splendid band of the Marines, and the inscription over the gateway, blazing with lights, told of the "unspeakable joy" of Southern Italy on this anniversary of the restoration of their liberties. The Palace square presented a most brilliant spectacle, at the head of

numbers of fig-trees. Most people were surprised with the gentle way he always spoke of the ex-king of Naples, blaming his education, his advisers, and thankfully recalling the young king's kindness to one of his staff, a prisoner at Gaeta. The presents he continued to receive were endless. One day some strangers begged him to accept gifts far too rich for his quiet tastes, which he courteously declined. Perceiving his visitors were

---

which San Francisco Paolo, the cupola of which sprang into light in a moment, stood out in all the beauty of its architectural decorations, traced in living fire. A band of music played national hymns, but a murmur continually rose until Garibaldi's Hymn was played, and then all joined in with a vigour which showed the love for their idol. The Luciani who live in the back streets burnt fires in little iron baskets, set up on a series of stands. The Toledo and all its *vicoli* glowed with light, so did every street and house in Naples, and looking across the port we could see Masaniello's tower and all the blocks of houses in that densely populated part glittering with lights. The demonstration was universal. At half-past eight o'clock I went down to the Questura, a place I was not in the habit of frequenting under the Bourbons, and looked down in a living ocean, as it was calculated, of from 30,000 to 40,000 persons. They were waiting for the exhibition of fireworks, and in the interval listened, more orderly than an aristocratic mob at an opera, to the national airs which were being performed, but here, as everywhere else, it was the "Hymn of Garibaldi" which was loudly called for, and if not repeated immediately murmurs arose in every direction; then, when the band struck up, there was clapping of hands and shouts of satisfaction, and all joined in. * * * * I went down into the thickest of the crowd, and formed a particle of the vast ocean; attraction and cohesion were pretty strong, and we moved about in a vast body—men, women, children, and babies in arms; but there was not a rude push, not a scream from the most timid, nor a single complaint, and I constantly heard the words "*con permesso, con licenza.*" Let me close my letter with some facts and observations suggested by what I have seen. *There was not one arrest yesterday for theft or quarrelling.* This is official.

The *Times* Correspondent at Naples writes, September 10:—"The brilliant and orderly fête of Saturday is so important a fact that I fear not to have said enough about it. Long as my letter was, I might have extended it much more, for there were many scenes which I have left undescribed, and many facts unrecorded. Take one: In the Via Baglio two men were quarrelling, backs up like two cats. One drew a knife, and the other rushed into his house to get some weapon. 'What is all this?' said a third; 'don't you know it's Garibaldi's day?' The men dropped their knives, and embraced amid cries of '*Viva Garibaldi!*' 'Tis a pretty little episode, on the truth of which you may depend. Often and often, as I gazed and listened on Saturday, I said to myself, 'This is the only true *plébiscite* I have witnessed;' for the first—be it said without any prejudice to the Italian cause—was a humbug, as all *plébiscites* must be, and as was the firstborn of that precious family. But the one that was taken on Saturday was spontaneous, universal, was voted by the heart, and clamoured for Garibaldi. It will have its consequences, and, unless I am mistaken, it will not be long before the cry will be raised, with irrepressible energy, 'To Rome with Garibaldi!'"

The *Times* Correspondent at Turin writes about the same time:—"The sway Garibaldi holds over his own people is grounded on boundless faith and love; he is accustomed to have his absolute will worshipped, not disputed; nay, his most passing thought guessed and forestalled. Though the most affable and condescending of men, the distance between him and his most intimate friends is immense, and never overstepped. None ever dare to offer him advice, none even to address him, when his brow is set and he broods over his venturous schemes. The very spell of the man is in his silence, and when he opens his lips the watchword must be 'to hear and to obey.'"

hurt, he said: "You might do me a great pleasure, if you would; there is much distress at present in part of the Austrian dominions; I have sent them a hundred francs only, it is all I can afford. If you would but sell these things, and give the money to these poor people who want it so much, I should be very grateful to you. The gentlemen who remembered the fearful death of Garibaldi's idolised wife, listened in astonishment, and at last said: "But they are Austrians!" "And is that the way you read Christ's gospel?" was the answer; "did He not die for all, and has He not said that all mankind are brothers, if they have not a good government the people ought rather to be pitied than blamed."† Of course his request was complied with, and the sufferers received 2,000 francs from the sale. So ended the winter in Caprera, and a quiet year for Garibaldi after the campaigns of 1860.

The same correspondent, alluding to the offers made by America to Garibaldi, has the following:—"It requires no very deep knowledge of Garibaldi's character, no very keen insight into the present state of affairs in Italy, and into the peculiar ties which bind the hermit of Caprera to his island home, to feel sure that no object in the world could induce him to quit his present position. Garibaldi and his party have full faith in the inevitable renewal of the final struggle between Italy and Austria early in the next spring; and what amount of honour and power could ever compensate that most disinterested of all men living, if on the first crack of a volunteer's rifle he were to be separated from the scene of action by the whole width of the Atlantic?

† A very different history went the round of the London Papers in November, 1863. Garibaldi had sent £60 to relieve the distress in Austria, and with the view of pleasing the Emperor the authorities refused to accept the money.

CHAPTER VIII.

Commencement of the year 1862—Address by Garibaldi to the Working Men's Association of London—The Pope endeavours to prevent the consolidation of a United Italy—He encourages Brigands—Garibaldi accepts the Presidency of the Rifle Association of Genoa—French attempt to break the Ricasoli Cabinet—Negotiations respecting Rome between France and Ricasoli—Rome captured would give freedom to all—The National Rifle Association, its objects—Garibaldi calls on the people of Naples to Arm—Enrollments in the name of Garibaldi—The failure of M. de Lavalette's mission to Rome—Napoleon's Speech at the opening of the Chamber—Demonstration against the temporal power of the Pope—Prince Napoleon expresses the true interests of France—Resignation of the Ricasoli Ministry—Garibaldi arrives at Turin—His entry into Cremona—Letter from him to Lord Palmerston—Celebration of his Birth-day—The adoration of the people for him—His reception at Milan—Napoleon desires that Italy should be divided—His Plan for a division—Attempt to destroy Garibaldi and those devoted to Italian Unity—Failure of the project—Another plan attempted—He urges the people to rally round the Standard of Victor Emmanuel—Garibaldi's reception and speech at Lecco—His celebrated address to the young men of Cremona—He urges the people to cry "Italy and Victor Emmanuel"—His address to the Ladies of Rome.

In the opening of the year 1862, the dissatisfaction in Naples was still great. General Garibaldi, who always turned to England for an example, and whose only aim was to secure for Italians an equal amount of freedom as that which the English nation enjoyed, had accepted the perpetual honorary presidency of the "United Associations of Working Men in Naples," with the intention of thereby assisting to spread abroad enlightened views of constitutional freedom. In such capacity he addressed a letter to the president of the General Working Men's Association in London. He told them that up to the present time, they had no schools, no liberty of speech, nor any free press in Italy, neither had they any right of association, in short, they had no air to breathe which they could call their own, but, that now, on the other hand, although they were still weighed down by the remnant of their ancient chains, they still enjoyed a far larger amount of freedom than they ever had done before. He pointed to the provinces that were overrun by brigands almost of every nation in the world, consecrated by Rome, to lay waste their country, to burn their villages and cities, and to slaughter unoffending citizens. There was consequently, in those parts, no security for life or property; work was very scarce and national activity languished. All this, he said, was the work of the Bourbons and of the priests. Rome did not belong to Italy. The Pope preyed upon the heart of Italy; foreign troops barred with their bayonets the way to the eternal city, and forbad the Italians to save themselves. The Italian nation was mortally wounded by the occupation of Rome, and in the midst of so many difficulties, Italians had turned their thoughts to their fellow workmen in England, and in the name of the love they bore to their own native land, in the name of the brotherhood of labor, of national rights, and of that universal freedom opposed so much by the Pope, he asked them to lend their assistance and join in the Italian cry, that Rome is no French land, that Rome does not belong to the priests, that Rome is Italian, and the capital of Italy, and that the voice of the people of England was strong and respected. He asked them, therefore, to join their protest against those flagrant violations of their rights, which were also the rights of all free people. The Italians could and would liberate their own country; they had to fight not only against their open foes, but also against their pretended friends; whilst the first sharpen and brandish their weapons, the others enfeeble and bind their arms. Let, he said, the French occupation of Rome be brought to a close, and Rome be restored to Italy. These, were the principles that the Garibaldians besought the people of England to respect. M. de Lavelette, the new

French Ambassador at Rome, had shown from official reports how the papacy was losing influence throughout the Italian Peninsula, by the anti-national policy of the Pope towards the Italian people, since Rome had been made the focus of intrigue, and the centre of Italy's worst enemies the abode of the ex-king, Francis II, and his reactionary partisans, who sent armed men into the Southern States to foment and massacre innocent citizens. It seems clear that the benevolent Pio Nono and his advisers had long made up their minds to refuse all reconciliation with Italy and her king; and that they had further resolved to use their utmost endeavours to prevent the consolidation of a united Italy. Meanwhile, funds were sent for the support of the bands of brigands that had been organized by the Cardinal Minister of State and the agents of king Francis. Bands of robbers had been let loose from Rome, and spread over some of the Italian cities in order to re-organize brigandage, and thus creating grave embarrassments for the Italian Government. In the Place Campo del Tiori, at Rome, an apothecary, named Vegnozzi, kept a register for the hiring of brigands, and in his cellars there was a manufactory for cartridges. In the Place Campo Vaccino might be seen every day troops of convicts, wretches with the shadow of the gallows already frowning over them. These men, under the name of workmen, were brigands engaged by the Neapolitan family, and maintained at their expense, or at that of the Roman police, ready to be drafted off by degrees into the Neapolitan provinces. On the previous 18th of December 200 of them had set out, furnished with regular passports from the Roman police, while the conveyances of the Roman Government took their arms and ammunition to some place that had been beforehand determined upon. Such was the way in which brigandage was perpetuated in the Neapolitan provinces. In reply to a parliamentary deputation that waited upon him, his Majesty said that notwithstanding the incubus that had been weighing down the energies of Italy during the past year, he was still sanguine in hoping that the new year would bring greater prosperity to the national cause.

Early in January, Garibaldi accepted the presidency of the Rifle Association of Genoa, and on doing so addressed a letter to the members of that body, in which he told them to make preparations for a national armament; for the moment was fast approaching when they would have to prove their patriotism by new deeds of valour. He also stated that Baron Ricasoli had demanded a credit of 2,000,000 livres to purchase arms for the National Guard. At the same time, it seemed as if foreign influence was intriguing at Turin to bring about complications amongst extreme parties. French influence was at work to break up the Ricasoli Cabinet. In Paris there seemed a disposition to discourage the progress of Italian unity and organization, whilst one or two writers of the semi-official Parisian press were allowed to indulge in detracting misrepresentations about Italian affairs. The difficulties in which Ricasoli found himself were pointed out with satisfaction. The unity of the Peninsula was again declared to be the work of England; a statement which alone would be sufficient to make it hateful in the eyes of the majority of Frenchmen.

The following is an extract from a letter written by Garibaldi to the Committee of Trecchina (a market town of Naples), about this period:—"You were among the first to throw down the glove to the tyrants of your country; yet upon you have fallen the greatest misfortunes. Such is often the reward of merit. There remains to us the approval of our consciences for having fulfilled our duty, and the inflexible resolve to fulfil it again before very long. The priests of Rome, with those who tolerate and protect them, are the cause of all your troubles. I should have gone to you some time since, but did not go for the same reasons as those which induced me to leave you. I hope however, soon to be with you, meanwhile, all of you arm yourselves with a musket or with whatever arms circumstances permit. You will find efficient officers amongst your valiant fellow-citizens. Let all of you take up arms. Let your example be followed by all the other provinces, and, all being armed and organized, brigands and malefactors of every kind, will disappear. Above all, do not abandon the programme which makes us strong, 'Italy and Victor Emmanuel!' and do not listen to the men of party. We do not belong to parties, but we all belong to one nation which desires to be consolidated."

The negotiations respecting Rome were re-opened by France with Baron Ricasoli; but he rejected them directly, declaring, without reserve, that Italy could never recognise the temporal power of the court of Rome. On the 8th of January, a numerously attended meeting of the members forming the majority of the Chamber of Deputies was held, for the purpose of considering whether the parliamentary majority should continue to support the ministry. The meeting unanimously resolved to place its confidence in them. It was said in Paris that if Ratazzi came into power the Emperor would no longer delay to resume the negotiations respecting Rome. Garibaldi, like his king, continued to be in good health and spirits, looking forward to the future with hopeful confidence.*

On the 15th of January, Baron Ricasoli stated in parliament that the destruction of the Papal power by the capture of Rome would give freedom, not to Italians only, but to the whole human race besides. It was not possible to determine the time of their triumph. It might be at that very moment their destinies were ripening. There certainly was no lack of activity in rousing the warlike propensities of the citizens. Prince Humbert had been appointed president of the National Rifle Association, General Garibaldi being the vice-president. The prince had expressed his great desire to be of some service to the country. The avowed object of the association was the augmentation of the national strength, by training the young Italians to the use of arms, so that all might strike a blow for the inde-

* Early in the year, Madam Alberta Mario came to England to give some lectures upon the state of Italy, and her doing so was sanctioned by Garibaldi. She gave, an interesting narrative of the progress of Garibaldi after the landing at Calabria, of his triumphs, and of the difficulties which had been thrown in his way and in the way of Italian unity by the party of Piedmont.

pendence of their fatherland. Italy required assurances that on the day of struggle and danger, she might find a soldier in every one of her citizens. The wonderful enterprises of the brave volunteers collected from all the provinces of Italy, proved what mighty deeds might be expected from the Italian people, if they were well instructed in the use of their arms, and had a thorough knowledge of military exercises. Garibaldi called upon the people of Naples to "Arm themselves for God's sake." He said, "Let every one take up arms, and I promise you that it will be an easy road that will lead Italy to the rank for which Providence has destined her." Garibaldi, though he had placed his sword permanently at the disposal of King Victor Emmanuel, yet, neither conspired, nor plotted, nor countenanced aggressive expeditions, and positively discountenanced those extreme patriots who might possibly by acting prematurely, bring disaster upon the new kingdom. There were some who were sanguine enough to think that France would not continue her garrison in Rome for a much longer period. Public demonstrations were organized in all the large towns in Italy against the Roman occupation, the people everywhere giving vent to their enthusiasm by shouting, "Rome, the capital of Italy." About the middle of February, Garibaldi wrote to the *Deritto*, stating from information he had received that in some towns clandestine enrolments were being made in his name, and requesting them to declare that the adoption of these proceedings had neither been authorised nor recommended by him. Things, meanwhile, had assumed an unquiet aspect; a great demonstration had taken place at Naples in favor of England; the same kind of demonstration had also taken place in almost every other town in Italy, and a great anti-papal Temporal power demonstration was set afoot at Milan, on which occasion a sermon was preached in the streets by Pantaleo, at the end of which the hymn of Garibaldi was sung. Brigandage was most extensively carried on in Naples. It was believed that if Garibaldi had had command it would have been at once suppressed, probably within a fortnight.

The old farce had again just been re-enacted between the Tuileries and the Vatican. Once more the French Emperor had been trying the effect of sympathetic and disinterested counsels, and once more he had been met with the stereotyped 'non possumus' of papal diplomacy. This time, however, the business presented more of the appearance of an ultimation than had yet been discernable in the greatest correspondence between Paris and Rome. Theoretically, the Popes final rejection of his Imperial patron's advice, ought to have led straight way to the evacuation of Rome, though practically, they did nothing in consequence. The utter impracticability of Papal diplomacy was never more strikingly illustrated than by the dispatch in which M. de Lavalette recorded the failure of his mission. "Let the French only evacuate the Italian capital, and the services of M. de Lavalette, and of all other diplomatists, will be totally superfluous," observed Garibaldi.

Italy was once more smiling in hope: the speech of the Emperor Napoleon at the opening of the legislative chambers was generally regarded in Turin as exhibiting a solicitude for Italy, which was regarded as the most certain pledge of success. The Italians immediately believed themselves on the high road to Rome; even at Vienna, the opinion was publicly expressed that the diplomatic correspondence with the Court of Rome just published was highly damaging to the Pope. But the suspense and agony of Italy were to be still further prolonged. Her anticipations of joy were premature. All the deductions which were drawn from the diplomatic notes of M. Thouvenel, the earnest appeal of M. de Lavalette, the insulting reply of the Papal Government, and the short paragraph in the Emperor's speech, were but delusions. French policy and French action in Italy were not then (nor are they now) to be construed by ordinary rules. The notion that a crisis in the Roman question had arrived, and that the French garrison would be promptly withdrawn from the Roman capital of Italy, were the foolish dreams of an impulsive people. The secret of the Emperor's policy in the affairs of Italy, and particularly of Rome, was not easy to be ascertained, nor was it probably clearly known to himself. Popular demonstrations shortly took place in Florence, Parma, Perugia, Ferrara, and Palermo, which had a very distinct and commendable object in view, namely, to contradict a falsehood and to make known the truth to the world, Cardinal Antonelli having had the audacity, in the face of all Europe, to assert, when replying to M. Thouvenel, "that the Pope had broken off all amicable relations with Turin, but found himself on the best possible terms with the people of Italy, who were the first to suffer for him, and the foremost to compassionate his grief." This impudent assertion sent the wildfire of indignation through the veins of all Italy, which was not abated by reiterated assertion given, "that there was no possible hope of accommodation with Rome, seeing that the whole college of cardinals, as well as the sovereign pontiff himself, had sworn not to yield a single inch of the temporal power under any circumstances whatsoever." This reckless assertion helped to swell the current of popular feeling into that angry torrent which has ever since been raging with unabated violence around the rock of St. Peter. Demonstrations were being prepared in nearly every city and town to show the unanimity of the people on this subject of the temporal power. The speech of Prince Napoleon in the French senate seemed a full expression of the sentiment of France. This attack was levelled against the Papal Government, and the exposure of the part which was played to General Goyon's knowledge at Rome. The very remarkable speeches delivered about that time in the senate by such undoubted imperialists as M. Pietri and Prince Napoleon, gave immediate support to the belief that the disposition of the Emperor to cultivate the confidence and good will of the liberal party was daily increasing; for it did not seem probable that either speaker would have given such prominent and forcible expression to views known to be so diametrically opposed to the Emperor's policy without sufficient grounds for doing so.

N

Garibaldi wrote to the young men of Italy, telling them that in 1860 their society numbered only 1,000, that in 1862 they must number 1,000,000, and that in this one object their whole energies must be concentrated. "Of the results of this," he adds, "we will talk together hereafter." In the first days of March, Baron Ricasoli resigned, and it was universally believed that this honest statesman fell a victim to a court intrigue, and to the personal influence exercised by Napoleon III. over Victor Emmanuel.

Madame la Princepe De Solms, grand daughter of Lucien Buonaparte, married in the early part of 1863, within one month of the death of her husband, Mons. Ratazzi. This requires no explanation to those who are acquainted with the questionable morality of high life in Turin. It is well known that Mr. Wise, protested both publicly and privately against the supposition that his brother, the Right Hon. Sir Thos. Wise, was the father of the lady in question.*

We now come to the most singular part of the whole of the affairs of 1862. General Garibaldi arrived in Turin on the 3rd March. It is much to be regretted that he should ever have been induced to place the slightest confidence in a ministry at the head of which presided Rattazzi, the acknowledged nominee of

---

* The following letter was addressed to the editor of the *Manchester Guardian*:—"Sir,—My attention has been called to a letter which has recently appeared in your Journal, from your London correspondent, in which he professes to give an account of the career of Madame Ratazzi—ci-divant De Solms—representing her to have been the daughter of my late lamented brother, Sir Thomas Wise. As the present head of the Wise family, I beg to give the most unqualified contradiction to that statement. Madame Wise and my brother were married in 1821, they lived together until 1828, when she separated herself from him; during that time, there were born only two children as issue of the said marriage, (both sons) namely, Alfred N. Wise, and William C. Wise, now living. My brother never saw his wife after their separation. The person to whom your correspondent refers, namely, Madame De Solms, was born at Weedon, in April, 1831. She is the daughter of an English officer then stationed there. My brother invariably repudiated the audaciously assumed relationship of that individual, and has left, in proof of it, the most satisfactory documents now in my possession, to be used as occasion may require, in refutation of these unfounded and scandalous fabrications. I may observe that the other statements of your correspondent, referring to my late brother, are a fiction on the part of his informant. I trust to your sense of justice to insert this contradiction to your correspondent's letter, and I hope that such of your contemporaries who published it will give equal publicity to my denial.—I remain, Sir, your obedient Servant, GEORGE WISE, 22, Upper Leeson-street, Dublin, February 20th, 1863."

the Emperor of the French.* A deputation waited upon Garibaldi to ask him his opinion with respect to the new government, and whether he thought it should be supported? The General answered, that the cabinet had entered into engagements with him, and had bound itself by pledges of the highest importance, which could not fail to be acceptable to the country: That one of these pledges was to be redeemed immediately, and until it was redeemed, he should never think of returning to Caprera. The General went on to say, that he trusted the day was at hand, when the miseries that distracted the southern provinces, would melt away before the sunny smile of order and tranquility, and concluded by telling them that until the accomplishment of these promises, great caution and tact were necessary. The ministry had faithfully promised him to act for itself, independently of all foreign influence. In its internal and external policy, it would labour for the accomplishment of the national programme, "Rome the capital of Italy." The Italian people, he said, must remain firm to their programme. "Italy and Victor Emmanuel." All letters from Genoa, written at this time, dwell upon the unbounded admiration of the Genoese for Garibaldi. Flags were hung from every window, and cries of "Viva Garibaldi!" resounded through the street. The appearance of his calm and dignified countenance in the carriage which conveyed him to the place of meeting at the Provvedimento society, excited the people to the highest pitch of enthusiasm. The platform in the hall was crowded with Garibaldian heroes,

* It is a positive fact that Signor Urbano Ratazzi endeavoured to approach and to come to an understanding with Garibaldi. We know that when, in December, 1861, there was an impression that the Ricasoli's ministry would fall on the return of Signor Ratazzi from Paris, the latter sent word to Garibaldi, through a friend, that he wished to speak with him. Garibaldi hastened to leave Caprera and went to Genoa, where he expected to find Signor Ratazzi, but in his stead, he found there another friend of his, who was afterwards to become a member of the Ratazzi ministry. This gentleman announced to Garibaldi his having received from the future Minister of Italy the mission of accompanying him to Turin. Garibaldi accepted to go, and when there he went from the railway station direct to the house of Ratazzi. From that moment Garibaldi advised his friends to support the Ratazzi ministry, and Ratazzi and his friends boasted of the friendship of Garibaldi. But Ratazzi's expectation was, for that time, disappointed, because Ricasoli received a vote of confidence, and Ratazzi failed to obtain office till February, 1862.

members of the celebrated thousand. The General said, "That the principal object for which the central committee had convoked the present gathering, was to consult about the organization and the uniting of all the free Italian societies; a holy end, which ought to lead to the accomplishment of the destinies of their country. They all knew that the cause of the misfortunes of Italy was internal dissension; the idea therefore of re-uniting all the members of the great Italian family was certainly a holy idea." At the conclusion of his speech, the whole assembly rose, and amid shouts of applause tendered to Garibaldi, the presidency of the association, which he willingly accepted. Garibaldi had the further intention of visiting all the chief towns of Italy in succession, including those of the South, and to urge the inhabitants to form rifle corps, where none had as yet been organized. When, however, he found that Victor Emmanuel was going to Naples, he abandoned the latter part of his programme, in order that the king might be better received. So long as Victor Emmanuel remains at Naples, he observed, I will remain in the north, out of his way. On his entry into Cremona, the National Guards, the Corps of exiles and carbineers, as well as an immense concourse of people were waiting to receive him. The General came in by All Saints' Church, where, in the open space, a touching spectacle presented itself; a considerable number of Neapolitan soldiers stopped the way, prostrating themselves before him, as the liberator and saviour of Naples. They clamoured to unharness the horses of his carriage, in order to draw it themselves, but this he would by no means permit, but continued his journey slowly through the turbulent mob of admirers that thronged around his carriage. A great number of carriages followed that of Garibaldi, three of which were filled with officers of the regular army, and in another was Steffanelli, General of Division, in black attire, accompanied by his aide-de-camp. On the arrival of the cortege, at the Trecchi palace, General Steffanelli descended from his carriage, to open the gates, which elicited from the people bursts of applause; Garibaldi soon appeared at one of the windows of the Palace, and addressed the crowd.

On the 5th May, he dispatched the following letter to Lord Palmerston from Trescorra. "My Lord, we have heard with joy and gratitude the words, replete with meaning, which you in the name of the great British nation, have uttered in the House of Commons in defence of the unity of Italy, and the principle of non-intervention. You have recognized the fact of the Napoleonic occupation of Rome to be a flagrant violation of non-intervention; it is an obstacle to the unity of Italy, and threatens the peace of Europe. If England only perseveres in her efforts to make this principle respected, the Italians will, unassisted, be able to obtain the entire deliverance of their country. Receive, my Lord, our respectful salutations.—The central Council of the Italian Association of Emancipation.—President, G. GARIBALDI."

Garibaldi's birthday passed quietly off at Naples. From the windows of the principal streets, floated thousands of flags, many of them bearing a portrait of their idol, or some inscription in his honour.

In many places alters were erected to him, as though he were a divinity, and burning candles were arranged around his statue, in testimony of their adoration. Many a doorway and window was illuminated by his colossal portrait in transparency.

One blaze of light o'erflowed the Theatre of San Carlo. Nine times did the frenzied audience clamour for the Hymn of Garibaldi, nor would they desist till the leader of the orchestra, sank exhausted with fatigue.

English people can form but a faint idea of the adoration which was paid by the Neapolitan people to their idol; he was worshipped, and what the Madonna is to the ignorant masses, so was Garibaldi to the throng of enthusiasts, who placed their only trust in him. It is no disparagement to King Victor Emmanuel, to say that the enthusiasm manifested on St. Joseph's day, was far greater than that with which he was greeted on his triumphal entry into Naples a few days before. Garibaldi's reception in Milan was most enthusiastic; the city was illuminated and presented a festive appearance. At the banquet at the Hotel de Ville, he spoke of the power of knowledge, and the future destinies of Italy, concluding by proposing the toast, "Victor Emmanuel."

Garibaldi had, however, other missions besides this avowed one, of promoting the purposes of the Rifle Association; he was on terms of the best understanding with the Government, and was surrounded by men in Rattazzi's confidence. It must be remembered that the plan of a united Italy was never that of the Emperor Napoleon, but that on the contrary, he wished Italy to be divided into three parts. On the 19th November, 1861, there appeared a statement in the *Daily News* to the effect that the project of an Italian confederation was by no means given up. The plan was to divide Italy into three parts; the northern part of Italy was to form a kingdom, of which Victor Emmanuel was to be king. The central portion was to constitute a Papal State, including Umbria and the Marches; the Southern was intended to constitute the kingdom of Naples: Venice would then be given up to Victor Emmanuel. The great obstacle to these designs at this period was Baron Ricasoli.*

There were many sensible politicians, who believed that the Emperor Napoleon still hoped to bring about this fatal project of dividing Italy into two or three separate states. It has been most confidently asserted that when Rattazzi went to Paris, shortly before he assumed office, he engaged to destroy the democratic element, and in a conversation with one of the most influential of the ministers, the eventuality of the detachment of Southern Italy was spoken of as a simple possibility. The greatest obstacle lay in Garibaldi and his friends, who were the

---

* Those who doubt the truth of this, have only to refer to Monsieur La Guerronierre's pamphlet published after Aspromonte, which gives us sufficient evidence of the fact, which is indeed intruded upon us in a more distinct and offensive form, than one would have easily supposed to be possible at the time.

most steadfast supporters of unity, "for the others, I care little," said the French Minister, and he had reason: It was therefore incumbent upon them to find some means to destroy the great obstacle. Two modes were open to consideration, one was the formation of an expedition to Greece, of which they hoped by soft words to prevail upon the general to take the command. The other was a design to bring him and his party into a snare; in their first object they had very nearly succeeded, an expedition was projected, for the East sanctioned, it is believed, by the ministry, and General Garibaldi consented to take the command. Enlistments were made, and the preparations were pressing steadily forward, when the statements of what had passed in Paris, were laid before Garibaldi, who then saw at a glance that all that was required of him was to leave the country with those chiefs most devoted to Italian unity, and with the bravest of his volunteers; he foresaw that most probably he would be surrounded by an overwhelming force, and his country left open to the machinations of an august ally, and of a ministry devoted to the French interests.

The Eastern expedition having thus fallen to the ground, the other plan was fallen back upon. An expedition into the Tyrol was organized, and it was hoped that when once hostilities had commenced Garibaldi would forget his old determination and place himself at their head. In the end the government turned and receiving information of this, and about 650 persons were arrested at Brescia, Pergamo, and Milan, on account of their connexion with the great conspiracy for invading the Tyrol and raising up an insurrection against Austria. Arms, ammunition, and some thousands of red shirts were also seized. Colonel Nullo, aide-de-camp to Garibaldi, was also arrested. Garibaldi wrote to the Milan *Gazette* the following note from Tuscora:—"In consequence of Colonel Nullo's arrest yesterday, I consider it my duty to declare that that officer acted exactly in conformity with my orders. G. Garibaldi."

An attempt was made on the part of the populace to restore the prisoners to liberty. It met, however, with no success, being immediately suppressed by the military. The number of killed and wounded at Brescia, Garibaldi wrote he could not discover, but he knew that there were boys and even women among their number. He could never believe that Italian soldiers could have killed unarmed women and children. The slayers must have been cut-throats of the police masquerading as soldiers; and as for their commander, who is chiefly answerable for this slaughter, "Oh!" said Garibaldi, "I would propose him for the office of Jack Ketch; and I would propose to the good citizens of Brescia to erect a monument to the Russian officer, Papoff, who broke his sabre when he had received orders to charge the unarmed people of Warsaw." The General afterwards wrote a letter, in which he said that some persons had wrongly interpreted the protest he had published in the *Diritto*. As an Italian soldier, he said he could never for a moment have harboured any intention of insulting the Italian army, which was the glory and hope of the nation; but he desired to say that soldiers ought to combat the enemies of their country, and not to massacre and wound unarmed men. If the commandant of Brescia had had permission to act according to the dictates of his heart they should not then have to lament these victims amongst the people. The duty of generals, he said, was to protect the frontier and to vanquish the enemies of their country; but they could never be justified in spilling the blood of citizens. Colonel Nullo and the rest were soon afterwards liberated and the General went to Varese, when he was received by the whole population, who refused for several hours to leave him. The General addressed them from the balcony of the Hotel de Ville, in the following terms:—"Good people of Varese, when I find myself amongst you I cannot help thinking that I have returned to my own home; for you always have received me in the same hospitable spirit, irrespective alike of the frowns of adversity or the smiles of prosperity. I thank you from the bottom of my heart for the affecting manner in which you have received me. In other parts of Lombardy, deplorable incidents have created indecision in the minds of Italians, and on that subject I am compelled to say a few words. The system of caste is unknown to Italian citizens. The army, national guard, and volunteers are brethren; our enemies are at Rome and Venice, and no one can usurp the monopoly of fighting the common enemies of us all. The cry, "Rome and Venice!" was in the mouth of everyone. "Yes, yes," replied the General, "we will go to Rome and Venice at the first summons from Victor Emmanuel; in the meantime, I urge you all to rally around his standard." A most enthusiastic reception awaited him at Lecco also, where the General delivered a speech, urging the people to make sacrifices for the redemption of their common country, and above everything else to cherish union and concord. The fever of excitement that the presence of the hero aroused wherever he chanced to be, is beyond all description. One day he addressed a deputation of young men from the various educational institutions of Cremona. He urged them not to indulge in vice, for vice, he said, was the disease of the soul. He told them that they should love instruction, because an uneducated man is little better than a monkey. He who acquires most knowledge rises the nearest to his Maker, from whom his soul springs; instruction should be grounded on solid moral education, and on this the social edifice should be built. Honour, he said, could only be acquired by virtue and instruction; nations, like individuals when weak, are insulted and enslaved. He advised them to bear with other people's weaknesses, to submit to no insults, to love instruction, for instruction is the mother of wealth and independence. Education had been of the greatest service to him, he said, in distant climes, and in exile had made him superior to poverty. Love knowledge, he continued, for it is the want of it that is the great obstacle to our national unity. Had

Italy been better instructed, her sons would long e'er this have discovered that they were not to be confined within the wall of a city, nor the hedge of a garden; but that the Alps and the broad sea were the only just and natural limits of their fatherland. They would have shaken off the fetters of slavery, and under the inspiration of freedom would long ago have hurled their tyrants into the dust.

It was decreed by the municipal and scholastic authorities that these memorable words should be written in letters of gold upon the threshold of their gymnasium. A Venetian exile asked the General when he would go to Venice, he replied, "I hope I shall be able to do so soon, but what am I? I am but one man." Oh! you are a thousand and hundreds of thousands; Italy is all yours, as are all our hearts and all our strength. "No," replied Garibaldi, severely, "This is the age of Victor Emmanuel, we are all one with our king, and will all work with him to liberate and unite Italy." To the Bishop and the clergy who had warmly espoused the national cause, and declared against the temporal power of the Pope, Garibaldi said, "You have nothing to learn from me, you have only to explain the word of God to the people; keep to the gospel, consult your oldest traditions, and you will be the fathers, instructors, and benefactors to the people, and they will kiss the prints of your footsteps; you will freely disavow those enemies of your country who falsely call themselves the priests of Christ." To the bishop who was ill, and whom he visited at his palace accompanied by his whole staff, he said, "I longed to see and know you, Monsignori, because I am aware that you are a true bishop, and a father to your people and your clergy; you are good and charitable, and have formed a clergy who edify me with their wise discourses, breathing a no less patriotic than energetic charity. Were all our clergy to follow your example, the redemption of our country would be an easy task." In all the towns he visited he took the greatest pains to urge the people to cry Italy and Victor Emmanuel, and at all the banquets, he, himself, proposed the health of the King, Prince Humbert, and the Royal Family.

Shortly before this, he had written a letter to the Italian clergy, from which the following is extracted:—"The real priests of Christ are invested with a sublime mission, without renouncing their character as Italians, they cannot remain accomplices of what is being done at Rome; let them consult their consciences regarding their duties, and finally let them disseminate the holy word of religion and truth amongst the multitudes, they will then earn the gratitude of millions of men, and they will restore the ancient Christianity, which proclaims self-denial and mutual forgiveness, and a grateful country will engrave their names amongst those of its heroic sons, by whom it has been redeemed."

When Ratazzi came into power, the fact of General Garibaldi having been consulted by the government, was a cause of public rejoicing at Florence, and had won over the hearts of the party, represented by Signor Dolfi; and after the first interview between the General and Rattazzi, the latter telegraphed to the prefect there, to say that Garibaldi was satisfied; that on Saint Joseph's day at Florence, the money usually expended on illuminations would this year be considered as a fund to relieve any Garibaldian soldiers in distress, or any families which had lost members during the last campaign; "this," said the circular "will be more pleasing to General Garibaldi than any rejoicings."

The *Italia* publishes an address from the Roman Ladies to Garibaldi, in which they said that "Rome may now be called the land of the dead," but that they looked for deliverance to Garibaldi.

Garibaldi replied in the following words:—

"Roman Matrons,—Rome or death! I have heard these words resound from the lovely slopes of Sebeto to the piled-up rocks of the Alps. Rome or death! That is the oath taken by the proud sons of Palestro and Palermo. Women! do not blaspheme by calling Rome the land of the dead. How could there be dead in the heart of Italy—in the heart of the world? The ashes of Rome, the ashes of her unhappy sons, have been buried, but these ashes are so impregnate with life as to be able to regenerate the world. Rome is a word that will arouse peoples as the tempest raises the waves. Rome, the mother of Italian grandeur. Was it not its history of giants, its wonderful ruins, that kindled in my young soul the flame of the beautiful, the ardour of generous designs? Rome! oh, Rome! who is not urged by thy very name to take arms for thy deliverance? Who feel not thus has not deserved the tender embrace of a mother, or the ardent kiss of a lover. Such a one has only to restore a base heart to its original clay. Ladies, I am with you to death."

The General tells us, that Ratazzi approved the plan of instituting national rifle clubs. It was desired to raise two battalions of Genoese carabineers; many young men hastened to enlist, but the project failed. Some hundreds not being able to return to their homes, associated themselves together in Lombardy for military training; the government, however, viewed their proceedings with suspicion, and made several arrests. The ministerial journals declared that it was intended to attempt an invasion of the Tyrol. This Garibaldi said was false. The cry was always, "Italy and Victor Emmanuel." It was, he continued, necessary to complete the armaments, in order to give the Italians an organization similar to that of Prussia and Switzerland The Italian Chamber of Deputies meanwhile occupied itself in discussing the question arising out of the recent arrests at Brescia and Bergamo. Bertani pressed for a full investigation into all the circumstances, and denied that the ministry possessed the confidence of the country. Crispi said that the expedition to the Tyrol was a phantom evoked by the government in order to render it easier to suppress the right of association in Italy. Garibaldi, said Crispi, never dreamt of passing the Mincio; the expedition was destined to cross the sea, and Ratazzi knew its destination: the minister promised a million of francs, arms, and ammunition. From Naples the minister had sent, only a few weeks previously, the following telegram to Garibaldi in cypher :—"The arms are ready, Garibaldi has only to sign a receipt and indicate the spot."

Crispi had asked for a secret committee, and the debate as to whether this should or should not be granted diverted the attention of the Chambers from the true question. One of the ministers, the Marquis Pepoli, who was cousin to the Emperor of the French, implored Crispi to be reserved, and not to ruin all. "Let me alone," said Crispi, who without doubt acted during the debate in the name of Garibaldi, "I will give names and dates and documents, and if you press me too far I will *bring the king also upon the scene.*" In the end the secret committee was rejected by the majority in the Chambers.

The general impression in Turin was that Ratazzi had consented to assist Garibaldi in an expedition to Dalmatia, which expedition should afterwards be directed wherever Garibaldi's genius might think fit, and it was generally supposed that these were the terms on which the left consented to support Ratazzi's ministry.

On the 15th of June (according to a letter of Madam Alberta Mario, from Casa Cairoli Belgirate, Lago Maggiore), Senator Plezza, the agent of the King, was waiting upon the General. They were closeted together some time, then they all dined together and went out for a row upon the lake. "The senator's whole soul," she says, "seemed bound up in the organization of the rifle clubs. If some of those pretended secretaries of Garibaldi were here, who write books full of falsehoods and nonsense, whereby they seek to gull the British public, they would be able to tell you the result of Plezza's conversation yesterday, of Sinco's this morning, as also the line of conduct established between the General and the members of the Emancipation Council, who have been closeted with him ever since six a.m."

CHAPTER IX.

State of parties in 1860—A united Italy in prospect—Garibaldi contemplates an Expedition—Great prospects of success—The Pope had ceased to be a Sovereign since 1860—The Romans had elected Garibaldi Chief of their Armies by Universal Suffrage—Garibaldi's opinion of the French Intervention in Mexico—He never contemplated an attack upon the French Troops at Rome—A belief entertained at Rome that an understanding existed between the King and Garibaldi—Reasons for some of the Piedmontese nobility for a Division of Italy—Garibaldi arrived at Palermo—His speech misreported—The Saturday Review on the French Emperor—Address of the people of Palermo—Arrival of Garibaldi at Marsala—His Speech to the People—Pallavicani recalled from Palermo—A deputation desires Garibaldi to march to Rome.

When, in the year 1860, General Giuseppi Garibaldi, against the consent of the government of King Victor Emmanuel, had invaded Sicily, few, probably, doubted the purity of his motives. Numbers, however, regarded the invasion as a most lawless proceeding. Naples was, at that period, a distinct kingdom. There never had been a United Italy since the time of the Roman Empire. In 1860 it was a phantom existing only in the brain of Garibaldi and the writings of Mazzini, and really believed in by very few of the followers of either; the Neapolitans themselves knew very little about constitutional governments, parliaments, or the responsibility of ministers, and the lower orders were sunk too low in the mire of ignorance and superstition to help themselves. Of the king, who lived at the foot of the snowy Alps, in the north, the vast majority had never heard. Towards Garibaldi personally there was certainly intense affection; an indistinct idea was prevalent that if he came he would deliver them from all oppression: as to how all this was to be brought about, their ideas were, indeed, very hazy. It was said that Naples should belong to Italy, or to Piedmont, because both countries spoke the same language, and even this was not correct. If this argument was tenable the Duchy of Saxe-Coburg, the kingdom of Hanover, the empire of Austria, ought all to be merged in one vast German empire. Francis II., whatever his faults might have been towards his own subjects, had given no cause of personal offence, either to Victor Emmanuel or to Garibaldi. The Neapolitan ambassador was on friendly terms with the Court of Turin, and a few of the ministers at the Neapolitan Court were apparently warmer in their professions of friendship than was the Sardinian ambassador. Yet in the face of all this the conquest of the Sicilies was effected and accepted by Victor Emmanuel and his ministry, and met with but feeble opposition from other nations. A united Italy, though still incomplete, was dawning in the horizon of European history. The expedition which Garibaldi now contemplated, although very little understood at the time, was far from being unconstitutional or illegal. Whatever the termination may have been it is certain that at the commencement there was a very reasonable prospect of success. In the first place, Rome was to have been the capital of the new kingdom. There was no Italian envoy at the papal court. On the contrary, one of the first acts of the Italian Parliament which obtained the royal consent, was to declare that Rome was the capital of Italy. The national committee at Rome, acting under instructions from Turin, had declared that no public debts contracted by the Pope after the declaration of the united parliament would ever be acknowledged by the government of Victor Emmanuel. The Pope virtually ceased to be a temporal sovereign as soon as this act became law. It was therefore to be supposed that the king would never oppose a movement to place in his hands the capital of his kingdom, which would constitute Italy upon a solid foundation. Garibaldi being the representative of the party that had both by arms and contributions brought about the annexation of Lombardy, the Emilia, Lucca, and the Tuscan provinces to the crown of Piedmont, might easily be excused, if he thought and that the acquisition of Rome would be a less difficult enterprise, that that city would be willingly accepted by the king, who had already received so much at his hands. There was also, a great difference in the condition of the Roman and of the Neapolitan people, the Neapolitans had never offered any very determined opposition to the misgovernment of their kings, however truly grateful they might have been when Garibaldi relieved them from it. The Romans, on the contrary, had protested by universal suffrage against the temporal dominion of the Pope, and had elected Garibaldi commander-in-chief of their armies.* Against the French occupation the Roman people had never ceased to protest, and they had implored Victor Emmanuel to deliver them from the most imbecile, corrupt, and tyrannical government the world had ever seen, and by continuing the occupation, Garibaldi protested that the Emperor was only prolonging the misery of the Roman people, and opposing a needless and most mischevious obstacle to the establishment of settled order throughout the peninsula. Garibaldi was fully prepared to protect the freedom

* After the disaster of Aspromonte Garibaldi wrote, "The Roman constituent assembly voted by universal suffrage, giving 143 against 5 votes for the perpetual downfall of that monstrous government. This legal vote cannot be cancelled either by the bayonets of Bonaparte or those of Austria. The right of Italy is still intact, and might be put in force by asking the Roman people again to declare their wishes by a direct vote; until a revocation of that act, I am the legal guardian of this popular right, for on me was conferred on the 30th of June, 1849, by the vote of the constituent assembly and by the triumvirate, the executive power of that time, and when they wounded me and took me prisoner at Aspromonte, I was marching towards the Eternal City, provided with those legal powers which my nation had already conferred upon me, to deliver it from the most wicked and loathsome government in the world; which every day blasphemes God in making merchandise "of Him." It is confidently believed by those who held offices of high trust about Garibaldi, in 1849, that if he had received the civil as well as the military power earlier, the history of Italy would have been written in different characters, and that very little would now been heard of the French occupation of Rome. In August, 1862, Garibaldi's greatest wish was to be engaged in transferring the legitimate power conferred upon him in 1849, into the hands of Victor Emmanuel.

and spiritual independence of the Holy Father, and was ready to give him a very large civil list, on the single condition that the inspired word of God might be open without restraint to all those Italians who might wish to peruse it. Again, during his recent tour through the northern provinces of Italy, Garibaldi had been received with a degree of enthusiasm which led him to suppose that he would have the entire support and concurrence of an immense majority of the Italian people; and it must always be remembered that in that tour he was accompanied by Senator Placca, who had been the confidential medium of communication between the king and himself throughout the campaigns of 1859, and on many subsequent occasions. Garibaldi never entertained much confidence in the ministry of Ratazzi. Their antecedents were strongly against them; but all this he had overlooked, and was willing to believe the explanations that they offered, to let the past be forgotten, and to judge them by their future actions only. It was not till after this period that he was made acquainted with Ratazzi's mission to Paris, and his plan for dividing Italy into three parts. To this plan he was himself naturally regarded as the chief obstacle. Hence the sudden abandonment of the Eastern Expedition, and the confusion and clashing of orders which so perplexed Colonel Nullo and the other chiefs who were engaged in it, and which ultimately led to the miserable affair of Sarnico. Garibaldi was fully aware that the ministers were the ministers of a foreign power, and that they sought not the union but the disunion of Italy. He believed, therefore, that he was fully justified in opposing them by any means at his command, and that by so doing he was best serving his king and his country. He was also perfectly well aware that Ratazzi did not dissolve the chambers on the ground that the answer to almost every letter and message sent to the departments, was that the Government had not the confidence of the people at large, and that members hostile to them would be returned in case of a general election.

The history of the occupation of Rome is known to all. It

commenced with the most deliberate violation of the most solemn promise,* on the part of the French National Assembly, the French ambassador, and the French general; and General Garibaldi maintained that such an occupation was to the dishonour and discredit of the French nation, and that to suppose that the majority of the educated classes in France were in favour of the maintenance of the temporal power of the Pope by French bayonets, against the will of the Roman people, was gross libel on the enlightenment of the French nation.

General Garibaldi never seriously contemplated it is supposed, any attack on the French troops in Rome, his reasons for this, will be given hereafter. The intelligence conveyed to the General of the secret transactions between the courts both of Rome and Paris was all but perfect.

* Having arrived before Rome, General Oudinot dispatched three of his officers to demand the admission of his troops, on the pretext that he had arrived to protect the city from the Austrians, and to ascertain the desire of the inhabitants with regard to the form of government they preferred. The French Assembly had, by a majority of eighty-seven votes, expressed its disapproval of the expedition to Rome. "My dear General," wrote Louis Napoleon, in bold defiance of the Assembly and its vote, "the telegraphic news announcing the unforeseen resistance you have met with under the walls of Rome, has greatly grieved me. I had hoped, as you know, that the inhabitants of Rome, opening their eyes to evidence, would receive with eagerness an army which had arrived there to accomplish a friendly and disinterested mission." Amongst other acts of friendship, the French soldiers destroyed by a mine the noted Acqua Paola aqueduct, one of the most interesting remains of old Rome then existing, an act of wanton vandalism.

The following anecdote may illustrate the General's feelings on this subject when lying very ill at the Hotel de Milan at Spezzia. He was informed that he had entirely mistaken the feelings of the French people in regard to the Roman occupation. "*The next Paris elections will best decide that point*," was the quiet reply. They did so, for of the thirty-five opposition members added to the French Chambers, thirty-four are stated to be opposed to the continued occupation of Rome.

At Spezzia the General stated to a French gentleman: "I should be sorry for it to be believed in France that at any period of my life I have desired to come into collision with the soldiers of France. I wish France to know what I now say to you, and I should be strangely forgetful of the history of the French people were I to suppose that they would see an enemy in any one who fights for the liberty of his country, whatever that country may be."

On the same day he was informed that the next mail would bring the news of the fall of Puebla. "I think you are in error respecting that, my friend," answered the General, "for I have been thinking the matter over; of course, should no European war come to distract them, the French are sure of success in the end, but I understand the kind of country in which they have to operate and the sort of people with which they have to deal, it will be some months yet before we shall hear of Puebla falling, and then, in my opinion, the real complications and difficulties of the affair will only commence." I mentioned General Garibaldi's opinion, respecting the French elections and Mexico, when in London on the 2nd of January, 1863, to my friend Mr. William Downing Bruce, of Lincoln's Inn, the Recorder of Wallingford, and to several other friends, I also called attention to these facts at the time to a gentleman connected with a London Newspaper. The opinion respecting Mexico

It was his firm belief that the Pope would never remain in Rome if the city was attacked, but would seek refuge elsewhere. He was well acquainted with the divided councils which led the Pope at a later period to summon to his presence Mr. Odo Russell,* and request the protection of a British man-of-war to convey him to Malta. He had, in fact, information of the very first summons conveyed to him by a cypher telegram, within a very few hours of its taking place; it is supposed that neither Mr. Odo Russell on the one side, nor the Pope on the other, was at all aware of this, but such was the fact. Garibaldi had his own agents in the Eternal City, his plans were fully formed, the organization was perfect, and many of the men who actually surrounded the Pontifical throne were in constant communication with them. The publication of the documents of Lansti trial also go far to prove the all but universal conspiracy in Rome against the Pontifical sovereignty.

The divisions in the counsels of the Emperor were equally well known to him, and he attached considerable importance to the brilliant speech made by Prince Napoleon, in the French Cham-

has proved correct, for from a letter by the Paris correspondent of the *Daily Telegraph* in December, 1863, that gentleman writes: "France, says the *Saturday Review*, does not like the ten millions she has to pay for her conquest, still less does she like her conquest being so uncertain after all."

Apropos of things parliamentary, I must tell you that Prince Napoleon, in his speech, will not confine himself to Poland; Italy and Mexico will each be alluded to in turn. Regarding the latter question, the following dialogue took place on Sunday, between the Prince and M. Fould: "Well, M. Fould, I am going to speak." "Yes, Sir, On Poland, no doubt." "On Poland, yes, and on Italy, and above all, on Mexico. about which I have a good deal to say that you will scarcely agree with or even like to hear." "Sir," replied the minister, "you cannot speak so badly of the business as I think of it, and if we could now retreat with honour without receiving a penny, I should be the first to say let us come away."

Another journal states, same date: "Private accounts from Mexico inform us that enormous supplies of men and money will be required to complete the conquest. The Mexicans, who are well officered, are prepared to continue a guerilla warfare to the last. * * * On the whole, this unfortunate Mexican expedition is giving the Emperor and his advisers more anxiety and annoyance than ever."

* As appears by the following letter from Mr. Layard to the secretary of the Admiralty Foreign Office, August, 26, 1862:—Sir, I am directed by Earl Russell, to request you to acquaint the Lords Commissioners of the Admiralty, that in the opinion of his lordship, Admiral Martin should have orders to accede to any request of the Pope to send a ship to Civita Vecchia to convey him to Malta. I am, &c., A. H. Layard.

bers, and to the apparent freedom of discussion which had been then allowed. He believed that Prince Napoleon, the Princess Mathilde, Monsieur Fould, and Count Persigny, held the healthy opinion that the Pope and the Italians ought to be left face to face, to settle their own difficulties in their own way; the Empress influenced by her Spanish education, Count Walewski and the majority of the Marshalls were on the other side for continuing the Roman occupation. The Pope himself and the clerical party in Turin firmly believed in a secret understanding between the king and Garibaldi, and this belief was without doubt supported by very good reasons. If Victor Emmanuel had but thrown himself into his Southern Capital of Naples, the enthusiasm of the people would have been so great, that there would have been no danger of the landing of a French Army; an entire nation would have appeared in arms, the Pope would have left Rome in an English vessel, and sought refuge in Malta, not a single French soldier would have been attacked then. Could France then have maintained her occupation, when the Pope had intrusted himself to English and not French protection. Under any circumstances the nature of the occupation must have been entirely altered, for Rome had been retained under the pretence of giving protection to the Pope. There were, however, men about Garibaldi who looked on the matter from a slightly different point of view. In the first place, with regard to the French ministry, they acknowledged the difference of opinion in the cabinet, but pointed out at the same time that, while the English ministers were responsible to parliament and the people, the French ministers were the servants, not of the country, but of the Emperor; and whatever might be their personal views and opinions, they would, when it came to the point, act in perfect conformity with his dictation.*

* The correspondent of the *Daily Telegraph*, before the outbreak of the war in 1859, prophesied that if ever Victor Emmanuel obtained a large kingdom, he would endeavour to obtain the good wishes of Napoleon, as an absolute sovereign. There were many persons in 1862 who thought they saw the first indications of the accomplishment of this prophecy. The complete Piedmontese education of the king, and

These sentiments of jealousy on the part of the king were utterly beyond the comprehension of Garibaldi, and so he refused to give them any credit. One day a letter was delivered to him, in which a distant allusion was made to this subject. Garibaldi tore it to pieces, and placed his foot upon the fragments.

There was another thing also which did not gain the consideration it deserved; that is to say, the ardent affection with which the Piedmontese regarded their capital. Even Cavour had spoken in the Chambers of the regret with which he should regard the abandonment of Turin for Rome. All the other Italian principalities had willingly resigned their capitals, believing in the early possession of Rome, and of this Turin had, up to that time, reaped the entire advantage. The value of house property was more than trebled, and the commerce and general prosperity of the chief town of a petty state were increased prodigiously through its sudden advancement to the dignity of being capital of a great kingdom. The British ambassador had the utmost difficulty in obtaining a house at any price. Suppose Rome was obtained by Garibaldi, what a change this would be for the Piedmontese. Turin would no longer be the chief city;* the

---

the ministers by whom he was surrounded, were not, they thought, properly taken into consideration,—for instance, Madlle. Rossins, the daughter of the corporal who taught the king fencing, had been created Countess of Miraflore, and some have thought that the king has since been privately married to her. The correspondent of the *Times*, writing from Turin, asserts that the king had not a single reputable companion. Mr. Dicey, in his life of Cavour, page 29, states:—"You could not find a life of Antony without alluding to Cleopatra, or draw a true character of Victor Emmanuel without referring to the *Chroniques Scandaleuses* of the city of Turin." The correspondent of the *Daily Telegraph*, writing in 1862, stated that the king had very few reputable companions, either men or women, about him. The personal jealousy he was supposed to have manifested towards Garibaldi, in 1860, was noticed by the correspondent of the *Times*, just before the first expedition to Sicily. The treatment which Garibaldi had received at the hands of the king was also remembered in Garibaldi's recent tour in the north of Italy. It has been remarked that amidst the deafening popular shouts for Garibaldi, the king's name was never heard, except from the lips of Garibaldi himself.

* On this subject the *Times*' correspondent, writing on the 31st of October, 1863, states, "Among the many changes which have taken place in Italy since 1859, none is perhaps more striking than that which has come over the town of Turin. The little capital of the Subalpine Kingdom, was notoriously the dullest town for its size in Italy the glory of being the capital of Italy may be short-lived, but it is well gilt while it lasts. The Piedmontese, as is but just, has got the lion's share in all good things, and Turin is making hay while the sun shines. Dozens of new hotels have been started, and the existing ones increased in many instances, and yet all are full. It was quite a piece of good luck that the town was too large for its resident population."

nobility who wished to follow the Court, would have to give up the houses in which their ancestors had dwelt for centuries; the establishments of the King would consequently be broken up, and he would be compelled to pass the greater part of the year at the seat of his Government. So complete, in short would be the change of life, habits and ideas, that there can be but little doubt that many of the nobility would have much preferred the adoption of the scheme proposed by Napoleon III. for dividing Italy into three parts, dissipating thereby their own ideas of the discomfort, which they imagined they should incur by a change of residence to Rome. Should there be any doubt that this statement correctly represents the views of a large party in Piedmont, the author would recommend the attentive perusal of a recent debate in the Italian Parliament, on which occasion the present ministers of the King of Italy speak of the French occupation of Rome with extreme tenderness, and in strange contrast to the straight forward manly declarations of Lord Palmerston respecting the acts of atrocious ruffianism perpetrated by the bandits at Rome.

Large bodies of brigands were in the habit of marching out of Rome fully armed and equipped, spreading devastation whereever they went. Was such a state of things to be tolerated in the nineteenth century? It was to redress these crying evils, and to introduce constitutional liberty in place of despotism that Garibaldi desired to obtain for his country the capital guaranteed by the parliament, and so to add the brightest gem he had yet gained to the diadem of the king. This it was that induced him to embark a second time at Genoa for Sicily, accompanied by many of his principal officers and advisers. These men fully participated in his views and in his hopes of success. He had been preceded by the Marquis Pallavicini, as governor of the island, who, when he accepted that post from the government, distinctly avowed his admiration of Garibaldi, and his irrevocable detemination to co-operate with him in every way. After this statement his appointment was confirmed,

Garibaldi wrote to the people of Sicily, the following letter:—

"People of Sicily!—Giorgio Pallavicini, the friend of my heart, is about to leave for Sicily to undertake the duties of the government which has been entrusted to him. This appointment of the martyr of Spielberg and the veteran of Italian liberty, is a good omen for your city of barricades, and in recommending him to you I fulfil a duty dedicated by my heart. Yours for life,

G. Garibaldi."

It was on the 28th of June that Garibaldi arrived at Palermo to raise his cry of "Rome or Death." The princes had preceded him a day or two before, and were then on a visit to the Marquis Pallavicini, who was just installed in his new office. His reception was most enthusiastic. The young princes were then at the opera, they had been well received and the house was crowded; all on a sudden everyone left the house, and the actors looked as though they wished to follow. The princes were left alone in the royal box, and on demanding the cause of the phenomenon, they were informed that Garibaldi had arrived. During his entire stay in the island it was always the same. Some of his speeches respecting the Emperor, were considered to be too violent to be politic, but it must be remembered in his defence, that he regarded Napoleon as the protector of the brigands, who were at that moment deluging his native land with blood. He was firmly persuaded of the Emperor's intention to divide Italy, and to secure a large portion of her territories for a prince of his house.

The speeches of Garibaldi were much misreported, and so strangely exaggerated that when he was shown a report of one of them, he answered with a smile—"This is really not worth contradicting. Every one who knows me will know at once that I am perfectly incapable of uttering such words." He spoke as follows, from the balcony of that palace from which he had so often previously addressed the people: "Two years since," said the General, "from this balcony I recounted to you a conference I had just held with two Bourbon generals. I told you the conditions accepted, because they were humane, such as the restitution of the wounded these I knew would awake an echo in your generous hearts, but when I came to certain humiliating conditions offered by them, I heard a sound that seemed a hoarse roar. No, those terms you refused to a man! That day the unity of Italy was irrevocably decreed! on that day the aspirations of 19 centuries were realized in the formula, "One Italy and Victor Emmanuel;" that formula is ours, we proclaimed it, amid the rude clash of arms on the plains of Calatafimi. We re-echoed it as we entered Palermo from the Termini gate. Let us now bring to a reality what was then but an idea. That principle gave us strength to fight our enemies, and to drive them out with the butt-end of our muskets. That principle will conduct us to Rome—yes, and to Venice also; I need not tell you that I am your friend, and that our friendship was created in the hour of danger and of glory; rely upon that friendship, give heed to my words, you know that I can never betray you. This principle of which I have spoken must lead us to the final victory. Human nature, alas! is not perfect, there are bad men who are influenced by bad motives, by ambition, by selfishness. These men are really like the cholera. Such men preach Muratism, which is one of the plagues of Italy, and would lead to a rupture of our national strength and end in despotism. Murat was a despot, and his relation still nourishes the cancer that consumes the heart of Italy. He engages mercenaries, and forms them into bands of hired brigands. I must tell you the truth. Napoleon, the autocrat, the powerful tyrant of France, is no friend of ours.* The people of Italy must be un-

* Garibaldi is not the only person who can say severe things of the Emperor, as will appear by the following extract from an article in the *Saturday Review*, of Dec. 19, 1863:—"When the year brought round the anniversary of the day which rewarded the Emperor for staking all his fortune on one last desperate cast, by permitting him to crush out the liberties of his country, he must have felt something of the weariness and despair which attend the never-ending struggle to retain a power ill-got and constantly threatened. The penalty which men like Louis Napoleon pay for their misdeeds is that they are never safe. He has done much in his time of which he may be reasonably proud. He has carried out some ideas to which he is sincerely attached. He has relieved the anxious melancholy of his temperament by a career of splendid excitement. But he has to work and to struggle for the main-

deceived; I do not speak to you of the French people: like ourselves they have need of liberty, to-day, unfortunately, they are dragged down by despotism, but they are our brethren, and you must learn to distinguish between the oppressor and the oppressed. The people of France, the people of Germany, the people everywhere are our brethren, another evil like the serpent in the grass is re-appearing. Bourbonism treated too tenderly, only abuses our forbearance. The General concluded by thanking the people for the affectionate manner in which they had treated him.

One object that Garibaldi had in remaining a few days at Palermo was to attend upon the young heir-apparent, and to be present with him at the inauguration of the rifle clubs. It produced an excellent impression upon the people to see their hero manifesting his affection for the young prince in so many ways, and treating him, at the same time, with the greatest respect. It was on the 29th day after his arrival that Garibaldi, accompanied by the royal princes and the Prefect of Palermo, inaugu-

---

tenance of his empire as much as he had ten years ago. He finds that, although France sees nothing but the empire before her, and acquiesces in the empire, and allows that the empire suits some of her tastes, yet she will not pay the price which the empire really costs. She will not give up all liberty of opinion, she will not mould herself wholly on the pattern of Imperialism, she even sometimes prefers giving a marked and open defiance to the empire rather than abandon all care for her own concerns. The second return of M. Pelletan for a central district of Paris is a great blow to the Emperor, and we may be sure that he feels it to be so. Every art was used, every decency was violated, every falsehood that could be devised was circulated, every possible abuse of power short of denying the liberty of voting was called in aid, in order that this dreaded defeat of the Government might be avoided. M. Pelletan was proclaimed in official placards to be the worst, the lowest, the most degraded of men. He was false to every tie of honour and patriotism. He hated France; he mourned for the victories of her glorious soldiery; he was the foe of the poor man; he was for getting up bloody, idle, and eternal revolutions. And, worse than all, he had been guilty of a new and peculiar crime. He had invented a special and original atrocity. He had actually dared to criticise Béranger. This awful announcement was supposed to be certain to thrill the hearts of Paris soldiers and Paris artisans. Other Frenchmen have been impious, Voltairian, atheistic; but M. Pelletan had gone further than this, and had published an unfavourable literary criticism on the poet who sang of French grissettes and French soldiers as no one else ever sang before or since. On the other hand, the Government candidate was the pearl and flower of Parisian mankind. He had been poor, and now was very rich. He was intensely respectable. He believed in the *Bon Dieu* and the Emperor' and was utterly incapable of writing any literary criticism whatever. And yet, in spite of all this, the district has gone wrong. It has taken the wicked critic and rejected the good industrial: it has endangered the cause of order, and affronted the Emperor, and wronged the precious memory of Lisette, by giving M.

rated the National Rifle Clubs. The fête was most splendid and the most perfect order, notwithstanding the volatile nature of the people (such was the ardent devotion they entertained for Garibaldi), reigned throughout this city of 200,000 inhabitants. The General several times addressed the multitude, and always upon the necessity of concord. "There are two men," he said, in conclusion of one of his addresses, "who will never deceive you. Listen to them: they are Victor Emmanuel and myself. Rome and Venice will be ours before long. To attain this object we must make any sacrifice with resignation. Italy must be one—one—one."

All accounts confirm the intense rapture of the reception given to Garibaldi. At Palermo the following address was delivered to nearly 100,000 people:—"My dear friends, I am deeply gratified for your enthusiasm and all your love for me, I owe you in return the most perfect openness and truth. My friends, I do not belong to the Church of the Pope, and I even desire to cleanse the Eternal City from the clerical abominations accumulated during a thousand years of temporal sovereignty and iniquitous misgovernment. I am, however, a member of that catholic church, the doctrines of which Christ our Saviour came on earth to preach, and I implore you to distinguish between the true servants of Christ and the servants of the Devil. Where

---

Pelletan a startling and overwhelming majority. Nor is it Paris only that has been false to the empire. Dijon—a great centre of trade, and one of the most rising towns in France—has also rejected the Government candidate, and taken a man who is not, perhaps, so lost to all that is good in humanity as to criticise Béranger, but who is pledged to support that Opposition which will soon make its voice heard in France. When the Opposition begins to speak, it will have plenty to say. Even in the Senate, things have been uttered that the Emperor can scarcely have liked. M. De la Guerronnière himself, who now holds a sort of semi-independent position, and has a court influence of his own, rebelled at the flagrant absurdity of complimenting the Emperor on the July elections. This was going too far. It was as if the House of Commons in the old days had been asked to pass a vote of thanks to George IV. for his conduct to Queen Caroline. The disgraceful scandals in the management of these elections which have lately been revealed may be passed over by fervent admirers of the Emperor in silence, as a sad necessity of the times, but surely they are among the things of which the less said the better."

Lord Palmerston stated in his place in the House, May 9, 1863:—"In Rome there is a French garrison, under its shelter there exists a committee of 200, whose practice is to organise a band of murderers, the scum and dross of every nation, and send them into the Neapolitan territory to commit every atrocity." Tolerably strong this, and certainly very true.

the priests are good the people are good. You have good priests, they are Christ's true followers, and therefore no one will ever deceive you who brings you the word of God open in his hand. What I want you fully to understand is that Christ came to redeem mankind, and his atonement is full and sufficient for those who believe the everlasting truths of the gospel. Freedom goes hand in hand with the gospel, and those only are Christ's followers who preach its entire doctrines. The great evil I pointed out long ago to the people of Naples, I point out to you to-day—that evil is the Pope, and I warn you again to distinguish the true priests from the false, between the priests who are the ministers of God, and the priests who are the ministers of the Devil. Remember above all that Christ called those who followed him brothers; therefore, city must not be divided from city, or family from family. Brotherhood not only means that we should work together for great things, but that we should live together in perfect concord, and in this concord will be our strength. No more jealousy between Sicilians and Neapolitans, between Piedmontese and Lombards. We are all one family, we are Italians, above all we are Christians. Concord between province and province becomes concord between family and family. Those who love their country and their God, must pardon each other. If any of you nourish hatred in your hearts, lay it bare, and forgive those who have injured you. I implore it of you in all affection, and now it only remains for me to thank you for your reception, and to tell you how happy I am to be once more amongst you. At the conclusion of the General's address, the enthusiasm of the people was unbounded—women wept—old men brought their sons to be blessed, all knelt; the General's manner was calm and solemn, his voice clear and ringing like a silver bell. The expression used about the Pope may, perhaps, be considered strong. It should always, however, be remembered that Garibaldi spoke with the full and perfect knowledge of the facts. It is to be hoped that the present committee on brigandage will give to the public those facts, proving, as they do, most fully, the complicity of the pontificial government with the support and payment of brigands and murderers, who are let loose in large bands to prey upon the peaceable inhabitants of lovely Naples ; their object being to upset the throne of King Victor Emmanuel, and to restore to the Bourbons their ancient dominions. A quiet, prosperous, and contented Italy would be to the reactionists what Paradise was to Satan, and they therefore resolved to make Italy, if possible, the dismal and terrible place they represent it to be. To effect this object they scruple not at the means, and deeds are continually being committed which would be a disgrace even to savages.*

The *Correspondance de Rome* has an article headed "Garibaldi and Palmerston." "The first of these two men," it stated, "is not in our eyes, worse company than the second. He is only less culpable, less loaded with horrible crimes, for which history and God have terrible judgments." The Filibuster with a red shirt, says, "that Rome is the ulcer of Italy, the impenitent octogenarian, cries out at table, that the Pope is the incubus of Italy, thus, they are both rivetted to the same chain and serve the same master. This excites in our hearts, hopes for a more complete vengance."

On the arrival of Garibaldi at Marsala, the municipality, the National Guard and its commander went out two leagues from the town to receive and to congratulate the General. Thousands of flags floated from the windows, and, in the midst of deaffening peals of cheering from ten thousand voices, the procession arrived at the cathedral, where the clergy awaited its entry. After a

* On the 3rd of February, 1863, news arrived that four officers who had been betrayed and murdered by the brigands, had their hearts torn out and carried about on the points of bayonets, amidst cries of "Viva il nostro Papa!" "Viva Francesco secondo il nostro rè!" Their ears were also cut off. The authority for this statement is E. Riccardi, deputy of the Italian parliament. On another occasion, forty soldiers of the line were shot, and Captain Rota, who commanded them (one of the thousand of Marsala) was burnt alive on a large heap of straw. This took place since the tragedy of Aspromonti, and is quoted to show there has been no change for the better, on the part of the Bourbons. The author could easily fill a volume with well-authenticated instances of robbery and murder that disgraced the early part of the year 1862.

hymn and benediction, Garibaldi was about to leave the church, when a strange scene took place. A monk ascended the pulpit and addressed the people in language so touching, that when he had concluded, Graibaldi went up to him and embraced him affectionately.

At Marsala, the General spoke as follows—in voice calm and solemn—which is the clear and powerful expression of the Italian idea which is incarnate in him :—"The time has come," said he, "when we can no longer permit the stranger on our soil, holding in slavery a portion of our brethren. Italy can no longer abide this shame: this is a shame for 25,000,000! and it must cease. Shortly, yes, shortly Rome is ours; yes, Rome, or death! It was from Marsala that the cry of liberty went forth; from Marsala let this cry go forth to-day—Rome, or death! and this cry will resound not only on the peninsula, but will find an echo throughout all Europe, and wherever the name of Liberty has not been profaned. We only want what belongs to us. Yes, that which belongs to us; for Rome is ours. [The crowd: 'Rome, or Death!'] This cry will weigh more in the balance of diplomacy than all the prayers in the world. He made the war of 1859 not for us, but for himself, we gave him our blood in the Crimean war, we paid him 60 millions, we go to him with Savoy and Nice; and he wanted more: I know it. He acted for the aggrandisement of his family; he has a petty prince ready for Rome, a petty lord for Naples, and so on: I know it. He wished us to be his subjects. He is the *enemy* of Italy; he has kept up and keeps up brigandage for the destruction of the Neapolitan provinces; he has scandalised all Europe in the vain hope of breaking the sinews of 25,000,000 of Italians. We need not stoop to solicit such a man. The French people are with us. Let Napoleon *fall*, and Rome is our own! I am happy to-day at being with you. I have good reason for being your friend. Adieu!"

The Marquis Pallavicini was recalled from Palermo by the government for applauding Garibaldi's speeches, in consequence of the protest of the French Consul at Palermo, against the attacks made upon the Emperor. Letters from Sicily stated that Garibaldi had won over all to his cause; he told them, that the time for words had gone, and the time for action had come, that more than twenty thousand of them had presented to him an address, telling him that they wanted no more vain talk, that they were convinced of the truth of his sayings, that their weapons were ready, and that they only waited for his summons. To this Garibaldi answered:—"You understand me and I understand you: provide yourselves each with a musket; practise, be silent, and when I call, let each one answer "present." Volunteers arrived without inconvenience at Palermo, and departed for Garibaldi's Camp, without the slightest hindrance. The garrisons went every where out of the General's way, but the mounted police, organized under military discipline, received him in full parade. A concert was announced at Palermo in support of Garibaldi's troops: about 3,000 tickets at a dollar a piece were sold; the Governor, General Lugia himself took fifty, and the Colonel of the Piedmontese regiment in the garrison, immediately complied with the request of lending the regimental Band for the purpose. Girgenti sent him 40,000 francs, voted by the common council, and subscriptions at Palermo were published every day in the papers; amongst others, we find the names of the Archbishop of Palermo, the cannons of the Chapter, and the Duke of St. Elie, who had hitherto been amongst the strongest supporters of the Ministry. Garribaldi also issued treasury bills, which were accepted by the community without hesitation. The public authorities did not interfere with his movements, nor did they hinder the augmentation of the volunteer army.

The following reply was made by Garibaldi to the Duke della Verdura and the Deputy Logia, who were commissioned by General Cugia, the Prefect of Palermo, to read to him the proclamation of the king:—"King Victor Emmanuel speaks as a king, and it is his duty to do so, when the circumstances of the nation and diplomacy require it. I respect the elect of the nation, but I go whither the aspirations of the Italians call me. If I had listened to the counsels of prudence and diplomacy, neither you or I would be in Sicily at this moment, and the Bourbon flag would still be floating over the strongholds of Francis II.

Shortly afterwards, Garibaldi received at his residence, a deputation of noblemen and gentlemen. He told them that his programme was always the same, and that no one would be able to change his design of marching upon Rome. The ministers could not, because he was acting by the will of the nation, and by the will of the king. On another occasion, he stated, that all was completely known to the king, and that therefore, nothing could stop him on the way to Rome, the city which had been proclaimed "the capital of Italy," by the will of the entire nation, confirmed by parliament, and recognised by several foreign powers.*

---

* The *Times'* correspondent at Turin had not recently favoured Garibaldi, nor did he look for his successes. The last enterprise he censured, and opposed from first to last with a vigour that seemed to some persons absolutely savage. Yet, what says he now? In another part of this paper will be found the statement of his belief that Garibaldi had good reason to believe himself backed by the king and government; that he had, and perhaps has, papers which sufficed to satisfy the local authorities wherever he went, that he was acting on high authority, and that the king himself corresponded with him so much a little before his last movement, that it is morally certain he must be in possession of very compromising confidences, and the king a party to very awkward, though easily broken understandings.—*Sept.*, 1862.

The correspondent of the *Daily Telegraph*, writing from Turin, September 2nd, 1863, says:—"I may, perhaps, be allowed to state in a few words that Ratazzi's hope was to get Garibaldi into the east, and to put him in a position in which, if successful, he might be backed, and if he failed, be betrayed and deserted. That design failing, Garibaldi was allowed, if not encouraged to go to Sicily. * * It was deliberately proposed to betray him. If the organs of that Government who planned Garibaldi's betrayal will re-open the question they must forgive us who unfortunately know some few of the details, if we do return to that unhappy subject. I close these remarks by saying that if circumstances had allowed Baron Ricasoli to retain office till the 3rd of March, there would then have been no Aspromonte. English readers must, I fear, take my word for this strong statement, but the Senator Plezza and Cavalier Celestino Bianchi are the authorities I offer in *confirmation to any Italian reader*.

The fact which may show, to a certain degree, that General Garibaldi had reason to reckon on the consent—on the silent consent at least—of the Turin Government, is the following:—

The General had gone, early in the morning, to *la Fienzza*. Everybody in Palermo knew his intention, and openly talked of it.

On the evening of that same day, many young men in red shirts and with guns on their shoulders, were walking about the town in the presence of the troops and of the royal gendarmes. They publicly greeted and embraced their relatives and their friends, announcing their departure for the camp.

Besides, two hundred volunteers, who had come from Upper Italy, principally

This was not the first time that there was a clashing of instructions in Sicily; in 1860, the king, at the request of the French Emperor, wrote, that he always disapproved of the expedition, and ordered Garibaldi not to cross over to the mainland; yet, on the 19th of June, in the same year, Cavour sent word to his confidential agent, La Farina, "Persano will aid you in everything *without compromising our flag*;" what a fine thing if Garibaldi should pass over into Calabria.

Had Garibaldi, when he crossed over in 1860, been defeated, he would not have had a line to show in defence of his conduct, for Cavour's letter was to his own confidential agent. So difficult is it to write with truth, modern Italian history.

Another curiosity of official correspondence was a letter from Admiral Albine, who commanded the Royal Italian Fleet, addressed to General Garibaldi, and written by order of the ministers at Turin. By this letter he placed the ships under his command at the General's disposal, and engaged to take him and his troops wherever he liked to go. The orders were, that he was to be taken to any port on the mainland he pleased. Just at the first instance Garibaldi was inclined to accept the offer, but the wonderful intelligence he received undeceived him. He was informed that the offer came from the ministers, and believing the ministers to be the servants of the Emperor, Garibaldi instantly suspected mischief, and returned to his original plan. When this letter came out, and was discussed in the Chambers, one of the ministers unblushingly asserted, 'Oh, if we had only got him on board we should have done what we liked with him, and taken him where we thought fit." So much for the honour of Italian statesmen of the Turin school.

Lombards and Tuscans, had remained at Palermo, consigned to Missor and Guergoni, to be organized into a special body, and armed. They assembled for this operation in a country-house, at the distance of a mile from Palermo, where the arms and equipments had been prepared. In order to be left free in their work, they had placed all round the place, sentries and outposts, who cried the *qui vive* to every person who approached the house. The Gendarmes themselves had to answer to the *qui vive* of the red shirts. Towards ten o'clock in the evening the armed columns of the Garibaldians began to move from Palermo, without meeting with any obstacle in their march.

Garibaldi did not receive at Aspromonte any summon to surrender. The fire began without any previous notice or message to signify the last decisions of the Government.

CHAPTER X.

Garibaldi's arrival at Catania—Great rejoicings—Father Pantaleone's address—Enthusiasm of the people—Garibaldi meets General Mella at Catania—The General declares he was not hostile—Garibaldi's communication to the king—The freedom of the press suppressed—The Commander of the National Guard declares in favour of the movement—Desertions from the Royal Army—Colonel La Porta resigns his seat in parliament to join the Garibaldians—Garibaldi writes twice to the king—The Royal Troops continue to desert—Volunteers increase—Rattazzi encourages and then turned against Garibaldi—Crispi denounces the ministers—50,000 of the people call upon the king to dismiss his ministers—Garibaldi seizes the French Postal Steamers—His volunteers embark in the Dispaccio and the General Abbalucci—No opposition offered by the French and Piedmont men of war—His proclamation previous to Aspromonti—Declares his hostility to the ministry—Is resolved to enter Rome a conqueror.

As soon as it became known that Garibaldi was coming, Catania became frantic; the bells were ringing a merry peal; every balcony was lit with lamps; torches rose in price, everybody sought to buy one; every cab in the city was occupied by the people who desired to meet the great hero, for his arrival could no longer be impeded. At midnight, on the heights of Mister bianca, a hundred torch-bearers were to be seen shouting and dancing: they knew the General was in sight. In a few minutes afterwards he arrived. On meeting Mordini, the latter observed: "General, the first step must be Catania; the second, Rome; the third, Venice." Garibaldi sent to the commander of the royal troops at Taterno to request an interview. The major came, and said he had positive orders not to allow the General to enter the town. The General replied, he did not intend to enter the borough, but he required provisions, his troops being weary and hungry after the long march: they would remain outside the town. The major gave his consent; but, whilst the provisions were being sought, the population, about 12,000 souls, grew excited, the bells were rung, processions bearing banners were formed, and deputations went down to Garibaldi inviting him to enter the town, whilst the women brought their children to be blessed by him. Many people knelt down before him in tears, overpowered as they were by emotion The young men of Catania went further. Armed with hatchets and big knives, they cut a path through the fig trees around the town. The proprietors of the gardens opened the doors, and Garibaldi and his men entered by that new way, through the upper end of the borough. The streets and the Market-place were thronged with a compact crowd, and the vivas announced to the royal troops that resistance was impossible. Garibaldi's troops took some refreshment and continued their forced march, but every one was happy. Many hours before the General arrived, great demonstrations were preparing. The people in the streets said to one another that Garibaldi was sure to come, that the Governor had his carriage ready to fly, in case of need. At five o'clock, several thousand men appeared in the streets, all of them wearing a card on their hats with the printed words, "Viva Vittorio Emanule, Viva Garibaldi, Abasso Rattazzi, Roma o Morte." Scarcely had they assembled on the Market place, when suddenly a carriage drove through the crowd to the Music stand of the band, and Father Pantaleone, Garibaldi's well known field chaplain ascended the steps; he was received with cheers, and he made a speech to the population, taking for his text the inscription on the printed card, which spoke out the feelings of the meeting. The governor did not interfere with the demonstration, or attempt to disperse it. The National Guard was not called out under arms, as it had been a few days back, upon a similar but less numerous demonstration. But to return to Garibaldi, at two at night he arrived at the gate. The illuminations, the flags, the torch light procession, and the frantic joy of the population was great; the Market place was illuminated with electric light. Garibaldi drove to the Club House, and made a speech from the balcony, in which he thanked the people of Catania for the hearty reception which had put the seal upon the liberation of Italy: "We shall soon certainly reach Rome:" said the General. The crowd shouted in reply, "Roma o Morte." "Yes, we shall reach Rome, the sacerdotal vampire shall cease to suck the life and blood of humanity, and Rome shall return to the pure gospel of Christ." This speech raised the enthusiasm to the highest pitch, priests and monks, men and women shouted Viva Garibaldi! Roma o Morte! At four we went to bed, but at seven, we were suddenly aroused by the information that the Royal troops were at only one hour's distance. The General ordered the alarm bell to be rung, and sent for the commander of the National Guard. In a quarter of an hour, barricades were building, the Volunteers and National Guard were under arms, and every means of defence was adopted. In about an hour it was known that the Royal troops who had advanced close to the outskirts of the town had again retired, and were encamped at Misterbianco. They had on the way arrested all Garibaldi's stragglers, and disarmed them as prisoners of war. In town, however, there was still one company whose commander came to Garibaldi with the request to be allowed to evacuate the barracks, and to join the army encamped at Misterbianco. Garibaldi gave at once orders not to molest those soldiers on their march. The members of the Italian Parliament present at Catania, nine in number, with Mordini at their head, went to the royal camp, and demanded of Major-General Mella, whether it was his intention to attack Catania. They returned in the evening; he had engaged himself not to attack the town, he declared he was not hostile to Garibaldi, and pretended not even to have known of his arrival at Catania. When the troops were marching to the vicinity of the town, he at once liberated his prisoners, those poor stragglers who had remained on the way, worn out by that terrible forced march from Regalbutto to Catania, and he requested Garibaldi to be allowed to get his provisions from Catania, which was at once granted. An Italian, extensively engaged in banking concerns, who had just arrived from Turin, stated that the general faith in the ultimate attainment of Italian unity was as great as ever it was throughout the whole country. The ministry, he said, and he was not in the least a party man, had entirely lost its prestige, owing to the insincerity with which it was discovered to have treated Garibaldi and the public, alike, and possibly the king also, and because it stood self-convicted of incompetency. The public in general did not fear any imperial treachery with regard to the threatened occupation of Naples by French troops, and this not because there was any very profound faith in the purity of the Emperor's intentions; but because Italy through its length and breadth believed that England (which it supposes upon points of vital policy in "dernier ressort" invariably influences Napoleon's policy) would never allow a breach of the principle of non-intervention. At the time this gentleman left Turin nothing was known as to the two fleets having been ordered to the bay of Naples; the reports, however, that the English had threatened to occupy Sicily, should a French armed force be ordered to land at Naples were perfectly correct. Such reports he ascribed to the fact that the act so threatened would simply be a necessity of the situation should the contingency contemplated arise. As to civil war in the proper sense of the term he stated the idea was only worthy of ridicule. There could be no civil war. Garibaldi was well known to have communicated to the king the sentiment that he would never *distract the country with civil war, and that he would rather die than draw his sword against an Italian soldier*. Garibaldi was merely striving on this occasion in his own way for what the government itself wanted, but which it was obviously unable to attain in its way. Garibaldi believed the country would speak out if he afforded it the means. As a strong proof of the confidence which animated the country at large, there was no slackening in the energy with which the new public works were urged forward. The Cavour Canal—a great irrigation work, the shares of which were at a considerable premium, not only in Turin, but in Milan and Genoa, although it had not then been commenced. The prestige of Garibaldi at Turin was every day increasing. He did not lose one moment's time in organizing his troops. The greatest calmness reigned in Catania. Though the governor had embarked on the *Maria Adelaide* he yet remained in port. The municipality performed their attributions as regularly as ever. All the shops were open, the courts of justice continued their business, and the town looked as quiet as before. A telegram had been intercepted, by which it appeared that the island of Sicily had been put into a state of siege. Rattazzi's infatuation became incredible, and Victor Emmanuel could not retain the fair name of the *Re-Galantuomo*, or could he bombard Messina, Catania and Palermo, like Ferdinand of Naples. Garibaldi's flag still bore the inscription "Italy and Victor Emmanuel." At last the freedom of the press, the right of association were suppressed, public meetings were forbidden. Rattazzi had evidently made his studies at Paris with great success; he was introducing into Italy liberty as it is understood in France and Dopretis, only lately one of the chiefs of the left was not ashamed to retain his seat in the cabinet. It was true that the proclamation by which the island was put in a state of siege, was signed by Gugia, but his want of decision was well known: he never would have undertaken the responsibility of such a serious step, unless he had received precise orders from Turin. In the meantime Catania was perfectly quiet, all the different political parties and classes were busy to further Garibaldi's plans. Marchese Cassalotto, the commander of the National Guard, and Messrs. Gravina and Candullo, the chiefs of the conservative party at Catania, visited the General, and told him openly, that though they disapproved of the movement when it was initiated, they now would do their best to add to its forces, since the will of the people could not any longer be doubted. As to the population, its sentiments were already expressed by the spontaneous illumination of all the streets for the fourth time, and by the frantic evvivas to Garibaldi as often as he showed himself. Desertion began to thin the ranks of the Royal troops; a sergeant, 28 men with bag and baggage came to exchange their good pay and fare for the fatigue and dangers of Garibaldi's camp; and eventually the commander of the garrison was obliged to withdraw, so that the soldiers might not pass over entirely to the volunteers. From Misterbianco, volunteers continued to arrive in great numbers, sixty within two days; thirty officers of the regular army resigned their commissions rather than march against Garibaldi. A battalion of Bersaglieri was placed at the outposts near the Garibaldians. On the next day it was discovered that a hundred men had gone over to Garibaldi. To avoid further desertions, the battalion was hastily embarked and sent to Genoa. On reaching Centorbi, the General's arrival surprised the population; they were not aware of his approach. It was Sunday, they were at home, and in a moment assembled around him with cheers and a hearty welcome; the bells rang joyous peals, the members of the band of the National Guard sought to make their way through the population, in order to form their rank whilst Garibaldi rode to church, and after short prayers took his way to a point which overlooked the country around. Returning to the town, the usual bustle of head-quarters recommenced: deputations to Garibaldi; persons waiting to be introduced; the mayor of the borough excusing himself about the scarcity of provisions for such unexpected guests; the officers of the staff seeking the quarters to which they had been billeted; Colonel Corte, the chief of the staff, commanding and bringing order out of the confusion; Civinini, the General's private secretary, writing orders; the young Marquis Maurigi copying them; Baron Varesano, a Sicilian nobleman, with a mediæval cast of features, enhanced by a splendid flowing beard, stretching his bulky body on a couch. Baron Nicotera, member of parliament, going about to seek information, whilst coffee, wine, and bread were served up to Colonels Nullo, Bruzzesi, and Missori, old Mignona, of Naples, Guerzoni, and others.

Garibaldi wrote twice to the king to assure him of his unshaken fidelity. He dined with the Cavaliere Marco the Prefect of Caltonesetta, with all his officers, after the king had issued a proclamation against him. The General proposed on this occasion: "To the health of Victor Emmanuel, crowned in the Campidoglio!" Garibaldi was in the habit of repeating *incessantly* "There will be *no civil war!*" From Palermo there was the astonishing information that, on Monday night, the population made a most summary demonstration, proclaiming Garibaldi's entry into Catania. The Governor-General, Cugia, sent his aides-de-camp to let the people know that such an event was impossible; but, whilst he was giving his orders, the dispatch arrived by the wires confirming the news which the Palermetans had guessed by instinct. There was a still more serious movement at Messina. The population literally flared-up. Such was the enthusiasm, that the governor was frightened, and sent his baggage on board the government steam boat. The three principal towns in Sicily having thus solemnly approved of Garibaldi's progress, the government forgetting that Victor Emmanuel was king, by the will of the nation, thought themselves authorized to declare the state of siege, but this proclamation was but a waste paper. The Sicilians who were not cowed by the Bourbons, cared little for Ratazzi's threats. The desertion from the royal army continued to increase. The generals of the royal army fearing a complete disorganization, retired from the neighbourhood of the town. At Messina the National Guard had been disarmed, because a general rising against the garrison was expected. With the exception of the commander of the National Guard, all the officers sided with Garibaldi. An English frigate arrived in the port of Catania, and cast anchor between the Duke of Genoa and the town. The English and French consuls sent a written protest to the captain of the royal frigate against any eventive attack. It was morally impossible to bombard any town in Sicily, since Victor Emmanuel's tenure of the island was only by good will, his title held good, though the Piedmontese bureaucracy were generally abhorred, because Garibaldi's name, which was deeply rooted in the hearts of the Sicilians, still covered that of the king, whose government treated the General as a rebel. The enlistment of the volunteers continued, and the organization of the army was in progress. The companies and battalions had commenced to take a regular form; a few days more and the army look most respectable. The officers wore no distinctive sign of rank; it was by the sabre alone that they were recognised. The Government telegrams of the *Agenzia Stefani* excited general indignation by their imprudent misstatements to the effect that Garibaldi had established everywhere a new administration, and assumed dictorial power.

It was about this period that Pulszky wrote, stating General Cialdini had had a conference, at Naples, with General La Marmora, and they were said to have taken measures to destroy* The *Popolo l'Italia*, of the 15th of August made the following statements:—"From the moment that Garibaldi began making the round of Sicily, he always urged the volunteer youths, hastening to join him, not to leave the continent. Ratazzi, on the contrary, and we have proofs in our hands, favoured the embarkation of these youths. The object was to place Garibaldi in an equivocal position, finding himself surrounded by ardent and willing youths, Garibaldi directed his friends, also, on the continent to prevent the departure of other youths, and we have always executed his orders, persuading the youths not to go. When Signor Ratazzi saw that his acts had attained the object in

* This telegram caused an uneasy feeling in the minds of those who believed in the reported jealousy which was said to have been infused into the mind of an illustrious personage, but when they had safely reached the mainland they all believed their doubts to have been groundless, and that success was certain.

uniting in Sicily the best and most ardent patriots, he turned round, sent an army, put the king forward, and threw down the apple of civil war. They wished to involve Garibaldi, and then to fight him, when they saw that the number of volunteers then dispatched heard the powerful voice of the General, and that the pure and Italian conception of Rome was giving a direction to the portion very different from that established in the Colloquies of Paris, then Ratazzi and the Emperor awoke: they thought they were near the realization of their plot, and the destruction of Garibaldi and the party of action." This was published on the 15th August. Some days later Monsieur Crispi, member of the Chambers, wrote a long letter to the *Diritto*, giving an account of the machinations of the ministers, and denouncing them to the country. In August a petition was signed at Palermo beseeching the king to put an end to the alarming crisis by dismissing the ministers. The petition was signed in two days by at least 50,000 persons; at the same time a Roman gentleman, late an officer in the Southern army, arrived in Sicily, to know at what moment the General desired an insurrection in the Papal States, and he gave in the names of the towns and boroughs where everything was already organized for such a purpose. The correspondent of a London paper wrote that he utterly disbelieved either in civil war in Italy, or in a mad attack by Garibaldi upon the French troops, the Italian Government, might, he said, send 60,000 or 100,000 soldiers to Sicily, place the island in a state of siege. Suspend the liberty of the press, but of what use would these measures be if Garibaldi effected his escape to the mainland, where forces were being organized for him then, as to the possibility of an encounter between Italian volunteers and French troops, no calmly judging politician admitted it. Meanwhile, the cabinet of Turin issued a proclamation signed by Ratazzi, stating that Garibaldi had raised the standard of revolt in Sicily in the King's name, to mislead the simple, for the purpose of exciting civil war* A subscription of 30,000 francs had just arrived from Turin, which, with the 2,800 muskets found in the castle of Catasria gave Garibaldi the means of arming and clothing his volunteers, whose numbers were considerably increased by the enthusiastic enlistment of the Catanese youth; the French packet, *le General Abbalucci* arrived in the port; the General went repeatedly on the Cupola of the Benedictine Abbey, to survey the movements both of the Italian Army in camp, around Mistr Bianco, and of the Government frigate the Duke of Genoa, which lay in the port. Early in the morning he was again on the cupola with a glass in his hand. Mordini greeted him with the words, "You take once more an eagle's view of them, General. When shall you pounce down?" Garibaldi smiled, and said, "Look here. Our difficulties are increasing indeed." We saw a second frigate, the *Maria Adelaide*, steaming towards the port, and at the same time a great stir in the camp of Mistr Bianco; but Garibaldi did not give any orders about the defence of Catania. He received as usual the reports of his officers, the deputations still thronging to him, and the volunteers of distinction, who presented themselves, among others, two Transylvanian magnates who had enlisted as privates among Menotti's guides. During the day Catania became somewhat alarmed. The royal troops left their camp at Mistr Bianco and slowly approached. The barricades discontinued on Tuesday were now raised a few inches; they did not, however, look very formidable as yet, still the higher classes became alarmed, and ladies and children commenced to leave the town. Garibaldi reassured everybody, and told those who came to him that there would be no attack. Many soldiers

---

* The Marchesa Maurigi went to Garibaldi to beg of him to persuade her only son to return home with her, but he answered: "I do not call any one, I do not keep any one, but I don't return any one who chooses to follow me." The old grandmother of the Duke Niscemi wrote to her grandson in the camp a letter in which she stated, that she would disinherit him, unless he returned at once. The young noblemen replied respectfully, that if any thing could have kept him at Palermo, it would have been his fear of wounding her feelings, and not the prospect of her property; he considered, however, that his duty to his country was even more sacred, and therefore, he resolved to follow Garibaldi's star for Victor Emmanuel and United Italy.

profited by the vicinity of the new camp and deserted to Garibaldi. The General, it was stated, had made a visit to the *Maria Adelaide.* On Sunday morning the *Dispaccio* of the Florio Company, bound to Malta, cast anchor under the guns of the *Maria Adelaide*, and, at the same time, the *Duke of Genoa* left the harbour to make her usual daily cruise, after having intimated to the captain of the port that any ship carrying Garibaldian volunteers would be stopped by her guns. Garibaldi paid a visit to the Italian and French postal steamers a few minutes later. At eleven o'clock they were invested with a packet of red shirts and the captains put under arrest, the General telling them that he had sequestered the steamers because he had need of them. The French captain declared that, of course, he could not offer any resistance, but that he desired solemnly to protest against such violence. "Just as you please," said the General: "You do your duty, and I will do mine." Accordingly the captain was escorted to town, when he made his protest in due form at the French Consulate, with all the formalities required by law. It must be remarked that although some of the volunteers were at this time on board the French steamer, the *Maria Adelaide* paid no attention to them, but at 4 p.m. steamed out of the port, cruising in the neighbourhood. At five the red shirts began to throng to the place facing the harbour, and with them all the people of Catania. In a few minutes the windows of the houses were densely packed with ladies, and about 5,000 persons had assembled on the place around the volunteers. The staff waited on the gallery of the bathing establishment on the lava rocks and about two boats lay close to the beach. At half past five the General arrived and the embarkation commenced. The staff, Menotti's Guides, the Tuscans, and the flower of the Sicilian volunteers now rowed to the *Despaccio;* the Sicilians of General Corrao occupied the larger vessel, the *General Abbatucci.* Garibaldi himself took the command of the former, though she was a slower ship; and put Burrattaini in command of the French packet, in the maintime it had grown dark, and the greatest confusion prevailed. Both ships were filled to suffocation, and there was no possibility of sitting or lying down, and still the boats were arriving and discharging their living cargoes on deck; at last, something like order was established, and at 10 the *Abbatucci* left her moorings, and slipt quietly out of the harbour. It must have been near midnight when the *Abbatucci* met the *Maria Adelaide*, but the man-of-war left her at once and steamed back to Catania.* At half past two, a.m., the Garibaldian steamers cast anchor. 1,300 volunteers had been left behind in Sicily; the staff were on the highest spirits. Menotti wrote to a gentleman in Liverpool, that in about three weeks they hoped to see Rome. Colonel Corte "All now goes on as well as possible." The volunteers were well-equipped, every man in his red shirt, and grey trousers; there were about 3,000 men, with a numerous staff of high spirited officers. Garibaldi breakfasted with the Captain of the French steamer, who afterwards told Count Pulzsky, that he thought from the first Garibaldi acted in full accord with the king, but that he had no longer the slightest doubt on the subject, from the moment he perceived the two Italian frigates had not offered the slightest opposition; at Messina, when La Seine had already announced that Garibaldi was at Calabria, Senator Mathieu, the Governor, sent for the Captain of the Abbatucci, and asked him where the frigates had been at the time when the volunteers were leaving Catania, "They were near enough," was the answer, "but they were blind, and the French cruisers, were out of the way." The chief of Garibaldi's staff has since stated, that when marching along the road by the sea side in Calabria, a steam-plated frigate was following, and might have utterly destroyed them, had they wished it; the officer in command of the vessel had applied for precise instruction, and had been furnished with these, "Do what is best for the King's service." They

* The *Maria Adelaide* was Admiral Persano's ship in 1860, when he had official orders to capture Garibaldi, and secret instructions to favour his landing in Sicily, both emanating from Cavour.

were afterwards tried at Genoa for allowing Garibaldi to escape, and honourably acquitted.*

On the 24th of August, Garibaldi issued the following proclamation: "Italians! my programme is always the same, so far as it depends upon me. I desire that the plebiscite of the 21st of October, 1860, may be a reality, that the compact entered into between the people and the king may receive full execution. I bow before the Majesty of Victor Emmanuel, king elect of the nation, but I am hostile to a ministry which has nothing Italian but the name, to a ministry which, to please diplomacy, ordered in May last, the arrests and the prosecutions of Sarnico as it now provokes civil war in the south, to keep in the good graces of the Emperor Napoleon. Such a ministry cannot, must not be supported, it deceives the king, it compromises him as it did in the proclamation of the 3rd instant, it deceives the country. The livery of a foreign master shall never be a title of honor and esteem for any ministry of ours. The Neapolitan provinces every one knows can only be kept down by an overwhelming military force. Love and good administration ought to found the unity of Italy; they have preferred the opposite way. Madmen, they wish, I know it, for civil war, that they may more easily stifle in blood the future of liberty, and immolate coveted victims upon the alter of despotism. For my part, I will not allow these guilty designs to be executed. Let the thought and action of all patriots be exclusively directed to the liberating enterprise of Rome. To Rome! then, to Rome! We shall be victorious, for we have with us reason, national law, and the universal conscience. I am sure the Italian people will not fail

---

* The *Maria Adelaide* threatened to blow the Volunteers to pieces. Garibaldi, however, sent an officer on board, who had an interview with the captain, and immediately afterwards the *Maria Adelaide* steamed out of harbour. Count Avogadvo and Signor Girod di Nizza, the commanders of the two frigates who followed Garibaldi to pass freely out of the port of Catania, had been arrested, and were tried by Court-martial; but these excellent officers had, probably, a very good answer to give to the charge against them. General Cialdini, was too old a fox to be caught in a trap, insisted on having written and very explicit orders before his departure, not choosing to rely on any given by word of mouth.—*Daily News.*

in their duty. May it please God that our valorous army may be with us also. If I have done anything for the country, believe my words,* I am resolved to enter Rome a conqueror, or to perish under its walls. But if I die, I am persuaded that you will worthily avenge my death, and will finish my work. Long live Italy! Hail to Victor Emmanuel at the Capital! †

G. GARIBALDI."

---

* The last part of the proclamation was intended to serve two purposes, to arouse the people, and to hasten the departure of the Pope from Rome.

† The following proclamation was issued by Garibaldi, dated Bos' co Ficuzza, 3rd August:—"Young comrades, the holy cause of our country unites us again to-day. Without asking where we are going, with smiles upon your lips you have hastened hither to fight against arrogant foreign rulers. I ask only of Providence to preserve me your confidence. I can promise nothing by toils and troubles, but I confidently rely upon your self-denial, for well do I know you. Oh! mutilated remnants of glorious battles, it is unnecessary to ask of you bravery in the fight, but I must ask you to preserve discipline, without which no army can exist. The Romans, by their discipline, were enabled to become the masters of the world. Strive to gain the affections of the people, as you knew how to do in 1860, as well as the esteem of our valiant army, in order to bring about the unity of the country. Upon this occasion also the brave Sicilians will be the forerunners of the great destinies to which the country is called. GARIBALDI."

CHAPTER XI.

The true story of Aspromonti—Colonel Pallavicino ordered to attack—How the General was wounded—The march after Aspromonti—The embarkation—Garibaldi's account of Aspromonti—Cialdini's report—Orders to destroy Garibaldi—Remarks on Cialdini's report—Government telegrams—Their inaccuracy—Arrival and reception of Garibaldi at Varignana—Disgraceful treatment of the prisoners—State of the prison—Dr. Partridge—The Mazzinians and Garibaldians—Pagliano's description of General Garibaldi.

The telegrams were in the hands of the Government, and we have seen how falsely they represented to Europe what was passing in Sicily. It was a great power in their favour to have the first telling of the story of Aspromonti. How they did tell that story, the following extracts from the Government papers will show—On the morning of the 30th of August, a telegram from Turin stated that at two the Minister of the Interior had received the news of the combat at Aspromonti, and of the capture of Garibaldi and his volunteers. The first dispatch was sent by General Cialdini, dated from Reggio. Other dispatches followed. From these it appeared that Colonel Pallavicini, who commanded the Bersaglieri, knowing that Garibaldi was at Aspromonti, resolved to attack him, and, despite the difficult nature of the ground, he led on his regiment of Bersaglieri, which he had reinforced by two battalions of the line. *Garibaldi was summoned to surrender; on his refusal, the fight commenced; it was long and desperate. The volunteers made a resistance which was not to be expected from such young and inexperienced troops. The position was carried at the point of the bayonet. As every issue was guarded, retreat was impossible*, and the result has been the unconditional surrender of all. Garibaldi asked leave to embark in an English steamer, but Colonel Pallavicini had no powers to decide in the matter. He referred to General Cialdini, who applied for instructions to the Government. Meantime, Garibaldi is on his way to Spezzia, a prisoner on board a man-of-war. He will be treated with *the highest consideration that circumstances will allow.* Every precaution has been taken to prevent a demonstration. A second telegram, dispatched from Turin on the afternoon of the same day, was: Colonel Pallavicini sent one of his aides to Garibaldi to enjoin him, in the name of the king and the law, to lay down his arms, with an intimation that he had orders to use force to make the law respected. Garibaldi returned an absolute refusal. Thereupon Colonel Pallavicini, although his soldiers were fatigued by the forced march, and had only had a halt of 40 minutes, gave the word, and his battalion divided into three close columns and marched at the double upon the volunteers, who held their ground resolutely. When the regulars came up, the volunteers fired; the Bersaglieri fired a few shots, then charged the position with the bayonet, and a terrible *mêlée* ensued; *Garibaldi evidently sought for death.* His son fought with extreme courage and determination. Again, in pursuance of orders from the Government, General Garibaldi is being conveyed to Spezzia in an Italian war vessel. Colonel Pallavicini has been appointed General." The Official Gazette of this evening publishes a dispatch from General Cialdini (which has been already given). The Gazette also contains the following :—"In order that the public may not credit false news, the Government declares that the Official Gazette is the the only organ of its news and acts. Garibaldi has asked to be put on board an English steamer, in order that he may leave his country." Again, on the 31st of August: "The state of seige will be maintained in the Neapolitan provinces and Sicily. The trial of Garibaldi and his followers will take place immediately. The deserters from the royal army to Garibaldi, who have been made prisoners, have been shot. The French Government has complimented the Cabinet of Turin, by telegraph, on the facts accomplished at Aspromonti." The *Moniteur* of the same date contained the following :—" The insurrection, which threatened to compromise the destinies of Italy, has terminated. Garibaldi after a very sharp contest, in which he was wounded, has been compelled to surrender with all his adherents."

Now what were the facts. Fortunately fourteen officers of General Garibaldi's staff drew up on the 31st of August the history of what really occurred: their account is as follows:—

"On board the steam frigate *Duke of Genoa*, which left Scylla in Calabria yesterday, at 4 p.m., the volunteers had received formal orders not to attack, not to defend themselves—to march rapidly, that was all. On the 29th, a little before mid-day, the General moved the camp from the Forestali of Aspromonte. The troops (of the King) had reached St. Stefano the night before. They had only a two hours' march to gain the heights on which we were. In the constant endeavour to avoid an encounter with the troops, the General gave orders to cross a little river, and to move northwards to the hill. We halted at midday, just at the entrance to a thick pine forest. When the column had arrived there it was face to face with the troops marching towards us, and already beginning to appear on the opposite height. We had not stationed outposts. The two houses of the Forestali had not been occupied. We took to the forest. It was thence more than evident that Garibaldi had no intention to fight, but sought, as he had always done, to prevent any encounter with the troops. Garibaldi was in the centre of the slope occupied by our column, and he sent his officers all along the front with repeated positive orders not to fire, and continued making observations on all sides through his telescope.

"The troops kept advancing; the riflemen in front with a running step, the troops of the line behind. The first ranks of riflemen were already within gunshot; they had taken aim. The whole column observed in silence. Not a cry, not a shot was heard. The General alone, standing erect, continued to take his observations, his large cloak of pale grey lined with red thrown over his broad shoulders; ever and anon he turned to repeat the command "Do not fire."

"But the *orders* given to the commanders of the troops to *attack us* were on the other hand *positive*. The riflemen commence firing—they advance. No preventive intimation whatever was transmitted. No parley was sought. The firing grows thicker and thicker. We hear the well-known whistle of the balls as they pass through the bushes and strike the trees around us. Unhappily, some inexperienced youths are unable to control themselves at the spectacle, so new to them, of this terrible game, and return a few ill-directed shots, which but too truly cause blood to flow. The rest do not move; he who is standing continues to stand; he who is sitting continues to sit. All the bugles without exception sound the signal for the fire to cease. All the officers give the same order by word of mouth. Such is the answer we send to the troops, which are sounding the advance, accompanying it with a well-sustained fire. The General from his post, erect amidst a thick shower of balls, repeats the cry 'Do not fire!' In that moment, two balls strike him. One a spent ball in the left thigh, another in full force in the instep of the right foot. The wound in the thigh is light—that in the foot is serious and complicated. Garibaldi, at the time he was wounded, not only remained standing, but drew himself up majestically. Friends, brothers, cousins, acquaintances, companions in recent battles fought for the country, meet and recognize each other. A lieutenant of the (royal) staff presses forward before the rest. He is conducted into the presence of the General, who, looking at him, commands him to lay down his sword. The lieutenant obeys, but observes that he came to parley. But why did he not come sooner? The General, with much dignity, reproved him in these words, 'I have known for 30 years, and better than you, in what war consists. Learn that those who come to parley do not present themselves in that guise.' Other officers of the rifles and of the line are led under the tree, where the General is laid. He orders their swords to be taken from them, but afterwards that they should be restored, which order is executed.

"All this passes in a very short time. Meanwhile, unmoved himself, and waving aloft his hat with his left hand, he cried out repeatedly, 'Long live Italy! Do not fire.' Some of his officers who were nearest to him carried him and laid him down under a tree. Then calmly, as was his wont, he continued to give orders. The most precise were ever these: 'Let them advance; do not fire.'

"Along our whole front the firing had ceased. A little while after Menotti is brought up, who is also struck with a spent ball in the calf of the left leg, causing a most painful contusion; he cannot stand. Father and son are both laid down under the same tree.

"A circle of officers and soldiers is made around Garibaldi, he lights a cigar and begins smoking, and repeats to all "Do not fight."

"The soldiers turn inquiring words and looks to the officers. The answer for all is the same 'Do not fight.'

"The bugles also continue to sound the *halt* and *cease firing*, no longer for our people but for the troops, that come nearer and nearer firing, and have already arrived.

"Volunteers, riflemen, and men of the line are at one moment confused together.

"From the first shot that was fired to this scene of confusion scarcely a quarter of an hour had elapsed. And the confusion is heightened by a spectacle worthy of consideration. The surgeons examine and dress the wounds of the General, who continues to smoke. He insists on their being continually kept wet, and water is brought from a neighbouring place.

"He asks repeatedly of the surgeons if it is a case for amputation, and tells them if it be, not to hesitate. The surgeons answer that it is not a case for amputation. The General then charges the chief of his staff to call to him the commander of the attacking body. For this purpose the staff officer who had come in the first instance, was dispatched, and he returned in twenty minutes accompanied by Colonel Pallavicino. The intentions of General Garibaldi are to treat, because we do not intend to fight the Italian army. Colonel Pallivicino, who, himself, like others meets with old acquaintances, declares in the first place, that he received positive orders to attack us under whatever circumstances, or wherever we might be found. He asks, 'If we acknowledge the king.' We answer, 'There is no occasion for any such declaration, that it is required only to refer to the programme of Garibaldi, and that his last proclamation from Catania is sufficient.' Colonel Pallavicino was conducted to the General. He presented himself uncovered, and expressed himself in respectful terms. In a short time he withdrew, and some staff officers of General Garibaldi went to propose to him, that the column should be disarmed, that so disarmed, it should be confided to the escort of his troops, and that it should be recommended in a particular manner to himself. It was agreed that General Garibaldi with a suite of officers, of whom he would have to present the list, and who should retain their swords, should proceed to Scylla, that on the journey they should stop wherever he wished to rest and have his wounds dressed. That at Scylla he would request to go on board an English ship with his followers. That the *cortège* should be escorted by a battalion of Rifles at a distance. With regard to the embarcation on board an English ship, Colonel Pallavicino saw no objection on his part, but said that he was obliged to ask for instructions from the Government.

"The body of troops which assaulted us consisted of— The 4th regiment: Commander Eberhardt present; the 4th battalion of the 29th regiment; the 4th battalion of the 57th regiment; the 6th battalion of Rifles; two companies of the 25th

Rifles; Maiedonio Pinelli, Commander, present. Commander-in-Chief of the corps, Colonel the Marquis Pallavicino di Priola. Several vessels of war and merchantmen were found at Scylla. General Cialdini was at Reggio. Vice-Admiral Albini commanded the fleet. The killed on either side are very few; the wounded also very few. It is too true that in the first instant of confusion, the taking away of arms was accompanied with acts and words of a brutal nature. We grieve for them and still more for those who were guilty of them. We cannot and will not recount them in detail, maintaining that they were suggested entirely by individual feelings.

"Almost the whole of the baggage went astray; it is true that no one thought of guarding it. It is also true that some purses were restored—that Colonel Pallavicino undertook as far as lay in his power to have them sought for, and immediately took measures to have them returned.

"On our side we caused a carbine that had been taken from rifleman to be restored. We have already said, that the swords which certain officers had been deprived of, were also given back to them. The disarming was effected. Evening was setting in. We contrived, in haste, a litter to transport the General. Carrying him was to be the sad and dutiful charge of the officers and soldiers who accompanied him. The riflemen commanded by Major Pinelli brought up the *cortege*. After about an hour's fatiguing march over a rough and broken way, we arrived at a ruined house, where several wounded were collected. The General was asked if he wished to stop there for the night. He answered, that he preferred to go farther on to some cottage or barn where he might be alone; a good distance farther on, on our right a little to the north we expected to find, as in fact we did, the cottage of the shepherd Vincenzo, an old acquaintance of some of our men, who first passed over to Calabria in August, 1860. We recommenced our progress, it was still longer and more disastrous than the first portion. The jolts produced by the windings and abrupt descent of the road occasioned much suffering for us, knowing what it must cause the General. He must have suffered agonies, but not a groan or a single murmur escaped his lips. For greater security, we sent scouts forward to light fires for the guidance of those who followed. Those who first reached the cottage arranged as well as they could, a bed of straw covered with cloaks. The *cortege* reached the cottage after upwards of three hours' march at a very late hour of the night. The moon shone sadly. There was deep silence, interrupted only from time to time by the howlings of shepherds' dogs. We asked for water to bathe the wounds. We had some broth prepared simply of goat's flesh. The surgeons proceeded to fulfil their duty. It was already midnight. At daylight we set ourselves to make a litter, more commodious and more solid. We moved on for Scylla at 6 a.m. It is useless to enter again or diffusely to speak of our journey. We marched on, almost constantly from rock to rock. At a place consisting of a few ruined houses, called St. Angelo, we decided to halt for half an hour that the General might have rest. The surgeons renew the bandages and the bathing. We prepare the broth and persuade him to take a mouthful. The General smiles and thanks us. When the sun begins to scorch we make an umbrella of laurel-branches to screen him. At length, at three p.m., we reach the small town of Scylla. We expected to find a house prepared in the higher part of the town in which the General might repose. It was not so. We were told that a house had been prepared lower down on the sea-coast. Colonel Pallavicino had arrived at Scylla the preceding evening, (29th,) and came to meet us. We found that the instructions received from the government were very severe. The colonel's words of the preceding day placed in greater contrast the brutal severity of the orders of the government. The General was not allowed to be put on board an English vessel. The officers named on the list were not to be allowed to accompany him. When the General heard this, he showed no surprise. He only said mildly to his officers, "Ah! you have deceived me!"

"The orders of the government were, that General Garibaldi should embark on board the steam frigate Duca di Genova, with his son; and that ten only of his officers might accompany him.*

"A request was made for orderlies to attend upon the General He declined to rest in the house that had been prepared, preferring to embark immediately. The steam frigate was ready to start; orders were accordingly given to send the boats; and we waited for them on the shore. Meanwhile we deposit the litter on which the General is placed on a large boat drawn up on the shore. The *cortège* is enclosed between the riflemen and the sea. In twenty minutes the two boats arrive; the sailors are armed as if in presence of an enemy. We embark and approach the vessel intended for us; we pass before the steamer Stella d'Italia; on the deck, in military uniform, stand General Cialdini and Vice-Admiral Albini, surrounded by a brilliant staff. No salute is given—we passed on and give none. The boat that carried General Garibaldi was allowed to pass; the second was stopped by Vice-Admiral Albini. It appeared to these gentlemen that there were two orderlies too many, and Vice-Admiral Albini in person came after us in a third boat to order in a coarse and rude manner, in the name of General Cialdini, that they should be made to disembark. A Vice-Admiral had been sent to bear these most highly important orders! we replied that rough manners were misplaced, seeing that we had embarked with every regularity, that is to say, in the order in which we were called. He rejoined that he was obliged to obey the orders of General Cialdini. The two orderlies were ordered to pass into a fourth boat, which would carry them ashore. The boat in which the General lay, conveyed him alongside, and he was carefully hoisted on board, the General steadying himself by a rope which he held in his hand, his head erect, and himself giving various orders to guard against accidents in the manœuvre. The sailors regarded him with astonishment and apparent admiration.

* From whom he was afterwards separated.

After we had been on board a few minutes the two orderlies that had been sent away returned. Colonel Pallavicino had made no objection to their embarcation; General Cialdini had, therefore, condescended to permit it. The parting with friends was a moving scene. All took off their hats and cried Viva Garibaldi a Roma! a Roma! The General waived his hand in return. We went on board; our companions went to the Castle of Scylla, it was stated for an hour only, after that they also would be embarked, for what destination we shall see. Whither are we bound? it is said to Spezzia, and afterwards, there are, it is said, certain government despatches, for the present sealed, containing instructions respecting us. Signed,

Bruzzesi, Bideschini, Corte, Cattabene, Cairoli, Guastalla, Manci, Ripari, Nullo, Albanese, Turillo Malato, Basile, Frigyesy, Basso.

Although prisoners, the officers of Garibaldi's staff succeeded in eluding the vigilance of their gaolers. The fact that even when prisoners, Garibaldi and his officers find means to communicate important documents to their friends, shows of itself how great is the influence the name of Garibaldi exercises over the country, and how wide-spread is the feeling of sympathy his sad fate has awakened. The above narrative was written by Colonel Guastalla, and revised by Colonel Corte.

Garibaldi's own comment on Aspromonti was contained in the following letter written on board the *Duke of Genoa*, September 1. "They thirsted for blood and I wished to spare it. Not the poor soldiers who obeyed, but the men of the clique who cannot forgive the revolution for being the revolution —it is that which disturbs their conservative digestion—and for having contributed to the re-establishment of our Italian family.

"Yes, they thirsted for blood; I perceived it with sorrow, and I endeavoured in consequence to the utmost to prevent that of our assailants from being shed.

"I ran along the front of our line crying out to them not to fire, and from the centre to the left, where my voice and those of my aides-de-camp could be heard, not a trigger was pulled. It was not thus on the attacking side. Having arrived at a distance of 200 metres, they began a tremendous fire, and the party of Bersaglieri who were in front of me, directing their shots against me, struck me with two balls, one in the left thigh, not serious, the other in the ankle of the right foot, making a serious wound.

"As all this happened at the opening of the conflict, and I was carried to the skirt of the wood after being wounded, I could see nothing more, a dense crowd having formed around me while my wound was being dressed. I feel certain, however, that up to the end of the line which was within my reach, and that of my aides-de-camp, not a single musket was fired. As there was no firing on our side, it was easy for the troops to approach and mingle with ours, and when I was told that they wished to disarm us, I replied that they should be themselves disarmed. The intentions of my companions were, however, so little hostile that I only succeeded in having a few officers and soldiers of the regulars disarmed.

"It was not so on our right. The *picciotti*, attacked by the regular troops, replied by a fire along the whole line, and although the trumpets sounded to cease firing, there was a smart fusillade, which, however, lasted not more than a quarter of an hour.

"My wounds led to some confusion in our line. Our soldiers, not seeing me, began to retreat into the wood, so that little by little the crowd round me broke up, and the most faithful alone remained. At this moment I learned that my staff and Colonel Pallavicini, who commanded the regular troops, were negotiating upon the following conditions:—First, that I should be free with my staff to withdraw where I pleased. (I replied, 'On board an English vessel.') Second, that having arrived at the sea shore, the rest of my companions should be set at liberty. Colonel Pallavicini conducted himself as a gallant and intelligent officer in all his military movements, and he has not been wanting in respect or courtesy towards me and my people. He showed his grief at having to shed Italian blood; but he had received peremptory orders and had to obey them. My arrangements had been purely defensive, and I had hoped to avoid a conflict, seeing the very strong position that I occupied, and entertaining the hope that the regular troops had received orders less sanguinary. If I had not been wounded at the outset, and if my people had not received the order under all circumstances to avoid any collision whatsoever with the regular troops, the contest between men of the same race might have been terrible. However, it is far better as it is. Whatever may be the result of my wounds, whatever fate the government prepares for me, I have the consciousness of having done my duty; and the sacrifice of my life is a very little thing if it has contributed to save that of a great number of my fellow countrymen.

"In the hazardous enterprise into which I and my companions had thrown ourselves headlong, I expected nothing good from the government of Rattazzi. But why should I not have hoped for less rigour on the part of the king, having altered in nothing the old programme, and having decided not to alter it at any price? What afflicts me most is, this fatal distrust, which contributes not a little to leave the national unity incomplete. However it may be, I once again present myself to Italy with head erect, assured of having done my duty. Once more my unimportant life and the more precious lifes of so many generous young men have been offered as a holocaust to the holiest of causes—pure from all vile personal interests.

"G. Garibaldi."

The publication of Garibaldi's letter upon the affair at Aspromonte brought a severe penalty upon the editor of the *Diritto* of Turin, viz., 2,000 francs fine and eighteen months' imprisonment.

Next in order may be given some extracts from the

"REPORT OF GENERAL CIALDINI TO THE MINISTER OF WAR AT TURIN.

"MESSINA, *September* 2.

"Having left Genoa on the 24th of August, at six p.m., for Sicily, with information that Garibaldi was still at Catania, out of which it did not seem possible for him to go; I resolved first to touch at Naples, in order to come to an understanding with General La Marmora, that we might act in concert in any contingency. On the 26th, at daybreak, I landed at Naples, and I was informed by General La Marmora that, contrary to all reasonable expectation, Garibaldi had left the port of Catania in two French postal steamers, on board of which as many had embarked as the vessels could hold, and that he had gained the shore of Melito, where he had disembarked with his followers.

"I had, in reality, no other orders than to combat with Garibaldi in Sicily. These orders might have been considered at an end from the moment when Catania, occupied by General Ricotti, had returned under the power of the Government, and Garibaldi was in Calabria, a territory under command of General La Marmora. * * *

"I accepted this second position, and, starting from the Gulf of Naples, I arrived at six next morning at Messina. There I learned the state of things, what troops and resources were disposable, and, after having left the necessary orders, I went to Reggio.

"Colonel Pallavicini, of the Bersaglieri, had reached Reggio some hours before me, and as senior officer had taken the command of the troops in the city.

"His first dispositions bore the stamp of the energetic resolution which is natural to him.

"Having long known him, I was happy to meet him so opportunely, and I ordered him to set out as soon as possible with a column of six or seven battalions, to make every effort to come up with Garibaldi, who was said to be encamped on the plateau of Aspromonte, *and to pursue him constantly without giving him a moment's repose; to attack him if he sought to escape, and destroy him if he accepted battle.* Forseeing, also, the possibility of a complete victory, I ordered him not to treat with Garibaldi, and only accept a surrender at discretion.

"There was no reason to believe that this column alone would be able to obtain the results which it did obtain. It was requisite, therefore, to close against Garibaldi every road by which he could penetrate into the interior of the Ulterior and Citerior Calabrias; it was requisite to form and put in movement other columns, which should act within a limited range, because thereby they would have *the greater chance of meeting with and destroying him.*"

General Cialdini concludes:

"Upon this feat of arms, which, by its consequences, acquires the importance of a battle, I send to your excellency the two original reports which I received at the moment from Colonel Pallavicini, and to which I abstain from adding or retrenching a single word.

"I feel that it only remains to me to recommend to the government and to the favour of the sovereign this distinguished colonel and the brave troops he commanded, for the services they have rendered can never be sufficiently recompensed.

"CIALDINI, General of Division.

"To his Excellency the Minister of War at Turin."

It would really be difficult to believe, upon any authority less than that of General Cialdini himself, that he thirsted for the blood of his old brother in arms to such a degree as to be guilty of acting wholly without orders (those which he had received to combat Garibaldi in Sicily, being as he stated at an end) in order that he might pursue Garibaldi "constantly, without giving him a moment's repose; *attack* him if he sought to escape, and *destroy* him if he accepted battle." Nothing can express the feeling better than his own words; and this attack took place upon the very ground which, two short years previously had formed a part only of one of the splendid gifts conferred by Garibaldi on Cialdini's king and master, whilst on the present occasion the worst fault that the worst enemy the General ever had, could lay to his charge, supposing everything urged against him to be gospel, amounted to this, that he, the legal ruler of the Romans by the will of the government and the people, ejected from that rule, against the will of the people, by French treachery and falsehood, was anxious to transfer to Cialdini's master the legal power placed in his hands, so confirming and supporting on this point at least, the latter policy of Count Cavour, who proclaimed in the chamber in one of his very last speeches that Italy was for the Italians, and that Rome was the only possible capital of Italy: carrying out also the vote of both chambers, proclaiming Victor Emmanuel king of Italy, and Rome the capital of the new kingdom. No person who has carefully perused the outspoken dispatches of Mr. Odo Russell, describing his interview with the Pope at the Pope's own request, can for an instant doubt that had Garibaldi been permitted to carry out his attempt, the Pope would at this instant, have been under British protection at Malta, and Napoleon either forced to hold Rome, the natural capital of Italy as a province of France or to restore it at once to Cialdini's master. Victor Emmanuel would have owed another crown to Garibaldi, under the circumstances that Garibaldi himself would have resigned his own rights to place the King in possession. But Piedmontese pride could not stand such an indignity, and the reader has the melancholy result before him.

What says General Durando in his circular from Turin to all the foreign powers? Why, that Garibaldi never ceased to invoke the name of the King, and that European cabinets must not misunderstand the true meaning of events; that the watchword of the volunteers was the expression of a want more imperative than ever; that the whole nation claimed the capital, and that the King's government had received a mandate from parliament respecting Rome. The problem may have changed its aspect, but the urgency of a solution becomes more cogent. General Durando concludes—

"Such a state of things is no longer tenable, and would end by entailing extreme consequences upon the government of the King, the responsibility of which could not weigh on us alone, and would seriously compromise the religious interests of catholicism and the tranquillity of Europe.

But it would be an unpardonable omision were we here to pass over the report of Colonel Pallavicini. It was generally but untruly reported that he had once served under Garibaldi. The fact is that, on the contrary, he never saw the General until the 29th of August, and his first address to him was, that he made his acquaintance on the most unfortunate day of his own life. He had his orders, and the General says he obeyed them like a good soldier. The responsibility never rested upon his shoulders; his personal treatment of his prisoner was everything that was respectful, kind, and courteous, and he shook hands heartily with some of his personal friends on the General's staff. His report is dated the first of September,* Beggio, and written after the General had left for Spezzia, and after he had himself conferred with General Cialdini. So rapid had been his promotion that he signed it as a Major-general. The wonder only is considering the necessity of supporting the official story and the great gain to him if he did so, not that the despatches in question contain many inaccuracies, but that they contain so much truth.

Having described his march, he writes:—"I then divided my troops into two columns, that on the right commanded by Lieutenant-Colonel Parrocchia, and that on the left by the colonel of the 4th Regiment, Chevalier Eberhart. The two columns arrived at the same time in view of the Garibaldi encampment, already abandoned by him, he having taken up a position on the crest of a steep hillock, to the east of the plateau of Aspromonte, I then sent an order to the commandant of the left column to attack the Garibaldian front, while making the right column fall

*Though Major General Pallavicini dates his despatches on the 1st of September, they were not given to the world by the Turin government until the 8th of that month.

back, and by a rapid movement I attacked the left flank of the rear of the rebels in order to cut off their retreat. The left column, with the 6th battalion of Bersaglieri at their head, after a smart fire, carried the position at the point of the bayonet, with cries of "Vivo il Re! Viva Italia!" while the left side was also attacked by our troops. General Garibaldi insisted with me that I should particularly recommend to the government the case of the deserters from the army. I promised him to do so, but I added that I had no hopes of success; because I knew the severe instructions given with regard to them. Of the documents which you demand from me, I can only transmit the two sent herewith, not having found any of greater importance. Possibly others of more significance may be discovered in the hands of the officers of Garibaldi's staff, whom I have not caused to be searched. According to the information I have received, other papers were torn up on the spot where the surrender took place. Some searches have been made, but no money has been found; however, each of the rebels was well provided. I have been informed that at the cascina where General Garibaldi passed the night, a considerable distribution of money was made to all present, about 150 in number. I must mention particularly to your excellency Lieutenant-Colonel Chevalier Eberhart, commandant of the 4th of the line, as having distinguished himself by his intelligence, and led his column with admirable spirit. I have to bestow the same praise on Lieutenant-Colonel Parrochia, who gave proofs of extraordinary energy and courage during the engagement. I must also mention to your excellency the valiant conduct of the two majors commanding the 6th and 25th battalions of Bersaglieri, Messrs. Giolitti and Pinelli, who always marched at the head of their columns, never ceasing to animate them by their example."

It is really hardly possible to help smiling, when it is remembered that all this zeal was wasted on attacking those who preferred death to civil war, and never attempted any defence, but this account makes it evident that the royal troops were the first to attack. In fact, Pallavicini faithfully carried out his instructions. Another part of the dispatch makes it equally clear that it was only after all firing had ceased that he sent the chief of his staff to Garibaldi, to summon him, in the name of the King, to surrender. He concludes:

"I then went to the wounded Garibaldi, who manifested no resentment against any one. On the contrary, he always avoided touching upon any subject of a political nature, and did not express towards the government either hatred or opposition. He adhered tacitly to the conditions I proposed; and demanded permission to embark in an English ship and leave the country. I replied that I would ask and wait for instructions on the subject. Having asked me what would be done with the prisoners, I replied that I was not the depository of the instructions of the government, but that, in my own opinion, the government, after causing the prisoners to be sent to Messina, would perhaps set them at liberty within twenty-four hours, in order not to be burdened by them. They agreed to surrender unconditionally. The General was conveyed, surrounded with his staff and a number of his adherents, under the escort of the 25th battalion of Bersaglieri, to a cascina called Marchesina, where he passed the night. Nex day he was conducted to Scilla, whither I had preceded him, and where I communicated to him the order of the government to put him on board the *Duca di Genova*. He half reproached me then with not having kept my promise to allow him to embark in an English ship, and reminded me that I had said his adherents would be set at liberty in twenty-four hours. I then said, with some heat, that I had never promised anything in the name of the government; that with regard to the embarkation I had said I would refer the matter to the ministry, whose answer I had at that moment communicated to the General; that as to what related to the future disposal of the prisoners I had only expressed my own personal opinion, which did not bind the government, which had given me no instructions upon the subject. He then suggested that, at a proper time, I should testify that I had expressed that hope. This I did not refuse, because the matter in question was a private opinion of my own. For the rest, as I have said above, General Garibaldi always kept silence, and broke it only to address these words to the people of Scilla, who happened to be in his way, 'Do you no longer recognise your general?' No cry answered this appeal."

It will be remembered that Cialdini's telegrams to the government, or at any rate the official telegrams the ministers had published to the world in Cialdini's name, had stated that Garibaldi was summoned to surrender; that on his refusal, the fight commenced, and was long and desperate; that when the regulars came up, the volunteers fired, and so forth. And the government assured the people that the *Official Gazette* published only the truth—the official truth as understood in Turin, they doubtless meant to imply.

Dr. Repardi, one of Garibaldi's companions, wrote to the editor of the *Diritto* in reference to some particulars in General Pallavicini's report. "The left column," he says, "of Major-general Pallavicini did not take the position with the bayonet. General Garibaldi's first order was, that all should remain at their posts, sitting or standing, as they happened to be. The General was wounded while he was walking on foot along the centre of his men calling out, 'do not fire,' and while all the bugles of the left and the centre were repeating the same command. The lieutenant of the royal staff sent to parley was followed by a company of riflemen who took their places on the esplanade at thirty paces from the General. It was under these circumstances that he was ordered to be disarmed. The ambulance chests were then opened by the royal troops, and the instruments for amputation, linen, and papers, were all carried away. Mention is made of a distribution of money having taken place amongst those who accompanied the General. I never heard nor do I know of any distribution of money.*

* There was no distribution of money, on the contrary, some of the staff subscribed money from their own pockets to enable several of the regimental officers to buy shoes for those of their men who were footsore.

The General is here without a farthing. None of our number, who were always at the side of the wounded General, heard him pronounce either at Scilla or elsewhere, 'do you no longer know your General.' And, indeed, for what object should he have said this, could it have been to awaken compassion? There was more than compassion; there was eloquence in the grave silence of the population. In conclusion, I testify that the words, 'do you no longer know your General,' never came from the lips of General Garibaldi." This letter is confirmed in every particular by eleven others, from different officers attending the General; all agree that Garibaldi never opened his lips to the people, but merely moved his hand to them; whilst an official communication, dictated by the medical staff, states that General Garibaldi received his wound while ordering his men not to fire, and when he was standing in front between his own soldiers and the royal troops.

The following extract of a letter from a Garibaldian officer, is confirmed by about forty other letters in the author's possession from persons present at Aspromonte: "When the General received the bullet he was passing along our front, ordering the men not to fire. I saw a slight shiver of his body, he took two or three steps, and then began to stagger. We ran to him, holding him up, he was regardless of his sufferings. Raising his cap, he cried, 'Viva Italia! Viva Italia!' I had his poor foot resting on my thigh, he called out to his assailants and asked them what they did with his people. I felt a shivering in all his limbs, and reminding him of his wound, I implored him to be quiet." One of the communications referred to adds that a battalion of the line, commanded by Heberhart, an Hungarian, who had been raised to the rank of Colonel by General Garibaldi himself, opened fire along with the Bersaglieri. After he was wounded Garibaldi never desisted for an instant in his efforts to stop the bloodshed; and 'Peace, peace, brethren, and long live Italy,' was his incessant cry.

The General himself wrote to a friend—"I was wounded

when I was not fighting, and when I had no intention of fighting." When in prison he observed to one of his earliest visitors—"Well, I hope Italy knows that there was not a fight at Aspromonte. I had given the strictest orders not to fire; some inexperienced boys did not obey, but happily, there were but few wounded amongst the brave Bersaglieri who captured me; as for my volunteers, they were needlessly fired at, and many of those brave fellows fell wounded with me, without discharging their muskets." When the General was informed that the official telegrams published by government told a very different story, he smiled and said, "Of course the gentlemen at Turin must make Europe believe that it was a serious fight and a bloody struggle. Don't be anxious, however, the truth will be known one day or other." To the Marchioness Pallavicini he said, "From my splendid position at Aspromonte I saw the Bersaglieri advancing for three quarters of an hour before they came up. Had I wished it, I could have crushed them completely, but I gave orders not to fire, and none near me did fire: I never willed civil war." It is thus placed beyond dispute that none of the volunteers fired until after they had seen Garibaldi wounded, and then only young recruits, mere boys, discharged their muskets, whilst the royal troops kept up a heavy fire for a quarter of an hour. And yet the number of wounded on both sides was nearly equal. The reason of this was that, though the volunteers fired few shots, those shots nearly all told, because the royal troops were below them, ascending the steep hill, the great advantage of position being with Garibaldi. For the same reason very few of the shots fired by the regular soldiers took effect; the majority of the bullets lodging in the ground. Had Garibaldi willed it, not one of the royal troops would ever have returned to tell the story of Aspromonte; but the service on which they were engaged had for them the twofold advantage of being both safe and profitable. The General had openly declared, before he left Turin, that he would die rather than draw his sword upon an Italian soldier. In Sicily he had incessantly repeated the same thing in slightly varying terms—there will be no civil war, there can be no civil war, there shall be no civil war, were his constant exclamations. Surely, never in the history of Europe has so safe a service as that of firing on men whom the will of an idolized chief rendered utterly defenceless, been so splendidly rewarded. It was really ten thousand pities to behold so much bravery and enthusiasm utterly thrown away.* Colonel Pallavicini and his officers, even if it were possible for them to plead ignorance of Garibaldi's ceaseless declarations, could not be ignorant of the scene passing before them. They must have observed that there were no outposts; that, instead of being drawn up in order of battle, the Garibaldians remained to a man without moving—some sitting, some standing, some lying on the ground; these facts must, therefore, have demonstrated that opposition was not even dreamt of. It was under these circumstances that, obeying the order given to destroy, the royal troops advanced and fired upon men whom honour made defenceless; and it was upon such feats as these that the Emperor Napoleon telegraphed his official congratulations to the King of Italy.

General Garibaldi was brought to Varignano, on board the *Duke of Genoa*. The captain was an Englishman, and did all in his power to promote the comfort of his prisoner; but he had only been appointed to the ship twenty-four hours previously, and was unable to do everything he wished, not being seconded by the whole of his officers. The voyage was a most painful one; the surgeon of the vessel vainly endeavouring to extract the bullet from the wound, the General fainting away at every fresh operation. Two other men-of-war, the *Italia* and the *Garibaldi*, which had been added to the royal navy by Garibaldi himself, followed the *Duke of Genoa* with Gari-

* The flag of Garibaldi in '62 was the same as in '60. It had for its motto "Italy and Victor Emmanuel," and all the administrative documents, some of which are in the author's possession, had printed at their head the following words—"Italia Vittorio Emmanuel," Roma o Morte only being added.

baldian prisoners on board. When they arrived at Varignano, the General was separated from his staff—a sorrowful parting it was on both sides. At Varignano the General was informed that no preparations had been made to receive him, and that he must remain on board the vessel twenty-four hours longer. Gentlemen residing in Spezzia have stated that when the inhabitants, who were perfectly unarmed, came in little boats to see the General, some of them bringing small offerings of fruit and flowers, they were fired upon.

Permission was asked the General to secure the services of a medical man in whom he had confidence, but the Government at Turin refused, informing him that they would send doctors to attend him. They further ordered the General to be separated from his wounded son, and Ripari, Basile and Albanese, and to be placed in separate confinement; but, to the credit of humanity be it said, these orders were not carried out. He was next told that he would be tried on the charge of treason, when he applied to have a legal adviser whom he named, but this request was also refused.

When General Garibaldi was landed at Varignano the women flocked around him, kissing his hands and the cloak in which he was wrapped; an eye-witness of this affecting scene writes that the air resounded with their sobs, Garibaldi was deeply affected. To some who pressed around him he said, "Patience, my children, hope for better times;" to others he said, "You see Garibaldi is not dead yet." After this excitement he again fainted.

At length he was carried, still in a fainting state, to the miserable apartment set apart for him in the convict prison. Here the paper on the walls was found hanging down with damp, and in the room there was a small dirty mattress covered with a few bed-clothes. Most providentially there were the two great coats, and the blanket on which the General was carried

* Now in the possession of Colonel Chambers.

from Aspromonte,* or he would have been in greater distress. Indeed, there was no change of linen, nor was there any lint for dressing the wound; therefore the old bandages could not be removed, and it appeared evident to the now disheartened medical man that there was little possibility of obtaining any of the requisite comforts for the wounded General. These facts are placed beyond a doubt by private letters. At length an Italian gentleman in the dockyard at Spezzia lent them an iron bedstead, and most fortunately Mrs. Schwabe, the widow of a wealthy Manchester merchant, who was one of the ladies on the Committee for the management of Garibaldi's schools at Naples, Turin, and elsewhere, arrived at Spezzia, and obtained permission to visit the General. When this kind-hearted lady found things in such a deplorable state, she immediately applied a remedy, not by any application to the Government at Turin, but by providing everything required from her own purse, and by her own personal industry.

Amongst the General's early visitors was the Signora Cairoli, the heroine of Pavia, a rich widow who had bestowed her four sons on Italy, two of whom had been killed, and the other two badly wounded, one of the latter, Henry, being now a prisoner. This true Italian mother, instead of lamenting over her misfortunes, exhorted her prisoner son to be confident in the future, and to do all in his power to carry out the wishes of his deceased brothers, who had died fighting for an united Italy. The third son of Signora Cairoli is now one of the most eloquent deputies in the Italian Parliament. He was wounded in Sicily and Naples in his breast, arms, and legs, is now compelled to walk with crutches, and has lost the use of his left arm. Few who were present with the General during his visit to the Palace Cairoli, in the spring of '62, can forget his almost distressing tenderness and affection towards this young man; how he would carry him in his arms, and place him with the greatest possible comfort in his boat on the lake; and would suffer no one to do anything for him which it was possible for him to do himself, so that in whatever way he was engaged, his eye was always turned towards young Cairoli, watchful for the least sign of weariness, and always anxious to render him every assistance in his power.

One day after dinner, Garibaldi, forgetting for an instant that poor Madame Cairoli was sitting by his side, proposed a toast "to the Italian Martyrs." All at once he turned to her, and perceiving that she was pale as a corpse and drowned in tears, he grasped her hand, and pressed it again and again to his lips, and unable to control his feelings, left the room. During the whole night he kept walking up and down his room, saying, "Has she not suffered enough without my awakening her grief by my thoughtlessness." The fourth son is an invalid for life, having received a wound in the head. He was taken prisoner with the rest of the followers of Garibaldi at Aspromonte, and in what manner he and his companions were treated, the following letter, addressed to M. Ratazzi by some of the Garibaldian prisoners, will show:—

"Fort of Monte-Ratti,

"Near Genoa, Sept. 11, 1862.

"Sir,—The Official Gazette recently contained a note, by which it appears that the government has declared that it gave the kindest orders with respect to the prisoners of Aspromonte. The undersigned declare that they consider as arbitrary and illegal the term "prisoners of war," which the government has applied to them, and which would withdraw them from the jurisdiction legally competent to try them. Upon this point, however, they reserve their protest for an opportune time, when they will invoke the laws and principles of public right sanctioned by the statutes. Meanwhile, in order that public opinion may not be led into error, and that there may exist a document to prove that the kind measures boasted of by the official gazette, if they ever were really ordered, were not executed; the undersigned wish to inform the minister that so far from they and their companions being treated with distinction and respect, on the contrary, from the very arrangement of the fort in which they are enclosed, 450 prisoners are crowded together without sufficient air or motion, prevented from walking outside the dormitories, and therefore compelled from want of space to remain always stretched, which is contrary to the very first principles of health. The undersigned, although specially watched, out of the personal deference of the commandant of the fort, are shut up to the number of thirteen, in a small room, three metres square, without ever being able to go out. They have not yet been able to receive a letter from their families, and they are not certain that any of the letters written by them have arrived at their address. They lie upon the ground; they are in want of everything necessary for personal cleanliness and the preservation of health. They are rigorously refused all external communication, and it becomes every day more and more difficult for them to write or procure any necessaries from without. This is how we are permitted to procure the conveniences to which we have been accustomed, as the Official Gazette alleges. The undersigned do not ask for any special favour for themselves from the minister, but in their own names and in the name of their companions, they protest against this unworthy treatment and this strange rigour, which have been suggested by an unreasonable fear. The government which treats us—us who have taken arms for the national unity to the cry of 'Italy and Victor Emmanuel'—worse than it would dare to treat the vilest criminals, is endeavouring to excuse itself to public opinion by official lies. We demand light, air, room, motion; permission to obtain necessaries at our own expense, and to make known to our relations and friends where we are and how we are. Grant us this; cease to tell lies and to deceive our families and country.

"(Signed) G. Civinini, Rocco Ricci Granito, Baron Turillo Malato, Enrico Cairoli, Nicolas Cortese Ferrugia, Leopold Sanza, G. Anzaldi, Marquis de Spadaro, Chevalier Bisignani, Achille di Villamena, Marquis R. Maurigi, Stefano Piraino, Prince Conrad Niscemi, Gabriel Colonna, De Fiumendisi Cesaro."

But to return to General Garibaldi: Colonel Santa Rosa wrote to one of the Italian papers denying any illtreatment on the part of the ministers towards the General, asserting that he was furnished with everything that he could require by the government, and that Mesdames Schwabe, Cairoli, and Montegazza had not supplied any comforts to the wounded soldier, but that the sub-prefect had furnished everything necessary. A letter from Spezzia, dated September the 6th, states :—"The apartments allotted to Garibaldi and his attendants (five in number, since the staff officers who accompanied him to Spezia have been removed to the fortress of Finestrella) consist of a suite of six rooms, but five of them are literally without furniture, except half a dozen *dirty matresses* placed on the floor on which the fellow prisoners of the General spend their long and tiresome nights. The kitchen is equally unfurnished. The General's chamber alone presents any appearance of furniture, the walls have been at one time covered with velvet paper, which now hangs down in shreds from the effect of time and damp. There are two great cupboards of wretched appearance and painted yellow, four or five chairs, a little table on which stands a brass candlestick, with a tallow candle, and the bed where Garibaldi is lying. This bed is worth notice ; the mattress is of doubtful thickness."

General Bixio writes from Genoa, "September the 5th. Having just returned from a visit to Spezzia, I read this morning in the papers the news taken from the *Official Gazette*, that Garibaldi had been carried to Varignano, to an apartment which had been expressly prepared for him* I do not know what in the language of the Minister Rattazi 'to prepare an apartment' can mean when the General remained several days without a change of bed, and only yesterday evening could such a bed be procured through the kindness of a private citizen, the shipbuilder of Spezzia dockyard. All the gentlemen who are at Varignano with the General have for their bed a mattress

* It will be remembered that the General was kept on board the steamer twenty-four hours after the arrival, under pretext that an apartment was being prepared for him.

stretched on the floor. Nothing has been as yet provided in the shape of linen bandages or leeches—nothing, in one word, of what is wanted to nurse a wounded man. Yesterday, Dr. Riboli was obliged to ask a lady of Spezzia for some linen. The minister, occupied as he is daily by sending a host of carbineers and policemen to this tranquil place, has not had time to occupy himself with the health of the prisoner. The surgeons themselves who had been sent to Varignano had the greatest difficulty in getting admitted into the room of the General for want of orders from the military commander." Signor Ratazzi may aspire to secure for himself the renown of being a defender of order; but he can have no claim to a reputation for humanity, and it would be better for him to conform his official news to the facts. Now, there is a telegraph from Varignano to Turin, by means of which the ministers were informed of everything that passed, and even of all that was said, in the General's room. It was on the 30th of August that the captain of the *Duke of Genoa* received orders from the ministers to take the wounded Garibaldi to Spezzia; yet General Bixio, writing of the facts as they existed on the night of the 4th of September, the sixth day afterwards, says, "*nothing* which was wanted for a wounded man had been provided; the General was without bandages, or a change of linen, and indebted to a ship-builder for a bed." It must also not be forgotten that Garibaldi had with him at Aspromonte everything which it was possible for wounded men to require, and that the royal troops not only plundered the medicine chests, but those containing linen for the wounded. Dr. Prandina applied to the Vice-Prefect, and he did supply him with two pairs of sheets, six pillow covers, eight towels, and several leeches; but this, let it be noted, was not until after the publication of Bixio's letter. Dr. Prandina also writes, "I had observed the difficulties to be encountered, and that I had need of much more than I received. Mesdames Mantegazza, Cairoli, Schwabe, and the Marchese Pallavicini arrived, and supplied at once everything which could be required." To this list the name of Madam Pulszky should be added.* Dr. Partridge writing from Spezzia on the 20th of September, states "The General's manner is very patient and tranquil, *his friends* have supplied him (and I hope will continue to do so) with those comforts necessary to his present condition." So much for the statements of the *Official Gazette* respecting the Italian government having provided everything required for Garibaldi's comfort.

Notwithstanding the circular of General Durando, which in itself amounted to an amnesty, if it had any meaning at all, the government journals still persisted in stating that General Garibaldi was to be placed upon his trial. No one about him, however, believed this for an instant. Letters had been received stating that his papers had been saved, and with these in Garibaldi's possession, it was next to impossible to try him on a charge of treason. Of course, this, like everything else, was known at Turin, and soon afterwards the public were informed that the king's daughters had implored their father to pardon Garibaldi.

It will be seen that General Durando accused Garibaldi in his circular of being mislead by Mazzini. "Led astray," said General Durando, "by sentiments which respect for law and a juster appreciation of the state of things ought to have restrained, and too accessible to the incitements of the sect better known by its victims than its successes, he did not quail before the prospect

---

* Extract of Letter from Spezzia:—" There have been also three Genoese ladies to see Garibaldi, who have at different times sent him large sums of money for the national cause; now, they have sold their jewels to provide for the distressed families of some of the Garibaldian volunteers. Singularly enough, their *names were Mary, Martha, and Magdalen.* When Madam Montegazzas arrived and found the General in want of everything and without a farthing, she gave him three hundred francs—all the money she had with her—intending it for his personal use. 'Give it to the commandant for my poor wounded,' was his instant order. Of himself he never appears to have thought for an instant. This lady arrived about three days after the General. The doctors were consulting at the time, and refused to admit her; but the patient hearing her voice, asked if she did not want to come in, and Col. Santa Rosa then interfered in her behalf. When she entered, she hastened to the General, and kneeling by his side, wept so bitterly that all present were infected by her example. Fearing that her presence might impede the doctors, she retired. While they were probing the wounds, the patient related how she had, when the Garibaldians were fighting the Austrians at Varnese, crossed over the lake amidst a shower of bullets to ask his leave to nurse his wounded."

of civil war, and wished to make himself the arbiter of the alliances and destinies of Italy. * * * * * * The facts that I have just briefly recapitulated will leave no other trace among us than a painful recollection."

One day a gentleman was the bearer of a letter* to the General, in which the writer had expressed himself strongly on the supposed intrigues of the Mazzinian party, which he accused of having betrayed the hero of Marsala; the General read it carefully, and then turning to his visitor observed: "Our friend is deceived, he must have got these ideas from those people at Turin." Then, after a pause, he resumed, in the deep tones which are natural to him when interested in his subject: "Mazzinians! Mazzini! 'tis folly. What has Mazzini to do with this question? I moved because it was my duty! After a hundred successful marches, I have now had one unsuccessful, and I am crippled, but for that, I should have entered Rome as I entered Naples."† The *Movimento* of Genoa published the following letter from Garibaldi. "I have read in No. 1,027 of the *Perseveranza*, a letter quoted from the *Esprit Public*, which is said to have been written to me by an agent of Mazzini's, on August 19, and to have been found upon me by the Royal troops at Aspromonte. These two bits of news form one lie." The Marquis Pallavicini also wrote, denying in the strongest possible terms that Mazzini had exercised the slightest influence over Garibaldi in the affair of Aspromonte. On the 22nd of August, Mazzini himself wrote to Mr. John M'Adam, of Glasgow, a letter, from which the following is extracted: "It is perfectly

* Mazzini, though he disapproved of the expedition to Rome, wrote afterwards, "Garibaldi has fought all the battles of Italian unity. Garibaldi has given that unity ten millions of citizens. Garibaldi is the living symbol of the desire of the whole nation; he was struck down, while he was moving not against you, but to where the Italian right has been proclaimed by you, and has been denied by the foreigner, not to change the orders of the state, or to combat your programme, but to the fulfilment of both one and the other; his imprisonment recalls to Europe that of Columbus."

† There is more in this answer than at first appears. Before Garibaldi entered Naples, the king left, and that capital was consequently entered without a drop of blood being spilt. Now, the intention of the Pope to leave Rome on Garibaldi's approach has been already alluded to, and the General therefore hoped ultimately to enter that capital in the same manner without bloodshed.

true that for eighteen months, I have been endeavouring to persuade Garibaldi that we ought to direct all our efforts towards Venice. Now, however, the die is cast, and all discussion on the matter would be out of place; as for me, I shall help the movement according to my power." Mazzini also wrote to the *Unita Italiana*, contradicting the statements of the *France*, the *Patrie*, and other French and Italian semi-official papers, that he had in any way influenced Garibaldi. He adds, "Garibaldi is no man's instrument." Mazzini declared at the house of a friend in London, in July, 1862, that he knew no more of Garibaldi's plans than an unborn infant, but that he would support him to the best of his power.

During the time Garibaldi was in Sicily, the *Official Gazette* stated "that his expedition alone prevented Rome from being given up, and that but for that expedition the Italian government would have had Rome at that time." Now the French minister, M. Trouville, in answer to the circular of General Durando, stated that at no time had the French Government ever given to the Italian Government the most remote idea that it would ever allow it to occupy Rome, and referred to a dispatch in the previous May for the confirmation of these statements. So much again for the truthfulness of the Ratazzi administration.

Three doctors in attendance on the General were made prisoners with him. One of the three was Pietro Ripari, who was surgeon to Garibaldi during the siege of Rome, proved equally brave on the field of Aspromonte, and intrepid in the manly endurance of seven years' imprisonment in the papal prison of Pagliano.* In

* He has since published a medical History of Garibaldi's wound. He thus describes his chief: A high open forehead, eyes, lively and eloquent, and suiting themselves to every thought of his mind; sight, intensely acute, and it is a singular fact, that when he gazes his eye horizontally on space as if in search of an idea, the iris contracts, and a very flame seems to shine from it. No living soul can read the depths of those thoughts. The General's temperament is the most enviable that nature can bestow on mortal, it is at once nervous, sanguine, and lymphatic. Hence, we may almost say, Garibaldi is composed of three men, namely:—The man of thought, the man of action, and the man of calm and secure determination. I have known and know the bravest soldiers, Ugo Bassi, who rushed with joy into danger; Manara, who exposed his great chest as though it were a delight; Bixio, who gallops

1859 he again joined his chief, and took part in the campaign on the lakes; in 1860 he was in Sicily and Naples, and being in attendance on the General at Aspromonte, he now shared his captivity.*

The General's sufferings in prison were great: he passed many sleepless nights; and during this painful period the ligatures and plasters were frequently unlaced, but without the slightest diminution of the agony. At length the talked of amnesty arrived; the exact terms of the telegram which conveyed it were these:—"His Majesty this day (Oct. 5th, 1862) signed the decree of amnesty to all the authors or accomplices of the late acts and attempts at rebellion which have taken place in the Southern provinces of the Kingdom, absolving them from the consequences, personal or otherwise, which might attach to them through the cause of justice. All the deserters from the land or sea service are actually excepted from the action of this amnesty, which, to-morrow, will be published in the *London Gazette.*" On Col. St. Rosa speaking to the General respecting the amnesty, he said "It is only the guilty that can be amnestied."

---

to seek for danger in the thickest battle; Menotti, who stood like a tower to be shot at by a regiment at point blank distance; Missori, that gallant soldier, who armed with a revolver, saved the General's life; Nullo, who smoothing his long moustache, galloped laughing, into the fight; and many others. But the solemn calmness, the supreme bravery of Garibaldi, I have seen in no other. The sentiment which prevails in him, and round which all other feelings concentrate, is love. He loves man individually, and collectively he loves humanity, he loves creation."

* The statement made in some of the papers that Garibaldi would have attempted his own life after Aspromonte is entirely destitute of foundation. What took place was this: While the surgeons were dressing his wound, and he was smoking a cigar, a lieutenant of the royal staff appeared before him armed, and all the usages of war demanded that a parlamentare should be unarmed. In this case, the gentleman was not only armed but accompanied by his men armed also. Garibaldi ordered him to be disarmed, saying he had made war for 30 years and never before saw a parlamentare appear in such a fashion. Those about the General, in their astonishment that he should notice such a trifle at such a time, did not instantly obey him. The General, to give emphasis to what he said, and to attract their attention, took a revolver which lay by his side, and slightly striking the ground with it, repeated the order, which was then obeyed; and he gave the revolver half-smiling to one of the surgeons, but saying at the same moment, "Who is this young man, and why did he not come before (meaning before the royal troops commenced firing); and what are they doing to my people?" When it was explained to him that the officer had really been sent as a parlamentare, he ordered his sword, and those of his companions, to be restored to them. A sergeant of the royal army, who had been one of the thousand, though he had not fired, implored his pardon for appearing in arms against him. The General said kindly, "My friend, you have nothing to ask pardon for, you have only done your duty."

The Government message did not reach the prison till nearly eleven at night, when the General slept, and the whole party were in bed except those who watched by his side. He awoke at a little past midnight, and hearing talking around him, enquired "what is it?"—the answer was, "the amnesty has arrived;" "has it," said Garibaldi, and turning on his side, he either slept or appeared to sleep. Many were surprised that Garibaldi accepted or refused the amnesty; but it must be remembered that from first to last, he protested that he had only done his duty to the best of his power, and he denied the justice of his imprisonment; but had he insisted on remaining a prisoner, his fellow prisoners would to a man have refused their liberty. And here let it be noted that about 1,500 of his followers were in confinement, most of them packed in close miserable rooms; they were wearied of their prison, and many of them dreadfully ill from the hardships of their lot. Speaking of the amnesty, old Repardi observed, "We are only pardoned by halves; why do not the ministers extend the act of grace and pardon us for all that we have done at Marsala, at Milatezza; for our crimes at Perlmo, and our rebellion at Capua; be assured that more than one of us regrets his share in the rebellion." The General's state became much worse after hearing of the condemnation to death of five Garibaldian soldiers, who had participated in the affair at Aspromonte, and who were proved to be deserters from the regular army. The charges against them were desertion and treason in bearing arms against the state. In the end however the sentence was commuted to transportation for life. After this change, the General's condition slightly improved. Mr. Taylor, M.P., who saw Garibaldi about this time, writes, "his calm, his wonderful serenity of demeanour seem not to heed, still less to be excited by the surroundings. I have already given you in two words the impression produced—that of wonderful serenity, calm, courteous, and tranquil; thankful for the least service rendered by any of his attendants; an utter absence of anything like the peevishness of a suffering man—yet without any appearance of pressure, or the exercise of control over himself—it was an atmosphere of moral elevation." A curious evidence of his stoical bearing of bodily pain was given when Zannetti first probed the wound. The surgeon knew the agony must be intense, but the patient did not move a muscle. "Does it not hurt you, General?" asked Zannetti, "Intensely," replied Garibaldi, almost smiling, and the operator was forced to ask him to show by some expression of his face where the severest pain was felt. Baron Zannetti is one of the first surgeons in Italy. During the reign of the Grand Duke, an Austrian sent for him, saying that he, the Grand Duke, was indisposed, and that the Baron must attend without delay. Zannetti replied, that he was about to visit a poor man who was very ill. On his return another messenger waited, Would he visit a sick soldier?—he went, performed an operation, and saved the soldier's life; he returned the large fee sent him by the Grand Duke, adding that he went to attend a poor soldier. General Garibaldi's visitors, despite the injunctions of the doctors, were undoubtedly too numerous; but it must be remembered that the General declared that the very sound of an English voice did him good, and that but for English sympathy he should have been dead. "The love of the people of England has saved my life," he one day observed. Knowing his father's fondness for children, one of the sons of the General took a little boy one day into his room—the child had on a red shirt over his white frock—"Oh! are you also a rebel, my poor darling," said Garibaldi, kissing him again and again, "don't you know that none but rebels and traitors wear that dress?"

The General, in his debilitated state, caused by a low wasting fever, sometimes fancied that it was the Emperor Napoleon's personal dislike to him that was the chief reason of the French occupation of Rome. One night, actuated by this feeling, he told one of his attendants, he had never in his life asked a favor of the King, but he thought he would do so now. He would ask to be shot; he was the object of suspicion and distrust to his own Sovereign, which no devotion, no obedience, no success even on his part haa oeen able to remove, and if he were only dead the Emperor might perhaps be induced to give up Rome. As he became weaker the anxiety of his medical attendants increased, and they implored him to permit them to summon others of their body to meet in a consultation. "Gentlemen," answered the General, "you have been trusted with my wounded when I could get no others to attend to them, if you could take care of my wounded, you can take care of me. I wish for no care, for no comfort, for no skill which I have been unable to obtain for the poorest of my wounded." Unable, however, to withstand the entreaties of his friends, he eventually gave way. Most anxious consultations were now held about the removal of the General to Spezzia, which was at last resolved upon, and the Hotel de Milan was taken for himself and friends. Some large rooms at the back of the Hotel had been previously let out as Government offices, and the Hotel itself had been sold to the Government to be given up in six months; before the Spring of which however the new Hotel de Milan was expected to be ready for occupation; so that should the General's health have detained him for so long a period as six months, it would have been easy to have moved him from one establishment to the other. Nevertheless, the Italian Government is said to have been of a different opinion; and the landlord was reminded that the Hotel de Milan must be given up at the time fixed, to a day. The excuse for this summary proceeding was that the General's health had compelled him to remain at Varignano, and that the same thing might occur again in Spezzia. They were told to have no fears on the subject, as the Hotel should be given up at the time fixed.

Garibaldi left Varignano on the morning of the 22nd of October. The following account of his removal to Spezzia from his prison is partly taken from an English newspaper:—"Garibaldi left Varignano on the morning of the 22nd of October. It was like a day of midsummer—the sea without a ripple, the sky cloudless, and the whole scenery of the beautiful bay in its brightest, freshest colouring. The marble mountains of Carrara absolutely blazed in the sun, and the villas, chapels, and vineyards of the surrounding shore were reflected as in a mirror in those quiet blue waters which are so treacherous, and can be so dangerous. To add to the beauty of the picture, three Italian line-of-battle ships float proudly on the bay. One of these vessels, too, suggests a curious reflection. The *San Giovanni*, the deck of which is crowded with officers and men, eager to see a hero who is not only a soldier but a sailor, is a Neapolitan vessel, and is part of the vast gift bestowed in 1860 by Garibaldi on the King of Italy. At half-past ten the little steamer engaged for Garibaldi steamed slowly out of the bay of Le Grazzie, in which is the lazzaretto of the Varignano, and took a direct course for the quay of La Spezzia. It had in tow a large boat, in which was a sort of canopy with some dozen men standing around it, partly in red shirts, partly in plain clothes. At the distance of about 500 yards from the Mole the steamer stopped. In the meantime the cry of "Garibaldi is come!" echoed through the little town, and soon the pier was crowded with Spezise, while cafés sent out their frequenters, and English tourists turned from unfinished breakfasts to see what will, perhaps, be the sensation of their journey. Had the arrival been as last night was anticipated, not a person within five miles would have been absent, but the idea had got abroad that the General would not be moored before mid-day. When the boat was cast off by the steamer, it was taken in tow by two boats, one manned with sailors from the *San Giovanni* war steamer, the other by amateurs, some in red shirts, among which was the Garibaldino whose official Spezzia had just imprisoned three days for crying 'Viva Garibaldi!' Stretched on an English mechanical bed lay the Italian martyr; the large boat in tow was escorted by two other boats full of men-of-wars men, and by a third boat manned by Spegese in red shirts, who had fought in those campaigns of Varese and Marsala. Round the canopy, under which reclined their patient, and from the sides of which hung two laurel chaplets, stood Albanese, Bresili, Ripardi, and Pandina the doctors, whose anxious, troubled faces told that the removal was not without peril. As the boat touched the quay, the scene was very curious; the pier was crowded up to the water's edge, and when the well-remembered face of Garibaldi was seen, a cheer half burst from the lips of the assembled multitude, but at a sign from Ripardi the crowd was dumb, and stood hushed in silent reverence. The people, too, fell back unordered before the red shirts, and preceded by a naval officer in full uniform, and surrounded by his doctors and staff, the bed was placed on a stretcher, and, supported by eight men, was raised above the heads of the bystanders and carried down the pier. The General was perfectly calm, and showed no signs of the pain he must have felt. As the litter was borne forward, it was halted under a cluster of acacia trees, that the crowd might see the hero—the man who, as Mr. Gladstone declared, 'Italy loved the best.' As he proceeded there was a dead silence; every head was uncovered. Once they paused to rest. It was a strange picture. The greatest man of his country wounded, and suffering, surrounded by the friends of his choice, around the silent crowd."

"I have seen," says the correspondent of the *Daily Telegraph*, "the General in his grandest moment—the idol of a people whom he had restored to freedom, the Dictator receiving homage which he did not covet, the soldier after the brilliant if bloody triumph, and finally, listening to expressions of sympathy from strangers and fellow-countrymen on the bed of sickness. But I have never seen himself more grand, or his reception more remarkable than to-day, when, as a traitor wounded for conspiring to increase the power and territory of his king, and pardoned for an error, which may even now cost him his life, and into which he was deluded by specious promises and semi-support—he was borne a shattered wreck, to what will be another lengthy imprisonment. When the General reached the

Hotel de Milan he was much exhausted. There was, too, some little difficulty in getting the bed up the stairs of the Hotel de Milan, and that added to the fatigue. Soon after the General's arrival at the Hotel de Milan, the Ministers it is said, sent to see if General Garibaldi would receive General de Medica. He did so and very kindly. The Marquis Repoli sending his best respects, the Ministers went to the General's sick couch to make friends, it was stated, in order that they might retain office. Dr. Nelaton came to Italy with a letter from M. Drouyn de Lhuys to the French ambassador at Turin, requesting him to arrange that the doctor might without delay, visit the 'most popular man of the day,' and give him the advantage of his skill. It at first created a feeling of surprise that a French minister so opposed to Italian unity should manifest so much sympathy with one who had devoted a life to the accomplishment of that unity: the explanation is this; M. Drouyn de Lhuys was at Monte Video when Garibaldi filled that part of the world with the fame of his heroic achievements in favour of liberty. The French Minister then had a near view of the General, who though calm and gentle in private life, proved such a lion on the battle field: all this made a deep impression on the mind of M. Drouyn de Lhuys; and, although his opinions are now widely different from those of Garibaldi, he remembers former times and former occurrences with a pleasure which he never attempts to conceal. Count Walewski also, Mr. Pulsyty informs me, was under the bewitching influence of Garibaldi's heroism and virtue in America. Before he arrived, Nelaton was by no means a warm admirer of Garibaldi. He was a man of cold and matter-of-fact character, not given to poetic ideas; he had never seen Garibaldi before he visited him professionally, and he went to him only as he would have done to any other patient in whom many people felt an interest. He left him, however, with very different feelings; he was perfectly charmed by his gentleness, his greatness of mind, and patient uncomplaining endurance of all the agony to which he was most unwillingly compelled to put him. Nelaton heard from the suffering patient not one word of anger or complaint; he found him perfectly calm, confident in the triumph of his cause, he listened to him praising the Italian army, to him speaking kindly of the King, and what wonder if Nelaton exclaimed in the excitement of the moment, 'Garibaldi is not a soldier, he is a saint! I am sure he will work miracles, he has worked one already, for he has moved me deeply by his very smile, and that is a miracle.' There was a Monte Videan gentleman, who came all the way to Italy to see Garibaldi. He arrived to find Aspromonte. He was never tired of talking of his boyish remembrances of how he had often sat on Garibaldi's knee, of his father, one of the ministers, had constantly told him that they should all have been murdered by Rosas but for Garibaldi. He spoke also much of the universal respect as well as affection entertained for him in those days. Certainly, his serenity under suffering, and his constant cheerful smiling patience, and the unfainting perfect temper with which he sustains his irksome captivity, are quite as wonderful as his muscles on the battle field, politics were ordered by the doctors to be entirely banished from his room. He usually reads the *Diritto*, but one day he saw quite a different paper on the table, namely, the *Official Gazette* of the kingdom of Italy; for an instant his eye flashed, and he enquired, with his usual calmness however, who had brought that paper into that room; Repardi explained that he was only using it to place the dressing upon it, and the General's expression returned to its usual gentle smile. Only he observed still smiling, adverting to the prospect of his long confinement, Ratazzi could not have chosen better the position and the mode of the wound.

"I have," continues the same correspondent, "mentioned before that the Italian fleet was in the bay. By none is the General more passionately beloved than by the sailors. Day by day they thronged the Hotel for tidings for some days before we left. From eleven to two there was one continued procession of sailors, and the pupils of the Royal

Naval Schools visiting the Hotel. The door of the General's room was left open, and they marched past, each being allowed a sight of him as he lay. Many a rough tar wiped a tear from his eye with his jacket sleeve. Many fairly broke down, and sobbed aloud in the anti-room. One man observes, after so much roughing it for Italy, this is the pension. All took their shoes off; and so gently did they come and leave, that one day it was only when the little pupils came, that the General was aware of what was being enacted around him, than he raised his head, and smiling that wonderful smile of his, kissed his hand to the children."

On the 29th of October there was a consultation of 17 doctors, and happily the majority were of opinion that amputation was unnecessary; an opinion confirmed the next day by the great Russian surgeon, Dr. Puogoff, but all joined in recommending the removal of the General to the milder climate of Pisa. This was affected early on the morning of the 8th of November, on board the steamer Moncahree, telegraphed for from Genoa. The plan was to sail to Leghorn, and proceed from thence to Pisa by railway.

Getting quietly through the city, he was informed, just as he was leaving Spezzia, that the Leghornese were preparing an ovation for him, to avoid which, he directed that the steamer should be at the mouth of the Arno, where, being carefully placed in a boat, he was towed up the river to Pisa. He was received with the greatest enthusiasm. Eight strong young men carried him in his bed to the Hotel, and an immense crowd remained for several hours under the windows. Meanwhile, the steamer with the General's luggage and part of the suite steamed round to Leghorn, where immense preparations had been made to receive the General. The ships were dressed with flags, and the harbour was a mass of boats, all crowded with gaily dressed people; the preparations in the town itself were perfect in every respect; the entire absence of military was, however, a remarkable feature—it was asserted that the soldiers were all confined to barracks, in order to prevent their taking part in the popular demonstration.

At Pisa the people insisted on having the Garibaldi Hymn repeated over and over again each night at the Opera. On one occasion the manager came forward and requested to know if the audience wished to have the hymn or the opera for the rest of the evening, and the hymn was resolved on unanimously. Upon this being mentioned to the General the next morning, some one remarked that the Government had prohibited the hymn. "Let that be ascertained without delay," said the General, "if it prove to be the case, I shall entreat the people, if they love me, not to insist upon the hymn. I wish the orders of the Government to be obeyed." It was, however, ascertained that although General La Marmora had prohibited the hymn in Naples, no orders of a similar nature had been received at Pisa.

The people of Pisa erected a marble slab at the place where Garibaldi landed to commemorate the event, stating that, wounded at Aspromonte, he had come to Pisa for the recovery of his health. This circumstance was considered by the authorities as casting a slur on the Royal army, and on the following day a picket of carbineers was sent to destroy the slab and erect another in its place, with the same inscription, omitting only the words "Wounded at Aspromonte." The next night the Government slab was broken into a hundred pieces by the inhabitants, and they were purposing to put up another which contained the obnoxious words, when General Garibaldi sent to entreat that they would comply with the wishes of the Government; adding, however, the significant words—"Where was I wounded, was it in Cochin China!"

The opening of the Italian Chambers now approached, and many were the speculations as to what would be the conduct of the Garabaldians. The chiefs of the liberal party arrived at Pisa to learn from Garibaldi his views. They were informed that, in every respect he adhered to his old programme, and that above all, he supported a Constitutional monarchy; he begged of them to behave with the greatest moderation, to offer no factious opposition even to the Government of Ratazzi, to vote upon each measure brought before the Chamber, on the merits of that measure itself, above all, to support the Government in any measures which might be brought forward for the augmentation of the Army and the Navy, the suppression of Brigandage, and the increase of Education. On the point of confidence in the ministry, however, there was no hesitation. Those who had so well proved themselves the servants of a Foreign power, could not represent the Constitutional King of a free state.

When the General's wound was alluded to, and he was suffering greatly at the time, he answered, "I cannot even think of such a trifle when we are discussing the interests of Italy." To questions about the state in which Bixio had found him at Varignano, he answered, "I can remember only the lovely view from the windows and the kindness of my friends." No wonder then that the debate which ended in the resignation of the Ratazzi ministry was so remarkable for its moderation.

In the end, however, Rome fell, and the republic was extinguished by the bayonets of republican France. Still unconquered, he led his men from the gates of Rome, but was finally overwhelmed by numbers, and for the time forced to succumb—the name of this man was Giuseppe Garibaldi, born at Nice, a faithful town of the Sardinian Kingdom. He was arrested at Genoa by order of Alfonse La Marmora. On the 10th of September, 1849, there was an animated discussion in the Chamber; it was asserted that the arrest of Garibaldi was in violation of the 26th article of the statute. The Minister stated that Garibaldi had fought for liberty in Rome—a foreign country—without the permission of the Government, and that his arrest had been deserved. Rattazzi and Depretis voted and spoke most eloquently in favour of Garibaldi, and the Chamber decided that the arrest of the General was opposed to the spirit of the Piedmontese constitution, the national sentiment, and the glory of Italy. Notwithstanding this decision, the General was ordered to leave Italy, and only permitted to remain for twenty-four hours at Nice to take leave of his children. A long debate in the Chambers ended in the resignation of the Rattazzi administration, to the satisfaction of the entire country.

On the 26th of September, Baron Lanettee successfully extracted the bullet from the wound in General Garibaldi's ancle, and the number of visits rendering it impossible to obtain the quite necessary for a speedy cure, his return to Caprera was decided upon. On the 11th of December, the general accepted the honorary presidency of a society at Pisa, on which occasion he wrote:—"I accept with pleasure the honorary presidency of your club. I accept it because I know that you will always be reconciled and united with all who sincerely wish our liberty and unity. Yes; let us obtain at any cost the liberty and unity of the country. After having gained the triumph of those two great principles which form your programme, it will be easy—by the light of liberty, which is civilisation—by the light of unity, which is strength—to occupy ourselves. And we shall succeed again with equal triumph by introducing modifications into, and by more fully developing, the institutions which should govern us. In this work you will see, and I will ensure it, we shall have a valiant coadjutor in the Italian army.—G. GARIBALDI."

On the 20th December the General embarked for Caprera. The general and suite filled two boats, which were manned by Garibaldians in red shirts, and were decked with banners, including that which was Garibaldi's standard at the siege of Rome. All Leghorn came out to witness the departure of the General, in spite of early hours and strong weather. The quays were densely peopled, and the water was covered with boats. Above the quays flaunted the great flag of the Trade Union of Italy, and the ensign of the Leghorn lodge of Free Masons, in which guild the General holds a high grade. Garibaldi's suite was composed of Coste, Bruzzesi, Missori, Busso, Guastalla, and an English friend. Unfortunately, it came on to blow so hard soon after the Sardegna had steamed out of harbour, that she could not keep her course, and was compelled to put back to Leghorn for twenty-four hours. The weather moderating, she finally cleared out on Sunday morning, and proceeded on her voyage to Caprera.

The following graphic description of the General's departure is from the pen of the correspondent of a London journal:—"Yesterday evening (Dec. 19) all was ready for the departure of the General. He wished to embark on the Arno and in that way reach Leghorn by a canal, an old work of the Medici which runs from Pisa to that city, and a boat was prepared for the purpose by his friends. This way of travelling, always long and tedious, would have been rendered more so by a heavy fall of rain; therefore, the General, yielding to the prayers of his friends, resolved to go by rail. As he wished to avoid the great demonstrations of popular feeling which are on no occasion wanting, he desired to go by special and to start earlier than the ordinary train. Yesterday he was very tired from receiving so many visitors, and suffered from being obliged to talk, which aggravated his wound by exciting the nervous system. Nevertheless he received all with singular affection and infinite benevolence; and indeed I did not once notice in his serene and calm bearing, I will not say a movement of impatience, but even of vexation or weariness. When all was decided for the departure by railway the weather changed, and therefore the General returned to his first plan of going by the canal. At half-past two in the morning his bed was taken on the shoulders of some of his Pisan volunteers, who claimed for themselves that honour, and with great care was carried down the stairs of the hotel and then by some neighbouring steps to the boat. All Pisa was alive, numerous parties filled the coffee-houses and other places, waiting the hours of departure in order to see their General. The streets, the banks of the Arno, and the bridges were full, and it was with difficulty they were able to make a path in the crowd through which to carry the illustrious wounded. Torches gleamed from all the windows. Bengal lights illuminated the beautiful Lung Arno, and the scene was truly picturesque. In the midst of this crowd which applauded and saluted the hero, we descended the Arno, and entered by the Ponte a Mare, in the canal called the Fosso der Vaicelli. Nothing I can say will give you any idea of this voyage. I can only tell you that for five or six miles, although the hour was so late all the fishermen and boatmen, the only inhabitants, were crowding along the waterside, which was illuminated by bonfires and torches. I who know this country, and know of what people the crowd was composed, find in these truly popular demonstrations, spontaneous, coming from the heart, a new proof of the immense influence which this singular man exercises. To see the wives of these fishermen and boatmen showing themselves in their balconies, lantern in hand, and crying with pleasure that at last they were able to see their hero; the boys and men throwing themselves into the water in order to salute him nearer. Indeed, we who have accompanied him in so many triumphs were astonished when we thought of the ovation through which we were passing, and at so unusual an hour. This demonstration lasted, I may say, during the whole journey, which was longer than we expected, I believe, by the cunning of the good Livornese who rowed the boat slowly, as they wished that the General should arrive at Leghorn by daylight. And here I despair of giving you any idea of the affectionate demonstration made by this good population. Immense crowds, great cheering, words of admiration and of love, women crying, blessings from all; the boats, the bridges, the banks of the canal, the windows, the roads, all were full of people who placed themselves everywhere and anywhere, even at some risks to their lives to see and salute Garibaldi. It is useless; no one who did not see it can have an idea of it. The postal steamer, Sardegna, on which the General wished to go was anchored in the Porto Nuovo; accompanied by a crowd of boats we arrived at the steamer. Here the roughness of the sea rendered difficult to approach, nevertheless, we got alongside. Strong rowers kept the boat firm. A cradle was let down in which the General's bed was put, and the ascent began. He was hardly raised a few inches, when a heavy sea struck the steamer, knocking it against the boat. It seemed as if it would crush him between the sides. Our hearts were in our throats. The boats tossing on the waves, the confusion, the cries, the cheers, formed an inexplicable tumult in this moment of peril. The General suspended in the air, tranquil and serene, turned himself to the people, drew his hand from under his clothes, and saluted them. Finally, the hour of departure arrived, the General's bed was placed on the deck, he saluted us and kissed us with affection; the parting pained us, and we returned sorrowfully to Leghorn."

CHAPTER XII.

Italy in 1863—The Duel between Minghetti and Ratazzi—The Russians in Poland—Noble Conduct of Mr. Ferguson—The Marquis Cavour and M. Passaglia—Opinions of the Italian Chambers—Mr. Stansfeld, M.P.—Dangers of a Franco-Italian Alliance—State of the Italian Volunteers—Lord H. Lennox on Prisons—The Anniversary of Aspromonte—Napoleon's proposal for a European Congress—Italian Brigandage—Proposed Division of Italy by the French Emperor—Victor Emmanuel's Visit to Naples—The Garibaldian Party—Constitutional Party—The Diritto, the Organ of Garibaldi.

The year 1863 was a quiet one for Italy. Farina, the Prime Minister, was obliged to retire from office by illness, ending in softening of the brain, and was succeeded by the Venosta Minogretti. Administration, the policy pursued by the Italian government, was still the same, based on the alliance and friendship of France. The marriage of Signor Ratazzi with the Princess Bonaparte de Solms, a relative of the Emperor's, has been previously alluded to. Shortly afterwards, Signor Minghetti charged Signor Ratazzi with having stated in the Chamber things which were "false, utterly false," and this led to a duel. To the correspondent of a leading London journal, we are indebted for the subjoined remarks on this encounter: Minghetti had given to Ratazzi the lie direct. The seconds of Minghetti were General Cialdini and Prince Simonetta, and having as challenged, the choice of arms, they chose cavalry sabres. Ratazzi is said never to have had a sabre in his hand before. Minghetti was nearly as much a novice as his adversary. What with cavalry sabres in the hands of civilians, the combatants themselves "stripped to their pants," the surgeon with his case of instruments, and General Cialdini with bushy moustaches, standing by, the *mise en scene* is as picturesque and lugubrious as a landscape by Salvator Rosa. But, in sober seriousness, the great onslaught sinks to the level of a grotesque and absurd scuffle. These two old gentlemen who did not know even the A B C of the sword exercise, appear to have dodged one another, and jumped about, backwards and forwards, in a manner much resembling the sham pugilistic encounters between the clowns in a circus; and in what has it all ended? Why Minghetti and Ratazzi remain still at enmity, notwithstanding the fierce assaults in tierce and carte, between them. Some good may, it is true, accrue from this ludicrous and unseeming exhibition. Ridicule kills, and let the ridiculous side of duelling only become apparent, and the day of its downfall may be computed."

Early in the year, Russian oppression and an utter disregard of existing treaties and conventions led to a revolt in Poland. General Garibaldi thereupon addressed a letter to the people of England, in which he says, "Englishmen! the sons of noble Poland require your aid and support. They have long been protected by you; do not let them perish under the knout—under the barbarous lance of the Cossack. They fight for the independence of their country and for liberty; for which you have already fought and triumphed. Proffer your hand unto them; you will end an oppression protested against so long—you will resuscitate a nation."

Collections were made throughout Italy, the proceeds of which are at the present time still being sent to the unhappy Poles. Garibaldi and the Liberals of Europe desire to have Poland liberated, in order that an ancient and high-spirited people, who were the champions of the Cross when the Crescent threatened it with extirpation, may recover their nationality*; and the

* The following letter was addressed by Garibaldi from Caprera to a young Russian:—"My dear child,—You ask me for a word of sympathy with Russia, the country of your birth. Our Saviour was born on the banks of the river Jordan, and

General in June, 1863, forwarded the subjoined touching letter from Caprera to poor Sierakowski, who died of his wounds while a Russian prisoner:—

"My worthy Friend—In three weeks, by your direction of the rising of the Palatinate of Kovno, and by your brilliant courage, you have gained the admiration of all Europe. Now prisoner in the hands of the Russians, and mortally wounded, you address yourself to me, recommending to my care your noble country. Would that I could actively display the great sympathy with which your holy cause inspires me! But, alas! I must remain inactive. Believe this, however—the people of Europe will not allow your country to be cruelly destroyed. I follow with heartfelt interest every movement of your insurrection. Bravest of the brave! your courage, your enthusiasm, and your daring, teach us how despots should be fought.—I pray you accept my friendship. "GARIBALDI."

In March the accounts of the General's health were gloomy, and it was apparent that he suffered greatly; the hero, however, never once repined, but answered all questioners, as to his health, with the cheering assurance that he was better. As it

---

when he proclaimed that all men are brothers, he did not ask whether their birthplace was the banks of the Neva or those of the Vistula. The Russians are therefore our brothers, because I have seen that the same sun ripens the fine grapes of Italy, and the splendid corn in the immense fields of your native land. I affectionately kiss your forehead.—GARIBALDI."

He was asked about the same time to give his autograph for a bazaar in Scotland; he wrote, "I hear with pleasure that you are about to build a new church in your district, and I pray that God may grant his blessing to it."

The following extract from a letter of the Paris correspondent of the *Daily Telegraph*, December 1863, exhibits the conduct of the Russians in Poland. "As soon as an overwhelming force has for an instant dislodged the insurrection from a parish, the troops and police begin to pillage the inhabitants; they take goods and chattels, horses and cattle, but the difficulty is to sell them. The only purchasers are the few Russian peasants who have been promised their share of the land, and are thus bribed to purchase, for a fifth of its value, the property of the ejected proprietor. Military officers of high grade have not neglected the opportunity, and one military commissioner, Protroff, has gained at least 30,000 francs. I could continue reciting horror after horror, but as they are mere repetitions of the infamies committed by the agents, military and civil, of the Russian Government during the last ten months, and as they are certainly not of a description which 'ten times repeated will still please,' I refrain merely adding, for the benefit of your readers, that I have in my desk letters telling of cruelties which I could not recount in the *Daily Telegraph*, and which if I wrote, and you would publish, I do not think would be credited. Very little scratching of the Russ still reveals the Tartar."

was feared he was rapidly becoming weaker, the distinguished English surgeon, Mr. Ferguson, was applied to by Mr. Downing Bruce, on the part of some of the General's friends, to know if he could visit Caprera in case no unprovement took place, offering at the same time to guarantee him a thousand pounds for the journey. Mr. Ferguson answered by placing himself unreservedly at the disposal of the General should his state of health require his assistance; the only thing this noble-minded doctor regretted was, that money had ever been mentioned to him in connection with attendance on Garibaldi, and he declined to accept even travelling expenses. In the meantime, the General's health improved, and the journey became unnecessary; but the *Movimento* of Genoa stated that the gratitude of the General for this further mark of English sympathy could hardly be exaggerated.

On the first of May Father Passaglia's project for a reform in the Italian Church was discussed in the Chambers, and opposed by the Ministry, and Father Passaglia withdrew his motion Immediately afterwards the Marquis Cavour, brother to the lamented statesman, hastily rose, and approaching M. Passaglia, addressed him in a menacing tone, accompanied by the most extravagant gestures. All the Members in the Chamber crowded to the scene of this unseemly altercation, and the business of the day was brought to a standstill. Amid the general confusion and the shouts of laughter that prevailed, it was impossible to obtain at the time any satisfactory account of the real cause of this disturbance; but after the close of the sitting, it was ascertained that the Marquis, whose guest Father Passaglia had been for some time, was in a state of indescribable fury at the course adopted in the Chambers by the great theologian. The sequel of this unlooked-for affair was, that before nightfall the Father indignantly left the house of a man by whom he had been subjected to so great an insult.

On May 14th, Signor Peruzzi defended the French Government against an accusation of duplicity which had been brought against it. The occupation of Rome, said the Signor, was a fact no less painful for the Government of the Emperor than for that of King Victor Emmanuel, but it was impossible to overlook the difficulties of the Emperor's position. He further added that brigandage had declined, and that the Italian Government employed its efforts in order that the French flag should no longer protect conspiracy in Rome. He ended by expressing his confidence in the Emperor, who, to his thinking, understood the spirit of the age. So then, the French flag had protected them—even the Italian Ministry could not deny that. Now let us bring another Parliament into court, and see what the Prime Minister of England has to say on this subject. "Under the shelter of the French garrison* there exists a committee of 200, whose employment is to organize bands of murderers, and send them forth to commit every sort of atrocity." On another occasion the same witness states—"This I mean to say, that at present, Rome being governed by a French garrison, and the Pope being only a puppet in their hands, it rests with the French garrison to prevent that committee from continuing this organized system of sending bodies of men, armed either before they go or to be armed when they get there, to commit outrages on Italian territory." Lord Palmerston did not make any charge against the Roman Government except one which could not be denied—that the authority of the Pope was wholly null, and over-ridden by 20,000 French troops, and that under that state of things, whether the fault lay with the Roman or the French Government, both were chargeable with responsibility for the acts committed by bands sallying forth from

* See Chapter XIV., given as a supplement, for the opinion of the *Times*, August 18, 1863.

† The French Emperor has recently been quoting the opinions of the founder of his house at St. Helena. It would be well if he would act on the following opinion:—"Napoleon himself said at St. Helena that 'Unity of manners, of language, of literature, must at a future, more or less remote, end in bringing her inhabitants under one government.' In 1814 Napoleon walking along the seashore of the island of Elba, with a young Italian, and looking across to the peninsula, suddenly asked, 'What do the Italians think of me?' They would love your majesty more had you given them unity,' was the reply; 'they are right,' said the Emperor; 'I did not think that they would go so far towards that goal. They have exceeded my expectations.'"

Rome for the purpose of committing outrages on the Neapolitan territory.†

The Italian Chambers, after the recess, were opened by the king in person, in an address which maintained utter silence on the subjects of Rome and Venetia, and which it was currently reported had been transmitted for imperial approbation, even before it was submitted to the king of Italy. The capture of five noted brigands at Genoa, on board the *Aunis*, with their passports signed by the Ambassadors of France and Spain, and their subsequent surrender to the French authorities and ultimate restoration to the Italian government, are matters which have been fully discussed, but the mention of the subject of brigandage naturally leads to the present state of feeling in Southern Italy. On this subject Mr. Stansfeld, M.P., shall be first heard:—

"The government," he states, "is hampered in its policy and confirmed in its antagonism to the national party by its alliance with France. Rome is still held by the French, and Italy is kept from the easy conquest of her natural and necessary capital, by her own ally. How can you expect the Italian people—how especially can you expect that southern population which does not owe its liberty either to France, or to Piedmont, but to Garibaldi and his volunteers, and which only gave itself to Piedmont in order to give itself to a united Italy,—to be content that the destinies of its country should hang expectant on a policy dictated from Paris through Turin? But enough of these differences and these difficulties, through which Italy has yet to work her way, and in spite of which she will, it is my profound conviction, conquer her salvation; but Italy must have Venice, she must have Rome, nor can she pause or dally long upon the road which leads to Venice and to Rome, at the risk of fatal internal dissensions and of national suicide; there are great dangers to Europe in a Franco-Italian war of independence, dangers of cessions of territory, dangers of Germany being brought into the field, and of our witnessing an active alliance between Italy and France, not only on the plains of Lombardy, but on the banks of the Rhine. There are great dangers to Italy, and therefore to Europe, in an exclusive Franco-Italian alliance. We all know that Rome in the occupation of the soldiers of the empire, is the focus of all reactionary intrigues and attempts. But this is not all. There is some truth in the statements of disaffection in the south, which have come from the other side of the house to-night—disaffection on the part not of the adherents of the exiled dynasty, but amongst the ranks of the patriots themselves, and which all the absolute fidelity to the cause of Italian unity, and all the unexampled self-abnegation of their leaders, has not sufficed to dispel or to prevent. I do not desire to criticise in a hostile spirit the faults of judgment or of intention on the part of the ministers of Turin which have caused this disaffection. I wish simply to indicate the sole remedy, which consists—I say it without fear of contradiction—in the pursuit of a truly national and independent policy, in trusting and not fearing the people, in rallying them to the aid of the government, and not, in obedience to the exigencies of an exclusive and subservient alliance, refusing to utilize and to organize the immense willing force of a nation which desires to be free. There are three practical bases on which such policy should rest. The first is friendly and open negotiations, in the face of Europe, with the French Emperor for the withdrawal of his troops from Rome. Secondly, in order to dispel the feeling in the south, that whereas of their own will and by volunteer force alone, they freed themselves and gave themselves to Italy, they find themselves treated as provinces of Sardinia; for such purpose, a clearly expressed understanding that, her capital once regained to the Italian nation, a national assembly seated at Rome shall revise in a national sense the laws of the country, in order that the 'statute' of Piedmont, borrowed for a time, may not permanently remain without revision and modification the law of the reconstituted nation. And lastly, the multiplication and the organization of the armed forces, regular and irregular of the country. * * * * Of the volunteer element there is no organization whatever at all worthy of the name.* And thus it comes to pass that Italy is kept in absolute dependence—in wrongful, foolish dependence—whatever confidence her ministers may have in his intentions—on the will and the power of her great ally." The foregoing extract is taken from a speech made by Mr. Stansfeld in the House of Commons in July 1861; but in December 1863, there appears little to alter.

The numerous advantages which the people have obtained in greater freedom, educational establishments,† liberty of conscience, increased development of the resources of the country, extension of railways, increase of trade, and the introduction of modern luxuries are at once and freely acknowledged. Still there is another side to this glowing picture. It has been seen how the Neapolitans loved Garibaldi, who freed them from a despotic rule and bestowed upon them the measure of freedom they enjoyed. Since the 29th of August, 1862, Garibaldi gained in popularity and influence. The correspondent of the *Daily Telegraph*, writing from Turin, April 9, states: "It is curious to take up the papers of Milan, Genoa, Naples, &c., and to read the appeals to Garibaldi. I have thought all along that once re-established in health, it would be found that the General was more powerful throughout Italy, excepting this metropolis, than ever, and that the hero of Varese was become the martyr of Aspromonte." Another gentleman, writing from Naples on the 3rd of February, says:—"For a moment last week, a stranger might have fancied himself in London. There was a public meeting in the winter gardens. A few paces distant, there was

* "The volunteers of Italy do not receive the same countenance from their Government that ours do," writes the correspondent of the *Daily Telegraph*, in December, 1863; "on the contrary, such a stringent, severe, disagreeable edict was enacted on the 11th October respecting them as to cause the society at Naples, which was beginning to be flourishing, to dissolve itself, an example which other of these societies threaten to follow."

† It must be, however, remembered, that the educational establishments founded by the Turin government, are few in number, and that nearly all those established by Garibaldi in Sicily have been abandoned by government.

a detachment of the national guards. The majority of the meeting were well-dressed, respectable men. There were many priests present. Count Ricciardi was in the chair. The Neapolitans instead of novices acted like adults in the school of liberty, for never, even in England, have I seen so large a body of men conduct themselves with more perfect order. The Emperor was treated without mercy, which was the signal for the consul to withdraw. England was described as the mistress of liberty, a sentiment which was received with shouts of applause. The government was spoken of in terms of great distrust and censure, while the bare mention of the name of Garibaldi drove the vast assembly frantic."

Now, how were those who followed the General treated by the government of the King of Italy? Let Lord H. Lennox speak. It had been stated that, from first to last, the nobleman in question had been surrounded by the agents of Mazzini during his visit to Naples, and that they had knowingly misrepresented the state of things. Be it so; but they could not deprive him of his eyes, so he will only be introduced to relate what came under his observation. When he visited the fourth prison the gaoler stated that it was capable of accommodating 650 persons, but that 1,359 were at that time incarcerated within its walls. Lord Lennox entered, and found in one cell eight or nine priests, about fourteen laymen suspected of political offences, and ten or twelve convicted felons. In the next cell there were about 157, the greater number of whom were untried. During the entire day, with the exception of a short time allowed for exercise in a wretched yard, and all night, they were kept in that cell, not knowing for what they were incarcerated; and with them was a man who had been convicted of murder, and who was condemned to be executed. In the next room he found 230 wretched men, in a state of wretchedness and squalor, which would require an abler and more eloquent tongue than his to describe. They were men of different classes, who had been condemned to that living tomb because they had listened to the voice of Garibaldi. Many of them had been imprisoned so long that their clothes were worn out, and they were without money to replace them. Lord Lennox is fully borne out in his statements by one who suffered the horrors of the Italian prisons.*

General Bixio, not generally too merciful, had stated in his place in the Turin Chambers, that a system of blood had been established in southern Italy, and had also expressed an opinion, that if Italy were to be made a nation, it must be done by justice, and not by the shedding of blood. The correspondent of the *Daily Telegraph*, writing from Turin, lets in a flood of light on the treatment of Garibaldi by the king of Italy. He says :—

" Before this letter reaches you, a year will have elapsed since Italy committed that great act of ingratitude which has almost

---

* The following is an extract from the *Daily News*, relating to the prisoners of Aspromonte. "In this favoured land, where our very criminals are pampered and petted in their prisons, if we are to be moved by a love of justice, with what horror should we read an account such as the following, of the treatment of the patriotic and unfortunate prisoners of Aspromonte, as given in the letter of one of their number. It is taken from the *Popolo d' Italia*, which states that in Nisida and other Bagni, more than forty Garibaldians groan as deserters, with a chain attached to their feet. " '12th January, 1863.

" 'After the day of Aspromonte, you know that I was condemned to death, with all my companions, with whom I had followed General Garibaldi. The punishment of death was commuted for me into forced labour for life. On the 21st of November I was torn from my colours, and confined in the civil prisons, where I have suffered from hunger, want of sleep, and from all kinds of insects. On the 19th of December I was dragged to Palermo, to the central prison, and for seven nights slept on the damp ground without shoes and even deprived of a shirt, asking in vain for bread, even on the day of the Nativity. On the 27th I was transferred to the Bagnio, where I had a chain of iron of 18 lbs. weight attached to my feet. In this state I have but one ray of hope left, the mercy of my sovereign, of which I do not doubt, 'unhappy one.' For if it be true that I deserted my regiment, it is very true besides, that I did not desert the banner of Italy and Victor Emmanuel. This was the banner of General Garibaldi, and was also mine—the banner of the King of Italy. Mine was no desertion from vileness to fight against Italy. The whole world has judged of our intentions. I resign myself, therefore, to my destiny, whatever it may be. Love ever the poor.

'Prisoner of Aspromonte.'

" What shall we think and say of the government of a country which thus rewards the best and bravest of its citizens?

" Senor Siccirdi also complained in the chamber on the 18th of April, of the bad administration of justice in the southern provinces, and of the summary executions of brigands. Mr. Layard, the under secretary for foreign affairs, in his place in the house, whilst he truly stated that the progress of the liberal movement had so far resulted beneficially for the Italian people, observed also that there were many things in that country which were to be deplored, 'that some of the prisons in Naples were no doubt in an unsatisfactory state, and he admitted also, that the condition of Italy was not satisfactory, at the same time, great things had never been accomplished without great trials, and Italy must be prepared to go through her day of trial.' "

cost her her greatest living citizen. The shot which struck Garibaldi, at Aspromonte, has produced some curious consequences. It cost a cabinet its power; a minister his career; a general, nay, two—for who has forgotten the picture of Cialdini, calmly watching the embarkation of his half-murdered brother-in-arms?—their popularity; moreover, it stamped its disgrace on a brave soldiery, in the shape of the 'medal for the campaign of Aspromonte;' and if it has not deprived the king of the assistance of his bravest subject, and sent Garibaldi for ever into the arms of his greatest enemies, it is only owing to the patience and long-suffering of that hero whom Napoleon, Ratazzi, La Marmora, and General Pallavicino, made a martyr. It is an unpleasant story, and tells against all Italy; but perhaps the worst part of it is that, up to this day, through all the months of severe suffering of the man who gave him Naples and Sicily, the King of Italy has never sent even an aide-de-camp to inquire after Garibaldi. The government has just suffered a defeat in the municipal elections of Naples, where strong and advanced Liberals have been returned in every case. Such names as those of the Duca di Saudonato, Lazzaro, Nicotera, Migogna, Sterbini, editor of the *Roma*, Morelli of Il Pensiero, Fanelli di Martino, and Barilla, must make a strong comment on the unpopularity of the government and of the continued popularity of Garibaldi. Nearly all the elected have served under him in the southern provinces. "My accounts from Naples speak of some trifling demonstrations—of crowds following the guard just relieved from the Palazzo Reale, and crying out for the 'Hymn of Garibaldi,' which of course the authorities were not wise enough to have played, and so end the dispute; and of patrols haunting Toledo the livelong night when they might have been in bed. Greater demonstrations are anticipated on the 29th, the fatal day of Aspromonte. Premising that when a government not only does such a brutal savage act, but commits itself by such an idiotic error as shooting the one great man of its country, it deserves all that may happen from it, and further adding that if the whole of the south of Italy should rise in open rebellion on Friday next, Signor Urbano Ratazzi should alone be arraigned for it."

The patriotism of Garibaldi prevented even the possibility of such an event, from the first instant when he lay wounded and bleeding at Aspromonte, he gave but one order, "If Italy loves me and trusts me, let her obey the law and submit to the government of the king;" so now, when the anniversary of that disgraceful scene approached, it became known through the length and breadth of the land that Garibaldi asked from those who loved him that there should be no public demonstrations, and the day passed off quietly and silently; as the people of Italy forgot all recollection of the treachery by which the Patriot of Italy was betrayed, they again plighted their fidelity to him, and therefore to national unity. It was wisely determined at Turin, however, that no official obstacles should be opposed to the demonstrations of popular feeling at the celebration of the anniversary of Garibaldi's entry into the southern capital, and the result entirely justified this act of deference to national sentiment. There was unbounded enthusiasm on the ever-memorable 7th of September, but there was nothing that could be otherwise than satisfactory to the most scrupulous and sensitive votary of law, order, and Victor Emmanuel. The hymn which bears the name of "National" was sung by tens of thousands of voices from morning till night and from night till morning. But the name of Garibaldi most assuredly represents the cause of Italy, one and indivisible, and struggling for the union and good of his beloved country, there can be no question, Garibaldi's highest aspiration is to crown Victor Emmanuel at the Capitol.

Again, the people of southern Italy dislike the French alliance. On the 5th of November the Emperor proposed a Congress to settle the affairs of Europe. The English ministers conceived that there was no good in disguising the fact that France, with her enormous standing armies and her autocratic form of government, was one of the chief causes of the disquiet which pervaded Europe. A Napoleon who appeared in the character of a general pacificator could not expect to command the confidence of Europe without palpable proofs of his honesty of purpose. Those proofs were, however, wanting. Example is more powerful than precept, and if Napoleon III. had followed the model set him by England with regard to the Ionian Islands, he would have met with more success as a preacher of a new International Congress. The withdrawal of the army of occupation from Rome, or a palpable reduction in the magnitude of the French forces stationed there, would have done more to inspire confidence than all the Napoleonic phrases in the world. Sceptics can hardly be blamed if they mistrusted a conversion which had not yet produced any fruits of repentance. The words, indeed, were as the words of Cobden, but the voice was the voice of Napoleon. England, therefore, declined in the most courteous terms to attend the Congress of Paris, and most of the great Powers followed her example. There was one monarch, however, who never for an instant wavered. The King of Italy returned to his glorious ally an answer of unconditional approbation, and made an unreserved promise of acquiescence. A letter from Paris, of the 27th of December, states, respecting the Congress:—"'A restricted assembly' is the phrase of the hour; but I think it was better defined by a politician last night as 'a duet between France and Italy.' The imperial organs, both living and printed, continue to assert that his majesty is determined that the performance shall take place; and so, I suppose, if he cannot command a full orchestra, he will even perform the 'duo' above mentioned."

Now, what are the services which the Emperor of the French has rendered to Italy, and which makes the King anxious to preserve an alliance with France in preference to any other country? First of all, in the year 1831, Prince Louis Napoleon fought against the Pope, and assisted to defeat the Papal forces. Let him have full credit and admiration for this, and let it be at once acknowledged that he deserves the warm thanks and gratitude of Italy. In 1849, however, the Roman people, without his aid, had got rid of the Pope, and had established a government similar to that of France, over which Napoleon presided; and yet, in the teeth of the article of the French constitution which he had sworn to uphold, and which asserted that France would respect foreign nationalities as she intended to cause her own to be respected, that she would undertake no war for the purpose of conquest, and would never employ her arms against the liberty of any people, he sent General Oudinot with a French army on what that general termed "a mission of peace, order, and conciliation," to Rome. This army attempted to enter the Captol against the will of the Roman government and people. The French troops were met and defeated by General Garibaldi, when the French General asked for a truce, which was granted by the victors. The French National Assembly disapproved of the conduct of the president, Prince Louis Napoleon, and he immediately despatched an ambassador to propose terms of peace, which terms were acceeded to by the Roman government against the advice of General Garibaldi.

The French General having now received supplies for which he had been waiting, repudiated the treaty signed by the ambassador extraordinary sent by his master, and declared that his orders were to attack Rome, but gave his promise in writing that he would not commence the attack before the 4th of June; instead of which he took the garrison by surprise, by attacking it on the night of Sunday the 2nd.* A garrison of 20,000 soldiers still holds Rome. Alas! where is the honuor of France? echo alone can return the answer. The opinion of the Premier of England on Imperial encouragement of brigandage has been fully given; but living in happy England few persons can even remotely comprehend the horrors inflicted on the Neapolitan

* All this is given at much greater length in Chapter XIV. as an appendix.

territory by the system supported by the French occupation of Rome. For the whole of these horrors, it is contended, the Emperor of the French is distinctly responsible by continuing, against the will of the Roman people, the French occupation of Rome.†

---

†The following details relating to the horrors of Italian brigandage are taken from the *Morning Post*:—"The capture of five noted brigands by the Government of Italy, and their subsequent surrender to the French authorities, are subjects with which most of our readers are familiar, but few are cognizant of the horrors which characterize the system of brigandage as practised in the southern provinces of Italy. The style of the labours of these men may be judged of by mentioning merely one day's work effected by Epriano La Gala and his band in the province of Avellino, where he murdered seven men, dishonoured nine women, set fire to two country houses, robbed fifteen families, and wantonly slaughtered more than 100 head of cattle and horses. His treatment of women in the presence of their husbands, fathers, or brothers, bound, beaten, and obliged to look on, will not bear particularizing. On the night of the 10th, eleven brigands, wearing masks, assaulted and sacked eight farms, only two miles distant from the town of Lanciano, and submitted all the women they found to the vilest treatment. After a week's campaigning the force sent out from Lanciano in pursuit of the villains returned with five whom they had captured. Two of these brigands were armed, and the other three laden with a portion of the booty they had seized on the farms. The two taken with arms in their hands were shot without delay."

A letter from Tropea, in the *Pungolo* of the 20th, states—"The brigands of the Sila, to revenge the shooting of five of their companions, laid wait on the road, and killed the first twenty-seven wayfarers who fell into their hands!"

On the farm of Prince San Severa, in the province of Capitanata, twelve brigands, a few days ago, bayonetted 265 sheep, tied the shepherd to a tree, and amused themselves by using him as a target to shoot at, from a distance, until he expired, riddled with balls. They then sent another shepherd, who had been forced to look on, with a letter to the prince's farm overseer, requesting 4000 ducates and a watch and chain without delay.

The expressively named brigand chief Miseria, on the 17th instant carried off a farmer named Lombardi from Tocco, in the province of Benevento, informing his family that he would be killed if 18,000 ducats were not sent without delay for his ransom.

If it happens that the brigands are attacked by troops whilst they have any prisoners waiting to be ransomed, they immediately slaughter them. The ferocious brigands commanded by Caruso, about sixty in number, well armed and mounted, had three prisoners with them when they were attacked near the forest of Tremleto, on the 19th instant, by a force of bersaglieri and hussars. The brigands directly slew two of these poor victims, named Luzi and Auzani; the third escaped the same fate by promising a heavy ransom. He subsequently sent the money by one of his farm servants, an ox driver, whom they killed after receiving the bag of ducats from him. In the engagement alluded to, Caruso's band lost ten men killed, a greater number wounded, and several horses, besides clothing and stores. Only one bersaglicre was killed, and one hussar wounded.

In the district of Rivensdalia, in the province of Acquila, alone, the farmers have had 4000 sheep stabbed during the present month, for it is one of the methods adopted by the Bourbonic brigands to impoverish every one who holds liberal opinions.

Upon the estate of a Neapolitan marchese, in the Capitanata, twenty two mares and eleven foals were killed by the brigands, and an extensive tract of ripe corn was set fire to and totally destroyed. The outlaws had a grudge against the marchese's men, one of whom, a native of Romagna, had successfully defended himself against an attack of the brigands by barricading his house door and firing from the roof. The assailants, after losing three or four men, decamped, vowing vengeance. Some weeks after the Romagnolo had to come to Naples, and was captured by a party of the same band; but, as he had let his beard grow meanwhile, and otherwise disguised himself, he was not recognised, but allowed to proceed after giving up 200 francs which he had on him. Three of the marchese's shepherds were still more successful in a recent affair with a noted brigand leader and two of his men, who visited the fold towards nightfall, and ordered the shepherds to get supper ready for them. This order, given by the bearers of three loaded muskets, was of course obeyed. The shepherds killed a lamb, lit a fire, and made arrangements for the repast with Homeric simplicity. Meanwhile the brigands sat moodily round the fire, watching the roast, each man with his musket resting on the ground between his legs. The shepherds, three brawny peasants from the Abruzzi mountains, exchanged significant glances, and, reading determination in each others eyes, sprang simultaneously on their unwelcome guests from behind, twisted their muskets upwards, and presenting them at the surprised brigands, ordering them not to move on pain of instant death. The brigands were of course cowed. After a few moments of this dumb show, one of the shepherds laid down his musket and proceeded to tie the arms of his brigand, whilst his companions continued to threaten the other two with instant death if they stirred. In this way all three were bound, and, without stopping to eat the roast lamb, were marched by the shepherds up to the town of Orsara, verified there by the authorities as old offenders, and summarily shot.

The revival of brigandage in Calabria, where Colonel Fumel had all but annihilated it, and especially in the province of Cosensa, has of late seriously interfered with the commercial development of that rich district, and even prevented the meeting of the provincial council. Two wealthy Calabrian proprietors recently captured by the brigands, had purchased their lives by paying a ransom of 15,000 ducats!

A whimsical notion of morality in brigandage is entertained by Serravalle, the captain of a band in the province of Basilicata, who robs, murders, and ransoms people himself, but allows nobody else in his beat to do so. He recently discovered that two pseudo-brigands were poaching on his manorial domains, passing themselves off for his nephews, and levying contributions in his name. He arrested them, and brought them to a rich farmer whom they had mulcted, proposing to shoot them in his presence. The farmer interceded for their lives, which were granted on condition of his engaging to take them handcuffed to the town of Anzi, to be shot in a more regular way.

On the 15th Serravalle sent three of his men to chastise two peasants who had ventured to appropriate two horses belonging to his band, which, being rather knocked up, he had left to graze in the neighbourhood of Grassano, a week before. The brigands, after upbraiding the peasants with their bad conduct in meddling with what they knew was not their own property, proceeded to punish them for their thievish propensities by cutting off their ears and beating them almost to death.

The correspondent of the *Daily Telegraph* wrote from Turin, August 28:—The publication of the brigandage Report, and the Royal decree by which military law supersedes civil law in certain provinces of Italy, has been the one event since I last had the pleasure of writing to you. It seems a good law—very long delayed—and published at least six weeks later than was necessary. It is a "fiasco" though, or, at least, a "fiascone," for nobody believes—not the chairman of the committee who signed the report—nor the Minister who received it, nor the King who had it read to him—that any law human or divine will stop brigandage so-called while the Pope is King of Rome, and the ex-King of Naples the guest of the Pope. The *Stampa*, which is as official as official can be, after praising the work of the commission in a vague sort of way, is forced to come to this very conclusion. I add some particulars of the Aunis, which may be depended on, and so are interesting. Here are some extracts from her log: "Carried from Malta to Civita Vechia, Antonio Ciccarelli." He was the chief of brigands in Foggia. "From Civita Vecchia to Corfu and Malta," and later "from Malta to Civita Vecchia," one Emanuele Gel, who brought a band of brigands—I regret to write it—from Corfu to Italy. Castellan and Pila, two notorious brigands, have also been accommodated with berths on the Aunis

With regard to the campaign of 1859, of which the history has been already given, no one can blame the French Government for making French interests the primary motive of its foreign policy, whether in Italy or in Mexico. This principle is common to all Governments. But all Governments do not propose to go to war from an impulse of pure, disinterested, chivalrous affection. Interests are one thing, and ideas another—except, indeed, the idea of taking two provinces from a weak ally in payment of two battles.*

Surely there can be no cause for gratitude here. The Emperor avowed that he fought for an idea, and the result demonstrated that he was most substantially paid, both in provinces and subsidies. In 1860 Napoleon warned Piedmont against aggrandizing herself, and prolonged the civil war in Southern Italy by sending a French fleet to protect Francis II. at Gaeta. On the 19th of

---

from Malta to the Papal Port. Luigi Raffaele and a friend also made the same voyage on the same steamer. When your readers remember that these men are all notorious robbers and murderers, it is no wonder that the Italians feel a little suspicious of the company to which the Aunis belongs, and still more so of the Government which rules that company.

From papers found upon a Spanish brigand, there is no doubt that the notorious La Gala, captured on board the Aunis, and whose arrest at one time threatened a rupture between the French and Italian Governments, was proceeding to Barcelona to organise a corps of brigands. The discovery has also been made that as many as 600 of these wretches have been organized into small bands, under the eyes of the Papal authorities, and have been sent into Italy, where their atrocities are already too painfully known.

On the other side of the question, a correspondent of the *Morning Herald*, writing from Naples under the heading of Destruction of Towns in Southern Italy, gives the extraordinary but circumstantial account of the devastation committed by the Italian troops in their efforts to destroy the horrible scourge of brigandage, which goes far to convey the idea that the remedy applied is nearly as bad as the disease. In the Terra de Molin the census of M. de Bellay, a clever and impartial engineer, who has lately made a survey of the Southern provinces, shows the towns destroyed to be four—Guaricia, of which the number of inhabitants was 1822; Campochiaro, 979; Casalduni, 3032; Pontelandolfo, 3917. In the Capitanata three—namely, Viesti, 5417; San Marco in Lainis, 10,012; Bignano, 1814. In Basilicata two—Venosa, 5952, and Basile, 3400. In Principato Citeriore two—Auletta, 2023; Eboli, 4175. In Principato Ulteriore two—Monte Falcione, 2018, and Monte Verde, 1788. Vico in the Terra di Lavoro, 730; and in Calabria Ulteriore Secundo—Cotrone, 1089, and Spinello, 250. Add to these the devastation of the following towns and communes of Basilicata to the extent of unroofing the houses and driving out the population: Vignola, Avigliano, Accerenza Pietragalla, Genzano, Lago Nege, Lauria, Molitano, Sant' Angelo, le Fratte, Monte Scaglioso, Ferrindina, San Fele, San Mauro, Accture, Tricarico, Monte Peloso, Tescopagano, Rionero, Atella, Lavella, and others. These communes contained above 150,000 inhabitants, so the misery occasioned by their devastation is easily conceived.

* It was only after the first part of this work had been printed that the Stansfeld pamphlet, "The Italian Movement, and Italian Parties," was placed in the author's hands. In it he gives the following history of the treaty of Plombières, so

November, 1861, the London *Daily News*, well knowing on what authority it made the statement, wrote: "The project of an Italian confederation is by no means given up, the plan devised in Paris was that Italy should be divided into three states, united in a confederation: the first, a Northern kingdom with Victor Emmanuel at its head; the second, the Papal states, including Umbria and the Marches; and the third, a Southern or Neapolitan kingdom, Venice being given to the Northern kingdom in November, 1861." This statement as was to be expected, met with the most emphatic denial; but in September, 1862, just after Aspromonte, appeared M. De la Guerronnier's third and most important letter, in which he demands a European Congress to settle the affairs of Italy, laying down the basis on which its deliberations are to proceed:—"First, the division of Italy into three states, united by a Federal tie. These States are, in the north, a monarchy worthy of the glory of the House of Savoy, with Florence for its capital, and to be augmented eventually by Venetia; in the south, Naples and the Two Sicilies, one of the

---

confirming the statements of the *Times* and *Economist*. "*We know the terms of the compact of Plombières*. You will think, perhaps, that I speak with too great confidence in saying that we *know* the terms. I will tell you the grounds, then, of that strength of assertion. You will remember when, on January 1, 1859, the Emperor Napoleon spoke those words of startling import to Baron Hübner, which first gave the alarm of war in Europe. Already before that day particulars of the compact and the general plan of the campaign had reached this country from two different but most reliable sources; they were essentially the same particulars as those which were first published, as a revelation in the columns of the *Times* sometime not earlier than the following month of March: and everything that has since happened or come to light has only tended to confirm their accuracy. A cause of war was to be sought with Austria, she was to be tempted to take the offensive, the campaign was to be a short one—if necessary peace on the Mincio. If Venice and Lombardy were gained to Piedmont, Nice and Savoy were to be yielded to France. Napoleon, the cousin, married to the king's daughter, was to find a kingdom in Tuscany. And now mark, all these particulars reached here, as I have given them, not as conjectures or beliefs, but as the reports, coming from two different sources, of what had been actually agreed upon between the Emperor and Cavour. I need hardly tell you that Napoleon, Jerome's son, with his separate *corps d'armée* operating across the Duchies, found that there was no hope for him; I need hardly remind you that peace was made upon the Mincio, and that Venice not being gained, Nice and Savoy did not become, by virtue of the bond, the due of France, but were claimed because the Duchies and Romagna persisted in giving themselves to the king."

It is impossible to acquit, after this distinct statement, either the King or Cavour, or the Emperor; all three must have been guilty of deception from first to last in the question of the session of Nice and Savoy.

finest capitals in the world, a magnificent bay, and an immense extent of coast commanding the Mediterranean; and, between the two, Rome—a power admirably fitted to unite them without subordinating one to the other; in a word, the Papacy would be the central and commanding Power of the Confederation, and Europe is to guarantee the Pontificial territory, and to secure a reservation of the Pope's sovereignty in the Marshes and Umbria, with a fixed tribute from the revenues of these provinces." At length, then, the position is known which the self-styled friend of the Italians holds towards Italy. It now appears, as many had all along believed, that Napoleon III. is the real, the only serious obstacle to the unity of the new kingdom. It is he, and not Austria or the Pope, that has arrested its progress, and unceasingly plotted to destroy it; and the worst features of the whole are that the prime minister of Italy should have stated in the Chamber that he "placed every confidence in the government of this man, who understood the requirements of the age in which he lived," and that Victor Emmanuel should at once and unconditionally have accepted his invitation to attend a Congress in Paris.*

To return to the state of feeling in the Neapolitan dominions, it must be confessed that the pocket is apt to exercise far too great an influence in most countries, and whatever advantages the Southern Italians may have gained (and they are very many) to them have been added a greatly increased taxation. Besides this, under Ferdinand the Second, the five per cents. were at 108 —a short time ago they were only 70; also, there had not been any conscription—all enlistments for the army had been voluntary, both in Naples and Sicily; the conscription was introduced by the law of Piedmont. Lastly, General de la Marmora, whose dislike and opposition to General Garibaldi and his volunteers has been manifested from first to last, is still retained in command at Naples.

* Can it be greatly wondered at that the opening of the railway from Castle Bolognesse to Ravenna, which was celebrated in the presence of Prince Carignane and some of the ministers was not a very brilliant affair. The prince, certainly not on his own account, for he is, and justly, most popular, had a very cool reception, but there were more allusions to Aspromonte than to the King of Italy.

"The other day" writes a correspondent, "a detachment of light cavalry, consisting of thirty-four men, under the command of Lieutenant Boromeo, was in the Basilicata, misled by its scouts into an ambush, where, totally surrounded by an overwhelming force of brigands, it lost twenty-two men killed and twenty-three horses. This affair has very naturally reawakened the feeling against General La Marmora, which has been never appeased since the affair of Aspromonte, and has given rise to a very temperate article in the *Diritto*. Giving General La Marmora credit for being a brave soldier, a good war minister, and for being influenced by the best and most patriotic feelings, the *Diritto* simply states that where he is, he is worse than useless. With 100,000 troops he cannot stand against 2,000 men, broken up into little gangs, and has several times had to report useless sacrifices of Italian life. It certainly does seem that the gallant general, whose Crimean laurels make him so justly a favourite with a large part of the Northern Italians, is a poor hand either at civil justice or guerilla warfare, and that he conducts the first like a soldier and the second like a civilian."

In the early part of the year it was stated in nearly all the European journals, Italian included, that the king had resolved to pardon, on the first favourable opportunity, the 600 deserters from the army, who, shortly before Aspromonte, left their regiments to join Garibaldi, believing that he was acting in concert with the king, and that they best served their country by so doing. Many had done the same in 1860, and had been rewarded for their conduct. The king's own birthday was the first date given, that passed; it might have been thought the 7th of September, when Garibaldi first entered Naples was the favourable date waited for, but that also passed; and lastly, the king's short visit to his southern capital, when Count Christian and Mr. Bishop, and all the other political prisoners were pardoned, also passed away, and these unfortunate men were left to their fate.* A private letter to the author gave the following account of this royal visit to Naples: "The reception given to the king has not been exactly what the official papers have reported. There was a sort of artificial enclosure fitted up, and everything was official—an official reception, official cheerings, official enthusiasm—and let me add that the bill of official expenses will prove to be very heavy indeed. At Leghorn, out of 3,000 national guards, less than two hundred joined their officers to meet the king."

A correspondent of the *Morning Herald*, writing from Southern Italy, supplies some information respecting the recent visit of Victor Emmanuel to Naples, which strikingly illustrates the state of public feeling in that part of Italy. He says: "I will only add two traits of the royal visit which are sufficiently characteristic of the country to be worth note, and for the truth of which I can amply vouch. At almost every point of the royal passage the cries of 'Viva il Ferrito d'Aspromonte' predominated over those of 'Viva Vittorio Emmanuele.' At the pontoon of San Giacamo a shot was fired from the crowd at the royal carriage, and a number of arrests were instantly made in consequence. The 'Hymn of Garibaldi' was vociferously applauded whenever heard, and the 'March of Savoy' received with the most sullen silence. Fifty thousand men were concentrated in Naples for the occasion, it being considered unsafe for the King of Italy to entrust his person in Naples with a less imposing force."

The correspondent of another journal writes: "After all, the bulletin of Garibaldi is the bulletin of Italy. Powerful before Aspromonte, he is irresistible now, as will be found when he once puts his foot on the continent of Italy. By the murderous policy—shall we say Franco-Piedmontese?—of Aspromonte, the

* Garibaldi, however, never forgets them, and constantly sends all the money he can collect for their use—(see *Bentley's Miscellany* for July, 1863). A remarkable testimony in favour of the Southern Italians is that of the generals and officers in the Italian army, who are unanimous in stating that the new Neapolitan recruits are more teachable and readier to undergo the hardships of military life than any from the upper provinces. And, as regards educational capacity, very satisfactory results have been obtained in the elementary schools—unhappily few in number up to the present—which have been instituted during the last three years—(see "Southern Italy"—its conditions and prospects, by Aurielo Saffi—*Macmillan's Magazine* for July, 1863.)

hero of Sicily became a martyr. The ministers of Italy would be wise to remember, and to recall, when making their future arrangements, that their predecessor, Monsieur de Ratazzi, has left them as a legacy, hostile instead of friendly, one of the most powerful agencies in Italy. A foolish and very short-sighted policy has of late 'pooh-poohed' Garibaldi and his influence. The party which asserts this perhaps may claim for its body the ultra-Piedmontese soldiers—men of a certain age—and for its leader, let us say, La Marmora. We, who are mere lookers-on, may perhaps be better judges than these men, who are not very politically wise, and who are certainly very politically and socially prejudiced. Was Italy in peril, more safety could come from the lifting of Garibaldi's finger than from the united wisdom of all the statesmanship of Turin, and this not so much from the great natural influence of Garibaldi as from the imbecility of official routine and the extreme care which government has taken to endeavour to turn a devoted adherent into a bitter foe, if he could be such, to Italy." Speaking of the ministers, the same correspondent adds: "Probable war and possible alliances—those are the points to which the Cabinet must pay its deepest attention if it wishes to keep office. Nor in the alliances to be formed out of Italy must it forget that most important one to be arranged in Italy between the Government and the people—a treaty which has been too much neglected during the last two years, but which bears in it the germ of Italian unity."

It must never be forgotten that the Garibaldians are a constitutional party, endeavouring to obtain for Italy an alliance with England, and for the Italian people the liberty enjoyed by England in contradistinction to the liberty enjoyed by France. It was once asked of General Garibaldi: "Is not your party the party of revolution?" "Precisely so," was the answer; "just as the English ministry is the ministry of a revolution, and as the monarch of England is seated on her throne in virtue of a revolution, and of a revolution alone." What friend of freedom has not rejoiced over the history of the glorious revolution of

1688, which secured to the British people their liberties, civil and religious, and called the House of Hanover to the throne of Great Britain? and to what does that solon of monarchs the King of the Belgians owe his crown?—to the revolution of 1830, which revolution secured the prosperity, and freedom, and independence of Belgium. Nay, to what does the Emperor Napoleon owe the throne of France?—certainly not to divine right, for his grandfather was a poor attorney in Corsica!—why, to the revolution of 1848 and the vote of the people. The monarchs of Spain and Portugal both owe their thrones to civil war and revolution: in the one case Don Carlos, and in the other Don Miguel, represented absolute power and the divine right of kings, and happily they were both, by the assistance of England, signally defeated. To what does Victor Emmanuel owe the title to by far the greatest part of his dominions? Why, to the revolution of 1859 and 1860; and his last and only true title to the throne of united Italy is the goodwill of his people: and, to conclude a list which might easily be lengthened, to what does the young brother of the Princess of Wales owe his classic crown? Why, to the successful revolution of 1862, which dethroned a monarch who basely forgot the obligations imposed on a king who also owed his crown to a revolution and the election of his people. Now, in case any red republicans on the one side, or any high tories on the other, should doubt the extreme moderation of the views entertained by Garibaldi and the party of which he is the only and acknowledged head, they are respectfully informed that as Napoleon speaks in the name of France, so the *Diritto* writes in the name of Garibaldi; its editor, Mons. Civinin, was one of his most trusted secretaries, and stood by his side at Aspromonte, when he was shot down as he pleaded for peace, exclaiming, "Brothers, do not fire!" The leading articles are contributed by the most trustworthy of the general's friends; nay, in a word, the *Diritto* is inspired by Garibaldi himself, and to its columns all doubters are confidently referred. If this evidence be not sufficient, let them carefully read the enlightened, statesmanlike and most moderate addresses delivered in the Chambers by Mordini, Matera, Coroli, and the other chiefs of an opposition which has faithfully supported the ministers on every question likely in their opinion to promote the welfare of Italy.

CHAPTER XIII.

The present state of parties as to the question on Rome and Venice—France the supporter of the Papacy—Proposed reformation of the Catholic Church—Venice and Rome the centre of re-action—Garibaldi's letter on Rome and Venice—Letter to Benedetto Caivoli—Present state of Venice—Garibaldi resigns his seat in the Italian Parliament—Garibaldi the leader of the party of action—The Italian Administration, reasons of their failure.

It is asserted that the Roman question is rapidly losing in the minds of the Italian people its purely political character, and is acquiring a most momentous religious aspect. Not only is the temporal power of the Pope impeached, but the people of Ita.y are now struggling to break the chains with which Roman superstition has enthralled their mind, for they feel that there is no security against the return of civil despotism whilst the reign of superstition continues. The recent proceedings of the Papal power, and especially its complicity with Italian brigandage, have done much to produce this state of mind; this change in popular feeling is, however, chiefly attributable to the information conveyed through the columns of the *Diritto*, the exponent of the views of Garibaldi. That journal recently published an article of irresistible power upon this question, which cannot fail to produce a great effect upon the Italian people. After tracing the whole history of the Italian struggle, and pointing out the pernicious effects, both temporally and spiritually, of the teachings of the Papacy, the *Diritto* concludes—

"Between Italy and the Romish Church, the question is life or death, to kill or let ourselves be killed. There can be no conciliation, no middle path. Italy has created, in part, to her own harm, and to the harm of the whole world, the Papacy. It is her destiny and her fitting expiation to undo her own work. To this task we are condemned—for this we live; and therefore in the performance of this task there lie at once our duty and our glory."

"The Italian question," observes Mr. Stansfeld, "is deeply, solemnly interesting to us as a Protestant community. I use the word in no narrow or antagonistic sense; I mean to us as a community believing in freedom of conscience as between man and man. We have not to wait for the destruction of the temporal power of the Papacy; the temporal power that now supports the Pope is not that of Papacy; it is that of France. The sham that still remains will ere long be swept away. But what we may with confidence look forward to as a future result of the conflict between Italy and the Papacy, as a first fruit of that new and conscious freedom and responsibility which this national uprising is already calling forth, is a Reformation of the catholic church—not our Reformation, for history does not repeat herself, and nothing spontaneous can be a copy of what has gone before, but, nevertheless, a movement of religious reformation pregnant with the most vital consequences to the Christian world, and certainly beneficial in its influence on the spirit of freedom and of faith; and this we shall owe to Italy—born again into the world, *not without purpose* in the evolution of the providential scheme." Cardinal d'Andrea, Bishop of Subiaco, and a liberal, has just issued a pastoral letter, in which he warns the Catholics not to believe in perspiring saints or blinking Virgins, under pain of being considered idiots themselves, and of turning their religion into a laughing-stock.

Again, Italy accuses the Vatican of sheltering all the "refactories" from the levy in Italy. *Il Giornale di Roma* speaks out boldly, and says that these men are deserters from an enemy's army, and therefore are the best friends of, and welcome and entitled to the best treatment from the Papal Government. One hundred and one of these defaulters are now living on the Papal bounty. In "assisting these parties," one is pleased to learn that "the Pontificial Government is moved by a sentiment of humanity." The Pope concludes the year of grace, 1863, by the confident assertion of his conviction that, before another year shall have rolled away, to the Church of Rome would be triumphantly restored the whole of its temporal possessions; and the Emperor Napoleon, the great and glorious ally of Victor Emmanuel, closed the same year by sending an additional 6,000 men to increase the French garrison at Rome!

Venice like Rome is a centre of reaction; arrangements were lately in progress in that city to despatch 150 men of the Ex-Duke of Modena's Army to Trieste, from which port they could be forwarded to the Papal States, in order to augment the brigand bands sent from the city of St. Peter to plunder and murder in Southern Italy. In July 1863, Garibaldi wrote the following letter on the subject of Rome and Venice: "The safety of Italy lies in the valour of her sons. Three years ago a spontaneous popular will proclaimed to the astonished world the kingdom of Italy. Since then the free sons of Italy have been waiting with expectant ears the voice that is to call them to Rome and Venice —that voice is silent. The cowards who should have raised it are dumb, and the generous sympathies of Italy are perishing in a disgraceful idleness. This must be put an end to at once. The slave has ever the right of rising against his tyrant and killing him. The hour must be close at hand when we shall be striving hand to hand against the occupiers of our land. Then we must be serious. We must all strike, and strike together, till the last link of the chain which binds us is severed. Our duty is a holy one. We shall be with you in action as in wish. Take example from noble Poland! Let your invaders know that you will be masters in your own house, and have nothing for them but the sword.

"GARIBALDI.

"Caprera, July 24."

The subjoined letter reporting the real intentions of General Goribaldi was written by Benedetto Caivoli, January 23, 1864:—"I have hitherto been silent from delicacy. I speak now to the honest men of every party in my right of defence, and in order that silence may not be interpreted hesitation. Those who attribute to the appeal of General Garibaldi, a far different purpose from that which has been clearly expressed, are either deceivers or deceived. His intent is, to collect means for helping our brothers oppressed by foreign domination, and to fight our national battles, which would be impossible without the paramount co-operation of our gallant army. Those, who endeavour to find the absurd intention of a dictatorship in the establishment of a central committee, whose only object is to collect money and to preach reconciliation, are, I repeat, either deceivers or deceived. This is a simple task, and it is not a new one. It dates from '48. But even in worse times, and through greater dangers, there never was a government in Piedmont, even when it was but a little state, who thought of proscribing committees, because they aimed only at providing means for the national independence. It was reserved to the Italian government, the very one intrusted by the revolution with this same national object through the formula of the plebiscito, to denounce our modest undertaking which such threats, as would belong more properly to Austria itself on the plea of her own defence. I do not intend to speak of myself, an obscure soldier of my country, when the outrage spares not even the venerable head of Garibaldi. This, alone, I will say to our accusers Remember for a moment his life. The man, who, in 1860, surrounded by his own army and by the love of a people, whom he had liberated, returns to the modest solicitude of private life for the sake of concord, if he now invokes it again, can it be suspected by any but unjust adversaries who pay the debt of gratitude with the poison of anger. This man, forgetting his own grievances, feels only the offence made to the national sentiment. Not yet restored to health, he devotes himself to the oppressed, and expresses the wish that they may renew the miracles of '48, thus giving through their own initiative, a signal of a war, which the government, tied by diplomatic obligations, could not perhaps otherwise declare. And for that object he demands the union of all parties in the holy name of the country. Such is his conception, and such are his words: aspiration to sacrifice, appeal to duty, a commission identical to that, which has been consented to in former days, and tending to the same end. Between Garibaldi and his unsincere accusers, the valiant, however, will judge. To them, in this period of baneful and inexplicable provocations, the remembrance of his sublime self-abnegation, will be a teaching and a comfort."

The following is the text of the manifesto of the Venetian Committee issued in December:—"Fellow Citizens, events so long looked for appear to be approaching. The question is no longer to excite enthusiasm by vain promises, and your Committee no longer does so. We have up to the present time told you that we must wait with constancy and patience; that the mute language of our sacrifices was a solemn protest against Austrian domination—an eloquent declaration of our faith in the King, in the Parliament, and in the destinies of Italy and a continual affirmation of our right, and of our firm determination to unite ourselves to the great Italian country. Now we tell you that the time of hard trials is about to cease, and that the hour for action draws near. Let us be united and await the signal."

When the Italian people guided by Garibaldi, set their hearts on becoming a nation, they hardly perhaps, calculated the cost. It was patriotism which, in the first instance, urged them on, certainly not arithmetic. Indeed they would have risen in generous indignation against any one who had attempted to draw their attention to so very commonplace and matter-of-fact a subject; and yet it is this very question of pounds, shillings, and pence, which at the present moment causes at one and the same time the greatest difficulty both of the government and of General Garibaldi, for if her successful revolution be only to terminate in bankruptcy, it certainly was hardly worth the venture.* It is utterly impossible for Italy to support an army on a war footing in times of peace, and that she had better boldly advance and challenge conclusions, is the opinion of some of her best friends; better do so, than be eaten up piecemeal by soldiers in barracks.

* The subjoined letter is from the correspondent of a London journal, who visited Venice during December, 1863. He is alone responsible for the ideas it contains:—"It is impossible to go on longer in the present condition. Excepting the Austrian soldiers, and the working corps attached to them, scarcely a living soul is to be seen after you leave Ferrara till you enter Venice. Never very lively, the drive after crossing the river is now like traversing a desert. On every side you see deserted houses, and around you whole farms thrown out of cultivation; for who can work his land so as to pay 60, 70, even 80 per cent. taxes? It is only at the military posts any life is to be found. Padua, where you take the train for Venice, is noisy, and even lively enough, and its enormous café is crowded from morning to night—not with natives though, for your Paduan is quiet, if not timid, and would. avoid the noisy resort of the military, even if he had no political reasons for so doing; but with horse, foot, and dragoons, whose talk is of war, and who "look big and swell their chests" when they see an Italian; and altogether it is like an Austrian garrison in an enemy's country. Going home by train you reach Venice, Perhaps the most striking sensation now to be found in Europe is the sudden transition from the screaming station, with its hissing engines, hurrying porters, and intrusive custom house officers, to the silent solitude of the Grand Canal. A stranger who sees it for the first time is only overwhelmed by the quaint beauty of the scene, and the dreamy sensation which Venice must produce on every well-regulated mind; but he who has been there before asks, "Where are the gondolas? Where are the people? Where is the life?" Instead of hundreds of those curious black "coffins clapt in a canoe," you see half-a-dozen "omnibus gondolas" returning empty from the station to the place from whence they came, that is, the hotels, and several boats full of stores and ammunition unwillingly propelled by Italians, under the immediate *surveillance* of Austrian soldiers armed with canes, which they are not above using. The further you go the worse you fare, and while your companion, in his inexperience, is revelling in a scene which, dull or gay, must be unequalled in Europe, you, in your disappointment, are inclined, according to your nature, either to cry or to quarrel with the next Austrian. "Can we have rooms—sitting-rooms —looking on the canal—nine bed-rooms, &c.?" Lord bless you! you might have ninety bed-rooms and salons to match. There are two Americans and three Irish travellers in the hotel. They are very much bored, and they, yourselves, and a spy, will form the party at table d'hôte. The conversation, too, will be dull, as the Americans have already been warned not to reflect on "Austrian institutions" before the silent gentleman who comes so regularly to his meals. The town itself is like Tadmor in the Wilderness. There is no business, no pleasure, of course no politics; nor do there seem to be any Venetians—certainly not one between sixteen and sixty. On the other hand, there are plenty of soldiers, and it must be some slight consolation to the few natives who remain in the city to see how dreadfully bored the Austrian officer or soldier is as he gapes away his time over "bock bier" in the front of a café in the Piazza di San Marco. You have great difficulty in extracting any information from the gagged Venetians who yet remain; but, if you succeed, you hear merely a repetition of what you have heard, seen, and felt since you crossed the frontier into fettered Italy, and come to the conclusion that this state of things cannot endure. Add to this, that an active agency is working for Venice throughout Italy; that Austria is known to be alarmed at the complicated state of Europe, and finally that Italy must fight in the spring for reasons of financial economy, and I think we really may come to the conclusion that Venetia in 1864, will be as interesting as Lombardy in 1859, and Naples in 1860.

At this present moment Italy, containing 22,000,000 inhabitants, has a peace establishment of one soldier out of every 83 men. With an income of 623,000,000 francs, Italy spends 259,000,000 francs on her soldiers alone. It is impossible for any country to keep up such a large standing army, without national bankruptcy and utter ruin staring her full in the face. There is yet another point of difficulty. The present Chambers do not fairly represent Italy. They were elected early in the spring of 1861, under the auspices of Count Cavour. It has always been conceded that Cavour worked for the good of his country; but, at the same time, he firmly believed that that good was dependent on his own retention of office; the minister who first authorised a certain course of action and then stated he should deny it, like St. Peter, was not likely to be overscrupulous in the methods he employed to secure the election of a subservient chamber. Nor did Garibaldi and his party offer any opposition. "Do what you will so you make Italy," was still his cry; besides, to use his own words, "at that time I had promises enough made to me."

Some time ago the Provincial Council of Potenza, one of the Neapolitan provinces afflicted with brigandage, unanimously voted a subsidy to aid the Polish revolution and a sum of money for a monument to Garibaldi. Garibaldi, in a letter published in the *Diritto*, applauds the subsidy but declines the monument. "As to the monument to me," he says, "I beg you will dismiss the thought of it. If you insist, you will put me to the pain of saying that I will not accept it. As long as the soldiers of two foreign armies riot on our soil, as long as a stream of civil blood flows from the Tronto to the Strait, as long as the glorious remains of our national battles die of hunger or by their own hand in the midst of the insane rejoicings of our cities, as long as the boy wants a school and the orphan an asylum, as long as there is in Italy misery, chains, and darkness, speak not of monuments, least of all of a monument to me." And the last news that reaches the main land from Caprera, as the year 1863 closes, is that the patient and long-enduring Garibaldi, almost broken-hearted at the sufferings of the Sicilian people, whom he induced to give themselves to Piedmont, has resigned his seat for Naples in the Italian Parliament. But there must be no misapprehension respecting the sentiments which influenced the General; he writes,

"Caprera, Dec. 21.

"Sir and very Honorable President of the Chamber of Deputies, Turin—For reasons, which will appear from the perusal of the enclosed letter to my constituents, I have thought it my duty to resign my seat, convinced that the Chamber will hasten to accept my resignation—I am, with the greatest respect,

"G. GARIBALDI."

"Caprera, Dec. 21.

"To the Electors of Naples—When I saw 229 deputies of the Italian Parliament confirm by their votes the sale of Italian territory, I felt sure I should not be able to remain long in an assembly which blindly severed the limbs of that country, to form which was its mission. Till now, however, the advice of friends, the hope of redeeming events, and an unalterable sentiment of devotion to my electors, kept me at my post. But now that I see the shame of Sicily succeed to the sale of Nice—of Sicily, which I love to call the country of my adoption—I feel myself compelled to restore to you electors, a trust which fetters my conscience, and renders me indirectly an accomplice of crimes which are not my own. It is not alone the love I bear to Sicily—the mother of so many revolutions—which decides me to this step; but the feeling that they have through her, wounded right and honour, and compromised the safety of all Italy. But no such acts or crimes as those will hinder me from being with the people in arms on the route to Rome and Venice.—Addio. "GARIBALDI."

It is easy to understand why in England, where it is next to impossible to encroach in any way upon the constitution, the present state of things in Southern Italy should not be clearly understood. The Italian House of Parliament passed last year a law for the repression of brigantage called after the name of the deputy who proposed it, the law Pica; this law placed the disturbed provinces almost in a state of siege, it was a part of the Neapolitan provinces only which the Italian Chamber subjected to the jurisdiction of this law, which was considered an exceptional one. But in Sicily, under pretext that there were a number of persons who were unwilling to submit to the conscription, this law was applied to Sicily by a decree of the ministers without the permission of the chamber. After this violation of the constitution, a military government was established in Sicily, which continues to this day—a number of violent acts which it is greatly feared will end in rendering nearly incurable the discontent of the Sicilians. Villages suspected of giving an asylum to the refractory have been deprived of water for four days. This fact being mentioned by a deputy in Parliament, obtained for answer that people did not die of thirst! Another fact, in an ancient country house, near a village called Pretralia Soprana, also in Sicily, they thought there was concealed a recruit, but in this they were deeeived, there was no recruit in the house. A patrole composed of troops of the line and the national guard, and commanded by an officer of the army, presented themselves at the door in the dead of the night, which they beat with the butt ends of their muskets, demandiug that it should be opened instantly. Now, it was a lonely house in the country, and the people in it roused suddenly from their slumbers by the noise, believed that they were attacked by thieves, and under this impression opened a window and discharged a musket. The officer in command set fire to the door and to a rick of straw. The door and the house were soon in flames, and when the soldiers afterwards entered the house, they found all the family, women and children included, dead—either burnt by the fire or suffocated by the smoke. Even this was not enough; on the bodies were found bayonet wounds. The deputy of the Italian Parliament and for the districot in question, was Fileppo Santo Canale, who wrote himself the history of this fact. Another fact, a young workman of Palermo, named Antonio Capello, is deaf and dumb, and has been so from his birth, a fact well known to all the town; in his twentieth year he fell under the law for the conscription, he drew the lot for a soldier, but by the law his infirmity protected him. The military doctor persisted in asserting that he only pretended to be deaf and dumb, and refused belief to the declarations of his friends and the evidence of the disclosures, he forced him to enter the hospital and to submit to every kind of proof; the Dr. Restelli, surgeon of the military district, ordered the application of red hot irons to the body of Capello in order to make him speak, 154 burns were inflicted upon the body of the unhappy mute, but of course he was unable to utter a single word. General Govene, charged with the military government of the Island, had not an exact list of the recruits in his list, he had the names of the dead, of women, of children, and of many who had emigrated in the service; for imaginary persons he caused to be arrested Dr. Albanese, one of the Drs. of General Garibaldi, they arrested this gentleman in the street and told him he was one of the refractory. I answered, Dr. Albanese, why I am 30 years old! That is nothing they answered, and they placed a sentry over his house, in the end they liberated him. They also accused the Duke de la Vegdura of protecting the delinquents, he pleaded the inviolability of his person as a senator, but this did not prevent them from placing sentries over his house. The government replied to the questions of the Deputies Maceli and la Borta, denying certain facts, and justifying others for reasons of State; they denied on the authority of Dr. Restelli, the wounds of the deaf and dumb Capello. In Palermo numbers of the population have seen these wounds. The author has in his possession a photograph of Capello, which he has just received from Palermo, which shows the burns and sufficiently answers this question. Garibaldi did not resign until the Italian Chambers had confirmed the unconstitutional conduct of the

Ministers in every respect. After the resignation of the General, the Government members in the house voted that it should be accepted, and virtually answered it by decorating Dr. Restelli, who ordered the torture to be inflicted.

The *Diritto* proclaims the following programme:—Admitting that in the hour of danger Garibaldi will neither ask the religion or the politics of those who are willing to aid him in the completion of the task to which he has devoted himself—the formation of an united Italy,—admitted that he will for the future never look whether the sword or the bayonet, which repulses the enemy of Italy and restores her unity, is wielded by a monarchal or republican hand, the *Diritto* proclaims that Italy under a king is the only idea existing in the minds of a party which, led by the saviour of Italy, and composed of her best, honestest, and most active citizens, has made the kingdom of the peninsula what it now is. The moderate party little knows, writes Civinni, the pernicious fault it commits when it insists on creating in Italy difficulties which do not exist, when by its own efforts it succeeds in reviving discords which can only profit the enemies of their country.

A leading London journal, the *Daily Telegraph*, of the 30th of December, has so able an article on the Italian Question, no apology is offered for giving it almost in its entirety:—

"Notwithstanding semi-official contradictions on the part of the Administration, and friendly explanations on the part of leading Italians, certain it is that the affairs of the peninsula are in a state which demands that rarest form of discretion—concentrated energy. The outward signs are embarrassing and anxious enough. The eloquently prompt response of King Victor Emmanuel, agreeing to take part in the Emperor Napoleon's Congress, has been followed up by plausible rumours that his Government is engaged in a vigorous augmentation and drilling of its army, with a view to active operations; and the condition of other countries has appeared to indicate the aim of these contemplated movements. Holstein is only the last of the points at which the conflagration seems likely to break forth, and whether the tumult is to take possession of Northern Germany or Hungary, Austria may have more on her hands than she bargains for; hence the deferred opportunity for Venetia seems to be not far distant. Again, should the Emperor Napoleon find his hands too full with Mexican expeditions, congresses, German complications, and perhaps a little affair to be accomplished on the Rhine, he might be glad enough of the ready, willing, and chivalrous support of the Rè Galantuomo; and would it be wonderful if, under such circumstances, he were to find other services for certain of his troops than that of lazily playing garrison in Rome? Letters have been seen flying about between Garibaldi and Victor Hugo; the 'Party of Action' is astir with fresh vitality; and everybody, from General La Marmora to the Sovereign Pontiff, is on the *qui vive* of hope or fear, as the case may be. There *is* something in the air, and people feel the electric influences of an approaching storm. Indeed, so nervously sensitive have they become, that they have actually anticipated things that are *not* to happen; reforms, for example, in the Pontifical Government. But there is even a darker side of the horizon. The Party of Action is anything but contented. The retirement of Dr. Bertani and a few friends from the Italian Parliament, to mark their indignation at the treatment of Sicily, is an untoward symptom; and, possibly, the retrogade strategy of the respectable members may be followed by other manifestations of the popular discontent. The Party of Reaction contributes its mite to the general uneasiness, the Pope having recently nominated fourteen new bishops, seven of them for posts in Italy, Bologna included; and since the Royal Government, as a matter of course, has refused the exequatur permitting the ecclesiastics to assume their offices, speculative politicians are already discussing the possibility of a new Protestant secession—a severance of the 'National Italian Church' from the local and provincial sect which still keeps its establishment on Monte Cavallo. Strange to say, while most of these threats of danger are visionary and fallacious, the condition of the peninsula is even more critical than the alarmists assert. As to the Party of Action, the most important leader of it is Garibaldi, and although the events of the day may prove very tantalising and tempting to his adventurous mind, we have some reason to believe that he does not contemplate any abrupt departure from the masterly position which he has preserved heretofore. The correspondence with Victor Hugo implies as much. It puts in an appearance for the tribunes of the people, French as well as Italian; it signifies that they are neither dead nor oblivious, and it shows them on the watch to seize any opportunity that may present itself; but that opportunity has not yet come. Their letters may be regarded less as cheques drawn at sight on the bank of revolution than as instruments to defer payment of the account—promissory notes, renewed for at least another year; though, of course, they will be taken up in the interval if the occasion should offer. The *Diritto*, the accredited organ of Garibaldi, has distinctly announced that, in the event of war breaking out elsewhere, the party for which it speaks would instantly place itself by the side of the national champions. 'Garibaldi,' says his mouthpiece, 'would be the first to say to his followers, Turn all your hatred against the enemies of Italy; and those followers would be the first to rush into action, crying United Italy under Victor Emmanuel.' Nay, the General himself has recently placed on record his distinctly constitutional convictions. Under his own hand he has not only expressed his attachment to England and her institutions, but has declared his thorough confidence in our Premier. I would give my life for England as freely as for Italy.' And not a doubt can be entertained that, should his country be assailed, should she be summoned to take her part in any great European challenge, or should destiny itself point the opportunity for her onward march, he will be found foremost amongst the officers of the Italian army, winning new victories, and laying both the throne and the people under new debts to his patriotism. It is not in these directions that the dangers of the kingdom lie. The Pope, who has not power enough to keep order in his own city, and remains there by favour of French patronage and the sufferance of his own lieges, may go to such aggressive lengths as the appointment of bishops; but what then? He knows beforehand that they are to remain in his own neighbourhood, as much mere titular dignitaries as Henry V. of France, or the Duke of Brunswick. Dr. Bertani is a clever man, but debate can go on without him. The capture of Caruso, however, does not end brigandage in Naples, nor is the retirement of Garibaldi from the Chamber of Deputies an insignificant occurrence. We may doubt the step as a question of sound policy, but the exciting cause is not to be ignored or despised. There may be 'faults on both sides,' but the very activity of General Pallavicini is evidence to the ugly fact that the Royal Government has not yet succeeded in winning the unreserved affections of the Neapolitans; and if some obscurity still hangs over the causes of the disorder in the southern part of the peninsula—if complaints can justly be alleged against local agitators in Sicily—if both provinces nourish some jealousy of northern ascendency—it is but too obvious that each is treated too much like a conquered dependency. To prove that certain individual ringleaders 'are in the wrong' would in no degree exonerate the Turin officials, whose business it was to compete with any such candidates for the affections of the people, and to beat every other competitor. With all their resources—with the means of inciting loyalty and patriotism, as opposed to discontent and provincialism—with their command of Italian zeal and Italian wit—the members of the Administration are damned by their own defence.* They confess that they have not

* Is it wonderful they don't succeed? see the following absurd story of Turin:—A Royal commission is named to organize a system of meteorological operations throughout the country. M. Matteucci, the senator, has been appointed president, and the chief seat of the institution is to be at Turin. Times are changed in Italy since Galileo said, *Non di meno gira*. Apropos of the Government having the "chief weather office" in Turin, a Florentine remarked, "Yes, it is the usual system of centralization; the Piedmontese believe that the sun rises, shines, and sets without leaving Savoy. Only lately a new official seal was required at Florence, the city of Cellini and of his descendants, and they had it made in the Via di Po at Turin!"

succeeded, where not to succeed is in itself an offence, and one of the gravest character. Nor are the reasons of their failure less palpable than the thing itself. Overlooking the example of our Richard II., they neglect to master the discontent by boldly and heartily crying, 'I will be your leader.' Their shortcomings and blunders are glaring, if we look only to the single case of Garibaldi. Granted that he erred at Aspromonte, surely he has paid the penalty many times over; and if he miscalculated there, his conduct did not differ very materially from certain sallies out of bounds which endowed the kingdom with the two provinces of Naples and Sicily, and made it really Italy. Admitting that a little official cold water might be cast on the one fault,* where has been the official tribute for the other splendid gifts?—where the national acknowledgment to the man that gave the nation existence and restored a country to its name? What his position, what his honours, what his share in the social intercourse and family councils of the Italians? He is no beggar for rewards—*he* does not need any of those honours which Royalty can bestow! but Royalty needs to bestow them, and that nation is defrauded whose rewards are withheld from its most devoted men. The founder of the State is consigned to a species of rustication; and the separate position into which he is thrust is an example of those laches which constitute the true weakness and peril of the kingdom."

* Respecting the one fault, the author begs to refer to the fact of the Pope's intention to leave Rome and go to Malta under English protection. What would the French have done then?

CHAPTER XIV.

Brief History of the events which led to the occupation of Rome—Italy at the peace of 1815—The insurrection of 1820—The Victor Emmanuel of that day—Pius IX—The revolution of 1848—The address of the assembly to England and France in 1849—The French Army under Oudinot, land in Italy—The defence of Rome entrusted to Garibaldi—Repulse of the French troops—Debate on the expedition to Rome in the French Assembly—Napoleon's letter to Oudinot—Garibaldi attacks the French—The King of Naples marches upon Rome—The Bourbon Army retreat and are defeated by Garibaldi—The Butchery at Villa Corsini—Defences of Rome abandoned—Garibaldi declared Dictator—Mr. Stansfeld on the defence of Rome.

Before concluding, I have thought it advisable to add, as an appendix, a brief history of the events which led to the occupation of Rome by the French army. At the peace of 1815 it is well known that Italy was parcelled out as part of the general spoil. The insurrection of 1820 at Naples followed. The king yielded in six days and granted a constitution. An Austrian army entered the kingdom the following year and restored despotism. A successful invasion by the Piedmontese took place, but the Victor Emmanuel of that day, bound by his oath to Austria not to grant any constitution, abdicated, and a constitutional government was in consequence proclaimed. The following April the king was however restored by the force of Austria. These movements were the works of the Carbonari. Charles Albert, then Prince of Carignano, father of the present king of Italy, and Prince Francis, of Naples, were members of this order. The Neapolitan Prince was a traitor from the first, and so things continued to go on till the national rising of 1848.

Pius IX ascended the Papal throne in 1846. He promised large administrative reforms, and a government in accordance with the requirements of the times, granted an amnesty, and appeared to be anxious to form a liberal and constitutional state, round which all parties might unite. So convinced was General Garibaldi of this, that he wrote offering his full and entire support to the Pope. This was Garibaldi's first attempt to support a constitutional monarchy in Italy. The resnlt is known to all. The Pope listened to evil councillors, returned to the old system, and had to fly from Rome in the disguise of a menial.

The Revolution of 1848, which dethroned Louis Philippe and the House of Orleans, establishing a republican government in France, was the signal for a general revolutionary movement throughout Europe. In Rome, a republican government was established, the same as in Paris, and Mazzini was appointed the Triumvir. The 5th article of the French Constitution stated, "The French Republic respects Foreign nationalities. She intends to cause her own to be respected; she will not undertake any sin for the purpose of conquest, and will never employ her arms against the liberty of any people." The President of the French Republic was Prince Louis Napoleon, who had himself fought for Italian liberty in the year 1831, when the Bolognese revolution broke out.* Louis Napoleon had taken an active part in the campaign, and, aided by General Sercognani, defeated the Papal forces in several places. His success was of short duration. He was deprived of his command, and banished from Italy, and only escaped the Austrian soldiers by assuming the disguise of a servant. It must also be borne in mind that the Emperor Napoleon, his uncle, had detained the Pope a prisoner in France. It could not be reasonably supposed, under these circumstances, that the President of the French Republic would do otherwise than rejoice at the formation of a sister republic in the Roman States. The Roman constituent assembly, elected by

* See "Vicissitudes of Families," second series, by Sir B. Burke, pages 294, 295 See also "The Autobiography of an Italian Rebel," by Riccalde

universal suffrage, voted by 143 against 5 votes, for the perpetual downfall of the temporal government of the Pope; it also resolved, in conformity with the new constitution, that, though firmly determined to resist the union of the temporal and ecclesiastical powers in one and the same person, they were ready to assume to the Pope the full and perfect exercise of all his ecclesiastical powers.

On the 18th of April, 1849, the constituent assembly voted that a manifesto should be addressed to the Governments and Parliaments of England and France. In this document it was stated, "That the Roman people had a right to give themselves the form of government which pleased them; that they had sanctioned the independence and free exercise of the spiritual authority of the Pope, and that they trusted that England and France would not assist in restoring a government irreconcilable by its nature with liberty and civilization, and morally destitute of all authority for many years past, and materially so during the previous five months."

Notwithstanding this, the French government dispatched a French army to Civita Vecchia, where they landed on the 27th April, 1849. General Oudinot declared that the flag which he had hoisted was that of peace, order, conciliation, and true liberty, and he invited the Roman people to co-operate in the accomplishment of this patriotic and sacred work. He also declared that the French had landed, not to defend the existing Pontifical government, but to avert great misfortunes from the country. France, he added, did not arrogate to herself the right to regulate the interests which belonged to the Roman people and extended to the whole Christian world. The prefect of the province replied, "Force may do much in this world, but I am averse to believe that republican France will employ its troops to overthrow the rights of a republic formed under the same auspices as her own. I am convinced that when you ascertain the truth you will feel assured that in our country the republic is supported by the immense majority of the people."

The Roman government resolved to oppose force by force, and the Assembly did not hesitate; on the 26th of April, at two o'clock in the afternoon, the following decree was voted amidst the applauses of all Rome:—"In the name of God and the people—The Assembly, after the communication received by the Triumvir, places in his hands the honour of the republic, and charges him to repel force by force."

The Triumvir entrusted to General Garibaldi, who arrived the same evening, the defence of the city of Rome.

It is impossible to describe the enthusiasm which took possession of the population at the sight of him. The courage of the people increased with their confidence, and it appeared as if the Assembly had not only decreed defence, but victory.

A few lines of the history of the Roman Revolution, by Biagio Miraglia, will give an idea of this enthusiasm: "This mysterious conqueror, surrounded by such a brilliant halo of glory, who entered Rome on the eve of the very day on which the republic was about to be attacked, was, in the minds of the Roman people, the only man capable of maintaining the decree of resistance; therefore the multitudes, on the very instant, united themselves with the man who personified the wants of the moment, and who was the hope of all."

He upheld for three months in the future capital of the nation the national flag, against the forces of France, Austria, Naples and Spain; twice were the French troops attacked at the point of the bayonet and repulsed far beyond the walls; it was afterwards stated by French writers, that the French soldiers only intended to make a recognizance and had fallen into a snare, this is not true; the French general had resolved upon a battle, his plan of which was found on the body of a French officer killed in the conflict, and transmitted to the Minister of War; it was after this victory that Garibaldi, seeing all the advantages of his situation, wrote to Avizzana, Minister of War, "Send me fresh troops, and as I promised to beat the French, and have kept my word, I promise you I will prevent any one of them from regaining their vessels." It was then that Mazzini, placing all his hopes on the French democratic party, of which Ledru Rollin was the chief, interposed his authority, he refused the fresh troops asked for, and ordered Garibaldi not to make a mortal enemy of France by a complete defeat. On Monday, 7th May, in the French National Assembly, there was an animated discussion on the French expedition to Rome; Mons. J. Favre having denounced its proceedings as contrary to the intention avowed by ministers, which was to prevent foreign interference at Rome; and as clearly opposed to wishes of the Roman people; he also stated, on the authority of private letters, that five unsuccessful assaults had been made, that 150 men had been killed and 600 wounded, and he ended by moving the appointment of a committee. Mons. Barrot, the president of the council, declared that the object of the expedition was, really, to prevent another power from interfering in the affairs of Rome, and expressed his belief that General Oudinot had not acted contrary to his instructions, though the army might have fallen into a snare, he opposed the committee as unconstitutional, and called upon the assembly to reject the motion. General Lamoriciere believed that General Oudinot might have been deceived as to the wishes of the people of Rome. M. Flocon announced that barricades had been erected at Rome, and that the French residents would fight against the new comers. After some further discussion Mons. Barrot acquiesced in the motion, and the members withdrew to appoint the committee. The sitting was resumed at 9 o'clock, when the report of the committee was presented. It stated that as the idea of the assembly had been that the expedition sent to Civita Vecchia ought to remain there, unless Austria moved on Rome, or a counter resolution in that city rendered an advance necessary. The committee considered that more had been done than had been intended, and it therefore proposed a resolution declaring that the national assembly requested the Government to take measures that the expedition to Italy be no longer turned aside from its real object. M. Drouyn de Lhuys on the part of the

Government, said he must positively refuse to order the troops to return to Civita Vecchia, their presence being required by events at Rome, the minister farther declared that the Government fully supported its agent, the general-in-chief, and the more so that the details of the encounter at Rome were wanting. M. Lenard accused the ministry of wishing to put down the Roman republic. After various amendments had been proposed and rejected, the resolution of the committee was carried against ministers by a majority of 328 to 241. The result was received with loud cheers, and cries of "Vive la Republique," and the chamber adjourned at a quarter past 1 o'clock.

Notwithstanding this vote of the French National Assembly, the president of the republic, Prince Louis Napoleon, addressed a letter to General Oudinot, in which he says: "I had hoped that the inhabitants of Rome would receive with eagerness an army which had arrived there to accomplish a friendly and disinterested mission. This has not been the case, our soldiers have been received as enemies, our military honour is engaged. I shall not suffer it to be assailed. Reinforcements shall not be wanting to you." The envoy of the Roman Government in Paris, addressed the following letter, in the name of the Roman people, to their brothers in France: "A sanguinary combat has taken place between the inhabitants of Rome and the children of France, whom rigorous orders urged against our homes; the sentiment of military honour commanded them to obey their chiefs, the sentiment of patriotism ordered us to defend our liberties and our country. Honour is saved, but at what a price! may the terrible responsibility be averted from us, who are united by the bonds of charity. May even the culpable be pardoned, they are punished sufficiently by remorse. Health and fraternity.—L. Tarpolei, Colonel Envoy Extraodinary of the Roman Republic in Paris.

In the next sitting of the French National Assembly, the subject of the president's letter to General Oudinot was brought forward by M. Grevy, in reply to whom M. Odillon Barrot stated that though the letter in question was not the act of the cabinet, he and his colleagues were ready to assume the whole responsibility of it. He declared that the object of the letter was merely to express sympathy with the army, and that it was not intended as the inauguration of a policy contrary to that of the assembly. General Changarnier placed the letter of the president of the republic to General Oudinot on the orders of the day of every regiment in the French service, although M. Odilon Barrot declared in the assembly that it was not official. Also General Foret refused to obey the orders of the president of the assembly by sending two battalions to guard it during its sitting; a breach of orders, which was brought under the notice of the assembly by M. Armand Manest, and apologised for by M. Odillon Barrot. On the 9th of May M. Ledru Rollin declared the letter of the president to General Oudinot to be an insolent defiance of the national assembly, and a violation of the constitution. Ultimately the debate was adjourned on the motion of M. Grevy and M. Fane, in consequence of M. Odilon Barrot having announced that M. Lesseps, the late minister from Paris at Madrid, had been sent by the government as an envoy to Rome, to express to the Roman people the wishes of the assembly, which showed that the government did not intend to oppose the assembly. The Paris correspondent of the *Morning Chronicle*, noticing the stormy debates in the French assembly says: "In the last three days troops have been pouring into Paris, and the number of men now garrisoning the capital is upwards of 100,000."

On the 12th of June a leading English provincial paper* wrote: "If the supposition be correct which attributed the delay in the appearance of the French president's message to the difficulties experienced by its framer in the endeavour to put a good face on the Roman expedition, we must say that the period of protracted gestation offers but a net result of labour lost. The document is now before the world, and the account which it

* The *Liverpool Mercury*.

gives of the transaction will not construe more favourably than General Oudinot's proclamations. The avowal just comes to this that France, unsolicited by any of the contending parties, arbitrarily intervened in Rome, in order 'to exercise a direct independent action by our own spontaneous movement.' This message also, as published in the *Moniteur*, differs from that published in the other French papers in a most essential point. In speaking of the resistance offered to General Oudinot by the Romans, the message as published in the *Moniteur*, says: 'This unexpected struggle, without making any change in the final aim of our enterprise, has paralysed our beneficent intentions, and rendered abortive the efforts of negociations.' The message, as published in the other journals, has, after the words 'beneficent intentions,' the following passage: 'Completely altered the state of the question, so that it is now only in Rome that it can be resolved in a manner consistent with the honour of France.' This latter version was the one originally laid upon the table of the assembly, but the president subsequently altered it as it appeared to explain somewhat too clearly his intentions with regard to Rome."

We will now return to that city, and to the day of the first victory over the French.

The joy which pervaded Rome in the evening and night which followed this first combat, may be easily supposed. The whole city was illuminated, and presented the aspect of a national fete. Songs and bands of music were heard in all directions. The next day, the first of May, Garibaldi received from the minister of war authority to attack the French with his legion; he took up a splendid position on a height, on the flank of the French army, but at the moment the Italians were about to charge, a French officer arrived and demanded a parley with Garibaldi, he stated that he was sent by the General Oudinot to treat for an armistice, and to be assured that the Roman people really accepted the republican government, and were determined to defend their rights. As a proof of his good intentions the French general offered to give up Garibaldi's favourite chaplain, Ugo Bœsso,* who (having the evening before refused to leave a dying man, whose head he was holding on his knee), had been taken prisoner. The Roman minister at war ordered Garibaldi to return to Rome, which he did, accompanied by the French officer. The armistice demanded of General Oudinot was accorded by the triumvir, and the republican government granted unconditional liberty to fully 500 French prisoners in their hands. A letter from Garibaldi, after speaking of the bravery displayed by the Roman troops, says, "A quantity of arms, drums, and other matters, have remained in our hands. The wounded French, before expiring, expressed their sorrow for having fought against their republican brethren."

The King of Naples, at the head of his army, was now marching upon Rome. Seeing this, Garibaldi, whom the armistice left unoccupied, demanded permission to employ his leisure in attacking the King of Naples. This permission was granted, and on the evening of the 4th of May, Garibaldi left the city with his legion, now 2,500 strong.

The rendezvous had been appointed at the Place of the People, and at six o'clock Garibaldi was there. A young Swiss, of German Switzerland, named Gustave de Hoffstiller, who has written an excellent history of the siege of Rome, gives the following account:—

"Just as six o'clock was striking, the General and his staff appeared, and was received with a thunder of *vivats*. I saw him for the first time. He is a man of middle height, his countenance scorched by the sun, but marked with lines of antique purity. He sat on his horse as calmly and firmly as if he had been born there; beneath his hat—broad-brimmed, with a narrow loop, and ornamented with a black ostrich feather—was spread a forest of hair. A red beard covered the whole of the lower

* Never did the unfortunate enter his house with extended hands and go out with those hands empty; but, likewise, never was his name seen on those subscription lists, much more frequently destined for the glorification of the subscribers than for the relief of the unfortunate.

part of his face. Over his red shirt was thrown an American poncho, white, lined with red, like his shirt. His staff wore the red blouse, and afterwards the whole Italian legion adopted that colour."

The papers of the day stated, "intelligence has been received from Rome up to the 9th. Garibaldi has marched into the Neapolitan territory, the Neapolitans have been forced to abandon Tracati and several other places, in order to provide for the defence of Naples against the advance of Garibaldi. The following official announcement of Garibaldi's victory, was published at Rome on the 10th. "Official bulletin: first Italian Legion of General Garibaldi, Palestrina, May 9th, quarter-past 8 o'clock, p.m. A complete victory. The enemy, 7,000 strong, entirely defeated. We have taken three pieces of artillery. The firing commenced at half-past 4 and finished at dusk. More detailed accounts shall be sent in an hour. Palestrina is illuminated from Daverio, chief of General Garibaldi's staff." The defeat of the Neapolitans by Garibaldi, was a perfect rout, not a Neapolitan soldier was to be found in the Roman republic; their success had, however, nearly cost the Italians dear. Garibaldi was wounded in the foot and the hand. "The head-quarters of the Neapolitan army are now at Naples, and the very excellently beaten Bomba is at Gaeta, pouring his sorrows into the bosom of the Pope." In Rome, Mazzini informed the Assembly that Garibaldi would confine his operations to the frontier, so as to be ready to fall back upon Rome whenever his presence might be needed; he was ordered to return, and did so, entering Rome on the morning of the 12th, having marched during the night 28 miles, without stopping an instant. The following account is greatly condensed from the account of the siege of Rome, written by Garibaldi, and by him given to Alexandre Dumas; the speaker is the General:—

"On the day Bologna fell, the ambassador extraordinary of the French republic, Ferdinand de Lesseps, entered Rome with Michael Accrusi, the envoy of the Roman republic to Paris.

"By means of the good offices of the French ambassador, the armistice, which had been agitated for a fortnight, and against which I had given so strong an opinion on the 1st of May, was concluded.

"The Roman government resolved to take advantage of this truce to get rid of the Neapolitan army.

"The government (Mazzini) first made Colonel Roselli a general, and then named him general in chief.

"Some of my friends urged me not to accept a secondary position under a man who the day before only was my inferior. But I confess I have been always inaccessible to these questions of self-love; whoever gives me an opportunity, if only as a simple soldier, of drawing my sword against the enemy, is entitled to my thanks. I therefore accepted with gratitude the post of general of division.

"On the 16th of May, in the evening, the whole army of the republic, that is to say, ten thousand men, with twelve pieces of cannon, marched out of the city of Rome by the San Giovanni gate. Of these ten thousand men, one thousand were cavalry."

General Garibaldi was ordered to proceed in advance.

"I had received," he continues, "information that the Neapolitan army was encamped at Velletri, with from 19 to 20,000 men, of whom two regiments were Swiss, and 30 pieces of cannon. It was likewise said that the King of Naples in person was in the city. In fact, the royals occupied Velletri, Albano, and Frascati; their advanced posts came as far as Fratvecchia. Their left wing was protected by the sea, their right wing leant upon the Appenines. After I had abandoned Palestrino, they had occupied it, and thus commanded the valley through which was the only practicable road for an army coming from Rome to attack them. They were, then, able to oppose to us a serious resistance, as they had over us the advantage of position, the advantage of numbers, the advantage of cannon, and that of cavalry. On the morning of the 19th, I quitted my position to march upon Velletri, to which city the whole Bourbon army had retreated."

In the end, the army of the King of Naples was again entirely defeated by General Garibaldi's division alone. In an early part of the day, he sent to the commander-in-chief for reinforcements, and received for answer that soldiers could not be sent, as they had not eaten their soup. He then resolved to do what he could with his own strength, and victory again crowned his efforts. Towards midnight, his troops took possession of Velletri itself.

"It was indeed deserted. A few prisoners had been too tardy, and from them and the people of the city, I learnt all I wanted to know—which was that, as soon as night came on, the Neapolitans had commenced their retreat, but in such disorder, that they had left the greater part of their wounded behind them. At daybreak I set off in pursuit of them, but it was impossible for me to overtake them. Besides, whilst I was on the high road to Terracina, I received orders to rejoin the column, half of which was returning to Rome. I re-entered Rome on the 24th of May, amidst an immense crowd, which hailed me with cries of wild joy."

In the meantime, General Oudinot, having received the reinforcements which he required, disavowed the treaty entered into by the Roman government and the envoy extraordinary of his master, the president of the French republic. It would have been thought that the dream of a French alliance would now have faded from the ideas of the Roman government, but they were only half convinced even yet, and they allowed their commander-in-chief, the newly-created General Roselli, to indite a letter, from which the following is an extract:—"General Oudinot, Duke de Reggio, citizen,—It is my perfect conviction that the army of the Roman republic will one day fight side by side with the army of the French republic to maintain the most sacred rights of peoples. This conviction leads me to make you proposals, which I hope you will accept. It is known to me

* The utter incompetence of General Roselli was evident from first to last. However, he shared the views of the Roman Government respecting the French, which, in their eyes, was at that time everything.

that a treaty has been signed between the government and plenipotentiary minister of France, a treaty which has not received your approbation." The letter goes on to request an unlimited armistice, with a notification of 15 days before the resumption of hostilities, asked in the name of the honour of the army and of the French republic, and concludes, "I have the honour to reqnest a prompt reply, General, begging you to accept the salutation of fraternity,—ROSELLI."

To this the French general replied:—"General,—The orders of my government are positive. They prescribe to me to enter Rome as soon as possible. * * * I defer the attack of the place until Monday morning at least. Receive, General, the assurance of my high consideration,—The general-in chief of the corps de l'armee of the Mediterranean, Oudinot Duc de Reggio."

According to this assurance, the attack would not commence before the 4th of June.

"It is true," writes Garibaldi, "that a French author, Foland, has said in his Commentaries upon Polybius, 'A general who goes to sleep on the faith of a treaty awakes a dupe.' I was roused at three o'clock by the sound of cannon. I found everything on fire. This is what had happened: Our advanced posts were at the Villa Pamphili. At the moment midnight was striking, and we were entering on the day of Sunday, the 3rd of June, a French column glided through the darkness towards the Villa Pamphili. 'Who goes there?' cried the sentinel, warned by the sound of footsteps. 'Viva l'Italia!' replied a voice. The sentinel, thinking he had to do with compatriots, suffered them to approach, and was poniarded. The column rushed into the Villa Pamphili. All they met with were either killed or made prisoners. Some men jumped through the windows into the garden, and when once in the garden, climbed over the walls. The most forward of them retired behind the convent of St. Pancrazio, shouting 'To arms! to arms!' whilst others ran off in the direction of the Villas Valentini and Corsini. Like the Villa Pamphili, these were carried by surprise, but not without making some resistance.

When I arrived at the St. Pancrazio gate, the Villa Pamphili, the Villa Corsini, and the Villa Valentini were all taken. The Vascello alone remained in our hands. Now the Villa Corsini being taken was an enormous loss to us; for as long as we were masters of that, the French could not draw their parallels. At any price, then, that must be retaken; it was for Rome a question of life and death. The firing between the cannoneers of the ramparts, the men of the Vascello, and the French of the Villa Corsini and the Villa Valentini, increased. But it was not a fusillade, or a cannonade that was necessary; it was an assault, a terrible but victorious assault, which might restore the Villa Corsini to us. For a moment the Villa Corsini was ours. That moment was short, but it was sublime! The French brought up all their reserve, and fell upon us all together before I could even repair the disorder inseparable from victory. The fight was renewed more desperately, more bloodily, more fatally than ever. I saw repass before me, repulsed by those irresistible powers of war, fire and steel, those whom I had seen pass on but a minute before, now bearing away their dead.

"I have seen very terrible fights. I saw the fight of Rio Grande, I saw the Bayada, I saw the Salto San-Antonio, but I never saw anything comparable to the butchery of the Villa Corsini.

"I came out the last, my puncho absolutely drilled with shot-holes; but without a single wound myself. Within ten minutes we were once more in the Vascello, in the line of houses which belonged to us, from all the windows of which we renewed our fire upon the Villa Corsini.

"We had suffered terrible losses. The Italian legion had, killed and wounded, five hundred men placed *nors de combat* The Bersaglieri, who had only six hundred men engaged, had a hundred and fifty killed. All the other losses were in the same proportion. The entire loss of my division of four thousand men was one thousand, of whom one hundred were officers. The Signor Bertani, in his report, reckons one hundred and eighty officers wounded at the Villa Corsini and the Gate of the People. The Bersaglieri alone had two officers killed, and eleven wounded."

It will be seen from this, the enormous advantages which the French general gained from his breach of faith. From this time there was no longer a question of any other general than Garibaldi defending Rome, although General Rosselli did not formally resign.

"Fearing an assault for the next day, I charged Giacomo Medici with the defence of all our advanced line, which now consisted of Vascello, and three or four small houses taken back from the French. I then passed the night in organizing our means of defence.

"There could be no longer any idea of saving Rome. From the moment an army of forty thousand men, having 36 pieces of siege cannon, can perform their works of approach, the taking of a city is nothing but a question of time. It must, one day or other fall; the only hope it has left is to fall gloriously.

"I that evening established my head-quarters in the Casino Savorelli, which, rising above the ramparts, overlooks the St. Pancrazio gate, and from its proximity permits everything to be seen that is passing in the Vascello, the Villa Corsini, and the Villa Valentini. It is true I was within half carbine shot of the French *tirailleurs*—but he who risks nothing wins nothing.

"This rage of the French artillerymen to riddle my poor head-quarters with bullets, balls, and obos, sometimes produced scenes sufficiently amusing."

It is not the object of this paper to give the history of the seige of Rome. General Garibaldi had lost his chief of the staff, Colonel Daverea, on the night of the 3rd, and he appointed Colonel Maneira to the vacant post; the reason the General gives shows the requirements he thinks a chief of the staff ought to possess, namely: great bravery and rare self possession, and quick eye in battle, and command of languages (Colonel Maneira spoke four), and above all that dignity which so well becomes superior rank. The new chief of the staff was mortally wounded on the 30th of June. Bertani and the other doctors were almost instantly in attendance, but it was useless; he was told to think of his Saviour, "I do think of him and much," was the answer. He then begged that his children might be brought up in the love of God and their country. On the day of his death, a letter arrived from his wife containing these words:—"Do not think of me, or of your children, think only of your country."

The conduct of the Roman people during these days of trial was worthy of ancient times. Whilst during the night, pursued by the showers of projectiles which crushed in the roofs of their houses, mothers flew from one place to another, pressing their children to their breasts; whilst the streets resounded with cries and lamentations, not a single voice spoke of surrendering. In the midst of all these cries, one jeering cry was frequently heard when a ball or an obus brought down the side of a house:—

"A Benediction from the Pope!"

During the evening of the 28th the French batteries appeared to rest for an instant as if to take breath, but on the day of the 29th they resumed their fire with fresh rage. Rome was intensely agitated; the day of the 27th had been terrible; our losses had been almost equal to those of the 3rd of June; the streets were choked with mutilated men. The sappers had no sooner taken the spade or the pickaxe in their hand than they were cut in two by balls or mutilated by obus. All our artillery-men—observe, *all*—had been killed at their guns: the duty of the artillery was performed by soldiers of the line. All the nocturnal guard being under arms, there was, a thing before unheard of, a reserve composed of the wounded, who, bleeding as they were, performed the duty. And yet all this time the assembly in permanence deliberated calmly and impassably in the Capitol under bullets and balls.

As long as one of our pieces of cannon remained upon its carriage it replied, but on the evening of the 29th the last was dismounted.

Garibaldi was summoned before the assembly, and this is his history of what happened.

"Mazzini had already announced to the assembly the position we now stood in: there remained, he said, but three parts to take: to treat with the French, to defend the city from barricade to barricade; or to leave the city, assembly, triumvirate, and army, carrying away with them the palladium of Roman liberty.

"When I appeared at the door of the chamber, all the deputies rose and applauded. I looked abont me, and upon myself to see what it was that awakened their enthusiasm. I was covered with blood; my clothes were pierced with balls and bayonet thrusts. They cried: 'To the tribune! to the tribune!' and I mounted it. I was interrogated on all sides.

"All defence is henceforth impossible," replied I, "unless we are resolved to make Rome another Saragossa. On the 9th of February I proposed a military dictatorship, that alone was able to place on foot a hundred thousand armed men. The living elements still subsisted; they were to be sought for, and they would have been found in one courageous man. If I had been attended to, the Roman eagle would again have made its eyrie upon the towers of the Capitol; and with my brave men—and my brave men know how to die, it is pretty well known—I might have changed the face of Italy. But there is no remedy for that which is done. Let us view with head erect the conflagration of which we no longer are the masters. Let us take with us from Rome all of the volunteer army who are willing to follow us. Where we shall be Rome will be. I pledge myself to nothing; but all that my men can do that I will do—and whilst it takes refuge in us our country shall not die."

In the end the following order was issued. "The Roman Republic, in the name of God and the People. The Roman Constituent Assembly discontinues a defence which has become impossible. It has its post. The triumvirate are charged with the execution of the present decree." On the 30th of June also, with a view to future emergencies, the constituent assembly, by formal vote, declared General Garibaldi the legal guardian of the rights of the Roman people, and conferred upon him the executive power of the state which the triumvirate resigned into his hands; and when he was wounded and taken prisoner at Aspromonti, when he was neither fighting or intending to fight, he was marching towards Rome provided with those legal powers which the representatives of the Roman people, elected themselves by universal suffrage, had already conferred upon him, anxious only to deliver these powers into the hands of Victor Emanuel, and to liberate the Roman people from a government which daily blasphemed God in making a merchandise of Him.

But to return. Garibaldi left Rome at the head of 4,000 foot and 900 horse, constituting two-thirds of the survivors of the defenders of Rome. At first successful, he was in the end forced to retreat before the overwhelming numbers of the Austrians, and finally to disband his forces. It was at this time that he lost, under circumstances the most painful that it is possible to conceive, his wife and unborn child. The first act of the French general on entering Rome was to send a French colonel to lay the keys of the city at the feet of the Pope. All the Roman physicians who attended the wounded patriots lost their diplomas. Mr. Stansfeld, now a Lord of the Admiralty, writes on this subject: "We can never forget the heroic defence of Rome, the brightest and saddest page in the history of the Italian movement; a defence which, hopeless as it proved to be, was the greatest moral victory which Italy has yet achieved. Rome fell after three months' siege to the overpowering force and the matchless perfidy of the French. I say that its hopeless defence was the greatest of all moral victories for Italy. It was so, because it gave to the unaided people a proof and a consciousness of its own dignity and of its own faculties; it was so because it upheld for three months against the forces of France, Austria, Naples and Spain, the national flag in Rome, the future capital of the nation, and because it showed what Italian volunteers could do against all present hope for the future of their country.

Twice were the French troops attacked at the point of the bayonet and repulsed far beyond the walls. The first occasion was on the 30th of April, 1849; within a few days a Neapolitan army of 15,000 men, led by the king in person, encamped at Albano, some fifteen miles from Rome, and on the 10th of May the French troops again attacked and were again repulsed. On the 19th of May an armistice was concluded, and negociations commenced with Lesseps, the French envoy, pending which the little army at Rome marched against the Neapolitan king a Velletri, and put him ignominiously to flight; laying the foundation for Garibaldi of that wondrous prestige which enabled him, years afterwards, to free Sicily and Naples, with a handful of volunteers opposed to an army of 100,000 men, to enter the capital alone, and to drive the son of Bomba to seek refuge in an almost impregnable fortress. On the 31st of May the French envoy signed a convention between the Roman assembly and himself, on the ratification of which, by General Oudinot and the French Government, the gates were to be opened to the army of France, with a new armistice to be, in case of non-ratification of the convention, prolonged for fifteen days. The general refused his assent and produced private instructions of his own, but promised not to recommence the attack before the 4th of June. To his eternal infamy, and that of the government which he served, he forfeited his word, attacked by surprise in the night of the 2nd. And throughout the whole of this unequal struggle, not only Rome but all the Roman states remained faithful to the assembly and government of their own choice, and to the flag of the nation which they had commissioned them to raise and to defend. That unanimity was the downfall of the temporal papacy, the thunders of the Vatican were henceforth to rank as stage tricks to an accustomed audience,—the papal chair must rest on French bayonets or tumble to the ground. And the protest of that sublime defence was more, it determined the nature of her future efforts to all Italy, it rendered impossible at any moment the adoption by Italy of any other goal but *unity* it bound Italy, without the possibility of being led, or driven, or compelled astray, to its accomplishment. Rome for her capital, the sea and the Alps her frontier lines, were the inevitable future of the Italian people."

M. Thouvenel, the French minister of foreign affairs, who resigned his post after Aspromonte, in the French Chamber, the commencement of 1863, says that Rome is the one black spot upon the political horizon of France, and the only way to dispel it is to act on the principle to which the French government owes its own existence.

What is the use the Emperor makes of his power in Rome on this subject? *The Times* of August 13th, 1863, states:—"From their own correspondent.—It would be a work of supererogation to attempt to show that the Papal authorities are accomplices in these acts of hostility to the Italian government. It can admit of no doubt, but what shall we say of the French under whose eyes these facts take place. At one time their authorities declare that no hostile preparations are made in Rome, and then, if pressed hard, admit that perhaps two or three recruits at a time, under the auspices of an over-zealous colonel, may leave the city for the Bourbon service, but they know nothing of it, and cannot prevent it. Now I have no hesitation in asserting that not a finger is raised in Rome without the fact being thoroughly known to the French police, which is the most lynx-eyed of its kind. Its vigilance is remarkable, and its success as great as its vigilance. Of course it saw those little knots of Spanish peasantry—whom everybody else saw in the streets—and knew all about them, and to say that they cannot prevent recruiting and the passage of these bands is simply absurd.

"A great flourish of trumpets has been made lately about the efforts of the French to discourage brigandage, but unfortunately for the credulity of those who hope all things, a band of escaped murderers leave Civita Vecchia just at this time, with passports *en regle*, signed by French and Spanish ambassadors bound for the great recruiting ground, and General Bosco leaves, it is reported, for Barcelonia, and fresh bands are coming over the frontier. The French authorities may know nothing of these proceedings, but it is an odous position which a great nation assumes when it acts as the protector of a nursery of brigands."

We have before alluded to the opinions expressed by Lord Palmerston, on the 8th of May, 1863, who stated:—"In Rome there is a French garrison; under its shelter there exists a committee of 200, whose practice is to organize a band of murderers, the scum and dregs of every nation, and send them forth into the Neapolitan territory to commit every atrocity."

In conclusion, the very fact that Italian unity has now arrived at the fourth year of its age may be assumed as a fair reason for believing that it will reach a vigorous manhood. The errors of statesmen, the opposition of open enemies, the underhand machinations of a faithless ally, all have failed to destroy its infancy, and when the time shall arrive for the nation to arm and free their brethren in Rome and Venetia, may the Italians be led again to battle and to victory by that unique pattern of ancient valour and of goodness, by that most true, most unselfish, and most noble-hearted of all Patriots, Giuseppe Garibaldi.

---

* An English gentleman, Mr. Tower, who was present at the siege of Rome, and accompanied the General to Liverpool in 1850, stated that the house in which Garibaldi lived was perfectly riddled with shot. He also related a curious incident which occurred during the escape of Garibaldi from the power of the Austrians. They knowing that Garibaldi was concealed in a certain town, had ordered that every person who wore a beard should be imprisoned. When the occupant of the house, in which Garibaldi was concealed learnt this, he urged the General to get rid of his beard. Instead of acting on this advice, Garibaldi ordered an open barouche, into which he and his aide-de-camp entered, and driving along the line of the Austrian forces, drawn up on the outskirts of the town, and as he passed them saluted the Austrian officers, who returned the salute, little imagining that the General was then making his daring escape. At another time, when Garibaldi, sunk in thought, was sitting with his elbows on a table, his face buried in his hands, a band of Austrian soldiers suddenly entered the house, crowding round and overwhelming him with inquiries, after the Rothen Zenfel, whose track they had been following for three quarters of an hour. He endured, however, all the importunities of these people, and answered their questions without allowing them to get a single glance of his face. Had he done so, notwithstanding his change of costume, it would instantly have cost him his life.

CPSIA information can be obtained
at www.ICGtesting.com
Printed in the USA
LVHW040027180422
716440LV00005B/381

9 783752 592047